HARLEY MERLIN AND THE MORTAL PACT

Harley Merlin 9

BELLA FORREST

ONE

Harley

Chaos had gone. Our veins were empty of it. There wasn't any pain, just a dull ache that had nothing to do with the actual, physical tear of having our abilities wrenched away. It was the dull ache of losing something that had always been part of us. I kept glancing at the others, waiting to feel their emotions, only to be hit with a wall of nothing.

It'd been less than an hour since our magic had been taken away, and we were all still reeling. Sure, we had a sliver of hope in the form of the Chaos-filled supernatural beings that existed on this earth, but that hadn't given us back our powers.

"How are those charms holding up?" I turned to Santana, who was doing an anxious round of the Catemacos' retreat in Mexico.

Santana shrugged. "No idea. Those *keris* O'Halloran took are glowing, so I'm going to guess that's a good thing? I just freaked out and assumed all the Chaos had gone, but that might not be true. If the weapons are still going, maybe the charms are as well."

Finch nodded. "Shiny-ass Chaos weapons should be a dead giveaway that there's some juice left in this cabin."

"*Keris?*" I frowned.

"Magical daggers, Indonesian origin. Pinched from the SDC museum, and probably never going to be returned." Santana flashed me a halfhearted smile. "Anyway, they're lighting up like nobody's business whenever I put them near these carved charms, so I'd say there's a chance we're still hidden out here."

The cabin was pretty much jam-packed, with Wade, Finch, Santana, Levi, Krieger, Raffe, Dylan, Tatyana, Astrid, Garrett, Alton, O'Halloran, and Jacob standing around, each one coming to terms with their lack of Chaos while trying to keep looking toward the options we had left.

Well, Jacob and Alton were lying down, one just about conscious, the other one totally out of it and being attended to by a helpless, magicless Krieger. Meanwhile, Isadora had been laid out on the sofa by Wade and Finch with a blanket covering her, her body so still I could hardly bring myself to look at her. Everyone was devastated, wearing the same lost expression. There was nothing anyone could do to resurrect Isadora this time. The only thing Krieger could do without his Organa magic was try to keep Alton comfortable.

We knew Katherine was responsible for our missing Chaos. Nobody else could've pulled that off. But at least we knew she wasn't coming after us, as long as those *keris* daggers kept glowing and the charms surrounding the cabin held. We all needed a moment to breathe, to wrap our heads around what had happened.

"Looks like my ancestors did one heck of a security job on this place," Santana said, glancing at me. "But I'm guessing we're not planning to hide out here and wait until this whole thing blows over? I mean, we'd probably end up crawling out to find that the end of the world had already happened."

Raffe smirked. "Fire and brimstone. Demons and pitchforks. And Katherine standing at the head of it all."

I shot him a curious look. Kadar and Raffe had started to slide so effortlessly between one another that it was harder to tell who was speaking. There wasn't always the faint tinge of red to give the djinn away if he was only popping up for a split second, and that recent utterance hadn't sounded like a Raffe thing to say.

Not that it mattered. In the days to come, we were going to need Kadar more than ever. He and Zalaam, Levi's djinn, still had their Chaos intact, separate from the magic that had been snatched away from Raffe and Levi. This made them two of our most valuable assets.

"I wish we could wait this out, but this isn't a wait-and-see kind of scenario anymore," I replied. "We need to get after Katherine with every supernatural, Chaos-filled creature and item we can muster: Kadar, Zalaam, Garrett's Avenging Angel sword, and those *keris* daggers included."

Jacob tried to drag himself to his feet, only to stumble and crash back down. He looked awful. His eyes were hollow and rimmed with red, his face pale. I rushed to him and helped him into a sitting position, leaning him up against the back of the sofa. He was breathing hard, his hands balled into fists.

"I should've woken up sooner," he said tightly. "I was trying so hard to fight the spell she put on me. I tried every single hour of every single day since she knocked me out. When that didn't work, I kept trying to get a message through to Louella, but it was like Katherine had put my head in a thick glass bubble. Louella could only hear scraps. And now... And now she's gone, because I wasn't strong enough to fight back. If I'd just gotten the right message to her, she might still be alive." Tears spilled down Jacob's cheeks, his chest wracked with choked sobs.

I struggled to hold back my own tears.

"There's nothing you could've done, Jacob," I managed. "Katherine was already one step ahead of us all, but she's not going to stay ahead of us. I promise you that. We're going to get her, for Louella, for Isadora, and for everyone else she's hurt." I put my arm around his shoulders and held him tight. "Isadora told me to tell you goodbye before she passed on again. She cared about you so much. We all do. They wouldn't want to see you sad; they'd want to see you getting your strength back, so you could join us in our final battle against Katherine."

He covered his face with his hands. "I almost got a message through to Louella about Imogene and Katherine before all of that happened in the infirmary. I fed the truth to her, but she was asleep and she didn't hear me. She was so tired, and I wasn't strong enough to get that message through again until... well, you know what happened. I should've known Katherine would've had backup ready."

"You did everything you could, just like the rest of us," I insisted. "We should've been focusing on the aftermath of her becoming a Child of Chaos from the very beginning, but we were so blinded by confidence that we thought we could cut her off before that point. This isn't your fault. Katherine is solely responsible."

"I'll kill her," Jacob spat. "I'll portal to wherever she is, and I'll throw her into another portal that goes nowhere so I can watch it crush her to death. It's what Louella and Isadora would've wanted. I'm not going to let them down."

I hugged him closer. He was just a brokenhearted teenager who'd lost his mentor and his friend and couldn't get them back. Louella had given up her life right after hitting Katherine where it hurt, getting in one last dig to make Katherine doubt herself. So, I could understand Jacob's anger and grief. We all felt it. But there was one thing he was forgetting...

I rubbed his back, as though he were a kid. "Nobody is portaling anywhere for a while, Jacob. But we will get her."

He frowned, and then realization dawned. "Oh, right. No Chaos. I forgot."

"I think that's going to happen a lot in the days to come." I was testament to that, constantly trying to feel out my friends' emotions only to remember my Empathy had gone, along with the rest of my abilities.

"This is hopeless!" Krieger threw down the first-aid kit he'd found in the cabin and ran a hand through his hair. He was shaking. "How am

I supposed to do anything without my Chaos? I've never in my life been without it!"

"Do you need some help?" Astrid approached tentatively.

As the only human amongst us, she was the only one not personally reeling from the Great Chaos Snatch. And, without her complete soul, she was the only one who still had the ability to examine things logically, without the overwhelming emotions that were bogging the rest of us down. We still had some fight left in us, but this was still a mammoth hurdle to climb over.

Krieger looked up at her and sighed. "I suppose you have almost as much medical knowledge as I do right now, especially without my supplies from the infirmary. Most of my knowledge comes from working with Chaos. Without it, I doubt I'd get through a single day in a human hospital."

"Is that a yes?" Astrid looked at her father, who wasn't doing well at all. His breathing was shallow, his body limp, his face ashen. If I'd put him beside Isadora, I wouldn't have been able to tell that Alton was the one who was still alive. Astrid seemed as close to sad as it was possible for her to get; her brow furrowed as she sank down beside her father and took little glass vials out of the first-aid kit.

Krieger nodded. "Please. I still have O'Halloran's injuries to look over, so I might need your help there, too."

O'Halloran raised his hands. "Hey, no need to worry about me, doc. A few scrapes. They look worse than they are, I swear. Weird to think I can't just patch myself up with a bit of magic, but I'll survive."

"Tough as nails, huh?" I remarked.

"O'Halloran's a beast!" Dylan chimed in.

O'Halloran smiled. "I'm more of a cockroach when it comes to fighting—impossible to wipe out. And when we're all breathing a little easier and we've got a plan of action, I'll be getting my ass back to that garden place and getting those other magicals out."

"Although they're still there with Katherine and Davin," Tatyana said.

"I'll be going back too, if there's a way." Wade stared at the wall intently, as if he were hoping a portal might suddenly appear. I didn't need my Empathy to feel his anger; it was bristling off him. "My parents are still there. The preceptors are all still there. And those Children. But how are we supposed to get back to the Garden of Hesperides without a Portal Opener? I need to get back there!"

"Remington is there, too," Dylan said, his body tensed up.

Finch sighed. "So what, you want to go in all angry and half-cocked? Half-cocked guns don't kill anyone. That's got 'bad idea' written all over it. Two djinn, a big, fiery sword, a couple of daggers, and a group of humans does not an army maketh. Katherine would just finish the job she wanted to start."

"Well, I can't just stand here and do nothing." Wade looked to me, his eyes desperate. I walked up to him and held his face in my hands, holding his gaze.

"We're not going to do *nothing*, Wade. We're going to get them all back, and we're going to make our final move against Katherine," I promised. "I've got the Grimoire, and even though I might not be able to read out of it, we've got avenues to call upon Erebus. He might be able to reach the other Children of Chaos. If we can get them on our side, *then* we'll have the firepower to take on Katherine. We need to remember that she can't become what she wants to be without my body, and that means the game isn't over. As long as I'm still me, and there are supernatural beings and weapons in the world, then we're not done yet, and we haven't lost."

"Do you have another one of those Mason jars?" Astrid's voice distracted me from Wade's sadness and fury.

Something was happening to Alton. A thin, weak stream of black smoke was spilling out of him, his back arching up from the floor as he Purged.

Santana ran for the cupboard and took out another jar. Raffe had already reached for the entrapment stones that Wade had used on my Purge beast, which was still slamming itself into the side of the glass of its own jar, seemingly unaffected by the Chaos sweep. However, it didn't look like Raffe was going to need them. The moment Santana unscrewed the lid, the withered wisps of black smoke poured into the jar with feeble obedience. No sooner had Santana screwed the lid back on than the black wisp dissipated completely, the smoke evaporating into thin air, leaving the jar empty.

"What just happened?" Levi peered over from the far side of the room where he'd been pacing silently. I could tell he was trying to come to terms with the fact that Zalaam wasn't going anywhere, since we would need that djinn for the battle to come. After so long holding Zalaam in silent submission and no longer having the Chaos to keep him pushed down, there was going to be a steep learning curve ahead for Levi.

"I think it died," Garrett replied, tapping the jar with the edge of his sword—the Avenging Angel. The blade didn't light up with a fiery flame, suggesting there was no Chaos to react to.

Krieger gasped. "Impossible!"

"Look for yourself." Garrett nodded at the empty jar. "There's nothing there."

"Has anyone ever seen a Purge beast die like that before?" Tatyana looked between the more senior members of the group.

"Since Krieger just screamed 'Impossible,' I'm guessing that's going to be a no," Finch replied.

"I didn't scream," Krieger muttered. "I've just never seen anything like that before. And if that Purge beast just died, then it means Alton is in a far worse state than I anticipated. He is practically drained dry."

"What does that mean?" Astrid had pulled her dad into her lap and was cradling his head gently. I wanted to know the answer just as much as everyone else in the room.

"He'll need some time to recover, or he'll die," Krieger replied. "He certainly won't be able to do another resurrection without killing himself in the process, even if he were to get his full Chaos back."

Finch shook his head. "A Necromancer who can't Necromance.

That's pretty crappy. He's not going to like that when he wakes up."

"He might not, but at least he'll live." Astrid brushed back the sweat-soaked tufts of Alton's hair.

"There's more." Krieger lowered his gaze. "The Purge beast that just died was the last sliver of Chaos Alton had. He's going to need a Chaos infusion as soon as possible with his body ailing the way it is. Being human won't help him in the healing process. If anyone desperately needs magic right now, it's Alton."

"Well, when you're swimming in crap, just keep your head up." I was determined not to let morale fall below a point where it'd be impossible to get back. I was grateful to have these people with me. This was how we'd started this fight against Katherine, and this was how we were going to finish it. Together, filled with that underdog flame of hope that refused to go out.

"What a way to put it, Sis." Finch flashed me a smile. He tapped the jar that held my Purge beast, making it bash even harder into the glass.

I smiled back. "We've still got chips, and we've still got cards to play."

"And you worked in a casino, so you know all about that." Wade forced some enthusiasm into his voice as he put his arm around my waist. "Although, what do you make of our odds?"

"I'm not saying it'd be wise to bet on us, but the payoff will be huge if we can do this." I leaned into him, glad to feel him beside me. This was where I was supposed to be. "Katherine will be expecting us to beg for mercy, but we're not going to do that. She's taken everything from us, which gives us one advantage."

Finch frowned. "You want to enlighten us all?"

"We've got nothing left to lose." Even though I said it confidently, the pseudo-premonition that the Chains of Truth had given me still nagged away at the back of my mind. Deep down, I knew we did still have something to lose. Each other. If we went after Katherine, I didn't know if we'd ever stand in a room like this again—all of us together.

"Whoa!" Finch staggered back from my Purge beast's jar. The beast had launched itself at the lid, making a faint dent in the metal. As it regrouped, it spread itself over every square inch of the jar in a seething mass of concentrated smoke, so thick it looked like black sand. And that glass was starting to look *really* flimsy.

"It can't get out, can it?" I stared at Krieger.

"I really don't know," he replied. "And, I have to say, I'm getting quite scared of that thing. I've never seen so much Chaos in one Purge before, not even from Alton or Katherine or any other great magical. And since it hasn't manifested as a solid, sentient being like Tobe or Naima, I've got to say, this appears to be something else entirely. For that reason alone, I can't promise the jar will hold."

I leveled my gaze at the gathered group. "We don't have any time to waste. Right now, Katherine is ninety-nine percent Child of Chaos, but she needs my body to bridge the gap between the human and magical world and the otherworlds. Without me, she'll end up drifting about until she's summoned, same as the other Children of Chaos. However, we know she's already taken her first step by taking Chaos away from people, which means her own body is still holding up for the time being. It's a temporary bridge. At this very moment, she's likely redistributing magic as she sees fit."

"It's creeping me out to think of my mom inhabiting my sister's body." Finch shivered. "How is she going to do that, anyway?"

"Considering she wanted me to read from the Grimoire and tortured me to within an inch of my life to get me to do it, I've got a feeling there's something in the final spell that she needs in order to take my body for herself," I explained. "It's the most powerful spell in there, from what I could gather. It *felt* the most powerful. Dangerous and dark. It gave me weird vibes in a way that none of the other spells did."

"Always go with your gut," Dylan affirmed.

"What have you got in mind?" Garrett asked.

"Basically, we're looking at a race against time." I took a breath. "I need to perform the final spell first, before Katherine can get to me.

This spell is supposed to destroy her, but clearly Katherine has found a way to harness its power and use it to her advantage. She wouldn't be stupid enough to get me to read it if that wasn't the case. So, we need to beat her to the punch."

Levi folded his arms across his chest. "I still don't understand what it is you expect us to do, or what *you* expect to do, for that matter. You can't read from the Grimoire anymore. Presumably, Katherine will want to pour magic back into you, temporarily, if she manages to get you back, so you can read it solely for her, but what are you supposed to do without any Chaos to help?"

I shot him a cold look. "I'm glad you brought that up. I can still read the hidden pages, but I can't read them out loud. Levi has a point there. On top of that, the text seems incomplete somehow." I'd skimmed the page again earlier to try and distract myself from the void of having no magic. "For a spell of this magnitude, it should be longer, but it seems to stop abruptly. There's definitely something missing, and without my Chaos, I can't attempt a state of Euphoria."

If I'd been able to do that, I would've been able to reach out to mini-me again, but that option was completely off the table. Still, I was convinced there was something missing, something I couldn't quite put my finger on.

"So, you're saying you're clueless?" Levi muttered. "Katherine is a Child of Chaos, more or less, we've all had our Chaos wiped from us, Isadora is dead, Louella is dead, Gaia is dead, I have to share my body with Zalaam again, and you don't have a single clue what you're doing. Forgive me for not leaping with enthusiasm, because that sounds like square one to me."

Hey, I don't see you coming up with any bright ideas.

I was about to open my mouth to reply, but the words were knocked clean out of my lungs as the jar holding my Purge beast exploded in a blast so violent it sent us all flying backward. The glass shattered. Shards rained across the ground. My first Purge erupted out, with nothing left to keep it captive.

TWO

Finch

Being Billy No-Magic was going to take some getting used to. And that wasn't the only thing. I seriously should've gone back to the box dye when I'd had the chance. Shapeshifting a new look always had its glitches, but my Shapeshifting had up and left, walked right out of the building and slammed all the doors on its way out. So, now, I was not only magicless, but I was also a friggin' redhead again. I wasn't sure which was worse. Red wasn't my color. I was a little too Shipton with this shade, which was going to ruin my lean toward a more Merlin vibe.

Your hair isn't really the biggest problem, though, is it? Ah, my messed-up mind, casually putting me back on the right path. No, it wasn't the biggest problem right now, and nobody had mentioned it, which meant darling Madre—emphasis on the "Mad"—had lobotomized everyone's sense of humor as well as their Chaos. They'd all been standing around with freaked-out stares, like they'd walked into a room and couldn't remember why.

Oh, and to add a great, big, fat cherry of panic onto this crapstorm gateau, we now had the whole jar-shattering-and-unleashing-a-big-old-tsunami-of-black-smoke thing to deal with. *Yeah, there's that. Priorities, Finch.*

At first, the smoke just hovered, no form to speak of, just a seething mass of black fog.

Then, it seemed to get an idea into its wispy head. Not that it had a head. Or a body. Or eyes. Or any distinguishing features, really. It spread out across the cabin, making me wonder if I was inhaling unseen body parts. A second later, I could barely see my own hand in front of my face as it went wall-to-wall with its rippling mass, seeping into every crevice.

"Guys?" I clamped my hand over my mouth just in case. "Everyone alive?"

"Yeah!" a bunch of voices chorused back. They sounded scared. Understandable, I guessed, since we had zero powers to fight this thing. If it wanted a fight, that was, but since it was a little ball of hate and fury and grief, that wasn't exactly improbable.

Harley had birthed something unpredictable, and her timing couldn't have been worse.

Right now, the foggy Purge beast wasn't exactly letting us know what its plan was. It just seemed content to pack itself into the cabin, blocking our view of each other. But what was it plotting? A sneak attack? A mass blinding? Did it just want to freak us out? If that was the case, then it was a job well done.

Ordinarily, this would've been where I came in with some hilarious joke to lighten the mood, but I didn't have one. The fog could have killed us at any moment. I'd read enough Stephen King to know what spooky mists could do to a chirpy band of barely surviving protagonists.

"Harley?" I couldn't see her. I waved my arms around and hit something solid.

"That'd be me, kid." O'Halloran's voice boomed back. "I'll save you the embarrassment of telling you where you're touching."

"Sorry." I snatched my hand back. "Harley? Can you hear me?"

"Yeah, I hear you." She sounded super panicked.

"You think you can get this beastie in order?"

"I don't know…" She trailed off.

"Fancy giving it a try before it chokes us all to death?" I prompted.

"*Obey me!*" There was none of the usual weird, echoey voice that was kind of Harley, but kind of not. I guessed, without Chaos, she couldn't control this thing. Even with it, she'd probably have struggled.

The beastie didn't give her the slightest bit of notice. Instead, it started to slip out through the windows, like it was trying to get away from her. *It's making a run for it!*

A few moments later, the cabin had emptied of any foggy remnants. We sprinted to the window. I'd expected the beast to get as far away from its proverbial mistress as possible, in case she tried that echoey thing again, so it was a bit of a surprise to see it slithering across the ground toward the nearby lake. There, it spread out again like weird, black butter until it was sitting on the surface of the lake and covering it entirely.

"Well, this is a load of crap, isn't it?" I muttered.

"Which part?" Santana replied curtly. Why did I get the feeling this *chiquita* still didn't like me too much? Did I have to prostate myself in front of her? *It's prostrate, Finch. Prostrate.* Cheers, brain, saving the day again.

Having no magic had put me in one heck of a foul mood. It had been a long time since I'd been made to feel so defenseless and weak, so easy to kill. And, guess what—drumroll, please—it was Katherine leading the charge. She'd been the one to make me feel useless once before, for so many years, and here she was doing it again. Only this time, she was doing it from a distance. *Coward.*

"All of it." I held Santana's gaze until she looked away. I was going to call that one-nil in favor of me, although it was a pretty hollow victory. The fact remained: this was all crap. Harley talked a good game, but we were all benched right now, and I didn't know if there *was* anything we could do, even if we could scrape together a band of misfit supernaturals. Worst of all, I had no clue how long I could actually live like this, without magic.

The anxiety wasn't doing my noggin any favors, that was for sure.

"What's it doing?" Captain Useless of the Clan Levi peered over my shoulder, getting a little too close for comfort.

"Personal space, Levi? Ever heard of it?" I shot him a warning look that made him take a step back.

"I don't know, but it's not moving," Krieger replied. We were all crowded around the window, trying to figure this Purge beast out. It just seemed to be sitting there, spread out in a film where the lake should've been.

"Hey, at least it's out of the house," Dylan said.

"But what the heck kind of Purge beast is it?" Harley frowned at the inky black mass.

I shrugged. "You Purged it. You tell us."

"I have no idea," she replied quietly. "And believe me, I'd rather have had a Tobe-like being come out of me. At least then we'd be able to talk to it."

"On the bright side, it's not moving or shooting deadly laser beams at people," Krieger added.

"Wait, there's a bright side?" I gave a mock gasp.

Krieger chuckled tightly. "We have to look for one wherever we can."

"Right," I said. "We have to be comforted by the fact that it isn't hurting anyone. It could've choked us all, or killed us all in one fell swoop, but it didn't. That means it isn't violent—unlike its mama."

Harley gave a half-smile, which was all I wanted to see. Being the jester of the group had its benefits, and if it meant I could take Harley's mind off what was going on, even for a second, then it was worth it.

"Well, not violent *yet*, anyway," Garrett corrected.

Krieger nodded. "Exactly, so all we can do is monitor it as best we can, given the circumstances."

"We can't stay here much longer." Santana cast a worried glance at the rest of us. "I know those charms are keeping us safe, but they won't hold *forever* with no Chaos to draw from."

"We can't stay here even if we did have unlimited charms to protect us," Harley replied. "We need to get the supernaturals together."

"Yes! I'm glad we're calling them that." I smiled with satisfaction, even if nobody else seemed impressed.

"I just got a text from my parents." Santana duly ignored me as she stared down at her phone. "They're trying to figure out what's going on, but we can't use normal comms anymore. They're saying we should break the phones we have, which means we're going to need burners."

To prove her point, she quickly took her phone apart and smashed the pieces with the heel of her boot.

"It's that bad?" Levi's voice trembled.

Keep up, dingus.

Santana nodded. "We already know that the cult's power and influence has spread to the highest levels of magical society. The friggin' president of the UCA was fighting on Katherine's side, and those who are left and haven't been brainwashed by the Queen of Evil are probably reeling after the stunt Katherine just pulled. If they're anything like us, they'll be panicking, which means they're open to the cult's persuasion. I mean, who's not going to jump at the chance to get their magic back, even if it means surrendering to a crazed megalomaniac?"

"Us." I smirked.

"Well, that was a given, Finch," she retorted. "I'm talking about the people who aren't in this room, the scared magicals who'll be in total disarray right now. I can only imagine what's going through their heads."

"Probably the same thing that's going through ours," I replied, knowing I was walking a thin line between cheeky and impudent.

To my surprise, Santana nodded again. "Then we know how terrified everyone must be feeling. Fear makes people do stupid, stupid things. So, the point I'm trying to make is, we need to move fast before

Katherine can rally all those frightened people to her cause. And everyone needs to get rid of their phones until we can get burners."

Everyone dutifully whipped out their devices and started smashing them to pieces like toddlers mid-tantrum. I reluctantly took mine out and crushed it to smithereens. The only people who didn't do anything were Harley and Jacob—Jacob for obvious reasons. He was too weak to crush a snowflake, let alone a phone. And Harley... well, I wasn't sure about that one.

"You not getting smashy, Harley?" I asked.

She shook her head. "I've already got a burner, remember?"

"Oh... yeah." Jacob, Harley, and I had received them as gifts when we'd visited my old pal Kenzie and her goldmine of stolen goods. Mine was back at the SDC, since I'd switched back to my usual phone from one of my secret stashes after returning. *So stupid.*

"My other phone is out of action, so no problem there," she added. Once the smashing had subsided, everyone's focus returned.

"If we're gathering supernaturals, then we need to get to Tobe and the Bestiary," Wade urged. "Krieger, you said Tobe was working on disconnecting the Bestiary from the SDC when Katherine hit the infirmary with that crumbling spell. Do you think he managed it?"

Krieger shook his head. "It would've been a temporary measure until the danger had passed. As soon as the crumbling spell stopped, Tobe would've reconnected the Bestiary. In hindsight, it would have been useful to keep it disconnected, but we didn't know what was going to happen."

"So there's one thing we need that we don't have: magic. And, what's more, we can't go back to the SDC to gather the beasts in the Bestiary. You can bet your ass Katherine will have her people surrounding the coven." Harley stared out of the window at the creature from the Black Lagoon.

"Plus, we're human now. I doubt the SDC would even let us in," O'Halloran pointed out.

"He's right." Wade shook his head. "Shoot, he's right."

Levi nodded. "And, if Katherine has taken Chaos away from all magicals, then that has some truly terrible implications."

"Like?" Raffe prompted.

It was Astrid who answered, the only one of us who wasn't losing her mind over what had just happened. I never thought, in all my life, that I'd ever call a human lucky, but this whole debacle definitely gave her an edge. She knew how to live like this. It was all she'd ever known.

"The covens across the globe will likely have already begun reacting to the influx of non-magicals. And by that I mean the former magicals who were inside the covens when their abilities were taken," she explained. "You have to think of covens as sentient organisms. They accept magicals based on their Chaos and having their names in the registry. If the magicals who were inside suddenly become powerless and human, the way it happened to all of you, then the covens will probably throw them out. It's like an automatic alarm system that can't be bypassed."

She'd gone full Spock, to the point where it was almost eerie, like she was an emotionless news anchor telling the masses about a zombie apocalypse.

"But Suri managed to get in, and the coven didn't kick her out," Jacob wheezed from across the room. The poor dude was a weak, shaking bag of nerves and grief, but I was kind of glad to have him back in the land of the conscious. My dear mother seemed to have a penchant for crushing the spirits of sixteen-year-old boys.

"Suri was one human," Krieger replied. "One human can get away with being inside the coven without being kicked out. The coven doesn't see one person as a threat, but an entire throng of humans is a different story. It'll view them as a disease and do what it can to fix the problem."

"Wait, that means the covens will be left empty." Levi frowned as understanding whacked me in the skull.

"Left empty so that Katherine can complete a hostile takeover with her magicals," I finished. "She'll stuff them with her people."

O'Halloran sucked in a sharp breath. "That's very possible. If I were in her position, the first thing I'd do is get the highest-ranking former magicals from each coven who had pledged themselves to me and give them just enough magic to enter. After that, I'd force them to open the covens to my cult members, basically repopulating them with my people. Or 'stuffing them,' as you put it, Finch."

"Well, there's a worrying insight into your mind," I replied. "Tell me you're not Katherine, masquerading as O'Halloran. I'm not sure I could take another Imogene revelation."

That one had really come at me from left field. All this time, I'd been so sure I knew all of Katherine's secrets, and then *bam!* I find out she was Imogene all along. To top off the initial horror, I'd had to deal with all the implications that came with this realization. I'd had some pretty saucy thoughts about Imogene. *Ugh, so disturbing. So gross.* 'Oedipus complex' didn't even cover the nightmarish reality. Freud would've kicked me out of his office and given up on psychology altogether.

"I'm definitely not." O'Halloran chuckled bitterly. "Having her fill my head full of drugs was bad enough."

"And they've all worn off now, right?" Wade eyed him suspiciously.

O'Halloran nodded. "I'm pretty sure. I can talk about Katherine and Echidna without having a total breakdown, so I'm going to take that as a good sign." He paused. "I think that the antidote she gave me was probably another mind-bending drug of some kind. Remember, I told you the water she kept giving me tasted weird, but I haven't drunk anything or taken any 'antidote' in a while, so hopefully I should be fine. I doubt I could've fought against her folks if I was still under her influence."

"If she's making moves, we have to match her." Harley turned away from the window to address everyone. I loved it when she went into badass leader mode. *Attagirl!* "We can't stay here going stir-crazy. We need to gather whatever allies we have left, even without our magic.

Someone, somewhere must know something. A way to get back at Katherine."

"Kenzie might be a good stop to get the revenge ball rolling," I suggested. "Especially as we've just stomped our phones to dust. She'll help us out, given the circumstances. How could she say no now?"

"Do you think she might have anything else in her stash that we could use? Ephemeras, maybe? Something that can help us get some juice back, even if it's just temporary?" She looked desperate. We all did.

Krieger shook his head. "Ephemeras won't be of much use to you. You would only be able to use the ability within them, and that is if you could even find a magical willing to put a fragment of their ability into the device." He paused. "Although..."

"Although?" the Rag Team chorused.

"There is a similar device, called a Hermetic Battery," he explained. "They are contraband items, given their nature. They are not confined to a single ability and can be used to draw raw Chaos from a magical, which can then be used by anyone who has the Hermetic Battery in their possession. Magicals have been known to use them illegally to create personal interdimensional pockets, as the battery refines the Chaos that is poured inside it, strengthening it beyond ordinary levels. Call it a boost to their ordinary power. There is a limit to the objects, however, as with any battery. And I don't know if this Kenzie would have such items in her possession."

I smiled. "Believe me, if anyone does, it's her. You name it, she's got it."

"Then that's definitely where we should go," Wade asserted.

"I should warn you," Krieger said. "You will need an actual magical in order to make the Hermetic Battery work, if you manage to find one. You won't be able to use Kadar or a Purge beast. Their energy is far too raw and, for lack of a better word, chaotic. It will tear the battery apart."

"Comforting," I muttered. "Any other fun challenges we should know about?"

"One more," he replied. "While this item may solve your Grimoire-reading problem, Harley, you will need to be careful to conserve as much of the Chaos as possible. A spell of the magnitude you have mentioned will require a full charge, to say the least."

"We don't even know if we can get these batteries yet, so we'll cross that bridge if and when we get to it," Harley said.

"Tobe may also be in possession of some, if you can find him," Krieger added thoughtfully. "I know Beast Masters in the past have used these items—it is the only circumstance in which they are permitted, given the need for boosts of energy in a Bestiary and repairs that need to be made quickly. He may have some on him, but that would mean entering the SDC, and we have already ruled that out."

"So Kenzie's our best bet then, unless we want to get ourselves captured at the SDC. She's our only bet, let's be honest." Harley turned to me. "Do you think she'll have any stolen charms or other items that could protect a few more humans?"

"Who've you got in mind?" I asked.

She shook her head. "First off, I'm going to text Ryann and the Smiths and tell them to get the hell out of San Diego. They need to hide somewhere, but they'll need protection in order to do that. And if Kenzie has any extra means of protection, then we can use those on ourselves."

"I'm sure Kenzie will have something up those neon sleeves of hers. They're deceptively spacious." I didn't know if that was entirely true. There was a chance she'd have none of the things we needed. But I wanted to give Harley some hope.

"Then what are we waiting for?" She looked around at us all, and her message was clear. There was no time left on the clock that had been clanging over our heads since the get-go.

We needed to move. Now.

THREE

Katherine

It wasn't in my nature to be a killjoy, especially not when I was the one who was supposed to be basking in glory. I was surrounded by respect and loyalty and fear—which came with its own delicious frisson of glee—so I should've been riding a wave of total bliss.

But instead, I was getting dragged back by the flimsy flesh that was holding me together. My beautiful body, being battered by all this exquisite energy. I couldn't have one without losing the other. Catch-22 didn't even cover it, and I was about ready to catch-22 the living daylights out of Chaos for doing this to me. *Sly devil.*

The cracks were already starting to show, and it was only going to get worse. That sweeping cull of snatching abilities had done the trick —letting the magical world know I was serious, if they hadn't caught on already—but it had taken a lot more out of me than I'd anticipated, and I was suffering the consequences of daring to go big. Why did the great always have to suffer? It hardly seemed fair.

Then again, Chaos had made sure that none of this was fair to me, even though I'd followed every instruction to the letter. Helping to write a book that was intended to destroy me wasn't exactly good sportsmanship, now, was it?

I supposed Chaos sensed I wouldn't be content to hover around in the ether somewhere, kicking cans and skipping stones until someone decided to call upon me. *Pfft, who would?* As if anyone would choose that when they could be so much more. I'd be lauding it over the lot of them right now, my fellow Children, if my irritating little loophole hadn't scurried away before I could get her to read out the Grimoire spell I needed to take advantage of. It was the one spell that could be used *for* me instead of *against* me, courtesy of Odette's brain of wonders, tortured out of her after great effort.

It had been designed to destroy me, naturally, but it was a spell that could be subverted to suit my needs, now that I was a Child of Chaos—a handy bit of fine print that had slipped under Chaos's radar. I had so many choice expletives to use for that parasite Harley, but I'd always thought swear words showed a lack of intelligent vocabulary.

It's slipping through my fingers.

I tried to shut my thoughts up, but that was the problem with brains. They chattered on as they pleased, pointing out the damned obvious. Nevertheless, pessimism wouldn't do me any favors. If I'd given in to negative thinking, I'd never have made it this far.

The only problem was, I'd been wracking my brain ever since I'd completed the Challenge, and I couldn't for the life of me figure out where I'd gone wrong. I'd planned everything down to the last detail, just as I always did. So how did it get to this—me falling apart like wet toilet paper with no body to pour my divine self into?

Harley's inferior figure should've been mine by now.

That stark, unyielding fact throbbed like a hangover in my head. *No, I know where I went wrong.* I'd clearly underestimated Harley and the foolish devotion of her friends. I'd put too much weight on their fear of death. Who wanted to die? Nobody. And they must have known that coming here to the Garden of Hesperides to save Harley was tantamount to suicide. They hadn't died, much to my annoyance, but the risk had been there, and they'd done it anyway.

This wasn't exactly the grand finale I'd had in mind, but that didn't mean the show was over. Far from it. This was nothing more than a technical glitch. Soon enough, I'd take my position in the spotlight—fully contained in Harley's body.

I turned to Davin who stood beside me. "How do I look? Be honest or I'll have your head."

I'd done my best to wipe the oozing black substance away from the cracks that splintered across my face, but the cracks were like fissures in a dam that couldn't be plugged. No matter how much I smeared it away, more replaced it. And let me tell you, having black goop trickling down your face is a killer for a woman's confidence.

Davin smiled and brushed away a stray glob of oily black. I thought I saw him shudder, but he covered it well. "You look majestic, Eris. You are glowing, as any soon-to-be goddess ought to." He paused. "And, I must say, the shine does a great deal to detract from the… let us call them imperfections. You have to be close to see them."

"Then make sure you keep everyone at a decent distance. I don't want anyone seeing my 'imperfections,' as you call them."

I looked at myself once more in the mirror I'd erected. Call it vanity, but I had to see the mess Chaos was making of me; it was like an itch that needed scratching or a zit that needed popping. I knew I should have smashed the mirror to pieces and ignored the ongoing damage, but hey, that would've meant seven years' bad luck. I wasn't superstitious, but I couldn't afford to risk more misfortune.

Besides, none of my cult suspected that this glorious physique was failing me yet. I'd made sure to keep them suitably busy so none of them would have time to notice.

I'd sent a third of the cultists who'd come to this otherworld back out to search for Harley and her band of morons. Another third was standing at a safe distance, awaiting orders. Meanwhile, the last third had the important task of finding the insurgents who'd come through the portal so I could tear them all to shreds. Well, someone else would have to do the tearing, in case I wound up losing an arm or worse, but at least I'd get some pleasure out of watching. The torture and execution of my enemies wasn't usually a spectator sport for me. I liked to get right in the middle of it and lead by example, but I could make an exception if it meant holding this body together until my replacement arrived.

"I am here to serve, Eris." Davin took my hand and kissed it. Black goo smeared his lips, but he didn't wipe it away. He wouldn't have dared. "We will see this remedied, and you will rise to true greatness, as you deserve."

"Thank you, Davin." I kept it cool, not showing just how grateful I was for his words. Even with him, I refused to look vulnerable, but having him here was a peculiar comfort in this time of enormous stress.

Still, the truth was the truth, and reality was biting me in the ass. My body was failing, actually failing, and soon enough it'd be crumbling at the seams, like a china doll that had been smashed full-force into a brick wall.

Without a vessel that had Primus Anglicus strength, a.k.a. the Merlin Parasite, my newfound Child of Chaos form would be uncontrollable. I'd be stuck here in this wasteland, with little to no direct influence on the human world. If I tried to leave, I'd be sucked back in. This was the exact opposite of why I'd become a Child in the first place. I'd done this for absolute liberty, not for a prison masquerading as an otherworld. Ethereal titles of immortality that did absolutely nothing could get stuffed. I wanted to be a goddess between worlds, gifted with all-powerful energy, not a wispy entity confined by friggin' Chaos rules.

"Have you considered Finch as an alternative for your current predicament?" Davin asked, finally wiping the black stain from his lips. "He might be suitable. After all, he shares the Shipton and Merlin blood, which would make him gifted with the same Primus Anglicus clout that you require."

I sighed. I had been doing that a lot lately. "I dislike the idea of being stuck in my son's body for all eternity. I hope I can use my

Shapeshifting to bring my own body back into play, but if not... well, Finch's face isn't exactly what I had in mind for the Goddess of Discord. The Merlin bitch isn't ideal, either, but it's a better fit. Anyway, I'm still fairly sure I can sway Finch back into my service once all of this is done, but I need to get rid of Harley first. That little Merlin scab is a veritable wedge in my family affairs, and she needs picking off."

"A delightful visual." Davin chuckled.

"Make no mistake, I *will* use Finch in Harley's place if I have no other choice." I glanced back at my reflection in the mirror and pulled a sour face. "I'd have to remove the Dempsey Suppressor first, though, and that'll require a lot of oomph." *Oomph I might not have in the tank, by that point.*

"None of us anticipated that Harley and her friends would put up such a fight," Davin mused. "Your plan was exceptional, but I suppose weeds can creep through even the tiniest of cracks."

"And these particular weeds are becoming a colossal pain in my ass," I muttered. "Before that Merlin thorn came along, the SDC was a big, ugly joke, always lagging at the bottom of the yearly scoreboard. They'd have been the first to bend, for sure, if she'd just stayed under whatever rock she was hiding under for all those years. I won't be making that mistake again. I won't be underestimating anyone's willingness to die for that insipid little maggot."

Davin smiled. "Very wise as ever, my sweet goddess."

"Say that again," I purred. This kitty was in need of a little ego stroke.

"My sweet, divine goddess." His blue eyes held my gaze, making my stomach turn somersaults. I couldn't help myself. What sort of red-blooded woman would I be if I didn't get all tingly at the sight of a tasty morsel like this, looking at me like *that*? He looked like he had all sorts of plans for what he wanted to do with me. With this face, oozing black all over the place, I had to take my kicks where I could get them.

I grabbed the lapels of his oh-so-sleek suit and pulled him toward me. His hands slid around my waist, firm and strong and manly as hell. It was good to be a goddess, for sure, but sometimes it was good to be a woman too. I snaked my hand up his chest and trailed my fingertips across his neck, wondering how easy it would be to snap if he ever betrayed me. An occupational hazard—I was always thinking of ways to kill people—but right now all I wanted to do was make out.

I pulled his head down and pressed my lips to his. He had a way of kissing that made me melt, which was probably a little risky since my body was already on the brink of collapse. But what a way to go, huh? I sank deeper into his embrace, his lips moving against mine, hungry and devout.

With this kiss, I do thee bind to my service.

I smiled against his mouth as he pulled me closer. He was loving every moment of this. After all, Davin already thought himself a god among men, and I was bringing him one step closer to making that a reality. He would never be a god in his own right, but he could stand beside a goddess and bathe in my glory.

I moved my head away, leaving him gasping for more.

"What do we do now?" he asked, dipping to place one last kiss on my neck.

I shivered. Maybe it was the Necromancer in him, or maybe it was just his impossibly good-looking face, but there was something so very vampiric about Davin that made his kisses all the more exciting.

"My body is cracking," I replied, catching my breath. "It's giving out, and there's not much I can do to stop it without my Merlin vessel. It means I'm annoyingly limited, unless I decide to go all-in and unravel before I can get a hold of that wily little imp. But that's not going to happen. This ball of twine is staying tight."

"It must be so very frustrating, my sweet." Davin wiped away another trickle of black ooze from my cheek.

"That's putting it mildly." I tilted my head from side to side to try and crack a bone back into place. "If I'm not careful, I'll miss my chance to catch Harley altogether, and you're the only one I trust to pull this off."

"Pull what off, my goddess?"

"Finding Harley." I'd have sent Naima, but Harley had murdered her. *Yet another reason to see her wiped off the face of this earth.* "You must go out and bring her back to me, while I strengthen my position as the new goddess of the magical world, as Eris, Child of Chaos and general badass who's going to tip the balance between humans and magicals."

Davin frowned. "I would be only too willing to comply, but how do you suggest I do that? You say she has disappeared, and we have received no word from the cultists who were already sent in pursuit of her. What can I do that they cannot?"

I rolled my eyes. "Think outside the box, Davin. For a powerful magical with an insane reputation, you can be rather dense sometimes. Little Miss Perfect is being protected somehow. I don't know how, but I'm inclined to think there's a plethora of protection spells on her— protection spells that haven't been affected by my Chaos sweep. Now, do you want me to hold your hand, or are you a big enough boy to figure the rest out?"

"A little nudge in the right direction might be useful," he replied sheepishly.

"Tap into every single intelligence source out there, in the US and beyond. I've already set it up for you after years of hard work, melding the minds of those in the upper echelons, so all you have to do is cherry pick and use all of that to your advantage. Every camera, every airport, every port of entry... but start in San Diego. This is Harley's home, and all little birds come home to roost. They can't help them-selves, no matter how idiotic it is. She's bound to stay close."

"And what should I do when I find her? After all, we know she won't be alone."

I was starting to get a little peeved. "It doesn't matter if she's alone or not. Haven't you been paying attention? She's powerless now.

They're all human, and if you can't take down a simple bunch of humans, then perhaps I ought to rethink your position here."

His eyes widened. "My apologies, Eris. It slipped my mind. I suppose, as I still have abilities, I forgot that you had taken magic from those who would defy you."

"Yes, well, you might be next in line to have your Chaos taken away if you disappoint me. Now, go after Harley and her irritating pals. Failure won't be tolerated. As soon as you have her, check in with me." It burned me up that I couldn't retrieve her myself.

He bowed. "Yes, Eris."

"Well then, what are you waiting for?"

Now that I've sent that delicious distraction on his merry way…

I was eager to make sure everything else was in place, and there was one specific thing on my mind. The Bestiary. It would only be a matter of time until all the covens belonged to me, but they would fall apart if I didn't have Tobe where he was supposed to be, taking care of all those precious creatures locked up and giving their power to my cause. Call me vain, but I didn't want Davin dropping his proverbial eaves on my concerns. He was loyal to me, but that loyalty came with provisions. He still hadn't pledged, and I wasn't about to give him another excuse to try to delay it.

I really should have just killed him. Men weren't good for me. But, without Naima, I had a gap to fill, and Davin was the perfect size.

I needed a solitary spot to gather my remaining strength. I would need it if I was going to force Tobe to obey me. Purge beasts like him didn't bend easily, and I could already sense the crack it was going to cause. So, I headed toward the far side of the ruins, where Gaia's waterfall had started to trickle again. *It's not Gaia's, it's mine.* I had to keep reminding myself that this otherworld belonged to me now.

I had almost reached my destination when two figures came

sprinting across the barren wasteland. They skidded to a halt beside me, stooping to catch their breath. *Weaklings.* However, it wasn't their stamina that concerned me—it was the looks on their faces.

"If you don't have good news for me, you can turn right back around and scurry off until you *do* have good news," I said stiffly, using one of the crumbling pillars of the old ruins to hide the oily black ooze that bled from every damned crack.

"We thought we should update you, Almighty Eris," the first one rasped. He was a young man who looked more like a skeleton than a person. I had no idea how his stick legs were holding up the weight of him.

The second nodded. "We can't find the Crowleys or Remington anywhere, and the Children have vanished. It's this terrain, Eris. This world is so big, and we've got no lay of the land. Even with magic, they're evading us."

She was an older woman, maybe in her forties, but looking good for it. She barely had a peroxide-blonde hair out of place or a smear of smudged makeup, which made me wonder if she'd really given her all in the previous battle. *I won't have shirkers in my cult.* I'd have to keep my eye on this one.

"Then you haven't been looking hard enough." My voice held a clear warning.

"We have, Goddess, I promise you," Skeletor replied. "We've tried to track them, but we're getting nothing back. It's like they've completely disappeared. You've seen the landscape for yourself—it's flat as a pancake. But we can't find any trace of them anywhere."

"Do I have to do *everything* myself?" I snapped. "What is the use of all of you if you can't even find the flashing neon sign of our enemy in a flattened haystack? Should I giftwrap them for you? Would that make it easier?"

"We really have been trying, Eris," the woman urged, her voice trembling.

I glared at her. "This is what I get for not vetting properly. A bunch of inept rookies who don't know their ass from their elbow!"

Anger was building inside me, making my blood boil. I knew who was responsible for this little game of hide and seek. *Gaia's Children.* Evidently, I wasn't the only one forgetting that this otherworld belonged to me now. They were still working for *her*, even though they'd seen me squeeze the life out of her. I'd dragged her back by her hair, just to serve her right for daring to prance around in my image, and left her to disintegrate. They should have been bending to me by now.

Why is nothing going the way I planned?!

"Please, have mercy. We're doing all we can," Skeletor begged.

At least these two were afraid of me, which was more than I could say for these impudent Children of Gaia. Clearly, they hadn't gotten a potent enough taste of my wrath earlier. Now, I was going to shove my power down their throats, until they friggin' choked on it.

A blast of fury-driven Telekinesis exploded out of me. I was way past playing nice, and if it meant a couple more cracks in my face, then so be it.

Shivering tendrils shot out of me, bursting every which way like a web. They hardened as they hit solid flesh. My hands clenched tightly into fists until my knuckles turned white and fissures splintered all the way across the backs of my hands. Bits of skin flaked away, leaving a rippling black mass beneath, but I didn't care. I wanted these sons of bitches, even if it cost me a few more hours of holding onto this body.

I yanked my arms up, the tendrils snapping right back like elastic bands, bringing my mortal enemies out of their hiding places. I didn't have the energy to deal with the Elementals right then, but their time would come.

However, in the distance, four large humanoid figures emerged. *Oh, well, out you come, then, you little worms.*

One was made from shimmering water, one was forged from clouds, the third bristled with fire, and the fourth seemed to be crafted from the rock beneath their feet. Earth, Air, Water, and Fire had come out to get a closer look at their new queen. The poor saps were scowling right at me, no doubt grieving for Mommy Dearest, whom I'd pummeled into dust. All that power, all that confidence, and all that history, and it hadn't done a single thing to save her.

I grinned at them, wanting them to feel my satisfaction, then approached the first line in the group I'd dragged out of their hidey-holes. Felicity and Cormac Crowley knelt beside Remington Knight-shade, with Hiro Nomura and the other preceptors flanking them.

"Get up!" I commanded the front line.

Nomura was drenched in the blood of my cultists—actually dripping, as if he'd walked out of an action movie. He would be the perfect candidate for what I had planned, to show these ingrates once and for all that disobedience wouldn't be tolerated.

The cultists who weren't on a mission gathered around, like the *tricoteuse* who used to gather around the guillotine during public executions in civil-war-ridden France, calmly knitting away while heads rolled. I could get on board with that sort of gal. I could feel the awe of those gathered around me, and it felt good to have them enraptured. This was why I'd done this. This respect and this nervous excitement were precisely the reason I'd set this goal of becoming a goddess. I was judge, jury, and executioner, and here was my salivating audience.

"Hold this one still," I ordered, pointing to Nomura.

A few giddy cultists volunteered, rushing forward to hold him steady. He didn't flinch. His eyes were fixed on mine, like he'd known this would happen. I supposed there was one exception to the "nobody wants to die" rule, and that was the rare individual who had nothing left to lose. Still, he'd serve his purpose.

"You may kill me, Katherine, but you will not kill the hope in those who still wish to see your defeat," Nomura asserted.

"You think anyone else wants to be put on the chopping block?" I smiled at him. "You pledged yourself to my cause. Or did you forget?"

A gasp went up from the now-standing insurgents, all of them staring at Nomura. I stifled a snort. News of his betrayal had spread, but it obviously hadn't spread far enough.

"You blackmailed me," Nomura replied calmly. "You threatened the life of my son. What else was I supposed to do? Anyone in my position would have done the same."

"And where did that get you? Shinsuke died anyway, and he died for me." I looked to the crowd. "Shinsuke was a member of my cult, and he attempted to betray me. He died for it, torn apart by Purge beasts. And so will you, though you'll be pleased to know I don't have a handy group of Purge beasts, so it'll just be plain old execution. Magic or blade, though? I haven't decided yet."

"Spare us a monologue, Katherine," Felicity Crowley spat. "What is it with you and the sound of your own voice? You've always loved it, but you never did realize that nobody was listening, did you? Jeez, most of us drowned you out before you even started."

I chuckled. "Perhaps, if you had been listening, you wouldn't be standing here now."

"And miss putting you back in your place? Never."

Felicity was a tough old boot. She was the kind of woman I would've ended up as if I'd taken a different path: strong, intelligent, beautiful, and good with words. I'd often admired her in the past, but she just gave off a vibe that smacked of a lack of ambition. She was the leader of a coven, but she could've been so much more.

"And what place would that be?" I replied.

"Six feet under."

I laughed. "Bring me Nomura's blades." She was on her high horse now, but she'd be toppling out of the saddle in a second.

The cultists wrenched the two katanas from their straps on Nomura's back and brought them over to me. I held their elaborate handles tightly, feeling the satisfying weight of the twin swords. I'd never been particularly good with weapons, always preferring the blissful shiver of pure magic, but this was going to look ever so dramatic.

Felicity, Cormac, and Remington had the decency to look pale. In fairness, I'd expected more from Remington, since he probably knew about my Imogene ruse by now. Maybe it was the shock that was rendering him silent. I tended to have that effect on people. Even Felicity seemed stunned enough to shut her trap.

"Not so chatty now, are we?" I mused as I took a step toward Nomura.

"You don't need to do this," Cormac cut in, his words hitting my ears with that soothing Irish lilt. I'd forgotten how intoxicating an Irish accent could be, and Cormac was a looker in his own right. Dark and mysterious, I'd have called him. He had nothing on Davin, but he wasn't too shabby.

"Ah, but it's not a matter of need, Cormac. This is purely a matter of want." I didn't wait for him to speak again. "Any last words, Nomura?"

"You will not be smiling when all of this comes to a close," he said quietly. "I have nothing more to say to you. Reunite me with my son. I pray my sins and his may be forgiven, so that he and I may be at peace."

"Oh, there's one more thing." I'd been waiting for this.

"Of course there is," Felicity muttered, but I ignored her.

"I was the one who killed your wife, Nomura. She was on a mission to retrieve a hidden cache of rare magical artifacts when I happened upon her research party. I killed them all. So let's call that three for three, shall we?"

Nomura's eyes widened, a look of overwhelming rage and horror washing over him. But before he could breathe a word, I raised the swords up and swiped them across his neck in a perfectly synchronized display of grace and precision. I didn't wait for his head to fall. Instead, I made my way past him to the secondary line, choosing victims at random. A few security magicals were cut down, just to hammer home my point. I meant business, and if these idiots didn't yield, they'd suffer the same fate.

"Is that the only way you know how to negotiate?" Cormac's sour tone called to me.

I turned back. "Productive, no?"

"You're a monster, not a goddess. You've always needed to be the center of attention, even when you were a student in New York. Looks like nothing has changed."

I'd known the Crowleys for a long time, but if they thought they could use little anecdotes to make me appear weak, they had another thing coming. The Katherine they'd known back then wasn't the one standing before them today. I wasn't Katherine anymore. I was Eris.

Regardless, my skin prickled with anger. "Are you really that eager for a taste of these blades, Cormac? Do you think you can get under my skin with a few choice words? Weaklings like you mean nothing to me. I could kill you all and it wouldn't make a dent in my day."

"You're desperate, Katherine," he replied. "I always knew you were power-mad, but even you must be able to see that it's not going to end well. You've got Chaos itself turning against you. This is all going to blow up in your face, mark my words."

"If you even have a face by the end of this." Remington had finally found his voice.

"He speaks!" I gave a mock gasp.

"And you probably won't want your precious followers to hear what I have to say," he shot back. "Look at you—you're falling apart. And if you lose your body before you can find a vessel to hold this new energy, you're pretty much done for. I would've thought someone like you would have something in place to stop that from happening. Apparently not." It seemed as though Odette had done more chattering than she'd let on. Evidently, Remington knew something of my plan, and there was only one person who could've given him that kind of information. Although, it looked like he'd only come to this realization now that he'd figured out something was off about me. These cracks weren't exactly subtle.

"I'll find my vessel, don't you worry." Rage burned in the pit of my stomach, and I was having a hard time controlling it. I couldn't afford another outburst, but these punks were making it very difficult to keep calm.

"When you fall, the cult will fall. What, do you think they'll follow you when you're a wisp of energy trapped in this otherworld? There's almost nothing you can do to affect the magicals in the human world when your body goes and you get stuck here. And I'll make sure *nobody* summons you when that day comes. There's a reason the Children of Chaos live apart from the human world and why they're holed up in these otherworlds. Or didn't you know that?"

I kept my cool. "Of course I know that. Why else would I be seeking a vessel?"

"It's because of people like you that it happened in the first place," Remington said. "And when you get trapped here, without a form, I wouldn't be surprised if Chaos tightens its belt even further. And don't think I haven't guessed which vessel you've got your eye on. You won't get her, Katherine. Harley's not yours to use."

I frowned. "Of course you'd know all about this, wouldn't you? I'm sure you got some rare morsels out of that girlfriend of yours. Well, so did I, when I tortured her and cracked open her brain and let all the goodies spill out. How else would I know what Harley can do for me? I would be stumped if it wasn't for dear, darling Odette and that incredible mind of hers. A shame I turned it to mulch when I was done getting what I wanted and made her into a babbling moron."

"You'd better wipe that smirk off your face, or—" Remington snarled. Funny how savage people could get when it came to the people they loved.

"Or what, Remington?" I interrupted. "There's nothing you can do about it. You can't bring her back. She's cold in the ground now, and she's staying there. And I've earned the right to a bit of satisfaction." His face had turned ashen with rage, but I just laughed. "Anyway, I did what was necessary. In the end, I'd call it a kindness that I had her killed; like putting down a sick dog. She wouldn't have wanted to carry on like that, a complete halfwit whose days were filled with rocking back and forth. I'd have been surprised if she could even remember you by then, Remington."

Remington fought against the cultists who held him back. "Your days of congratulating yourself are numbered, Katherine. You made the mistake of using Odette and casting her aside. You should have delved deeper; you should have kept her alive. But that's your problem, isn't it? You're so fixated on one goal that you don't see the rest. There might have been a simpler solution in her mind, but you didn't bother to look. And now you've got no way of finding that out. You'll fail. You'll fail no matter what you do."

"Simpler solutions? Like what?" I held Nomura's blades at the neck of another security magical. "I suggest you start talking, or this guy gets it. In fact, I'll just keep killing people until you decide you want to say something worthy enough to get me to stop."

I killed the security magical there and then, just to let him know I was serious. A flicker of panic crossed Remington's face. *Good.* If he thought he knew more than me, then this was his opportunity to shorten my kill list.

"Just stop!" Remington shouted hoarsely. "I don't know anything. All I know is what you're planning—I realized it as soon as I saw those cracks on your face. I said there *might* have been another solution, but you killed the only person who could've told you."

"Do you have a nugget for me or not? Make it a good one, or I'll keep going." He seemed like he was telling the truth, which bugged me, but I wanted to be sure. And the threat of murder was a surefire way to get someone to speak.

I rested the blades on the shoulders of one of the SDC's preceptors. Lasher Ickes, I believe his name was. He was trembling like a dog, his glasses slipping right down to the bridge of his hawkish nose. He was a beanpole of a man, with stringy blond hair and weak, watery blue eyes. *You must be the historian.* I didn't go in for stereotypes, but there was no denying this one.

"The Children of Chaos used to roam the earth freely before, in ancient days," Remington said in a low voice. "Some, like Erebus, tried to rule over the Primus Anglicus, but Chaos cut in and cast the Children from Earth and into their otherworlds. Ever since, the Children's reach into the human world has been limited, even though Chaos flows through everything. Clearly, there are still loopholes, like the Challenge you completed, and Portal Openers who can reach these otherworlds... but the universe, as it is today, is different from the early days of Chaos, because of individuals like you who ruined it for everyone else."

"I said I wanted information that I *didn't* know." I edged the blades closer to Lasher Ickes's neck, and he began to sob uncontrollably. I wanted to shake him by the shoulders and tell him to man the heck up, but that would have been a waste of effort, since he was about to die.

"There could have been other loopholes, but you didn't bother to look. You wanted it to be something from the Grimoire because you're obsessed with it," he replied more quickly. "You're obsessed with punishing the Merlins and the Shiptons."

"I can force you to—" I stopped mid-sentence as a blinding pain shot through me. Light seeped through the cracks in my skin, the oily black beneath my torn-up hands transforming into a bronzed glow.

"No, you can't." Remington smiled. "I don't have Odette's memories and thoughts. I don't know what she would've known. But you should've been wiser. Now you're doomed to fail because you won't be able to find Harley in time!"

I gathered myself as the pain subsided just enough to let me continue. "I'd be doing you all a favor if I killed you right now, but I'm guessing that's what you want: fuel to stoke the fires of all those who seek to resist me. Well, you can keep your kindling to yourselves." I forced a grin onto my face. "Instead, you're going to show everyone how glorious it is to be in my service. Waste not, want not, right? There'll be no death for you today. No, I'm going to turn you into my obedient servants."

"No!" Felicity shouted, as if that was going to stop me.

"Videte nunc mihi. Servite mihi aut putrefaciunt. Tantum audi vocem meam, sed credunt mihi caros pati. Erunt, et in ministerium, et exsultate in ea tranquillitas est in te. Obedientia postulavit."

The curse rippled out of me and settled over the group of insurgents. They fell silent, their heads dipping forward, their eyes staring dead ahead like zombies. Lovely, obedient zombies.

"Look to me." Their eyes all turned up, bloodshot, irises glimmering purple. *Perfect.*

However, Remington's words nagged at the back of my mind. Had I missed something important? Had I missed another loophole that might have taken the need for Harley out of the equation? Or had he just been bluffing to annoy me? I didn't know, but I supposed I didn't care, really. I'd made my choice and I was sticking to it. I'd rather enjoy the bed I'd made once I had Harley's body.

For now, however, I had a list as long as my arm to get through. And, as Remington had so kindly pointed out, not a whole lot of time in which to get it all done. I was barely holding myself together. But, as the British would say, I had to keep calm and carry on. Chin up, back straight, socks up, and all that weird stuff Davin came out with.

First and foremost on my list was the repopulation of the covens, and making sure the Bestiary was in good working order with its Beast Master in place. The covens would be empty now that I'd taken Chaos away from the magicals, since they would have identified their residents as humans and kicked them out. *Ah, security protocols, how I do love thee.*

I turned to my gathered minions.

"I need you to track down the highest ranking former magicals from each coven and give them an Ephemera. It will grant them enough Chaos to get all of your teams inside the covens. Force them in whatever way you have to and burn the old registries. Create new registries and add your names, then see to it that the high-ranking magicals are restrained—or bend them to our cause. If they refuse, lock them up. If they relent, bring them to me. If any of you high-ranking individuals are already among us, then select a coven and begin, taking a team with you," I ordered. "The cult must spread out and occupy the vacant covens. From there, you must hijack the systems and turn everything to our cause."

"Yes, Eris," the gathered cultists chorused.

How I loved the sound of unadulterated loyalty.

"For now, however, we keep all of this secret from the humans. They shouldn't know of our plans just yet. That battle will come later, and will be easily won once we've infiltrated every city in the United States and beyond." I smiled at the thought. "We conquer the magical world first, and the human world will follow." And, after I got my new body, the real show would begin.

"Yes, Eris," they chorused again.

They had all had enough of their Chaos restored to be able to gain entry into the covens, and those who chose to serve along the way would be granted the same gift. I was a magnanimous goddess, after all.

As they made their way through portals created by those to whom I'd given that ability, I turned back to Lasher Ickes. He stared up at me with those feeble eyes, now a satisfying shade of purple. With a swipe, I lifted the curse from him. There was something about the way he'd been trembling that gave me an idea. He seemed like exactly the sort of person who could be made to change sides, now that he'd seen what I was about. The weakest minds were always the first to fold.

He flung himself down on the ground at my feet.

"Mighty Eris, spare me," he begged. "Preceptor Bellmore tried to get me to come with her to join you. I refused then, but that was before I understood your strength and your wisdom. Please, spare me, and I'll be your loyal follower. I swear it."

"Why should I trust you?"

"Because you have made me see the light. I understand now, in a way I didn't before. I have seen your kind across the years in my history books, and I know there would be no use in disobeying you. I would rather be on the winning side, Eris. I would rather live and have my Chaos returned."

I smiled.

I'd known taking magic would be a useful tool of persuasion, and it seemed to be working out rather nicely. Although, that didn't mean I was foolish enough to just outright trust someone who'd fought against me barely a few hours ago.

"I will give you a task so that you can prove yourself to me."

He nodded effusively. "Anything, Eris. Anything."

"You will be the one to lead the way into the SDC." I nodded to a small cluster of cultists who stood nearby. "This will be your team. If you try and betray me, they will kill you on the spot. Understood?"

"Understood, Eris." He was practically licking my shoes.

"Take this, and it will allow you inside the SDC." I took an Ephemera out of my dress and handed it to him. It was charged with enough Chaos to get him into the coven and keep him there.

He frowned. "But… what about my own abilities?"

"They'll be returned once I'm certain you can be trusted." I had trouble trusting anyone from the SDC, to be quite honest, given their track record. Bellmore had tried to doubt me, and now she was dead. Ickes would go the same way if he slipped up. *Ickes is the perfect name for you.* Just looking at his weaselly face made me shudder, but at least he could be useful.

He bowed down again. "Yes, Eris. Of course, Eris. I won't disappoint, Eris." *Yes, sir. No, sir. Three bags full, sir.* I abhorred grovelers, but I could swallow that contempt for now.

"We have work to do, so I suggest we get on with it. I won't be far away, so don't think you can run off and sound any alarms. That won't end well for you. I doubt you're too keen on becoming Ickes the Headless Historian, are you?"

"No, Eris." He looked about ready to pee his pants, which meant he was at the perfect stage of loyalty.

"Good, then let's get to it."

I held up my palm and opened a portal into the SDC. A risky neces-sity, but it didn't seem to be making too much of a mess of me. This was small stuff in comparison to a blanket curse or a blast of spidery Telekinesis. Other cult members had been gifted with the ability to open portals, but they were handling their own missions.

Walking through the portal into Imogene's old stomping grounds, I braced myself for the hard work that was yet to come. Namely, using just enough power to get Tobe to obey me without tearing myself to shreds. Harley's allies were still too numerous for my liking, but I'd deal with them as the opportunity arose.

I put on the guise of Imogene for what I hoped would be the last time, and the coven accepted me at face value as Ickes and the small group of cultists followed me inside.

"As I mentioned, see to it that the registry is burned and create a new one. Add your names to it, and add mine for good measure," I ordered.

"You aren't joining us, Eris?" one of the cultists replied.

I shook my head. "No, I have my own business to attend to." Rear-ranging the magical hierarchy and burning registries was a small-fry operation compared to what I had to do. I needed to make sure my power source was all in order so these covens would keep running the way they were supposed to. Without that measure in place, it wouldn't just be me who would start to fall apart.

Leaving them to it, I headed straight for the Bestiary, reveling in the silence of the empty hallways. When I reached the doorways, I pushed them open in the most dramatic way possible, feeling like an ancient warrior about to break down the stronghold of my enemy.

That heroic sensation died as I froze on the threshold, swearing so loudly that it echoed across the vast atrium. The boxes were open. Lots of the monsters were running free, but I knew a ruse when I saw one, and I was willing to bet my left ass cheek that there would be some missing when we did a head count.

Tobe included.

FOUR

Harley

We had to get moving, but I couldn't help staring back out of the window at my misty Purge beast, still stretched over the lake in a foggy mass.

What was it doing out there? Why was it just… sitting like that? It wasn't like any creature I'd ever seen. The black smog creature that had almost wiped us out in the French church was the closest thing to it, but that beast had at least had eyes. And it had made its intentions majorly understood when it swept toward me like it wanted me dead. If it hadn't been for Finch, it might've finished the job.

But this creature didn't give me the same vibe. I had no clue whatsoever what it wanted or what it was doing.

"Someone needs to stay here and watch over this thing," I said.

The others were gathering supplies. Garrett had his sword and O'Halloran had his daggers, but the rest of us were pretty much defenseless. Santana's family had a few extra bits and pieces around the cabin, but they weren't nearly as impressive as the weapons from the SDC museum. Santana had managed to find a shotgun, which she had slung over her shoulder. Dylan had a crossbow and a sparse quiver of bolts. Meanwhile, Tatyana and Wade had knives from the kitchen, and

Finch had a baseball bat. Levi and Raffe didn't have any weapons—they *were* the weapons. Well, their djinn were. As for me, I didn't have anything.

"Harley Quinn, I'm coming for your crown." Finch chuckled to himself as he made a few practice swings.

"Harley, take this." Santana passed me a switchblade.

At least it was a tool I was vaguely familiar with. I'd gotten out of several scrapes involving these things. *Stick 'em with the sharp end, right?*

"I'll stay here and keep an eye on the Purge beast," Krieger said. I'd noticed his reluctance to gear up and had sort of been expecting him to volunteer. "Someone will need to keep watch over Jacob and Alton also, and I suppose I'm meant to be the one with the most medical knowledge."

This loss of Chaos thing had really hit Krieger hard, but he was doing his best with the tools he had. Namely, a fairly impressive first-aid kit, courtesy of the Catemacos.

Jacob shook his head and tried to get up. "I'm coming with you."

"Sorry, Jacob, you're going to have to sit this one out," Wade replied, his tone soft.

I nodded. "You're still recovering. If you go out there with us, you'll get hurt." He looked heartbroken but stayed silent. "You should stay here and keep an eye on our misty friend, make sure it doesn't do anything it's, uh, not supposed to." I had no idea what would qualify as unusual behavior, but it was the only thing I could think of to say that might give him a sense of purpose.

"I would also like to volunteer to stay," Levi chimed in unexpectedly. "I still have Zalaam at my disposal." His face twisted up, letting us all know that the djinn didn't take kindly to his phrasing. "I mean, I still have Zalaam working alongside me. While djinn aren't normally versed in magic spells, nor do they possess Elemental abilities, they are still products of Chaos, as we know; they have stemmed from Erebus directly. For that reason, they can resist the attack of another creature forged of Chaos. Should the black mist become hostile, it will be useful to have a line of defense."

"Pfft, and he calls himself the wise one," Kadar muttered, Raffe's skin flushing a pale shade of red. "Don't you know anything about our history?"

Levi frowned. "I haven't taken much time to speak with Zalaam about it, nor did I seek to learn much before he was... restrained. He always wanted to talk before then, but I figured out a number of ways to shut him out fairly early on. I suppose I was never comfortable with having a djinn." His face twisted up again, a hint of red peeking through his skin.

"Well, if you had bothered to listen to him, and if you had accepted your union, you'd know that there were ancient djinn who used to perform crazy powerful magic and curses." Kadar still had a big chip on his shoulder, that much was obvious.

"That is a thing of the past." Zalaam's voice boomed through, turning Levi a dark crimson. "These days, ordinary djinn—those who roam free of such parasitical unions as ours—lead much more secluded lives. Many are locked within the Bestiary, as it happens, and have been for many a year, despite the fact that we are so much more than generic Purge beasts. I suppose magicals rarely care to make the distinction."

Looks like Papa Djinn has a chip too.

"So, Jacob, Levi, you're going to stay here with Krieger and watch the black mist? And take care of Alton?" I glanced at them, realizing that Astrid hadn't said anything at all. She was just staring at her father like she was urging herself to feel *something*. I could see the strain on her face.

"Astrid?" Garrett stepped in, putting his hand on her shoulder.

She jumped in surprise. "What? Sorry, I was miles away."

"Are you staying here?" he asked.

She paused for a moment. "Yes... Yes, I think I should stay here and look after my father, help him recover." She took Smartie out and swiped her fingertips across the screen. "I've got Smartie, so I can assist you all remotely with anything you need. He's still linked to the covens, so I should be able to gather a bunch of intel and send it over to you. I've already got the number for Harley's burner. If you text me everyone else's numbers when you've got new phones, I'll be able to communicate efficiently."

I nodded. "Will do."

"Wait, won't Katherine be able to trace Smartie?" Tatyana peered at the device.

Astrid shook her head. "He's untraceable. I made him that way."

"Then the four of you will stay here to watch Misty and Alton." I looked back out at the rippling fog, still baffled by the thing.

"Misty?" Finch chuckled. "A bit too sappy for something that could choke us all to death, don't you think? It's like calling a polar bear Marshmallow."

I shrugged. "I like it. Subverting expectations."

"Names are important," Kadar cut in. "Misty is practical."

"Okay, if everyone's ready, then we need to talk logistics." Wade jumped into business mode. "Our first destination should be neutral ground, and Kenzie is definitely our best option so far in terms of getting some temporary Chaos back. Thanks for that tip, Krieger, Finch."

Finch gave a comical bow. "No problem, guv'nor."

"I hope you can find the items you need," Krieger replied.

"Yeah, she's got burners and all kinds of not-so-legal stuff that we can hopefully use to move around. So, even if we don't get any of those Hermetic Batteries, we'll at least have a bit more freedom," I added, looking at our motley crew. We didn't exactly look formidable, but appearances could be deceiving. And I really, really hoped Kenzie did have some Hermetic Batteries, otherwise we'd still be screwed Chaos-wise.

"From there, we'll have to assess our options." O'Halloran came in as the military man. At least he looked the part. "As non-magicals, we're not just locked out of the covens. We're locked out of Waterfront Park and every other interdimensional bubble you can think of. The barriers have gone up, lads and lasses, and we're going to have to get creative to move forward. A little military improv—nothing we can't handle, I'm sure."

"Like black ops?" Finch's eyes widened like he was a little kid.

O'Halloran smiled. "If you like, aye."

"I'm... I'm coming with you."

All of us whipped around to see Alton gripping the side of the sofa and pushing himself up, his chest heaving as he struggled to stand.

"No offense, Alton, but you look like hell," O'Halloran replied. "You'd slow us down."

He shook his head defiantly. "I'm coming with you. I'm not leaving you to do this alone, and I won't slow you down." He let go of the sofa and somehow managed to stand on his own two feet, a sense of determination radiating off him. "Astrid, you should still stay here and be our command center, but I'm coming whether you like it or not. You'll need all the help you can get out there, especially where covens and interdimensional access points are concerned. The SDC's secret passageways aren't the only things I've got up my sleeves."

"You were practically dead a moment ago, Alton!" Santana pleaded. "You need to rest."

"Not until Katherine is *actually* dead," he retorted. "This isn't negotiable."

"And what if you keel over while we're out there? We don't have a way of sending you back to Krieger." I was worried. Really worried.

He looked me straight in the eyes. "I'll manage, Harley."

"Dad, maybe it would be best if you stayed." Astrid put her hand on Alton's arm in a vain attempt to get him to sit back down.

"I can't stay here. There's too much at stake," he insisted. "Plus, I'm the only person who knows where Tobe will have gone. If this Kenzie individual doesn't have any Hermetic Batteries, or doesn't have enough for our needs, then Tobe will be our last option for getting more."

I frowned. "What do you mean? Tobe was at the SDC."

"He was, yes," Alton replied with a smirk. "Did you honestly think he'd just sit there in the Bestiary and wait for Katherine to come in and stake her claim on him and his wards, too?"

"Would I look really stupid if I said yeah?" Finch murmured.

Alton gave a weak laugh. "Tobe is a highly intelligent creature. As soon as he heard about Harley being taken, he'd have begun his exit protocols. He won't have been able to take all of the monsters with him, but he'll have taken as many as he could and gone into hiding. I discussed these protocols with him myself, as soon as Katherine's victory started to become more than a possibility. We had them set in stone after you all returned from the Tartarus mission. And, fortunately, I didn't say anything about them to Imogene, and neither did Tobe. It was purely between the two of us." He paused, as if about to land a winning swing. "So, if you want to find Tobe, you need me."

"Or, you know, you could just tell us where he is," O'Halloran shot back. "Save yourself an aneurysm or cardiac arrest."

"Chaos is still out there, in little pockets. I need some of that in order to recover from this state I'm in." Alton leveled his gaze at O'Halloran. "It's the only way I'll heal faster. If I stay here, I'll get worse, so I'm choosing to act instead of languish. These Hermetic Batteries may be my only remedy."

"You're hoodwinking us is what you're doing," O'Halloran complained. "I didn't think you capable of blackmail, Alton. Shame on you." His tone was half teasing, half deadly serious.

"You'd leave me here otherwise." Alton smiled. "Don't pretend you wouldn't."

"Who's pretending? I'd leave you here in a heartbeat—you know, since that'd be more likely to save your life. But, hey, it's your funeral. Don't let me stand in the way. And don't expect a eulogy, because you won't be getting one. I'll just have 'should've listened' carved on your headstone." O'Halloran shook his head, but what more could we say?

We needed all the supernaturals we could get our hands on, and that included Tobe and his menagerie of beasts.

Alton chuckled. "Noted."

"So… Alton, you're with us, then." I sighed reluctantly. "And if our first port of call is Kenzie, then we need to get to San Diego." I was about to suggest we just go straight to Tobe to get those battery things from him, but we still needed burners and any other protective items she might have. Plus, if Kenzie *did* have some Hermetic Batteries, then backups would always be useful.

"The cult will be eyeing up every single port of entry, every single train and bus station. If there's a mode of transport leading to San Diego, you can bet your ass that the cult is watching it. I wouldn't be surprised if they've popped holes in every hot air balloon they can find, just to be on the safe side." O'Halloran glanced at us all as if we were soldiers in front of a general. "Katherine wants you, Harley. Obsessed would be an understatement. So, we're going to have to be careful."

"And let's not forget we're human now," Wade added.

Finch smirked. "Yup, straight up *Homo sapiens*. No *Homo magicus*."

Wade cut back in. "Which begs the question—how on earth do we get from Southern Mexico to San Diego without being detected?"

"I'm insulted." Kadar folded his arms across his chest. "You think I'm stuck in Raffe's body for the good of my health? All this tasty Chaos, and you're likely thinking about hitchhiking to San Diego, or worse. I am pure, rippling Chaos, ladies and gentlemen. And I've been part of Raffe for long enough to know how to perform that curious little chalk-door spell."

"Sorry," we chorused. With our magic gone, it was hard not to paint everyone with the same magicless brush.

"Apology accepted." He smirked. "The only problem is, I don't know exactly where this Kenzie lives. If I have to think our way there, we may end up in Dubai."

"Problem solved." Astrid brandished Smartie at the djinn. On the screen, she'd dragged up a satellite view of Kenzie's apartment building.

"Who needs magic when you have technical wizardry?" Finch chirped, though I could tell his heart wasn't in it.

We do, that's who. But we'd get it back, one way or another. We'd definitely get it back… right?

FIVE

Harley

Taking the chalk Finch had stolen from Remington's office, Kadar approached the nearest wall and began to draw.

As he whispered the *Aperi Si Ostium* spell, the lines crackled, sinking into the wooden planks and forging the three-dimensional doorway. The whole time, he kept looking back at the picture on Smartie's screen, no doubt fixing the location in his head to make sure we ended up in the right place. Well, there was only one way to find out.

He pulled the handle and swung the door outward, revealing the shady grime of a back alley. I recognized the neighborhood.

"You did it!" I gasped. This could be chalked up, quite literally, as a win for us.

Kadar shot me a withering look. "Gratitude for the vote of confidence. I get the feeling this won't be the last time you forget how useful I can be."

He stepped through to the alleyway, the rest of us following close behind. I brought up the rear, casting a glance back at the weird mist on the lake before crossing the threshold. *Please don't let it kill anyone.* The four who were remaining at the cabin might've had Zalaam, but my Purge beast was crazy powerful. I hoped they'd never find out just how powerful.

Running up to the front of the line, I ducked down beside Wade and Kadar and peered out over the dilapidated yards. Like last time, there were a few groups of shady-looking characters clustered along the street, but none of them were too close to Kenzie's derelict apartment building. In fact, we had a direct line to her littered front yard, which still had a crusty old refrigerator and a moldy sofa as garden ornaments.

Jacob's Sensate ability would've come in handy right about now, so we could pick out the cultists from the ordinary folk. They'd be hiding everywhere, if I knew Katherine the way I hoped I did. She wanted to get me as quickly as she could, and that meant having boots on the ground, covering as wide an area as possible. Any one of these hood rats could be a cultist, and we wouldn't know about it until it was too late.

"Keep your heads down. Don't draw attention," I whispered, pulling a World Cup Mexico '86 cap down over my head. Yet another treasure from the Catemaco stores.

Wade had the shades that his parents had given him and a battered old denim jacket to put over his fancy suit. Although, he couldn't use them to see hidden charms; the lenses would still be picking them up, for sure, but his eyes no longer had the magical capacity to see the secret sigils.

Finch had a worn fedora twinned with a pair of Ray Bans that made him look like a Miami mobster, which he was clearly delighted by. Santana, Tatyana, Dylan, Raffe, Garrett, O'Halloran, and Alton had a mishmash of clothes that had been found in the cabin: jackets, hats, coats, shades, anything that would marginally hide our identities. It'd have to be enough.

As we crept out of the alley and made our way toward Kenzie's apartment building, I took in our surroundings, trying to get a feel for anything dangerous. Everything *seemed* normal, exactly like it had before. Just the bad side of town—a place I knew well.

"Why isn't there a bunch of Eris propaganda plastered all over the place?" Santana whispered. "Didn't she say she wanted to be the ruler of the magical *and* the human world? Or has she given up on the last bit?"

Finch grinned. "Katherine? Give up? As if. She's biding her time, waiting for her big entrance. There'd be no point in announcing herself as their overlord only to disintegrate into a billion little pieces before she actually got to do anything to them. She needs Harley first. She needs a body that's not going to fall apart before she declares herself a goddess, or she'd just end up a laughingstock, a goddess who suddenly drifted away and never came back."

"He's right," I replied as full understanding hit me. "I saw the toll that Katherine's Child of Chaos form was taking on her body. That's why she needs me, so she can keep it all together. Chaos is ripping her apart."

Finch nodded. "And, knowing my mother, she wouldn't dream of asserting herself as an almighty goddess unless she had her caboose well and truly covered. Like I said, biding her sweet time."

"So, she's having problems with her form," Wade said. "That's only going to spur her on to find Harley as quickly as possible. All it gives us is the equivalent of a five-second head start. This is literally our last shot."

"I'm sure you'll keep reminding us, Captain Stopwatch." Finch smirked, but I could tell he was worried.

Hurrying across the yard, we entered the hollowed-out husk of Kenzie's apartment block through the same iron door that was hanging half off its hinges. It smelled the same; that eclectic mix of urine, decay, and misery.

Together, we moved up the darkened stairs, and I wished I had my Fire, if only to light the way for us. Even though I knew there was nothing to be afraid of, I kept thinking something was going to jump out at us.

We reached Kenzie's floor and approached the solid metal door where she lived. Wade knocked, and we waited for an answer.

"Who's there?" a quiet, frightened voice asked from the other side.

"It's Finch." He stepped up, taking Wade's position. "I'm a friend of Kenzie's. Do you remember me from last time? I was here with two of my friends."

The door creaked open, and a small, puffy face appeared in the gap. It was Kenzie's little sister. I couldn't remember her name, but she looked so much like Kenzie that the connection was impossible to mistake. She was even wearing one of Kenzie's cropped hoodies, complete with an expletive emblazoned across the front, though it looked full-size on her.

"Are you here to help her?" the girl whimpered.

Finch frowned. "What do you mean, Inez? Where's your sister?"

The little girl grasped Finch's hand and yanked him into the apartment, not stopping until they reached the crumbling front room where I'd seen her engrossed in a rerun of *SpongeBob*. Only, the vibe was completely different. The TV was off, and Kenzie was lying on the sofa, her eyes wide open and milky white, staring blindly upward.

Finch ran to her and started shaking her by the shoulders, but Kenzie wouldn't wake up. She was unconscious.

"She… she was morphing… out of her body. Then… then the magic went." Inez sobbed, holding onto Finch's shirt. "And… and my mom… she's getting really sick. More sick than ever. She's… in the bedroom. She's asleep, and she's… really sick. Kenzie said your… talisman thingie didn't work. She said… she needed to get someone else to help… but then… then the magic went out and she… she didn't wake up again."

"Crap," Finch said. "I'm not sure why the talisman wouldn't have worked if you tried it before Chaos went out. As for Kenzie, she must have been mid-morph when the Chaos sweep happened. Her consciousness is probably out there, stuck in a pigeon or something."

"This is bad. Very bad." Alton stumbled forward and placed his hand on Kenzie's forehead. I didn't know if he'd forgotten that he didn't have any powers or if he was just checking her temperature. Either way, his face spoke a thousand words. Kenzie had been our only option for communications, but she was out of the game.

Nope, not going to let this get to me.

"Inez, maybe you could help us instead?" I asked gently. "We came to speak to your sister about something very important, and it's something that could help fix her."

Inez eyed me suspiciously. "Help you with what?"

"Do you know where Kenzie keeps her stash of stuff?"

"Yeah, but you can't have it," she replied.

Wow, she is so like her sister.

"Hey, Inez, you trust me, right?" Finch held the girl by her shoulders. "And we really need you to do us a favor, or else your sister is never going to be okay. We've got a way to bring her back, but that means you're going to have to step up. Can you do that?" He was a little too matter of fact, considering what Inez must have been going through.

She frowned. "I wouldn't trust you as far as I could throw you, but… if you think you can fix Kenzie, then I'll help."

"Where'd you learn that line, huh?" Finch smirked. "Your sister?"

Inez flushed. "Maybe."

"Come on, show us where Kenzie keeps the good stuff," he urged.

Still snuffling, Inez led us through to Kenzie's phone stash, the plastic boxes piled just as high as ever. Finch leapt into action, pulling down boxes and handing out burner cells and SIM cards. As soon as everyone had theirs working, I texted the numbers to Astrid, who was waiting. Now at least we'd be able to communicate with our eye in the sky.

"Will you help Kenzie now?" Inez's eyes were wide with hope.

Finch shrugged. "We've got a lot to do first, but if we get that done, then I'm sure she'll come back around."

"You said you'd help!" Inez protested.

"I am helping, but it's not a quick fix. Sorry to disappoint." Finch started rummaging in some of the other boxes. "The only way to help her is to kill the woman who caused all of this. Once we've done that, then we can worry about your sister."

"Finch!" Tatyana hissed.

He glanced over his shoulder. "What?"

"You could try a little empathy."

"I'm not going to lie, am I?" he replied.

"No, but there's a way of doing things," Santana cut in. "Show some compassion, you turd. How would you like it if your sister was in danger and nobody knew if she'd make it through?"

Finch arched an eyebrow. "Been there, done that. Still living it, to be honest."

"Jeez, Finch." Wade frowned. "I thought you were done with that 'don't give a crap' attitude?"

Finch sighed and turned around. "Look, it's not that I'm heartless. I'm not. But we need to keep our eyes on the big prize. Is it sad that Kenzie is trapped somewhere? Sure. Do we have time to worry about it? No. We need to find these Hermetic Batteries, and that's all there is to it. Kenzie's predicament can come later, once we've figured the rest out." He looked down at Inez. "Sorry, kiddo."

"You watch who you're calling kiddo," Inez hissed back.

"Before you all make me out to be the big bad wolf here, get your heads in the game and see the bigger picture," he continued. "We need to be as cold and calculated as Katherine if we want to beat her to a pulp. Wasting time on the small stuff is only going to hold us back. We need to compartmentalize, because if we don't make this work, then we can all kiss our asses goodbye. Like Wonderboy said, we can't forget that this is our last shot. Our actual last shot. This is the part in the game where we're on half a heart and we're about to face the big final boss, only we don't get to start again if we fail."

He turned back to the stack of boxes and continued his rummaging, leaving the rest of us dumbfounded. His analogy was so very Finch, but it struck a chord. I couldn't have put it better myself.

"Do you even know what you're looking for, Finch?" Dylan asked.

"Just give me a sec. Aha, found it!" He tugged a smaller, blue plastic box out of the pile and held it up like a trophy. A label on the side said *Power Sources*. Bringing it back down, he tore off the lid and set it on the side so we could all peer inside.

"Are these the Hermetic Batteries?" I gasped.

"Yo, Alton!" Finch called through to the kitchen, where Alton was leaning against the counter. "Are these what we're looking for?" He brandished one of the objects—a thick brass cuff that looked like it would cover the entirety of my forearm, with glass windows revealing tiny metal mechanisms inside. There were five of them inside the box. Not enough for the whole crew, but it would be a start if these were the right objects.

Alton nodded wearily. "Yes… they are Hermetic Batteries."

Finch punched the air. "Yes! Thank you, Finch. Oh, not a problem. Just doing my job."

"Yeah, but they're empty," Dylan replied.

"I'm aware of that." Finch rolled his eyes. "We're going to need some help filling these babies up. Kadar, care to work your magic? I'm sure Krieger was just being cautious about the whole exploding thing."

Raffe stepped forward, changing into the djinn. He stared at the five Hermetic Batteries and shook his head. "I'm afraid he was not being cautious. He spoke the truth. My raw Chaos, even in a small quantity, would cause this to explode once the refining process started. I was uncertain when Dr. Krieger said that, but now that I've seen them, I know he is right. Do you see that brass disc inside?"

We nodded.

"That is, as far as I can tell from my vague knowledge of magical objects, a Chaos gauge. It should work as a circuit breaker for energy that is too strong, like mine. Hence, an explosion. However, I should be able to use my djinn abilities to draw Chaos from a magical and fill them up. I suspect it would be a similar process to Ephemeras. I just can't put my own Chaos inside them."

"I thought you said you were useful." Finch looked frustrated.

I shrugged. "Look, let's not get bogged down by operational details. The fact is, we've got these things, but we've got no way of using them or filling them because we aren't magicals anymore, unless we want to go around ambushing cultists to get their Chaos out of them. Who else might be able to fill these things? There has to be someone."

"What about the message Kenzie was trying to write? Do you think she might've been writing it for you? Did she know you were coming?" All of us turned to Inez, who suddenly went shy.

"What message?" I was trying hard not to sound too desperate.

"She usually takes notes when she's out doing her morph stuff," Inez explained. "I took the pen and paper out of her hands, but she was writing something. Like, she's unconscious and everything, but her fingers kept twitching and moving the pen a bit. There were some letters, but I don't know if they mean anything."

"Show us," Wade urged.

Heading back into the front room, Inez fetched the piece of paper and held it out. There, in shaky black ink, was a word. Well, one word and the start of another, to be precise:

Marie L

"Marie Laveau," I whispered. She had Chaos by the truckload—the kind that Katherine couldn't take away, because she wasn't a magical in the ordinary sense. Would her Chaos be more suitable than the djinn's?

"And you said Kenzie had gone out to seek further help for your mother?" Alton asked the girl.

Inez nodded. "Yeah. Don't know where, though, so don't ask."

Alton smiled. "Kenzie probably went to Marie Laveau for help and used an animal's body to get there quicker."

"What did I say? She's stuck in a pigeon!" Finch punched the air in excitement.

"If anyone can help us with the Hermetic Batteries and the

Grimoire, not to mention everything else, it's Marie Laveau," I admitted. "She might even be able to fill them up for us, since her Chaos is likely still intact." I wasn't going to let myself get too excited yet, though. We still had a long way to go and, apparently, more hoops to jump through. *Great.*

"New Orleans, here we come!" Finch whooped.

Just then, my phone beeped. I took it out of my pocket, expecting a reply from Astrid. Instead, Ryann's name flashed up with a message attached:

Out of San Diego. We're safe. Are you? Worried sick. Love you. Mom and Dad say love you, too.

I sighed with relief. At least that was one less thing to worry about. Knowing they were safely out of the way would give me the peace of mind that I needed to stay focused on what was ahead, because that was going to be one heck of a mountain to climb.

I typed back quickly, wanting to give them that same peace of mind.

Am safe. Don't worry. Sending love to you all. Stay hidden.

"So, which way do we go first?" Tatyana asked. "Marie Laveau or Tobe?"

"I don't think it's wise for us to split up," O'Halloran added.

Alton nodded. "No splitting up. We should head to New Orleans first. It'll be easier to get to Tobe from there, and we should be able to split the Chaos from these Hermetic Batteries to any he might have, if Marie Laveau can help us. I've seen it done before. Besides, he will know not to move from his position until we find him, as we agreed. He won't go anywhere until he hears from me."

"Is he *in* New Orleans?" O'Halloran peered at Alton suspiciously.

Alton smiled. "Nope. I'm not going to tell you where he is yet—so don't even think about sending me back."

"New Orleans it is, then," Wade said.

Garrett raised his hand. Or, rather, his sword. "Last time we went to Marie Laveau's place, her burial site was inside an interdimensional pocket. If we're human now, how are we supposed to access it?"

Raffe cleared his throat, but Kadar's voice came out. "Hello? Now, this is really getting insulting."

"You can get us in?" Wade asked.

"I might not be as powerful as some djinn, since I'm forced to have a host, and said host is currently lacking his Chaos, which makes me even less powerful. But, come on…"

"Point taken." Wade smiled apologetically.

Finch grinned from ear to ear. "Yass, time for a bit of tomb raiding!"

"Finch, don't touch anything when we get to Marie Laveau's garden," I warned.

"Killjoy," he mumbled.

"Nope, just trying to stop *you* from getting killed." I smiled back at him, though my insides were jangling with nerves.

It was time to visit an old friend, though "friend" might have been pushing it. Marie Laveau was a law unto herself, and we had to remember that. She was a Voodoo Queen, after all, and that dark streak in her was unpredictable at best, dangerous at worst.

It was anyone's guess what kind of welcome we'd receive.

SIX

Finch

"Yo, hold your horses for a sec." I waggled my phone at the group just as everyone else's phone pinged in a jarring clamor. It was the human Whiz-Kid. Otherwise known as Astrid. "You all seeing what I'm seeing?"

"A text from Astrid." Dylan stared at the screen. *Slow claps for the genius.*

"It's an email address and a password. She says we need to get to a computer or a tablet or a smartphone." Wade nodded.

"So glad we've got Einstein with us." I flashed him a grin.

He rolled his eyes. This was our usual rhythm of banter. I'd never have admitted it, but Wonderboy was growing on me way more than I'd expected him to. Posh boys were always joyless muppets, but Wade was turning out to be okay. An exception to the rule. I liked to think Harley had a part in that. I mean, he'd been insufferable before she arrived at the SDC, prancing about the place like a prized donkey. *Ah, the things love can do.*

The thought made me glance at Harley's jacket. I was still getting used to seeing her wear it when the last person I'd seen in it was Adley. But it made a weird kind of sense. Adley had been the only person I'd ever truly cared about. Now, Harley had taken that painfully vacant spot. Although, not in the same way, naturally. This wasn't *Game of Thrones*.

"Inez, you got a computer we can use?" I turned to the little girl. "None of our burners are smartphones."

She was scowling at me, as per usual. As if I could've known the talisman would be a flop. I wasn't some collector of ancient artifacts. I'd stolen a few in my time, sure, but did I know how they worked? Barely. And it wasn't like I wanted Kenzie to be trapped in a bird brain. Looked like I was *El Scapegoat* once again. All because I had the common sense to keep my emotions on the back burner.

"Yeah," she replied.

"Do you want to show us where it is?"

She shrugged. "Whatever." Ah, the Hayvon sass was strong with this one.

Still, she led us through the apartment to a tiny, box-shaped room in the back. An anemic bulb lit the place up. Ahead, a PC as old as Alton sat on a dusty desk. I doubted it'd even have Windows 95 installed by the looks of the thing. I'd almost forgotten PCs had ever looked like this—it was genuinely massive, and bulky as anything.

"Does it have access to the Internet?" I asked dubiously.

"Of course it does," Inez shot back, turning the old machine on. The clatter that came from inside it was almost laughable. *Is it coal-powered or what?*

"I see." I dialed Astrid's number and waited for her to answer.

"Finch?"

"Yup, though we should probably use call signs. I'll be Professor X, and you can be Whiz-Kid," I replied. I could've sworn I heard her eyes roll. The others were staring at me. "What? It makes total sense."

"What do you need... Professor X?" The reluctance in her voice made me smirk.

"We've got a computer, though it's probably going to take a million years to boot up. How do we access the email account you gave us without bringing the cultists down on us?"

"Listen very carefully. The email account is protected, so it shouldn't alert anyone," she replied. As she spoke, telling me how to navigate through firewalls and get into the dark web, I typed away on the painfully slow computer. Eventually, I reached the page that we needed and opened up the email account. "Do you have it?"

"Yep, *B-I-N-G-O* and Bingo was his name-o." I clicked the link and the email account opened, showing a list of new messages.

"Then I'll go before anyone can trace this call. They shouldn't be able to, but we should limit calls to a few minutes, just in case. And, as much as I hate to admit it, you're right about the call signs. Get everyone to send me theirs."

I smiled. "Will do." Hanging up, I turned to the others. "Astrid says you've got to text her your call signs. Pick good ones. This is your moment."

As they did that, I clicked through the messages in the email account, hoping for something juicy. Unfortunately, Astrid's gathered intel had been entirely squeezed of the good juice. It left a dry, miserable husk of a list, complete with depressing photos from the covens' surveillance systems. And, more of it kept coming in. Cultists had been spotted everywhere. There were groups of them at every seaport, airport, and every kind of port you could think of. They clearly thought they were being discreet, but they stood out like sore thumbs. Davin hadn't been seen, and neither had Katherine. So that was one little spark of goodness. We needed all the intel we could get before we headed to the Big Easy.

"Does someone else want to sift through this mess? It's making my eyes hurt." I stepped away from the PC, and Garrett took my place. He'd spent enough time fawning over Astrid in the SDC's command center to know what to do. Listening to the steady *tap-tap* of keys, I made my way back through the dingy apartment.

Inez had retreated to the kitchen and was standing on a crate to reach the stovetop. Something was frying in a pan, and O'Halloran was scooping about a ton of coffee into a mug beside her. Alton was leaning over the kitchen table, his head in his hands. I guessed the breakfast was for him. He looked like he'd had one heck of a heavy night.

"Rough night?" I smiled as Alton lifted his head.

"Worse than Hogmanay in Edinburgh, circa 2006," he replied.

"I'm going to pretend I know what that means." I walked toward Inez and peered over her shoulder. "What's cooking, small fry?"

She shot lasers out of her eyes. "I'm not a small fry!"

"Well, you're small, and you're frying something, so I'd say you are."

A small smile tugged at the corners of her lips. "Just some mush-rooms for the sick one over there, and maybe some toast if I can find bread that hasn't gone moldy. It always made my mom feel better."

"You got anything stronger for the poor dude?" I eyed the cabinets.

She frowned and clambered down from her crate. Dragging it with her, she climbed back up and reached on tiptoe for some plastic canis-ters in the nearby cupboard. Taking them down, she set them on the kitchen counter.

"These might help. They're my mom's pills, and I used to give them to her when Kenzie wasn't around." Her voice caught in her throat. "I know what they do. They're supposed to boost your immune system and stop things from fighting other things. So they might work on your friend."

"So wise for one so tiny." I grinned at her, but she didn't look impressed.

"I'll smack you with this pan if you call me small again," she warned.

I raised my hands in surrender. "Okay, okay, no more small jabs!" If she was anything like Kenzie, she was a genius in the making. A tough but adorable one, like a furious hamster or a mildly pissed-off honey badger. Those suckers were lethal, but oh so cute.

While Harley and the others were still busy with the images Astrid had sent, I crossed the room to sit beside Kenzie. The clang of pans filled the air. Midget Chef was scraping the breakfast onto a plate while O'Halloran mixed the coffee and set it in front of Alton. He drank deep, like a student the night before a last-minute essay was due. Cracking open a few of the medicine bottles, he popped a few pills, too. I didn't know if they'd help much. Nothing but a whack of Chaos could fix Alton—like, really fix him—but I supposed beggars couldn't be choosers.

"Yo, Tiny, you in there?" I made sure nobody was looking and pushed a strand of Kenzie's hair out of her face. "I've got no idea if you can hear me, but, if you can... sorry for ransacking your supplies. I know you'd understand if you were here. We took phones and Hermetic Batteries, so sorry for that." I glanced at Alton, who was shoveling down food like there was no tomorrow. "And sorry for ransacking your fridge. Oh, and your mom's medicine cabinet, too. I'll replace it all, if we make it back."

I felt a bit stupid chatting to an unconscious girl, but who knew, maybe she'd remember this when she woke up. Unless she was going to wake up a vegetable. If the Chaos sweep had caught her mid-morph, then there was no telling what kind of damage was going on in her head. It could be irreversible.

Nah, Kenzie's a tough cookie, I told myself. Kenzie had been a pal, or the closest thing to it, for a while now. I wasn't about to let Katherine destroy her.

"I just wanted you to know," I continued. "My friends and I are going to do everything we can to bring Chaos back, so we can fix you. Your family needs you, and I'm not going to let them suffer. In the meantime, I'll make sure your sister and your mom have everything they need."

I realized it was the first time I'd referred to the Rag Team as my friends out loud. It was a weird feeling. Were they my friends? I didn't really have much to compare it to. There was Kenzie, though she'd always been more of a business pal. Me and Garrett had been pals, once upon a time, but that'd been different. It had been layered with the ruse of me working for Katherine. How real can a friendship be if it's built on lies? I looked at them, all crammed into the box room like sardines.

If I care about what happens to them, then maybe that's what friendship is.

Man, this was getting a little too after-school-special for my liking. It was what happened when you spent too much time with the Muppet Babies.

"Whoa!" Harley's voice drew my attention back.

"What is it?" I leapt over the sofa, James Bond-style, and ran to the box room. Muscling my way in, I squished myself beside Raffe and Santana and looked at the screen.

Stilted videos were playing, struggling through the ancient PC— scenes of magicals being brought to their knees. There wasn't any sound, but their horrified faces said everything. This was the moment Chaos had been snatched away. A few seconds later, they disappeared. The covens had kicked them out.

"Sneaky little creeps," I muttered as the video changed. Cult members flooded in through portals, while others just waltzed in on their own two feet. At the head of each group, there was always some poor chump who'd been wrangled into submission, and each of those chumps held a very familiar object in their hands. "She's given them Ephemeras to get around the coven protocols."

Wade nodded. "It would appear so."

The video buffered for a few moments, and all of us held our breaths. As it started to play again, it revealed the cult members tearing apart the registries. They had new books ready, fully prepared to establish their dominance over the covens they'd taken over. They started writing feverishly, putting in new names so the covens would accept their new inhabitants. *Well, this is bad.*

"We knew she'd do this," Santana hissed. "Taking over the magical world first, before she sets her sights on the human world. It'll be like taking candy from a baby."

"This is what I'd call a power move," I agreed. "I have another name for it, but there are children present."

"Garrett, click on that email there." Santana pointed to a new file that had appeared.

He did as she asked, and a new window popped up. In the bottom right-hand corner, the footage was location stamped: *Paris Coven.* Garrett clicked on more as they came in: Seoul Coven, Hong Kong Coven, Edinburgh Coven, Vilnius Coven, Seville Coven, Belfast Coven, Frankfurt Coven, Berlin Coven, Brussels Coven, Warsaw Coven, Johannesburg Coven, Manila Coven, Cairo Coven, Algiers Coven, Dubai Coven...

The list went on and on. It was happening everywhere. All over the world, on every continent.

"Is there a link to Moscow?" Tatyana's voice made my blood run cold. That was fear in its purest state, right there.

"I think so." Garrett clicked through a few more emails until he found it. Sure enough, the same thing was happening there.

"My parents!" Tatyana gasped. "My parents—they're right there."

She pointed to a group of frightened people on the screen. They disappeared a second before cult members came crashing in. But that wasn't the worst of it. There were exterior cameras showing some of the former magicals being killed outside the covens by additional cultists. Not just in Moscow, but in countries all across the globe. I knew Katherine well enough to know that these people weren't being picked at random. They were likely old grudges—old scores that Katherine and her cult needed to settle. After all, who was going to stop them? Katherine was the big kahuna now, and they were her little kahunas. Of course they were going to let that swell their egos. It was The Agentic State 101. The same thing that had happened in World War II with everyone's favorite villains—the Nazis.

"Do you see them?" Harley put her hand on Tatyana's shoulder. "Are they among the dead?" The footage from the exterior cameras turned grainy, making it hard to recognize specific faces.

She shook her head. "No… no, I don't think so. I need to call them. I need to speak to them." She took out her burner and began dialing frantically. I could hear the "Your call could not be connected" woman echoing from where I stood. That robotic voice rubbing a truckload of salt into a very open wound. Tatyana kept trying, pausing to remember numbers, but that voice kept echoing back. And we couldn't do anything but stare at her and hope that one call would get through.

"Any luck?" Dylan put his arm around her waist and let her collapse into him.

She shook her head. "No, no, I can't get through. I'll send some texts and try again later. They have to be okay; they just have to be."

I didn't want to add insult to injury by stating the obvious. Tatyana's parents were high up in the Moscow Coven. If Katherine's minions were killing important people, paving their mistress's way to all-consuming authority, they'd probably be the first to go. Unless they pledged themselves. That would be the only way they could save their lives. But, for once, I kept my mouth shut. Nobody wanted to hear the stark truth when it came to family, and I wasn't going to be the asshole who pointed it out.

"So, the whole magical world is against us, then? No pressure," I murmured instead.

"And we've got a few old friends to contend with," Santana added, urging Garrett to bring the SDC video back up.

There, in the fuzzy image, stood Lasher Ickes. I'd always avoided his optional lectures like the plague when I'd come into the SDC. He was as dusty as the books he gushed himself silly over. *Yeesh, that voice.* He could have put a bull elephant to sleep with his monotone drone. No need for tranquilizers with that dull weasel around. He looked like a weasel, too—all stringy and slithery. It didn't surprise me that he'd crumbled under Katherine's pressure like week-old cake.

"Is that…" Harley trailed off. Her eyes were like saucers.

Someone stepped into the frame. The goddess herself, only wearing Imogene's disguise. A way to trick the SDC security protocols, no doubt. It was funny to think that, once upon a time, I'd have done anything for that witch. Now, I just wanted to throw up the entire contents of my stomach when I saw her face. Or smash it to pieces. Even in disguise.

We all watched, hooked, as she left the band of minions to rip up registries and cause general mayhem. The videos switched between cameras, following Katherine through the SDC. It was weird to see it so empty. I immediately knew where she was headed. She didn't need any guides. After playing Imogene for so long, she knew this place like the back of her hand. I still couldn't believe I hadn't figured her out sooner. *Ugh.* So much therapy was going to be needed after this was over.

She pushed open the Bestiary doors like Aragorn during his epic entry into Helm's Deep. *Geek. Shut up, brain.* I knew she was doing it to be dramatic. It would've been crazy cool if it had been someone else doing it. But, from her, it just looked pathetic. There was nobody around to watch her, and she was still acting like a prize drama queen. I got a wave of satisfaction a few moments later when she froze completely. Creatures were running wild in the Bestiary, their boxes open, and Tobe was nowhere to be seen. She wouldn't find him, either, since he'd already jumped ship.

A blinding light pulsed out of her chest and spread outward in powerful ripples which hit the camera and made it glitch for a moment. Puffs of black smoke dissipated into the atmosphere while the remaining creatures skidded to a halt and stared at Katherine. Had she just killed a bunch of them? It looked like it.

She turned on her heel and stormed back the way she'd come, the Imogene guise gone. With the registries ripped up, she didn't need it now.

Even through the grainy footage, I could see the cracks in her face. Big ones, running all the way down to her neck. Her hands barely had a few scraps of skin left on them, making them look like black skeleton claws that flickered with a subtle glow. *Just when you thought she couldn't get any creepier.*

"So it's true, then," I said. "Katherine's falling apart at the seams. World, meet Zombie Katherine, Queen of the Damned."

"This is why she wants you so badly, Harley." Wade glanced at her, looking worried.

She nodded. "Yep." *Short and to the point.*

It looked like Mother Dearest was finally getting the body she deserved, a deathly, decaying corpse to match her personality. But she wasn't dead yet, and I wasn't going to stop until she was. I wouldn't rest until the name Katherine Shipton became a distant memory—a near-miss in magical history. This asteroid wasn't going to wipe us out, no matter how determined she was. It sickened me to remember how much I'd loved her. I'd have given my life for her. Now, all I felt was hate. Hate so pure and intense I couldn't even quantify it. *Ooh, big word.* I needed to take my pills again, to shut that little voice up. But the fact remained, I loathed her with every particle of my not-so-magic being. And one throbbing truth came rising out of the ashes of our past relationship. I wanted to be the one to end her. I'd earned that right. Even if I died with her, so be it. I'd promised the Chains of Truth as much.

I wanted to be the one to avenge the pain she'd caused me and the life she'd stolen from me. I wanted to be the one to avenge my dad, and my sister, my aunt, and everyone else she'd hurt or murdered along the way. *The expendables*, in her mind.

Maybe I could be a hero, just once. Forgotten over time, but alive in the memories of those I loved. That would be enough. If I could just do that, I'd die a happy man.

SEVEN

Katherine

T*hat double-crossing monstrosity.*

I tried to keep my cool as I sat behind the desk in my old office, a handful of cultists standing guard. Well, Imogene's old office, but I'd put in the hard work. This office, and every director's office, belonged to me. I might have enjoyed it if I didn't have thoughts of Tobe running through my head. A Bestiary required a Beast Master to keep things running smoothly, and that meant I had to find Tobe and the missing monsters before it sputtered out on me. Still, the Bestiary could run itself for the moment, at least. And I could make do with the beasts that remained.

The main pressing issue was… where was he? Had that flying kitty gone to help Harley? I couldn't have that, which was why I'd sent cultists to try and track him down before he could cause more complications.

Keeping things running smoothly was going to present more of a problem in the coming days. I probably shouldn't have killed a bunch of the Purge beasts, but it had made me feel so much better to let loose with a bit of this intoxicating power. A temporary satisfaction, considering my whole, shattering body was now aching like I'd been hit by a fourteen-wheeler. I should've listened to Davin's constant fixation on delayed gratification, but what could I say, I could be an impulsive woman when I wanted to be, and Tobe had pushed all the right buttons to get me to explode.

I wish Naima was here.

It was hard not to have that true loyalty at my side every hour of the day. I kept turning to speak to her, only to find her absent. Then again, I wasn't sentimental by nature. It would just take some getting used to. Another part of my learning curve in the pursuit of absolute power.

"It's lonely at the top." Harley's words came hurtling back into my mind, only to be soundly shoved down like an irksome jack-in-the-box. *You won't get to me, parasite.* I wasn't going to allow any weakling to get under my skin.

Putting on my most charming smile, I leaned back in the comfortable chair and rested my feet on the desk. My eager cultists came rushing forward to refill the flute of champagne in my hand, and I let out a calming sigh. Despite this body hiccup, my plans were coming together, and the Chaos sweep had ensured that nobody got in my way. There was one more thing, on top of Tobe and the Bestiary, that I had to attend to, but I was waiting for the all-clear from Mallenberg before I dealt with that. Until then, all I could do was sip champagne and hope that Davin was closing in on Harley. That didn't sit well with me, leaving it in the hands of others, but what could I do?

"Goddess." A cultist burst into the room and bowed so low I thought he might crack his spine in two. He was in his mid-forties, tall and broad, with a scar running across his face.

"Yes?" I sipped the champagne and tried not to grimace. I'd never liked the taste, or the effect it had on me, but you had to have champagne at a celebration, right? This was the sour, fizzy flavor of triumph, and I'd down the whole magnum of it if it showed how unperturbed I was by my missing loophole.

"The covens are all yours," he replied, bowing again. "All of the former magicals have been removed. And, uh, some of them were killed. There were a few unresolved arguments, and some of your loyal followers thought it best that they were dealt with immediately."

"Not to worry." I giggled. *Oof, there go the bubbles.* That was why I rarely drank. A drunken goddess wasn't a particularly inspiring sight. Plus, the last time I'd allowed myself to get a bit merry, I'd wound up snogging Alton's face off. Well, I wouldn't be snogging anyone's face off, not until Davin got back with my gift-wrapped loyalty present. "I did promise my followers the chance to get retribution for any wrongs that had been done to them. Why not start now? It'll send a clear message, which will only swell my ranks."

I was somewhat envious of Davin and my other cultists, tying a neat bow on all my plans. I'd hoped to be the one to get everything in order, but if I tried to go out there and do everything myself, my body would disappear. And, hey, optimal delegation was the sign of any good leader. Even if I wanted to be the one to shock the living daylights out of Harley when I turned up to wherever she was hiding and dragged her back to the otherworld, kicking and screaming and...

My body started to glow again. I took a few deep breaths, and it fortunately eased up. I couldn't have another impulsive moment, not yet. I needed to save up all this beautiful energy for when Davin brought that parasite here.

"They'll be grateful to know that." The man bowed again. *Seriously, if he keeps doing that, he's going to need a chiropractor.*

"What's your name?" I asked.

The man froze. "Me?"

"No, the guy standing next to you. Of course I mean you."

"My name is Gregoire LaSalle, Eris."

I smiled. "You're French?"

"Belgian, actually." His accent wasn't very thick at all, just a hint of something not quite American. Evidently, he'd been in the US too long. "I was an Angel for the European Security Services, stationed in Brussels, but that was a different life."

I nodded. "So, you must know some tantalizing secret spells, then?"

"I suppose so."

"Good." I needed to delegate again. It was relentlessly infuriating, to have this much power and not be able to use it properly. I couldn't even make a quick shift to fix my beautiful face.

"Was there something you had in mind?" He eyed me nervously.

I took up my hand mirror and stared at my reflection. *Magic mirror on the wall...* I definitely wasn't the fairest anymore. And, just to annoy me that little bit further, I had a nice new crack in my face to deal with —a big fissure running from my right temple to the bottom of my jaw. *Well, that's just great, isn't it?* My anger spiked again, prompting me to take a few meditative breaths. I'd been thinking about delving into a state of Euphoria until Davin came back, but that wouldn't set a particularly admirable example. A goddess who was totally out of it? No, thanks.

"I'd like to give you a task, LaSalle."

He frowned. "Of course."

"Cook something up for me. A spell, anything, that I can use on my skin. Call it magical makeup, if you will, only it's going to need a little more heft than your average foundation."

"Surely, Goddess, you can do that yourself?"

I threw the mirror at his head and enjoyed watching the glass smash. "Are you going to question every order that I give you, or are you going to be as loyal as you claimed to be when I branded you with the Apple of Discord?"

Blood trickled down his face, and a shard of mirror stuck out of his forehead like a miniature shark fin. He was shaking so violently that it'd rendered him silent. I missed Naima even more. She might have been relatively useless, but she'd been a damn sight better than most of these lazy idiots. And she'd definitely never have dared to question a direct order.

I sucked in a sharp breath to try and stop myself from exploding. "You were an Angel, right? You should be used to following orders without a single question. Or has it been so long that you've forgotten how to obey? If you'd prefer an execution, I'd be only too happy to oblige."

He shook his head. "No, Goddess. That won't be necessary. I... I'll whip something up to help you."

"See that you do, or I'll be the one doing the whipping." I downed the rest of my champagne, hoping it'd settle my boiling anger. "Get to it immediately. I've got places to be, as soon as Mallenberg calls, and I can't show up with a load of cracks in my face, can I? I wouldn't want anyone thinking there's something wrong when there isn't. But people always go on first impressions, and I'd like to make a good one. Understood?"

"Yes. Right away." LaSalle bowed again, a drop of blood splashing on the floor.

"And clean that up before you go. What am I, your chambermaid?" One last snark to make myself feel better.

"Yes. Of course." He took off his own sweater to wipe up the blood and collect the shattered pieces of the mirror. I enjoyed watching him scrabble around in desperation. This was precisely the effect I wanted to have on people. The rest of the magical world, those who'd already pledged and those who hadn't, needed to see a healthy and confident ruler, or they'd never follow me.

I was going to be that ruler, light cracks and oily goop be damned.

You really are an Angel, LaSalle.

"Oh yes, that'll do nicely." I admired myself in a brand-new hand mirror as I sat at the desk in the director's office. He'd done an admittedly great job of fixing my face. No cracks, no imperfections, just smooth, porcelain skin, exactly the way I liked it. And it wasn't just my face he'd fixed, either. My hands were now covered in silky skin again, and the wreckage that my divine cleavage had become was now all as it should be. The substance was best described as flesh-toned silicone, and it was working wonders. I couldn't even feel it.

"You're pleased?" LaSalle looked pale and shaky, with good reason. Any glimmer of failure and I'd be calling for another cultist to clean him off the floor.

Speaking of that, it had only been a few hours since I'd sent him away, so I had to admire his speed and efficiency. I'd have hated to lose such a valuable asset.

I flashed him a winning smile. "Very."

"I'm glad, Goddess."

I clicked my fingers, and another henchman came running. Emphasis on the 'hench.' This guy was built like a tank.

"Goddess." The man dipped his head.

"Please hold Mr. LaSalle still for me," I replied with a flick of my newly smoothed wrist.

LaSalle looked like he was about to make a run for it, but Tank was quick for his size. He grasped LaSalle tight and his arms wrapped around him, squeezing him like a boa constrictor. *Why do people instantly think I want someone dead?*

"Don't kill him, idiot," I said. Tank loosened his grip, though not so much that LaSalle could slip out of his grasp.

"What do you want me to do with him?" Tank sounded confused.

"Recite this spell, if you would: *Surrexit lingua vestra cattus.*" LaSalle's eyes opened wide in panic. "Ah, so you're familiar with this one?"

"No, please…" he begged. It wasn't going to change anything.

"Please, recite what I told you." I stared at Tank, waiting for him to comply.

He frowned and did as he was told. "*Surrexit lingua vestra cattus.*"

Instantly, LaSalle started to struggle, but Tank held him in a vise. He wasn't getting out of this one, despite all of his Angel training. I watched, amused, as the spell twisted out of Tank's hands and poured into LaSalle's mouth in a tendril of red. As it entwined itself around his tongue, the muscle began to decay, disintegrating into black crumbs until there was nothing left for him to speak with. He howled the whole way through, naturally, until his voice became little more than a gargle. He stared at me in disbelief, pained tears streaming down his cheeks.

"While you did an exemplary job, let this be a lesson to you: if you question me, you'll pay the price for your insolence. No exceptions." I flashed a look at the four other cultists who stood guard around the room, and they all bowed their heads quickly.

LaSalle whimpered as he stuck his fingers in his mouth, checking to see if there was anything there. *You won't find it.*

"And stop your sniveling while you're at it," I snapped. "Your tongue will grow out again… eventually. In the meantime, I suggest you learn to obey your mistress—your goddess—unless you want to lose another body part you're particularly fond of."

LaSalle fell silent and nodded slowly. He made a gargling noise that sounded a bit like, "Yes, Goddess," but with his tongue gone, it was anybody's guess.

"Now, what can you tell me about Tobe and the missing monsters?" I turned to the other cultists. I'd had the SDC minions do a headcount in the Bestiary, and sure enough, there'd been some beasties unaccounted for; Tobe being the main one, as I'd expected.

A female cultist stepped forward. She was almost as big as Tank and wore her hair shaved into a floppy mohawk. Two stripes of violet eyeliner bordered her jet-black eyes, making them stand out like a cat's. *Could this be my new Naima? A better substitute than Davin? Perhaps.* At the moment, she was shaking far too much for me to make that kind of decision.

"There is no news so far," she said. Her voice was high and sweet, in stark contrast to the way she looked. "We can't find Tobe anywhere, and we haven't been able to track him or any of the missing beasts. It looks like he took the tracker device for the Purge beasts with him."

I swallowed a wave of anger. "And what methods have you used to track him so far?" I needed him sooner rather than later, before things started to go awry in the Bestiary.

"We've used three separate tracking spells, and we even employed some humans who are loyal to the cult, to help find him in San Diego. At the moment, we've got nothing, Goddess."

"Are you cold?" I held her gaze.

She frowned. "No, Goddess."

"Then why are you shaking?"

"Uh… I don't know."

"Do you fear me?"

She nodded nervously. "Yes, Goddess."

"Good. Just checking." I smiled. "Now, why don't you tell me your name?"

"Naomi Brakes," she replied. *Ooh, promising.* Naima, Naomi—maybe this girl had potential, after all. I could certainly use a bodyguard who was built like a brick. Well, for as long as I had a body, anyway.

"Well, Naomi, how about you join me on a little trip back to the Bestiary? I'd like to see the state it's in. I trust it is still running as it should be?"

"Yes, Goddess."

Well, that was the second slice of good news I'd had today. First, my beautiful face had been restored. Second, the Bestiary hadn't packed it in yet, although I knew that wouldn't last. *Always darting around like a headless chicken.* I wouldn't have minded sipping a few more glasses of champagne, but at least this was something I could actually do with my own fair hands, with minimal effort.

"Come on, then. No time to waste." I kicked my legs down off the table and got up. I had another idea if regular tracking hadn't worked.

I didn't bother to look back as I exited; I knew she'd be following me. The Eurydice to my Orpheus, only I didn't much care if she wound up dead.

She didn't say a word as we walked through the empty labyrinth of the SDC, passing a couple of cultists on the way. Naturally, they bowed and scraped, which pleased me greatly, but I didn't stop to exchange pleasantries. Instead, I pressed on to the Bestiary, listening for the echo of Naomi's footsteps behind me. It was like having an elephant stampeding at your back, but it was oddly comforting. Another good sign of her bodyguard material.

"Tell me, are the gargoyles back in their box?" I pushed through the doors of the Bestiary, eager to pay a visit to my leathery little beauties. If there were any left, that was.

"Yes, Goddess," Naomi replied. "I had them rounded up myself."

"Wonderful news." I breezed along toward their menagerie. "You know, I've always had a special relationship with gargoyles."

"You have?"

"They're quite easy to control, once you have the knack." I came to a halt beside their large enclosure. Tobe had put all kinds of bells and whistles on the lock, but it was simple enough to pick with this amount of power pounding through me. As soon as the lock clicked, I let myself in. The dark wisps of smoke unfurled, growing limbs and wings and faces, until I had a twelve-strong cluster of gargoyles staring right at me. They made no attempt to harm me. They knew better than that. These were my babies—they'd never do anything to hurt me. *You hear that, Finch? A gargoyle is more trustworthy than you.*

"Hello, my pretties." The leathery creatures swept toward me, landing on the ground with wet thuds and starting to nuzzle at my legs. "Mommy's got a job for you." They looked up eagerly. "I need you all to go out and find Tobe, do you understand?"

If anyone could track that winged half-lion, half-whatever traitor, it was a bunch of revenge-thirsty gargoyles. And they'd never let their Momma down. Of course, they'd feared Tobe while he was the Beast Master, but he'd up and left that post of his own accord. Now, I was here. I was going to be their mistress, their mother, their ruler. Even when they dragged Tobe back, he'd work under my rules. I'd pin his wings to the wall of my office, clipping them for good, just to make sure he didn't go flapping off again. He could've made things easy on himself, but he'd chosen to play hardball. So, now, the Bestiary was mine.

"Excuse me, Goddess?" Naomi said meekly.

I turned. "Yes?"

"Won't letting more monsters loose jeopardize the other covens' energy sources?" *Ah, she's smart, too.* That was very encouraging.

I smirked. "I've had at least twenty covens in America disabled and destroyed completely. Who needs a coven in Anchorage, anyway? I'm doing them a favor. And that means there is plenty of extra juice in the Bestiary to compensate for a few missing monsters."

"Can I ask which other covens you destroyed?" Her eyes shone with curiosity. I was liking this girl more and more.

"Little Rock, Tallahassee, Des Moines, Baton Rouge, New Orleans, Houston, Nashville, Jackson, Concord, New Jersey, Lincoln, Boulder, Fargo, Bismarck, Columbus, Austin, Richmond, Montpelier. And the jewel in the crown—New York. I'm probably missing a few, but it's not up to me to keep track."

She paled. "New York?"

"Yes, New York."

"That's where I came from."

"I could tell from the slapped-fish look on your face," I replied. "Don't worry, I had all of the precious contents transferred back to Washington. But, make no mistake, New York will never be magical again."

"Why?" She frowned. "I don't mean any disrespect, but why not fill it with your followers, the way you've done here?"

"Because of the Merlin dynasty." I shrugged. It really was that simple. "If you were an inhabitant of the New York Coven, then that's likely where you first heard of me. Am I right?"

She nodded.

"So, you should already know that New York treated me like garbage. They spurned my name and called me a villainess, dragging my name through the mud. Correct?"

"Yes, Goddess." Understanding had dawned across her bulldog-esque features. "But I never believed a word of it, not for a second."

"You wouldn't be here if you had," I replied. "Anyway, call this a dose of long-overdue payback. And they only have themselves to blame."

"But what about the Children of Chaos?" Naomi continued.

Hmm... maybe a bit too inquisitive. At least Naima had known when to keep quiet. But then, there'd never be another quite like her, not unless I Purged a replacement right out of me. *Ugh, the closest thing to childbirth these feeble men will ever get.* And with my body like this, that didn't seem like too sharp an idea.

I gave her a hard look. "What about them?"

"Well, aren't you worried they might intervene or attack you again?"

"You're talking about the creatures in the otherworld, aren't you?"

She nodded.

"First of all, they weren't Children of Chaos. Easy mistake to make. They were Gaia's Children—a hefty bout of Earth, Wind, Air, and Fire. But definitely not Children of Chaos." I paused. "And, secondly, no Child can kill another Child. Chaos rules. The worst they can do is piss me off or conspire against me in some super-secret squad, but they can't kill me. To help with that, I've already made some shiny new Portal Openers who are hiding in all the otherworlds, so they can give me the heads-up if these tantrum-throwing kiddies decide to go rogue on me. If a single one of them so much as sneezes, I'll know about it."

"You're a remarkable woman." Naomi smiled nervously.

"I am, aren't I?" I turned back to the gargoyles, who were engrossed in rubbing themselves all over me. I wouldn't have minded so much if I hadn't been so worried about them rubbing my skin right off. By the time I had Harley back, I'd have to slather myself in that ointment LaSalle had made—or dip myself in a vat of it.

I clicked my fingers, and their heads snapped up, their sweet tongues lolling out of their heads. "Oh, Davin would be so very jealous of all of you. Oh, yes he would." I tickled the closest one under the jaw, and his wing-hooks tapped against the floor in happiness. "Now, get out there and find Tobe. You can pick up a snack along the way, if you're feeling hungry, but be discreet about it. We don't want the humans screaming and causing a fuss, okay?"

I had a special revelation planned for the human world. In the meantime, the magical world had to be secured first.

The gargoyles swept up into the air and barreled out of the enclosure, crashing through the first window they came across and smashing it to pieces. They forced their way out into the real world and hurtled away from the coven, with one goal set in their minds. That was what I adored about gargoyles. They were simple creatures, and they wouldn't stop until they'd executed my command.

"Naomi, could you gather a few cultists and fix that window for me?"

She nodded. "Of course, Goddess. Right away." She was about to leave when I called her back.

"Actually, there's one more thing you can do for me. Call this a test, to see if you're worthy of standing at my side." I dangled the carrot, knowing she'd bite.

"Anything, Goddess!" she screeched with excitement. She'd be the one smashing windows if her voice got any higher.

"Once you're finished with the window, I'd like you to go out and assemble a global task force. These people don't understand when they've been beaten, you see. There'll be former magicals all over the place trying to form an alliance—a rebellion against me. Some are still foolish enough to think they can destroy me, but that's not going to happen. Shame to rain on their parade, but those are the facts. The cult is to check every corner of the magical world and capture anyone who's voicing any kind of dissent. Understood?"

"Yes, Goddess." She paused. "But where would you like us to imprison these rebels? In the coven basements? Are there enough cells across the covens for that?"

I chuckled. "Oh no, sweet-cheeks. We're going to put them in Purgatory."

"Isn't Purgatory quite full?"

"You're asking all the right questions today, Naomi." I laughed louder, swept up in the excitement of my next step. "It is right now, but it won't be for long. There will be plenty of cells to fill once I'm done with it."

Just then, my phone beeped. A message from Mallenberg.

Oh yes... right on time.

EIGHT

Harley

———

S till reeling from the shock of seeing Astrid's videos, the only thing we could do was keep going.

New Orleans and Marie Laveau awaited us, though I had no idea what we'd find when we got there. With no charms to protect us, and five of us wearing the empty Hermetic Battery cuffs, we were down to the wire against Katherine and her pursuit of me. There were cultists everywhere, scouring the globe for us. Or more specifically, for me.

Wielding the charmed chalk like a paintbrush, Kadar deftly swept it across the wall of Kenzie's apartment and whispered the *Aperi Si Ostium* spell. He'd been told to keep New Orleans in his mind, namely St. Mary's Chapel in the Garden District, where we'd encountered Marie Laveau's lily garden last time. Still, there were no guarantees we'd end up there.

As the chalk lines fizzed and cut out the three-dimensional door-way, Santana leaned up against the wall. "Are you going to let Raffe back out this time?" she asked. "You're useful to have around and all, but I'd like to see my boyfriend once in a while, if it's not too much trouble!"

Kadar smirked. "My feisty Mexican temptress, Raffe and I come as a package deal. You like one, you've got to like the other, too. Those are the rules."

"Oh really? You got that rulebook handy?"

He laughed. "Consider this the perfect opportunity for us to get to know one another a little better. It's been a while since it was just you and me, and I've missed it so very, very much."

"Yeah? I've missed it like a hole in the head." She rolled her eyes for added effect, making us all smile despite our nerves.

"Now, now, is that any way to speak to the djinn who is taking such good care of your love?" He leaned over and wrapped a strand of her hair around his index finger. Naturally, Santana immediately slapped his hand away.

"Yes, Raffe's *mi amor*, not you."

"See, that's the kind of talk I can get on board with. The way you roll your Rs. It's intoxicating." He grinned at her. "Call me selfish, but I wouldn't mind having you all to myself. As you can see, I haven't lost an ounce of interest in you, even though you've been reduced to nothing more than a puny human. But don't worry, I'll give Raffe back when I've had enough time to really get under your skin."

Finch interrupted before Santana could retort. "Yo, you two should just stick it on a Valentine's card and send it in the mail. We've got places to be."

Chuckling, Kadar pushed open the door, leading us out onto the street in front of St. Mary's Chapel. I hurried to the front, with Wade, Tatyana, and Garrett flanking me. This was familiar territory for us.

Glancing at Tatyana, I'd expected to see terror after what had happened to her the last time we were here. Marie Laveau had taken over her body, after all. Instead, I saw grim determination, and a flicker of sadness in her eyes. I knew she was hoping that her parents were somewhere safe, but nobody had called her back. Even for an eternal optimist, that didn't look good.

We sprinted up the whitewashed steps and burst through the pinewood doors, entering the eerily quiet chapel. Slowing down, we crept down the main aisle, my eyes seeking out the Veves of Erzulie that were carved into the upside-down shield adornments.

There they were, just as before, etched beneath the crucifixes. I glanced over my shoulder to make sure everyone was with us, then peered up at the balcony which overlooked the main aisle to double-check we were alone. I shivered. Churches had that effect on me, especially after the France incident.

"So, where's this garden that Laveau is buried in?" Dylan asked. "I don't see one. Is it around back?"

"In a way, yeah. And I wouldn't call her 'Laveau' unless you want to end up crippled by a nasty curse. We need to be hyper-respectful around her," I replied, remembering the decaying spell that she'd put on Wade. "To get to the garden, we have to get through that door over there. Only problem is, it's charmed."

I pointed to the doorway on the right-hand side of the altar, tucked away in the wall. Being here again was giving me major déjà vu.

"I can help with that." Kadar smiled smugly.

"Hold up on that for a second," I said.

Something felt wrong here, and I was pretty sure it wasn't just my paranoia. The church had been empty the last time we were here, but it hadn't felt like this. It was almost like they had the AC on too high. It felt cold... cold and wrong.

"What's up?" Wade came to my side, his brow furrowed.

"I don't know. It's just a feeling." I looked around again. The chapel was tiny by ecclesiastical standards, and there definitely wasn't anyone here. "Let's scope the place out first, make sure there aren't any cultists hiding."

"Where, in the pulpit?" Finch joked. "Or how about stuffed in the organ?"

I shot him a serious look. "Maybe."

The humor instantly faded from his face. "Sure. What she said— let's check this chapel out."

As the others ducked down to check under the pews, Finch darted up the stairs to the organ balcony. Meanwhile, I headed for the altar. No sooner had I stepped around it than I saw a figure curled up on the ground.

I almost screamed. It was the priest, gagged and tied up, totally unconscious. *What the—?*

I whirled around as the double doors exploded open and Davin made an entrance. *Why am I not freaking surprised?* The others jumped in alarm, Dylan smacking his head on the underside of the pew in shock.

Davin wasn't wasting any time. He cast magic left and right, the hexes and Air whizzing past the Rag Team's heads. Being painfully human, all we could do was try to dodge the curses that came our way. He wanted me. Katherine had sent him here. I didn't even need to hear him speak to know that. Not that he was prone to shutting his mouth.

"You should always be careful where you tread, Ms. Merlin," he chided as he shot a pulse of Air at Tatyana, knocking her back into the wall. "You never know who might be watching."

I backed away toward the wall, as if that would somehow protect me. He was advancing down the main aisle, though the Rag Team was doing everything they could to get close to him. Garrett's Avenging Angel was on fire again. As he brought it down toward Davin's head, the British pain in my ass ducked right under it, Matrix-style, the blade skimming so close to his face that I could almost hear the sound of his designer stubble singeing. It knocked Garrett off balance, though he was quick to recover. As he brought the blade back around, Davin shot a blast of Air into his face and sent him tumbling over the pews.

O'Halloran swooped in next, his daggers moving with blurring speed. A well-timed hex left him spasming on the floor, where Davin simply stepped over him and kept advancing.

"What are you talking about?" I shouted, trying to buy the others some time.

"I have been watching you, Harley, from the moment you set foot back in San Diego. And there were some rather plump tidbits to be found in what you had to say when you entered that vulgar little apartment. Thin walls, Ms. Merlin. Very thin walls." He chuckled. However, his laughter was cut short by the ear-splitting explosion of a shotgun going off. The spray of bullets tore the sleeve of Davin's expensive suit, and his eyes narrowed with anger as he checked the damage.

Meanwhile, Santana had both barrels aimed at his head. I didn't know if that had been a warning shot, or if her aim had been off, but I doubted he'd escape another blast. Beside her, Kadar was about to let loose, judging by the deep red color of his skin. Santana had one hand on his shoulder, keeping him back, protecting Raffe's body in case he got hit by the pellets.

What does he mean about tidbits? I tried to wrack my brain, only to be distracted as another gunshot went off, the echo ricocheting around the room. Davin was too quick for that. He put up a wall of rippling Air, and the pellets swerved away from him, peppering the ceiling with small thuds.

"A valiant attempt." He smirked as he hurled a hex at Santana. Her knees crumpled as she hit the deck, writhing like a worm on a hook. Evidently, Katherine didn't want them dead, otherwise Davin could have killed them already. No, why would she give up perfectly good collateral? My friends, for whom I would have done anything. *Even read from the Grimoire for her?* I couldn't think about that now.

"She's not getting me, Davin! She can rot away, and I'll be only too happy to watch!" I shouted as the others tore in with their assortment of makeshift weapons.

O'Halloran, Santana, and Garrett were still down, but they wouldn't be for long. Garrett was already getting back to his feet, ready to give Davin hell. Kadar leapt through the air, only to be swept aside by a gust of Air.

"That is simply not an option, dear girl," Davin purred as he continued to advance. All the while, my friends tried to fight him. My eyes widened as I noticed Finch balancing precariously on the edge of the balcony, perching like a cat about to pounce. *No!*

He did exactly that a moment later, springing forward and landing right on Davin's back. As crazy as it was, Finch managed to bring Davin down, if only for a moment. They wrestled in the aisle until Davin punched his fists into Finch's chest, sending him arcing upward through the air. He came down hard on the stone floor.

"Finch!" I yelled, as Garrett, Kadar, and Wade lunged for Davin. Another blast of Air sent them right back, all three of them slamming into the wall.

Unable to hold back any longer, I sprinted at Davin, flicking out my switchblade as I ran. *Don't run with knives, right?* I skidded to my knees at the last minute, trying to swipe the blade at Davin's legs. He looked down in shock as I managed to rake the knife across his thigh.

"You should have aimed higher," he said, bringing his palms up.

Purple tendrils snaked out of his hands, and I scrambled backward, darting for shelter behind the nearest pew. That was when I noticed Alton hiding, ducking low between two pews so Davin wouldn't see him. As Davin's footsteps pounded closer, Alton darted out. I rose to see him tackling Davin's legs. Davin staggered backward, Alton on top of him and trying to get hold of his neck.

"You?" Davin roared. "I thought I finished you off in France."

"Think again," Alton replied, squeezing with all his might. But it wasn't enough. Davin pounded his fists into Alton's chest, hitting him with the brutal brunt of his Air. Alton went sailing upward, soaring right over the aisle and crashing down against the wall to my left. I ran to him instantly to check that he was breathing. He looked up at me with pained eyes, his mouth opening as though he wanted to say something.

"Save your strength," I urged. "Please. We can't do this without you."

He fell silent, grimacing as he tried to move.

Glancing over my shoulder, I saw Kadar barrel right into Davin. In a flash of fangs and claws, the djinn laid into the man, mangling his suit jacket until it was nothing but threads. I saw blood spring up from beneath, soaking the material in crimson.

"Yes, Kadar!" I yelled.

He spiraled into a frenzy, punching and kicking and biting for all he was worth. For the first time since he'd entered the church, Davin seemed to be struggling. The djinn was strong, still filled with the Chaos that the rest of us were lacking. But Davin wasn't done yet. He smacked hex after hex into Kadar. The djinn howled in pain but refused to stop.

The rest of the Rag Team rallied while Davin was distracted. Tatyana sprinted for the upside-down shields on the wall and tore them off to lob at Davin's head. A couple of them hit Kadar, earning her a choice growl, but several hit their mark. Following suit, Santana set down her shotgun, which she couldn't fire without hitting Raffe, and started hurling whatever she could find, knowing it'd make an impact without hurting Kadar too badly. Dylan rushed to pick up a pew, presumably to crash down on Davin, only to remember that he wasn't a Herculean anymore. A look of confusion crossed his face as he hurried to join the girls in their throwing escapades. O'Halloran was just about back on his feet, his daggers at the ready, while Garrett ran beside him, the two of them heading for Davin.

To my relief, Finch was stirring. He picked himself up off the pews, shaking off the pain he must've been in. Wade ran to check on him. I wanted to go to my brother, too, but Alton looked like he was in a far worse state, and I didn't feel comfortable leaving his side. We were so close to getting the Hermetic Batteries filled. So freaking close.

"All good?" Wade asked.

Finch nodded. "I'm going to need a six-hour massage, but I don't think anything's broken. My legs are still working, so I'll call that a win." *Thank God he's okay.* I looked at the crucifixes that covered the church. If He was ever going to hear me, this was the place.

I was itching to get involved as the mayhem continued, but Alton was swaying weakly, sweat dripping off his face, his eyes rolling back into his head. Crouching down, I kept my hands on his shoulders, trying to get him to focus.

Meanwhile, Kadar was literally tearing Davin to pieces. Black smoke billowed off the djinn's back as he raked at Davin's flesh. *Are we... winning?*

Davin shoved his hand across Kadar's mouth and pummeled a hex right into his throat. For a split second, Kadar's eyes looked like they were on fire, flames licking out of his eyeballs. He howled in agony as he reeled back, toppling off Davin.

Santana ran to him, giving Davin the opportunity he needed. He leapt to his feet and grabbed Santana by the neck, smacking her head into the nearest pew. She staggered, gripping the sides of the pew to steady herself, while Davin breezed past, heading toward his target. Me.

He was a complete mess, his bare torso showing through what remained of his suit. "You won't triumph, Harley," he rasped. "Katherine already knows what she needs. The only thing she requires to make it work is you. Chaos made a mistake. A fatal one."

"I won't read it out," I choked.

"So you admit it. You know there is a spell she can use." Davin smirked. "Chaos paved the way to make this possible."

I stayed silent, not wanting to give anything away unnecessarily. I knew her plan had something to do with the strange, unfinished spell my dad had written. But I still didn't completely understand how Katherine could use something that was intended to destroy her. Evidently, she did, which was the most worrying thing. What mistake had Chaos made? A thousand thoughts pulsed through my brain, but he was getting closer by the second.

Then I noticed Garrett and O'Halloran creeping up behind him. They moved to strike, just as he twisted around and launched a barrage of hexes at them. They hit the deck, writhing in pain. Even Kadar, who was still spouting pockets of fire through his skin. I had no idea what curse Davin was using, but it was effective, to say the least.

"And then there was one." He grinned like the cat who'd gotten the cream.

I shuddered, remembering where I'd heard that before. *Louella...* He and Katherine were so alike that it sickened me—both of them only out for themselves. *You deserve each other, you sick monsters.* I should've sensed he was a treacherous piece of crap the moment he'd smarmed into the French church.

"How did you find me?" I refused to let my voice tremble.

He smiled. "As I said, sweeting, I've been trailing you since you first set foot in San Diego. A foolish error, returning home. Facial recognition technology is a wondrous thing." He paused. "Do you realize, you could have stopped all of this by simply hiding away and staying put until my divine mistress's body gave out? But you are not that sort of hero, are you? Do you know what they say about heroes, Harley?"

"That nobody remembers them." I glanced at Finch, who'd told me that same thing. He was still on the floor in pain, hugging his knees to his chest.

"No, dear heart. They are always the first to die." He was so close now that I could feel his breath on my face.

NINE

Harley

"But you're not going to kill me," I shot back, brandishing my blade. "Katherine needs me. We all know that by now."

"I didn't say *I* was going to kill you," he replied, taking a small step back. "Though I will be more than happy to assist my beautiful goddess when the moment of your demise comes. And there will be plenty more that I can kill in the meantime, to whet my appetite."

I frowned at him, feigning confusion. "How could you have followed us from San Diego? How did you even *find* us in San Diego?" I needed to buy more time, and giving him an opportunity to gloat was the best way to do that.

His right palm opened suddenly, and the blade shot out of my grasp. "Eris has boots on the ground everywhere you turn," he replied smoothly, sending the knife skittering across the floor with a kick of his boot. "As I said, some of that wonderful facial recognition technology worked in our favor. An alert reached me immediately. I have eyes on all the cameras you can think of, sweetheart."

So do we. I had to pray he didn't know about Astrid and Smartie. That, at least, would give us an advantage.

"I got wind of your whereabouts as soon as you were spotted in that gritty little neighborhood. I trailed you there and watched you enter the apartment of this Kenzie girl, but I made sure to bide my time and keep my distance so I could see what plans you had in mind." He chuckled to himself. "My goddess will want to hear of all your vain attempts, if only to amuse her. She finds it rather hilarious that you refuse to accept defeat. I must say, I find it somewhat admirable to see such dedication to a cause. You remind me of her in that regard. But your pursuits, I'm afraid, are emphatically fruitless."

"Why not stop us sooner?" *Come on, keep talking, you smug little rat.*

"It is better to listen and choose a perfect moment than strike too soon and miss out on valuable new information," he explained. "Thanks to my eavesdropping, I discovered your plans to come here, to New Orleans, to visit with Ms. Marie Laveau. I have yet to understand what this Kenzie character means to you, but I made sure to put a cult security detail on the apartment in case anyone attempted to escape. Further collateral for my goddess's use."

My heart plummeted. "If you touch a hair on any of their heads, I'll make sure you're opening your pickle jars with stumps!" I snarled.

"What a vulgar visual." Davin grinned. "Though I haven't decided what to do with those girls. I thought I might use them as leverage later, but if you continue to threaten me, I may be more inclined to just kill them outright. Nevertheless, I'm certain they are involved in some way. That cannot go unpunished. Those who spectate are just as guilty as those who act."

He doesn't know about Astrid... does he? By the sounds of it, he'd heard some of the conversation we'd had at Kenzie's apartment, but not all of it. He'd only heard the last bit, that we were coming to Marie Laveau's garden, but he clearly had no idea why.

Still, it meant Kenzie was now in grave danger.

I caught a slight movement behind him from the corner of my eye, and it took everything I had to keep my gaze fixed on his. The hexes Davin had been throwing didn't last that long. Wade was creeping out from behind a pew. His hand reached for Garrett's sword, which had fallen when Garrett had. It didn't make a sound as he picked it up and stood to his full height.

"You were nearly a spectator, though, weren't you?" I asked quickly, as Davin grabbed me by the arm. I'd be portaling out of here if I didn't do everything I could to drag my heels. Either that or he'd be shoving me through a chalk door. I guessed it was the former, since he wasn't reaching for any charmed chalk.

He frowned. "What do you mean?"

"Back there in the Garden of Hesperides, when Katherine told you to get after us, you hesitated. You just stood there looking at us, like you didn't want to obey her. You want to tell me why that is? Are you not as loyal as you seem?"

"I misheard her, that is all," he replied, a little too quickly.

"Where's your tattoo?" I blurted out.

His frown deepened as he stilled. A flicker of irritation crossed his face. "I do not have one yet," he replied curtly.

"Why's that? Do you think you're too important to permanently mark your precious skin?" I smirked, pulling up my sleeve to show mine. He gasped audibly, his irritation turning to shock. "Even I've got one of those, and I don't freaking want it. I'd tear it right out of my arm if I could. But it's my reminder, to keep my focus on what I'm doing and why. And don't pretend you wouldn't have kept looking for me if I'd chosen to hide. You think I would've just sat there like a sitting duck and made your job easier? Don't make me laugh." Wade's blade was raised to strike.

"I will receive my tattoo in due course, I am sure," Davin replied coldly.

"How can Katherine trust you if you refuse to get one?"

"She trusts me. You will be my gift to her."

Wade leapt through the air and brought the blade down against Davin's shoulder.

But he ducked just in time, feinting out of the way of the blow. Wade stumbled forward, and Davin rounded on him. He gripped him by the throat and lifted him up into the air with impossible strength. Maybe I should have seen it coming, based on his earlier performance. *Has Katherine given him extra juice?!*

"I will snap your lover's neck clean in two if you do not agree to come with me." He squeezed tighter, Wade's face turning purple as he choked and tried to tear Davin's hands away.

"Let him go!" I growled. I knew Davin could just take me if he wanted to, given that I had zero magic left and he had it by the bucketload. This was just another ego display, to try and crush me mentally before he snatched me away and gifted me to Katherine—bow included.

"Agree to go with me, and I will." Davin smirked. *You son of a bitch.*

"Let him go—let everyone live—and I will," I shouted. The words felt like poison as they left my tongue, but I couldn't stand by and watch him kill Wade. This was my weakness, and we all knew it, Wade, Davin, and I. It would *always* be my weakness. Which made me wonder why the Chains of Truth had let me live, since I clearly didn't have it in me to sacrifice everyone and everything to end Katherine. I was starting to doubt I could, even if we were face-to-face.

"Gratitude, Ms. Merlin." Davin dropped Wade like a stone. He hit the deck, clawing at his throat as he dragged oxygen back into his lungs.

"Harley, no..." Wade rasped.

"You heard her, Crowley. She has made her choice, and it has saved all of your lives—for now, at least." Davin gave an icy chuckle as he snapped his fingers.

Cultists entered the church, though I had no clue where they'd come from. Had they been waiting all this time? Had Davin wanted to take us on singlehandedly, so he could have all the glory when he recounted the tale to Katherine? Or did he now have the ability to summon cultists at will? None of those options were very comforting.

"Harley..." Wade croaked.

"I'm sorry." I shook my head, barely able to form the words. "I couldn't watch you die!"

"Take these rebels away, and have them thrown in Purgatory," Davin commanded the newcomers.

"Wait, what? Purgatory?" My voice came out as a squawk.

He nodded. "That is where all those who oppose our goddess go nowadays."

"How?" I gasped.

"How do you think?" He snorted. "Our divine goddess had the Purgatory prisoners released and offered them the same choice that she has offered everyone else. The empty cells are now being filled with non-magical dissidents. An efficient use of space, don't you think?"

She's still making moves. Even with her body falling apart, it didn't look like she was showing any sign of slowing down. And that kind of determination was deadly.

"Now then, shall we return to my goddess?" Davin yanked me toward him.

Suddenly, his wasn't the only voice I could hear. Kadar sat off to my right, propped against the wall, a strange grin on his face that Davin hadn't noticed. His lips were moving, whispering something under his breath.

A moment later, the door that opened onto Marie Laveau's garden swung outward, unleashing a violent windstorm that swept into the church. The pews went flying. Every candlestick and bit of furniture that wasn't bolted down spiraled up as the powerful gale hit. The balcony splintered, the walls trembled, and the windows smashed to pieces. Shadowed spirits chased after the storm, tearing into the church and lunging for every cultist they came across. They weren't solid, so it was hard to tell what they were, but they reminded me of strange, twisted hounds.

The cultists didn't even have time to scream as the Voodoo spirits silenced them, shadows snaking around their necks and wispy limbs disappearing right down their throats. I didn't want to know what those limbs were doing to the cultists' insides.

As Davin whirled around, eyes bulging as he took in the scene, someone sailed through the air toward him. I saw the glint of a blade a split second before the knife buried itself in Davin's chest.

Finch.

He was clinging to Davin's back like a rabid monkey, holding the blade steady as Davin flailed helplessly. All the magic in the world couldn't spare him from death. Nothing could. And Finch had aimed true, almost as if he'd done it before... but I didn't let myself dwell on that. Instead, I shot him a weary, grateful smile as Davin sank to his knees and slumped forward. Finch had saved me again. He'd saved all of us. Although, these last-minute rescues really weren't doing my heart any favors.

"What was that?" I gasped. I rushed straight to Wade and helped him up, holding his face in my hands and kissing him desperately. He'd almost died. I'd earned a moment's reprieve.

"Who'd ye think, *brav nanm?*" A familiar, eerie laugh drifted in through the open doorway.

That nickname. *Brave soul.* I'd have known it anywhere.

Draped in red silk and looking as stunning as ever with her ebony skin and jet-black eyes that glinted with a center of violet, Marie Laveau stood on the threshold between her world and ours and watched as her Voodoo hounds tore the cultists to shreds, until there were none left standing.

TEN

Finch

Man, Kadar had saved our butts on this one. I couldn't stop staring at the Voodoo Queen. What an entrance. And, turns out, Voodoo hounds did a way better job of getting rid of pesky cultists than we ever could have, now that we were measly humans. Plus, smarmy-chops Doncaster was on the floor in a pool of his own blood. Satisfying didn't even cover it. I'd killed him. Even feeling like I'd been smacked in the back with a wrecking ball, I'd managed to down him. *Suck on that, Davin.*

"Are ye all goin' te stand around with ya mouths hangin' open, or are ye goin' te join me in me garden? I don't think it's fair likely that ya here by accident. Nobody darkens me door 'less they be wantin' somethin' of Marie Laveau."

She gave a strange laugh that seemed to echo through the church. Even in spirit form, she was a force to be reckoned with. I could feel her power pulsing like a beacon.

"Thank you, Ms. Laveau." Harley bowed to her. She was the only one who didn't look like she was about to drop dead of exhaustion. Fear, sure, but not exhaustion. Trying to protect her had taken a lot out of us. It wasn't an easy pill to swallow, and I was used to swallowing pills, but we weren't as strong as we used to be. *Stupid no-magic.*

"I would've come te ya aid of me own volition, but that be the trouble with doors of the magical sort. I can't be openin' them on me lonesome. Only a magical can do the act. 'Tis why I've been safe in me garden of lilies so long. Not that too many of ya sort know I be buried here." Her voice was intoxicating. Rich and amazing and terrifying all at once, and flirting with a Cajun flavor. *Tasty.*

"You saved us," Wade said, breathless.

"I wouldn't be leavin' them fools te have their wicked way with ye. I been itchin' te get through, waitin' for one of ye te open the door. Patience is me virtue, but not when I don't care for the behavior of them *kochon vye*." I had no idea what that meant, but her tone needed no explanation. Marie Laveau wasn't happy about the cultist intrusion. *Same, Marie... same.* "Me spirits took a fair strain on me juju, in truth. It be sappin' me of me defenses. Facin' Kassrine ain't goin' te end well for me, if she should darken me door, so you should hurry yaselves and come on in. Time be runnin' out."

Kadar dragged himself to his feet. "Then what are we waiting for?"

"A djinn?" Marie sniffed at him. "I don't care for ya ilk, but I can make an exception. Ye opened me door, after all. And if ye be lingerin' with me *brav nanm*, I suppose ye can't be all wrong."

I raised a hand. "Ms. Laveau, what's a *brav nanm*?" She kept calling Harley that. I wanted to make sure it wasn't some Cajun swear word.

"It means 'brave soul,' Finch," Harley replied.

"Right." Wow. Looked like my sister was actually pals with this awesome queen. She certainly rolled in some crazy circles. Ours, for one. The biggest band of misfits you've ever seen.

"Ye must be the brother?" Marie smiled. The way she said it, it sounded more like "brudder," and I had to say, it sounded cool. "Chaos be workin' in mysterious ways, bringin' two *nanm pèdi* together. But it always does. It always has. It always will."

I raised my hand again. "Are you calling us both brave souls?"

She chuckled. "It be meanin' 'lost souls,' brother of the *brav nanm*."

"Right… sorry. I promise I won't keep asking. I just like to keep up with things, that's all," I replied.

"There's honor in seekin' te learn of other cultures, *frè pèdi*. That be meanin' 'lost brother' before ye ask. No harm te be found in askin' the right questions, mind. The wrong ones, avoid them where ye can." She beckoned for us to step through the door. "Now come. I be a busy woman."

As a weary group, we followed her into her garden. The door closed behind us with a slam. *Suitably ominous.*

I hadn't expected to see such beautiful digs out here, but Marie Laveau had a sweet setup. A lily pond, a bunch of flowers everywhere, and a shiny mausoleum up on top of a low hill. Not quite what I'd pictured for a woman who'd once been the most powerful dark magical in existence. I'd been envisioning fire and brimstone. Shadows and darkness. A black castle, maybe. But this would do.

She led us across a stone walkway between the lily ponds and paused on the hill. There, she turned. Man, this woman was majestic. I had no other word for her. She moved like water, all graceful and fluid. And her presence packed a hell of a punch. I could've watched her all day… if Katherine hadn't been about to murder us all.

"Are you going to take over my body again?" Tatyana asked.

Eh? I was clearly missing something.

Marie laughed. "I will keep me form as it is for as long as I can. If I start te weaken, I may jump in. At least ye get a warnin' this time."

"I'll brace for it, then," Tatyana replied.

"Do you know what's going on?" Harley cut in. At least someone was in business mode.

Marie's expression darkened. A scary sight, for sure. "Aye, I know of what be goin' on. Kassrine has achieved her dark desire te ascend. She's taken Chaos away from those born te it. A fair monstrous act. It be why I've allowed ya djinn te come into me garden. He be the only one with Chaos still pulsin' in his veins." She paused. "But it ain't all doom and gloom, *brav nanm*. I see ya worry, and it pains me in me heart of hearts. But where there be fighters, there be hope."

"What kind of hope?" Santana asked.

"What Kassrine Shipton don't know—or maybe does know, but ain't about te acknowledge—is the raw truth of Chaos. The ties that bind. It is known among those like me, those who live in the soul of Chaos, that ye can never truly sever the ties between ya magicals and ya Chaos. It ain't possible." An amused smile tugged at her lips. It was halfway between eerie and hysterical. "Ye may be wallowin' in ya sorrows of bein' powerless now, me *timoun vanyan sòlda*, but that be only temporary. The floodgates be closed... well, closed may be the wrong word. They be switched off. Anyone Kassrine gives Chaos to, who don't be a natural magical, will never be a full magical. They will always be feelin' incomplete. And Chaos, if it be restored, it will always find its way back te all them magicals what had it before. It knows where home be."

Harley sighed. "That sounds nice, but it's not going to help us right now. Right now, we *are* powerless, and we don't have Chaos winging its way back to us anytime soon. The only thing we've got left is the Grimoire, but I can't perform the spells. I can barely understand what's in these pages." She lifted the satchel with the book inside.

"Such power in one *piti* book," Marie purred. Her eyes glowed. "But tell me, *brav nanm*, how were ye plannin' te use the Grimoire before ya Chaos were snatched away? Think as if nothin' has changed."

"There's a final spell in here that I know I can use, but I don't understand it. It's... I don't know for sure, but I think it's incomplete. It just sort of breaks off." Harley took out the book and turned to the right page. Marie swept forward but turned her face away as she looked at the words.

"Me eyes want te see, but they can't." She sounded annoyed.

She can't read it? It baffled me. This woman was beyond powerful, even dead as a doornail. There was no way she should have still been here, on this earth, but she'd even managed to scare the Grim Reaper away. Well, the spirit version. Having never been dead, I had no idea what that was—the big light at the end of the tunnel. But it seemed she'd been beaten by a book.

Marie sighed, staring at each of us. I felt exposed, like my clothes had just vanished and I was standing totally nude in front of her. I'd had that dream before, though it hadn't been Marie I'd been naked in front of. It had been Miss Jenkins from fourth grade homeroom. The kids had laughed. It was a bad time all around, and I'd woken up in a cold sweat. The same cold sweat I was feeling now.

What if she thought I was unworthy or something? Did she have that kind of power? Or was I getting her mixed up with those irritating Chains? *Prying little snakes.* Judging by the concerned faces of the Muppet Babies, I wasn't the only one feeling exposed.

"There be nothin' so troublin' as havin' ya Chaos torn out like ya guts," she mused. "I'll help ye however I can. I don't care te involve myself in the quarrels of magicals, but I won't be acceptin' a world where Kassrine Shipton reigns as a Child of Chaos. That *li-dyab* deserves te be in the hands of hell. She already been disruptin' the natural balance of the magical world for longer than I'm like te permit." She'd spat the word *li-dyab*, so I guessed she wasn't calling Mother Dearest an angelic ray of sunshine.

"Thank you, Marie." Harley heaved out a sigh of relief. This would've been a pretty useless trip if she'd said no. Well, maybe not completely useless. I'd still killed Davin. That had been worth schlepping all the way to New Orleans.

"There's somethin' more that ye might want te be knowin'." Marie turned toward the mausoleum. "A *zanmi* of yours found their way into me private realm. They been keepin' me company. And it's been said, in all the history what's gone before, that cats be close te the gods, protectin' spirits."

I frowned. "A cat?"

Right on cue, a sleek, gray-and-black cat darted out from behind the mausoleum and sprinted down the hill. It made a beeline for me.

No idea why. I hated cats. Always had. I almost bolted as it started rubbing its furry little head against my legs. *Ugh.*

"You've got an admirer there, lad." O'Halloran chuckled. "Didn't take you for a cat person."

I shot him a look. "I'm not."

"Looks like you're going to be," Dylan added.

"Catnip Shipton." O'Halloran grinned.

I rolled my eyes. "I'm not going by Shipton anymore. It's… Merlin. Finch Merlin." It felt awkward as ass to say out loud, but it was something I'd been wanting to say for a while. I didn't know if it was meeting my dad or what, but Shipton just didn't sit right anymore. Not that it ever really had. That name had never belonged to me. But maybe Merlin could.

"Well, you better call the name change bureau." Santana smirked, though I didn't get the usual snarky vibe from her.

"I'm working on it," I replied.

"It suits you much better." Harley gave me a small smile that made me feel like less of a tool.

"Wait…" I ducked down and held the cat at arm's length. There was something about the eyes that didn't seem right. Where a black iris should've been, there was a white dot. Milky white. The same shade that Kenzie's eyes had been back at the apartment. *Ah man, I was so sure you were stuck in a pigeon.* "Kenzie?!"

The cat mewled. Why did I get the feeling she was calling me an idiot? There was a tone to the mewl that I didn't like. A sassy mewl.

"Is it her?" Harley rushed over.

I nodded. "Yeah, I think so. Can't you hear the sarcasm? It's got to be."

"Are you a cat-whisperer now?" Dylan laughed.

"Kenzie?" I ignored their jokes. I was the resident comedian, not them. And their jokes weren't even good. "Kenzie? Give me two meows if it's really you." I could've sworn the damn thing rolled its eyes at me as it let out two sharp meows.

"It's definitely her." Harley looked back at the others. "She must have gotten stuck like this when she came to see you, Marie."

Marie nodded. "She'd just come into me garden when Chaos got stolen away. I can hear the thoughts of her spirit, so we've been havin' talks, puss and me." Her striking eyes fixed on me. "She came te me, as the charm ye gave her didn't work on the ails of her *manman*. But it wasn't ya fault, *frè pèdi*."

I frowned. "It wasn't?" I'd only had a vague idea of what that talisman could actually do, so it hadn't been a *massive* surprise to find out that it was a dud. Was Marie trying to tell me that it wasn't a dud? Man, I wished she'd call me something cooler than *frè pèdi*, though. How come Harley got "brave soul" and I got "lost brother"? It hardly seemed fair.

"The ails of this *ti fi's manman* ain't of natural origin," Marie explained. "I been chattin' with her, as I've said. A gift given to them that continues to defy death. A gift of speakin' with all creatures, and readin' into they souls. Someone put a Voodoo curse on Kenzie's *manman*. I can sense Voodoo a world away. It be me forte, after all." She gave one of her eerie cackles.

"So you can fix Kenzie's mom?" I gaped at her. All this time, it hadn't been Alzheimer's at all. It had been some Voodoo juju. But from where?

"Not so easy, *frè pèdi*. Te get a feel for what plagues her *manman*, I'd need her te come te me garden. But that won't be no possibility now." She turned her hypnotic stare on Harley. "But that ain't of importance now. Ye must hurry in ya pursuit of Kassrine. Them *kochon vye* won't be the last te come after ye. And the Grimoire can only do so much te hide ye, *brav nanm*, from Kassrine's intent eye, 'specially without ya Chaos."

Harley nodded thoughtfully. "So, it is the Grimoire."

"You knew about this?" I stared at her. "You didn't think you should tell us that you had your own spooky, dusty-book bodyguards?"

"I only had a suspicion that the Grimoire was protecting me. I started to wonder when Katherine didn't immediately turn up at our door, demanding that I hand my body over. I didn't want to say anything, in case I was wrong," she replied.

"Wise *ti fi*," Marie said with a smirk. "There be power in them pages. I'd give up a night with me *renmen* te be able te read it or touch it."

"Your who said what now?" I couldn't help it. I didn't like not knowing what was being said.

"Me true love. The other half of me soul," she replied.

"Papa Legba," Harley chimed in. "Did you get to see him this All Hallows' Eve? He was pretty angry when we left him, on our last visit."

"Aye, ye robbed him of a vessel. Though it sounded like he deserved what ye did." She giggled. "He told me all when we'd devoured each other beneath the moonlight, entwinin' our souls once more. Ye really should try it, *brav nanm*, now that ye have the same love in ya heart. But he told all, and I scolded him for bein' a trickster. I do love him, with all me heart, but he's always had traits that I never cared for. He holds no grudge, if that makes ye feel better. He found another vessel, right enough."

Ooh... juicy. Harley really did know the Voodoo Queen. Intimately, by the sounds of it. They'd clearly discussed the gory details of spiritual hanky-panky. And, I had to say, I was intrigued. By Marie's stories, not Harley's. I was still struggling not to barf whenever I saw her and Wade getting all cozy.

Harley went beet red, and Wade looked shifty. "I'll keep that in mind, Marie. Glad to hear you got to see him again. I know you were looking forward to it."

"It were all I could've hoped for, until the sun came up." Marie sighed. "But we've no time te talk of me *renmen* now. There's something I'd like te ask of ye, *brav nanm*."

"What?" she replied.

"Why don't ye read me some of them pages, since I can't read them with me own eyes? I'd do the spells of me own free will, but me juju ain't what it should be, and that book be beyond me. It ain't intended for me, but ye already knew that."

Hey, if anyone's going to know what to do with that thing, it's the Voodoo Queen. I looked at Harley to try and pass on the message. She was already settling down on the grass and spreading the weighty book over her lap. Looked like we were on the same wavelength. *Go team!*

The Muppet Babies and I listened as Harley read out the first spell. I half expected it to come out of her in a big old boom, but it was just my sister's usual voice. No weird smoke, no chilling echo, just her words tumbling out. Sure enough, the spell was cut short. Well, it seemed like it was. I didn't know what was supposed to be written in there, so maybe I was wrong. But it did sound like someone had half-assed the job. Namely, our daddio.

"That be a spell for summonin' a Child of Chaos, if memory do serve. 'Tis in the language—a nuance others might miss, but not Marie Laveau. 'Tis the sort to be used for summonin' Darkness, and since Erebus is ya Child of Darkness, me guess is, it's meant for him. Mighty dangerous territory, *brav nanm.*" Marie glanced up at the sky as though she expected the dark kiddo to appear at any moment.

"But I've summoned Erebus before, and this wasn't the spell I used," Harley said.

"There be many ways te skin a cat, *brav nanm.* And there be more than one way te summon Erebus. This ain't specifically writ for him, but 'tis in the nuances, as I did say. 'Tis for Darkness. That be why the spell is different." She paused. "Tell me, be there another spell what mentions a Child of Chaos? Or mentions bringin' a Child of Chaos te ye?"

Harley flipped through the pages and paused. "Yes... yes, there is!" It came out as a squeak.

"Read for me," Marie urged.

"*Light in the Dark, yield to me. Come through rain or shine.*
Light in the Dark, yield to me. Come into being and be mine.
Light in the Dark, yield to me. Seize the moment here before you.

Light in the Dark, yield to me. Speak of that which is true.

Light in the Dark, yield to me. I stand before you, holding back the tide.

Light in the Dark, yield to me. I am here for you, to abide.

Light in the Dark, yield to me. Let us be as one in our course.

Light in the Dark, yield to me. Lest we fail and must gather in our remorse."

Harley looked up hopefully. "Does that mean anything to you? This one seems complete."

"That be the summonin' of Lux, *brav nanm*. That one be more specific, for certain." Marie smiled strangely. "Now, tell me, what is it Kassrine be wantin' of ye?"

"My body." Harley didn't miss a beat.

She was way more casual about it than I would've been. I almost felt grateful that I didn't have the same kind of juice she had, otherwise Mama Shipton would've been after me like a shot. And I really wouldn't have wanted to spend the rest of my days trapped with her inside my body. *No, thanks.* So, I supposed there were some slightly selfish benefits to being pretty ordinary.

"Aye, 'tis as I thought." Marie nodded to the book. "Look for a spell that talks of giving ya body, or havin' ya body used by a Child of Chaos. Me guess is, Chaos were not expectin' Kassrine te get so far in the game. There may be a *piti* scrap of somethin' what they overlooked. Kassrine's rise to ascension, te be specific."

Harley continued to flip through the pages until she paused. Her shoulders stiffened. "I think this might be it."

I went over what Harley had told me about Kassrine—crap, now I was doing it. She'd ransacked Odette's mind and plucked out a spell of some kind, a spell she could use for her own benefit. If there really was a spell in that book that was meant for a Child of Chaos, giving them the ability to use a magical's body, then we were screwed.

"Read for me." Marie waited patiently.

"What's yours is mine, what's mine is yours. Hold dominion over me, and take what is owed, to see this tyranny brought to a close.

What's mine is yours, what's yours is mine. You are invited, at my behest, to put this evil firmly to rest.

What's yours is mine, what's mine is yours. Take temporary control, and cross the divide, within my body may you reside.

What's mine is yours, what's yours is mine. We make this last stand as one, you and I, to ensure that our peace will never die.

What's yours is mine, what's mine is yours. I have the blood, you have the power. Help us overcome in our final hour," Harley finished, her voice going a little shaky.

She hadn't had much time to look over the pages with everything else going on. I guessed it was as much of a shock to her as it was to the rest of us, that Katherine's harebrained plan could actually be made a reality. But that was my mother for you. Always putting things in order, down to the last detail. This was the spell she'd torn out of Odette's head. It had to be.

"This is the one Kassrine be wantin' te use, I'd stake all me All Hallows on it." Marie shook her head. "And ye say that first one be incomplete?"

Harley nodded. "It feels like it, right?"

"Aye, it do." She closed her eyes, humming softly to herself. A moment later, she lit up like the Fourth of freaking July. Light poured out of her. I staggered back, terrified that Katherine might pop out. At the moment, she was the queen of pouring light. And we'd been fooled before. As the light ebbed, Marie's eyes burned so bright they were impossible to look at. *Shame.* But at least she wasn't Katherine. "Describe the unfinished page te me. Tell me if there's somethin' that be out of place. A symbol in the corner, or somethin' of that sort?"

Harley scanned the page and gasped. "There's a tiny lily in the corner. I must have missed it before."

"Do them other pages have the same symbol? I love a lily, as ye well know." Marie chuckled.

Harley flipped back and forth. "Yes! Yes, they do!"

Marie's chuckle turned into a terrifying howl of hysterics. "Tell me, *brav nanm*, who wrote them spells? Ya *manman* or ya *papa?*"

She frowned. "I think my mom wrote the Lux spell—the handwriting is different. As for the other two, I know my dad wrote the first, the Erebus one. I heard him write it." She paused. "It's a long story, and I probably don't have time to tell it. Anyway, that means he must've written the body spell, too. The handwriting is the same."

"Then ye have ya answer, *brav nanm*." Marie laughed again. It hit me like a gunshot. "It be a spell of three parts. Complicated, secretive—a combination that nay magicals would dare te make happen. Few of them, anyway. Me and me *renmen* wouldn't even dare it. 'Tis why them pages be marked as they be. Me thinkin' is, ya *papa* ran out of time before he could bring them pages together. He left them broke, because he couldn't tie them together. That curse that Kassrine put on him must've gotten te him before he could finish, and them forces of Chaos would've left his body before he surrendered te Kassrine's control. *Nanm pòv*."

"These spells are all connected?" Harley blinked in confusion. She wasn't the only one. Man, Chaos really loved its triads.

Marie nodded. "Take them pages out and put them on top of ya Erebus spell."

"You mean, *tear* them out?" She frowned.

"Aye. I don't think I did stutter."

Harley hesitated. "Are you sure? I don't know if I can do that."

"Like I be sayin'—did I stutter? Ye tear them pages out, ye get what ye be lookin' for. If ye can't, then I can't help ye. 'Tis simple. Simpler than facin' Kassrine with no Chaos te speak of."

Come on, cut her a break! I could understand Harley's reluctance. Tearing those pages out meant much more than a simple bit of ripping. This was her parents' book. It was sacrilege. I mean, it was sacrilege to rip up any book, but this was twice as bad.

Harley chewed her lip. The rest of the Muppet Babies had gone silent. Even Wonderboy didn't seem to know what to say.

"Ye thinkin' somethin' bad is goin' te happen?" Marie snickered. "The Grimoire be more powerful than ye be givin' it credit for. It'll fix its own self after ye cast ya three-part spell. Ye may trust me on that, though I don't think I've ever given ye reason not te trust me, have I?"

"No… I guess not." Harley took a breath and did as instructed.

I could practically feel her pain as she tore the Lux spell and the body spell out of the book. It was like tearing off a limb. Maybe not your favorite limb, but a pretty important one. All of us held our breath. Even the lilies had stopped swaying. Carefully, Harley placed the two pages on top of the Erebus spell—our dad's last legacy. I almost crapped my pants as white light surged out of the book. *People and objects really need to stop doing that!*

The light faded, and the pages began to meld together. Like puzzle pieces, they found the right edges. The texts nudged each other out of the way, overlapping and shoving like teenyboppers in front of their favorite boy band, creating something entirely new. And once they'd settled, the final spell emerged.

A particular expletive jumped to mind, dancing on the tip of my tongue. But that would have ruined the moment. And this moment belonged entirely to my sister.

ELEVEN

Harley

I stared at the melded spell and couldn't muster a single word. It was oddly beautiful, and all I could do was read over it again and again, hardly believing that it was real and in my hands at last.

The words had shifted into one another, forging an entirely new spell that wasn't incomplete, and had a list of herbs and crystals down one side. It was a perfectly formed entity that made me want to cry and scream and laugh all at once. I should've realized the Grimoire would hide this inside itself—it had hidden everything else.

"Ye be mesmerized, *non?*" Marie gave her usual frightening laugh.

"A little, yeah." I looked up at her, grinning.

"Ah, but ye be happy. It'd be a shame te knock ya smile off ya lips." *Why do I get the feeling you're going to?* "But there's more to yon spell than meets the eye, *brav nanm.* 'Tis all about balance and gettin' that balance all good."

I frowned. "What do you mean?"

"'Tis a question of balancin' Light and Darkness. If ye only summon the Darkness, ye get hurt. That be the truth." She said "truth" like "troot," her accent just as mysterious and ancient as ever. It made me wonder what she'd been like in her heyday, with Papa Legba by her side. I was pretty sure they'd have put Wade and me to shame… even without all that "entwinin' souls" stuff she kept insisting on telling me about.

"So, you're saying it's dangerous to summon Erebus on his own?" I replied. I knew that firsthand, after the debacle in the Special Collections room of the New York Coven, not to mention our encounter in Tartarus. Erebus was a bad egg, but I clearly needed him for what was to come. *Comforting…*

"Aye, it be right dangerous to summon him on his lonesome. He be wily and temperamental, and has nay respect for human life. Nor magical life—not much, anyhow. He strides te the beat of his own drum. 'Tis why ye be needin' the balance, ye see? Though Lux ain't no better, in truth. Her only saving grace is that her moral code be slightly less rough around the edges. She be needed te keep Erebus in his place."

I nodded. "So, I summon Lux first or Erebus?"

"Ye summon the Dark first, and then the Light te even the score," she replied. "When ye gots them both on this plane of existence, ye strike a deal with ya man Erebus. Ye offer him the goods what be laid out in the body spell. Te cut down Kassrine, ye need more than ye human self can muster. More than ye magical self could muster, if ye still had ya juju. He be ya weapon, *brav nanm.* But it don't stop there. Ye got te strike ya deal, and Lux has te approve of ya deal. Only then will ye be able te use ya weapon and give ya body to his cause—the only cause left te stand for."

"Wait, so I have to give my body to *Erebus*?" I stared at her. "How is that any different from giving my body to Katherine?"

"'Tis only temporary, *brav nanm.* Is why ye be needin' Lux te mediate. She'll be makin' sure he gives back what be taken, as part of ya deal. His power will be yours for the length of ya deal, 'til the job be done. But heed me warnin': make sure ye word ya deal properly, so he can't weasel through it like a worm. It's got te be tight. Nay gaps for him te make himself a loophole te hang ye by."

I glanced down at the page, reading every new line. One particular section kept catching my eye:

As it is wrong to kill the blood of one's blood, so it is for the Children of Chaos. But exceptions may be made when the future may be lost. In a vessel of ancient origin, the lines may be crossed. To defeat the evil that would cause great loss.

"Ye look mighty curious, *brav nanm*." Marie stared at the book. I still couldn't quite believe, with all her power, that she wasn't able to read it.

"It's just this section." I read the part out to her, noticing the others leaning forward to hear better. "*'In a vessel of ancient origin'*—it's talking about the Primus Anglicus, right? My Shipton side and my Merlin side; both of those are descended from the Primus Anglicus, I think. So, it's basically saying that as long as a Child of Chaos can find a vessel who has my bloodlines, they can kill another Child of Chaos?" I hadn't realized, until now, just how full of loopholes this book was. It might as well have been the Swiss cheese of magical spell-writing. *I've been spending too much time with my brother.* That was a line he'd have given.

"That be right," Marie replied. "Ya bloodline is rare. I always told ye so, from the first moment we met. Though this one gots a whiff of the same flavor, too." She nodded to Finch, who looked startled to be met with that violet gaze. To my surprise, he didn't say anything back. He just stood there like he was hypnotized. Technically speaking, he and I shared the same bloodlines, which meant we were the closest things this world would ever get to a Primus Anglicus, especially as I didn't see any of them rising up to save us.

"I've got one more question." I turned back to the task at hand, leaving Finch to his staring contest.

"As ye wish," Marie replied.

"Katherine wants to use the body spell on *me*, right?"

"Aye."

"Well, how would that be possible without the other parts? It's a three-part spell." I was hoping for some major blow from Marie that I could use to crush Katherine like a snail under my boot. A sure sign that she couldn't use it, and that she'd somehow gotten the wrong end of the stick. *Come on, Marie. Make my freaking day.*

Marie smiled, though it wasn't a comforting smile. It was borderline devilish.

"Them parts can be used separate, make no mistake 'bout that. The only one that can't would be that unfinished one. But that ain't ye problem. That body spell wouldn't work on its lonesome. It'd give her ya body for an hour or two, but nay more, and she be wantin' a permanent fix. The kind that ye can only get from all three."

"Are you saying Erebus will be able to take over my body permanently?" My gut wrenched. I didn't want that!

"Nay, *brav nanm.* It involves the trickiness of blood, ye see. Blood got power like ye wouldn't believe. Erebus can't take ye body permanently, as he ain't of ya blood. It be different for Kassrine. Her blood runs in ya veins, which gives her the means of takin' ye fer good. A match, so te speak, like donatin' ya organs. Only this be a body donation."

I grimaced.

"If I were te bet, she'll be wantin' ye to read the spell te her, as a Child of Chaos, in place of Erebus," Marie went on. "Chaos made a mess there—they didn't specify which Child of Chaos had te be called. Just a Dark one. And Kassrine be the darkest of the bunch. What she may not know is that ye need the approval of Lux. And Lux ain't going te give her that approval, unless forced te. Kassrine might have her plans for that, but I don't have facts for ye, nor what the *kochon vye* might have up her sleeve. Either that, or she's got some hold over ya man Erebus, and don't need to call no Child of Light te mediate. It could be done with two parts, but it'd be mighty dangerous."

"If she made a past deal with Erebus, would that be enough to control him?" My heart was pounding in my chest.

Marie shrugged. "Could be enough. 'Tis tricky te tell. Children of Chaos be fickle at the best of times."

"But you're saying she might not know that she has to leave Lux out to avoid a mediator?" That flicker of hope refused to go out.

"Aye, 'tis what I'm sayin'. All depends what she managed te pluck out of the head of that poor *ti fi*. And I can't tell ye that, 'cause I don't know in full. I just has bits of it, floatin' about through the spirits that come through me garden."

"Then we've got a freaking chance!" I almost punched the air.

If Katherine didn't know about the Lux factor, then that gave us a definite edge. Even if I read this whole page out to her, she'd have Lux to contend with, with no assurances that Lux would let it pass. And that meant things might not be as dire as they appeared. Chaos might have messed up by not specifying a Child of Chaos in the Dark part of the spell, meaning Katherine could use it for her own ends, but it had already put the safeguard of Lux in place.

"Ya heard tell in them books of old that Arthur would come on back when the world were in its time of greatest need, aye?" Marie continued.

"I think I remember something like that, yeah," I replied.

"Well, it ain't Arthur. Never were. It were always Merlin... or *a* Merlin." She paused. "Te use this spell as it were intended, a Merlin must make a deal with Erebus te destroy Kassrine. That be the gist. But it must be made on ground that be neutral."

I looked over the spell, as though it would have the answer. "Like an otherworld?"

"*Wi* and *non, brav nanm*. Them otherworlds ain't neutral. Not those ye been te before, anyway."

"Then where is?" I had no clue.

"Stonehenge be ya best bet," she replied. "'Tis rare knowledge, but

Stonehenge be the closed portal te Elysium. That be the neutral ground of the Children, but it ain't a place ye can portal te. It's solely for the use of Children. Nay magicals, nor humans, nor any other sort be allowed there, not without a Child of Chaos te give the invite. 'Tis safest for ye te summon Erebus and Lux in Stonehenge, that gray area between this world and theirs, so ye be on equal footin'. They'll hear ye, crystal clear, and they won't be able te ignore ye. If ye call from Stonehenge, they have te come."

"And the terms of this deal? Is there more to it than letting Erebus use my body?" I asked. The spell wasn't exactly specific, just a load more flowery poetry that I'd need an English degree to figure out. And literature had never been my best subject.

"That I can't say." Marie gave another devilish smile. *Is she telling the truth?*

"But you mentioned earlier that I should make sure there are no loopholes—as if you *did* know more about the spell."

"Aye, but I can't be tellin' ye more, *brav nanm*. By now, ye know the rules of Chaos. I be beholden te them, as we all be. I can't tell ye what them terms will be, in full. Although, I can tell ye one thing: this ain't somethin' that's been done te often. Most magicals know where their place be. Even I never had the gall te try me hand at bein' a Child of Chaos, and I once had more power in me pinkie than Kassrine has in her whole bein'." *No, you just defied the laws of the living and the dead instead.* Still, each to their own. "Although, whatever it be, maybe it don't matter. All ya wantin' te do is destroy Kassrine, aye?"

"Uh... yeah," I replied.

"Then give all te the cause. Whatever be needed, give it. This be your only chance."

"Right... of course." The words stuck in my throat.

I knew what was required of me. I'd known since it became clear that I was the only one who could do this whole thing. But did that mean I was ready to die? No. In the history of mankind, I didn't think there was anyone who'd truly been ready to give up their life, no matter what the reason. Life was precious and fragile, filled with incredible moments, and there was no way of knowing if we'd get to do it all again in another life. But all those heroes throughout history had done it anyway, and I knew I might have to as well, if it came to that. Still, I could maintain the right to walk into this wanting to survive, couldn't I?

"So, does that mean we've got a plan?" Wade glanced at me nervously.

I knew he wouldn't like the idea of me giving everything for this, either. But we had no choice.

"I guess we do," Garrett replied.

"Man, it feels good to have some decent news." Dylan smiled at Tatyana, though she still looked nervous, as though Marie might still sweep into her body at a moment's notice.

Santana raised her hand. "Hate to be the voice of doom and gloom, but how in the royal heck do we perform all this stuff without magic?"

"Yeah, I mean, we almost had our asses kicked by those cultists in the church, and they're small potatoes compared to what we're talking about doing," O'Halloran chimed in.

"Ms. Laveau." Finch tugged up the edge of his sleeve to reveal the empty Hermetic Battery clamped across his forearm. Wade, me, Santana, and Tatyana had the others. "We were hoping you could fill these up with some of your Voodoo juice. You know, since you've still got your Chaos and you're not a Purge beast, so you hopefully won't make them go boom."

"Me juju won't do ye no good," Marie replied, staring at the object. "Ye need ordinary magicals for them kinds of objects. Mortal magicals, not spirits of great power like meself. My Chaos would be as likely te make them explode as a djinn. To fill them batteries, ye be needin' powerful magicals or a couple of Mediocres. It be takin' a lot of power te make that spell work, especially for a Merlin."

"Damn." Finch looked as exasperated as I felt.

"Sorry te disappoint ye." She smiled.

"Then it's going to have to be cultists," Santana cut in. "We need cultists. We can take them down and steal their Chaos, going back to plan A. If we can be subtle about it, we won't alert anyone. Sounds like a fair exchange to me. Katherine is giving Chaos away like it's going out of fashion, so we take some back."

"Djinn, come te Marie." We all turned in surprise at the command. Kadar looked like he'd rather have taken a running leap than approach Marie, but we all needed to do our part, djinn included. Slowly, he made his way toward her.

"What do you want from me?" he asked.

"Ah hush, and let Marie get a feel for ye." She reached out and placed her hands against Kadar's temples. Her eyes closed for a moment, and Kadar's face morphed into a mask of absolute agony as tiny threads of violet energy slithered under his skin. The red shade of his body darkened, and the black smoke billowed like crazy out of his pores. Soon, the lily garden filled with the bestial grunts of his pain, though he was helpless to do anything to get her to stop.

"Raffe!" Santana lunged to step in, but Finch caught her around the waist and held her back. She smacked at his face, trying to get him to let go, but he wouldn't budge. I had to agree with Finch on this one. Marie was clearly doing something worthwhile. After all, she'd already told us how much disdain she had for the djinn.

"She's hurting him, Finch. Let go!" Santana pummeled his hands.

"Just let her do her thing," Finch urged. "This is the Voodoo Queen we're talking about. She isn't messing with his head for the good of her own health." He snapped his neck back, avoiding a punch to the face.

"Let me go!" Santana roared.

"Would ye calm down, *ti fi*." Marie's eyes shot open again. "Listen te ya man there. I don't trouble myself te hurt folk, unless it be necessary."

Santana's eyes narrowed. "What have you done to him?"

"All I did were give the djinn the juju te draw the Chaos out of any cultists ye descend upon—a marker, so te speak, te fool them batteries into thinkin' he be a magical operating them, else ye'll not get them te work. They ain't so simple as Ephemeras, but I guess ye didn't know that. Me Chaos rules don't apply te djinn, so I can give him a bit extra te help him along. A *mèsi* wouldn't go amiss. Ye don't want te be gettin' on the wrong side of me." As she spoke, Kadar pulled back and collapsed in a heap on the floor. He looked up at Marie, totally stunned, as understanding dawned across his bright red face.

"She definitely did something," Kadar said, his voice a weird mix of his own and Raffe's. "I can feel it. It's like a second energy running through me... a small spark that wasn't there before."

"I be waitin' for that *mèsi*." Marie gave Santana a hard, petrifying stare.

Sheepishly, Santana bowed her head. "Thank you, Ms. Laveau."

"Ah, that weren't so hard, were it?" Marie gave one of her unique, blood-chilling chuckles that set the hairs on the back of my neck on end. "Now, how 'bout the rest of ye?"

"Thank you, Ms. Laveau," we chorused. Even Alton managed to find the strength to speak. He was looking even worse than before, though he wouldn't have admitted it.

"Seriously, thank you," I added. "We wouldn't have this glimmer of hope without you. It means a lot."

"Well then, what ye be waitin' for? Get out and get the world saved, *brav nanm*." She cackled to her heart's content, only to cut off mid-laugh in a way that scared the life out of me. "I should add one thing. If ye fail, don't even darken me door again. I've given ye all ye need, and now it be up to ye. I don't have no more for ye—there ain't no second chances after this. Then again, there be a strong chance ye will all get yaselves killed, anyway, if ye fail."

I smiled. "And if we succeed?"

"I'll throw ye a party, in ya honor. Cajun-style. The only way te party." She grinned at me.

"Then there's probably one more thing I should tell you, before we go." I knew we didn't have much time, but I felt I owed it to her after all of her help. "You once told me that when life is done, nobody knows what comes after. You said that was why you'd always stayed here, in case you and Papa Legba were separated in whatever comes next."

She frowned. "Aye, that I did."

"Well, I know what comes next. Alton brought my mom and dad back from the afterlife, and, let me tell you this, they weren't separated. They were together in the afterlife, because their souls were bound to each other by love. If ever there comes a time when you're sick of being here, only able to see your *renmen* once a year, just know that, with a love as strong as yours, there's no way that anything could separate you."

She stared at me in silence for several painfully long minutes. Then, to my surprise, I noticed a tear rolling down her cheek. It fell to the ground, and from the spot where it landed, a lily began to grow, pushing through the earth and opening out, the petals a deep, blood red. It hit me then. All of these flowers, growing in this garden, were the tears that Marie Laveau had shed for her love. This wasn't just her mausoleum, it was a shrine to the life she'd led before this, and the love that was kept from her 364 days a year.

"Can this be true?" Marie looked at Alton, who nodded slowly.

"It is, Ms. Laveau. The souls of Hiram and Hester Merlin were reunited in the afterlife, and I doubt they were an exception. It's always been said that two souls, joined on Earth, remain joined in the next life. And now, I know that it's true."

"Ye have done me a great service in this, *brav nanm*. But I be waitin' te see how this turns out before I make me decision. We've been here so long, maybe we been here te long te change." She let another tear fall, a lily spiraling up through the soil.

"Could you give us a hand, in case there are any cultists left lurking in the church?" O'Halloran was back in military mode. Either that, or he'd missed this emotional moment for Marie.

She wiped away the rest of her tears and walked toward the church door. As she swiped her hand across it, the wood disappeared, turning transparent.

Beyond, the church was completely empty. The Voodoo hounds had made a total mess of the cultists who'd bombarded us, but I'd still expected to see bodies on the floor. Davin's, in particular, right where Finch had left him... he wasn't there anymore. His body was gone. All of the cultists were gone, even the ones who'd been left in tiny pieces.

"Did you clear them away?" Wade turned to Marie.

"No, I didn't," she replied, a strange expression of amusement on her face. "Mighty odd, but at least ye don't have more of them te deal with."

Yeah, that's not particularly comforting. Where the heck had they gone? Bodies didn't just get up and walk off, especially ones that had been missing heads and limbs of all sorts. In fairness, I hadn't actually *seen* Davin die. He'd *looked* dead, sure, but maybe he'd somehow survived the wound. It seemed extremely unlikely, but that man was as crafty as they came. Still, *if* that was the case and he'd somehow resurrected the other cultists, what the heck did they look like now? Patchwork people? I shuddered at the thought.

Before we could say another word, Marie clapped her hands together. Our own bodies twisted up, right out of the lily garden, and were spat back out into the church. I'd forgotten she liked to do that. And I'd forgotten just how much it hurt.

As I dragged myself to my feet, I looked around, wondering if the transparent door had altered our view of the church somehow. But the bodies of the cultists, and Davin, were still gone.

"Davin's a Necromancer, right?" Finch said, rising to his feet. "Can he Necromance *himself*? It wouldn't surprise me. He likes to romance himself, so why not add the necro? That sounded better in my head."

Alton shook his head. "No, that's not possible. He'd need another Necromancer to revive him. We can't turn our powers on ourselves when we're already dead."

"Then where the heck are they?" I asked, stooping to pick up my switchblade.

I couldn't make any sense of it, but it made our latest task that little bit harder. Not that we could have used those torn-up bodies anyway.

Davin and the cultists were gone, and now we needed to find some more so we could knock them out and take their Chaos. *Fair's fair, right, Katherine?*

TWELVE

Katherine

---

*A*h, *would you look at that?*

When I was younger, it had been my dream to own a Bestiary. Back then, my parents had laughed. I never understood why. Well, I was the one laughing now. And they were... well, dead.

As I'd gotten older, I'd always fancied a Bestiary full of humans, to taunt as I pleased. Magicals, somehow, were even more satisfying. They had a bit more bite to them.

And now, I had that twisted Bestiary that I'd always wanted. Purgatory belonged to me. It hadn't taken long. Joined by a few of the gargoyles who'd apparently been put in Tobe's naughty corner, now freed from their individual boxes, I'd gathered a horde of cultists to help me take control. Naturally, I'd had to keep exertions to a minimum for the sake of my porcelain skin.

Armed with magic, my cultists had overwhelmed Purgatory before they'd even known what had hit them. I'd rigged it perfectly. See, I'd only taken away some of the magic belonging to the idiot officers in this place, so as not to arouse too much suspicion—they wouldn't have even felt it leave. And I'd had Mallenberg rig the comms and President Caldwell keep the news of my Chaos sweep from reaching Purgatory, so they wouldn't have heard anything from the outside world until we were already bearing down on them. A bold move, perhaps, but I hadn't wanted to lose the element of surprise.

Security magicals and officers had been taken down before they could even blink while I'd watched from the open foyer by the mirrors, admiring their blind willingness to follow orders. The perfect followers.

In the aftermath, I'd worked my enslavement magic on the warden, a man named Kristof Furdík. Hilarious surname, and it had gotten a whole lot funnier when he'd bent to my will so easily. After that, I'd had my cultists separate the former prisoners into those who wanted to follow me and those who didn't. The latter would be stuck inside their cells until the end of time, while the former were whooping and hollering from the walkways, relishing their new freedom as they cheered on their shiny new goddess. Even if I wasn't looking my shiniest.

My cultists were bringing more prisoners into Purgatory en masse —former magicals who'd chosen poorly, deciding their "morals" were somehow more important than their Chaos, their freedom, their goddess, and a peaceful future. Already, the rebels were rising, like scum. *Ah, so that's why they're called Rebel Scum?* Finch had forever been harping on about something called *Star Wars*. I still had no idea what it was about, but at least I understood the meaning of the term now. And, boy, did it fit perfectly for these dissidents. *Wait, does that make me Darth Mutter?* I pushed the stupid thought away. Why was I thinking about Finch at a time like this, when this part of my plan was coming together in such delicious harmony?

These ingrates had already started to conspire against me, rallying other former magicals to try and take my cult on. It felt so very good to snuff out their ridiculous attempt at bravery. Bravery got people killed; everyone knew that.

"Isn't this wonderful?" I glanced at Juno Laurier. She'd been one of the mousier members of the Mage Council, sitting side by side with sweet, sappy Imogene for years, never realizing that I was right under her pointy witch-nose. Dramatic irony was one of my favorite pastimes.

"Which part? The mass murder? The enslavement of thousands? You taking away our rightful Chaos?" Juno spat back. She looked about ready to lunge, but that was the beauty of having a personal army and a strong set of Atomic Cuffs to use on just about everyone who tried to cross me.

"I'm glad you agree." I chuckled.

Juno scowled. "You disgust me."

"Sorry, what was that? You've discussed me? Only good things, I hope." Toying with dissidents was another favorite pastime.

"Pride comes before a fall, Katherine, and we're all going to applaud when you fall."

"Oh, you'll be applauding all right, when you see me rise to great ness." *Not like scum, just for reference.* I was going to rise like cream. Rich, luxurious, delicious cream. I was already most of the way there, if I could just avoid the rampant energy that was making said cream curdle. I'd had to get LaSalle to touch me up a few times since the prisoners had started flooding in.

"You'll be smiling on the other side of your face when this is over, Katherine," Juno hissed. "Not all of us are weak, and not all of us are afraid of you. And we won't forget the things you've done."

I rolled my eyes. "You really need to drop the whole Imogene thing. You barely even knew the real one, so stop acting all wounded about it. You were closer to me than you ever were to her."

"You killed her, you evil bitch."

"Your point being? Like I said, you barely even knew the real one." I gave a casual shrug. "So, how about you get to your pretty little knees and swear fealty to me? There's a good girl. You always followed me before. What, you need the boring draped clothes to swear allegiance? What difference does it make?"

"You betrayed us all. You were playing us, all this time. I'd never swear allegiance to you." Juno pulled against the cultists who held her, which only made me laugh.

"Well, don't say I didn't give you the choice." Before she could say another vapid word, I swiped my hand across her face. Purple tendrils snaked out and washed over her. A moment later, her eyes were that charming shade of indigo that the Crowleys and Remington showed in their eyes—the sign of an obedient slave. Ironic, since the color indigo was supposed to reflect great devotion, wisdom, and justice. I'd just ignore the fairness, impartiality, and defender of people's rights part for now. That bit would come, when I had my world exactly the way I wanted it.

I envisioned a throng of excellent women around me, once I was a true, world-straddling goddess.

"Go on, take a good look at your fellow cursed friends." I smirked as I pointed to my most recent additions.

Felicity and Cormac Crowley were standing to the side, their heads bowed, along with Remington, a cluster of security magicals, and the preceptors who hadn't begged for my favor. Juno stared blankly at them.

"You see, Juno, I'm letting them live because I'm saving them for something special. Also, I have zero respect for them. You, on the other hand—oh, I've got some respect for you. Hence why I'm putting you in a safe little cell until you make the right choice and give yourself to Eris."

As the cultists took Juno away to put her in said safe little cell, I watched the procession of miserable former magicals as they were marched through Purgatory to their own cells. A grin of pure glee spread across my face, though I had to be careful not to let it spread too wide—I didn't want to be adding any wrinkles to these irritating cracks.

The former prisoners cheered and applauded at the top of their lungs, howling at the sight of their enemies—a couple of whom had put them in this place to begin with—now clad in Atomic Cuffs and being shoved behind bars. Well, glass and steel. The sound was incredible.

I was just getting into the swing of the blissful moment when a portal tore open nearby, and Davin staggered through. A few cultists followed him, looking utterly horrifying. They looked as though they'd been pieced back together like a puzzle. Each made Frankenstein's monster look like a damned swimsuit model. Blood smeared every inch of their torn-up faces, making it look like they were wearing warpaint.

"Davin? What happened?" I wanted to say, "It had better be good news," but the sight of him spoke a thousand words. It wasn't good news. Clearly.

"We pursued Harley to New Orleans, but they had the djinn with them. He and I entered into close combat, as you may be able to tell from my ruined suit! However, somehow he managed to speak the correct words to open the door to Marie Laveau's burial site, and she unleashed her Voodoo hounds upon us. Some of your cultists may even fall to pieces again, as I had to rush the job. We barely escaped with our lives!"

He clutched at my hands and held them tight. *Dammit!* I'd been so ready to tear him a new one, in addition to what that irksome djinn had done, but his touch did something strange to my insides.

"Marie Laveau?" That brought a very different sensation to my broiling guts. And not a good one. "I will deal with that sour-faced cow when I get my body. Which I'm guessing I'm not getting right now, since I don't see that Merlin parasite anywhere."

"Forgive me, my darling goddess," Davin said. "I was killed in your name. I was stabbed in pursuit of your endeavors. You must know how fervently dedicated I am to your cause."

I frowned. "Am I missing something? Because you seem fairly alive and kicking to me."

"I am able to resurrect myself, divine Goddess." Davin gripped my hands tighter. "You remember what I told you, when we took my boat down the Thames? That has not changed, my love. My deal still stands, and it has allowed me to return to you and gaze into your beautiful eyes once more. I resurrected as many of your cultists as I could, also, so that your forces would not be diminished. And partially for fear of Marie Laveau's additional retribution against us, if I left their bodies lying around. You know what these Voodoo sorts are like. They can use dead bodies."

"I will put that foul witch's spirit in a jar!" I snarled. How dare she involve herself in mortal affairs? "And *where* is my body, Davin? Where is it? I told you not to come back without it, yet here you are—without her! Did I not make myself clear enough?"

Fury shot through my chest like a full quiver of arrows. I'd been having such a good couple of hours, and then *he* showed up and ruined it all. And the angrier I got, the more cracks began to appear on my body. I could feel them tearing open through the magical makeup, like a series of awkward wounds that refused to close. I was going to need one hell of a touch-up after this.

"Goddess, I did all I—" Davin tried to speak, but I cut him off.

"Don't you dare tell me that you did all you could, because obviously you didn't!" I barked, losing control. "Why are you here, Davin? Hmm? If you can resurrect yourself, why aren't you back there, giving Marie Laveau hell? And do you think they're just going to hole themselves up in that place and wait for this to blow over? If you *do* think that, then you must have left your brain behind when you came back to life!" I realized, a second too late, that Purgatory had fallen completely silent.

"Goddess, you need to calm down," he said, giving me a knowing look.

"When, in the history of being told to calm down, has anyone actually calmed down?" I shot back.

"You make an excellent point, Goddess. But, please, I urge you to take a breath and gather yourself." He stood between me and the silent-as-a-grave Purgatory. "I am on your side. I would like to take this moment to remind you of that. I am not your enemy. We are all doing everything we can to make your dreams a reality."

A lightbulb exploded in my head. "We need to change our tactics," I said, attempting to draw in a deep, calming breath. "If you're going to get Harley, following her around like a puppy isn't going to do any good. She's a sneaky little turd who always seems to wiggle her way out of tight corners. We have another avenue. One you seem to be forgetting." It was amazing, the beautiful ideas that could spring from overwhelming rage.

"What is your plan, Goddess?" Davin asked, his brow furrowed.

I chuckled, satisfied as the chatter began to return to Purgatory.

"A plan that has already proven itself to work," I replied.

THIRTEEN

Harley

We needed to leave New Orleans as fast as possible, to reach Tobe and hopefully get our hands on more of these Hermetic Batteries. Then, we could track some cultists and fill them up. A full set was preferable to five.

Kadar made another chalk door, working under Alton's instruction. Stepping through, I didn't recognize the terrain at all. We were standing in the middle of an evergreen forest, overlooking a crashing waterfall that tumbled violently into the river below. For a crazy moment, panic hit me right in the chest. Had we somehow made it back to the Garden of Hesperides? As common sense returned, I realized the Garden of Hesperides didn't have any greenery left. Katherine had destroyed it all, and Gaia too, leaving a barren wasteland.

"I hate to sound geographically dense, but where are we?" Finch whispered, Kenzie wrapped around his neck like a furry scarf.

Alton smiled. "Yellowstone National Park."

"Huh? Why?" I asked.

Alton grinned. "Just follow me."

He started to pick his way through the woodland. A faint path led through the trees, following the treacherous precipice that would see us all wind up in a watery grave. Since Alton was the only one who knew where Tobe actually was, all we could do was follow him. Although, I had to say, there could have been worse views.

Beautiful scenery stretched out toward the horizon: snow-dusted peaks, swaying evergreens, streams and rivers meandering through valleys, bordered by pebbled shorelines. I couldn't help but smile as I walked along. Being a resident of San Diego pretty much my whole life, I hadn't spent much time out in rural America. It brought back the faint memories of another expanse of beautiful, rural scenery, where I'd played beside the river, chasing minnows with a net and being thrown up into the air by my dad. This was what we were trying to save. The peaceful, serene beauty that Katherine wanted to destroy, and the warts-and-all cities that we came to these kinds of places to escape. The rural and the urban. The worst and the best of Earth and humanity, magical and otherwise.

"My mom and dad used to bring me to a cabin here during summer break," Wade said as he walked alongside me.

"They did?" I liked to hear about his childhood, putting the pieces together to figure out how he'd become the amazing, sweet man he was now.

He nodded. "I used to love it. One time, my dad left some bread outside, and this massive bear came snuffling into the campsite. I remember being so excited and so scared, pressing my face up to the glass to get a closer look. Rangers came and chased it away, but I've never forgotten it. I love this part of the world."

"Maybe we can have a vacation when all this is over." I laughed tightly. The moment I said it, it felt impossible. We weren't supposed to be ordinary, no matter how much I would've liked to have an ordinary life with him. *Then again, you'd never have met him if that was the case.*

"If we're having a vacation, we're not spending it in a cabin." Wade smiled, taking my hand. "I was thinking Hawaii, with your family. You missed out on that trip with them, and I'd like to get to know them better once we've gotten rid of Katherine. Maybe my parents can come, too." His voice caught in his throat. He was trying so hard to be brave, but I knew it must've been hard for him, not knowing what had happened to them.

"They'll make it out, Wade." I squeezed his hand tighter. "And they can come with us. After I've had that dinner that I promised to have with your mom."

He chuckled faintly. "I forgot about that."

"I haven't. We're going to have dinner with her, and we're going to go on vacation, and we're going to live out our lives after Katherine is gone. Or else, what are we fighting for?"

He leaned in to kiss my cheek. "I love you, Harley."

"I love you more."

"Is anyone else worried about bears?" Garrett's voice echoed behind us, making Wade and me laugh.

Finch snorted. "You're the one with the big, fiery sword, Garrett. I think you'll be fine."

"I'm actually getting a bit hungry, now that you mention it." Kadar grinned.

"You're not eating a bear, Kadar!" Santana shot back. At least they were walking side by side, which had to mean progress.

"Why not? I bet they're delicious." Kadar nudged Santana in the arm, but I still wasn't entirely sure he was joking.

"There's no signal out here," Tatyana muttered, waggling her phone in the air as if that would make a difference. My heart went out to her. She was suffering too, not knowing where her family members were, or if they were even alive.

"They'll be okay, Taty." Dylan put his arm around her shoulders and gave her a squeeze. "I promise."

"How can you be so optimistic all the time?" She stared up at him.

He smiled. "Because I've got you."

"Geez, it's like a Hallmark card around here." O'Halloran chuckled. "You're making me miss my wife."

I gaped at him. "You've got a wife, O'Halloran?"

"You think a stud like me would be a bachelor?" He grinned, though it didn't truly reach his eyes. "My wife lives in Ohio. I haven't seen her in a while—she's human, so she doesn't mix much with the magical world. But yeah, I have a wife. Happily married for twelve years."

"Hang on a sec, you can't just drop a bombshell like that!" Finch protested.

"She's human?" Garrett chimed in, his eyes wide. "Does she know what you are?"

He shook his head. "She thinks I work for the Armed Forces. Those were the terms I was given by the coven, so I had to stick to them. But I get back whenever I can. She's fine, and doesn't know there's anything up, so I guess Katherine isn't trying to make her move on the human world yet."

"You got a message from her?" Tatyana sounded heartbroken.

"I'm sure it's just a problem with international comms," he replied apologetically. "You'll get through to your family soon, I'm sure."

As a stilted silence settled over the group, we continued to follow a staggering Alton down the steep path. It cut through the jagged outcrop of the cliffs that surrounded the waterfall and the river below, leading to the shore, and it was a wonder to me how Alton was managing this. My thighs were already starting to burn, and I felt the path crumbling under my feet. Hiking really wasn't my jam.

Twenty minutes later, we reached the flat riverbank and walked along the shore. The trees were densely packed, shadows shifting between the trunks while the river swept past. I almost jumped out of my skin as a fish leapt out of the water, half expecting to come face-to-face with Davin or the cultists again. I'd almost gotten my breath back when Alton suddenly came to a halt and whistled loudly, the echo of it ricocheting through the shady woodland. Beneath the piercing sound, the steady rhythm of the waterfall thundered.

A moment later, a figure emerged through the trees, and my heart lurched with happiness.

Tobe.

"Beast Man, yes!" Dylan whooped.

More figures emerged behind Tobe, flanking him on all sides. There were about three dozen Purge beasts obediently following him —a handful of gargoyles, including one familiar beastie. *Yeesh, anyone but Murray.* A leprechaun tapped its foot impatiently beside Tobe's talons while four changelings crouched low, staring up at us with weird, gray eyes. Some goblins waited in the wings, their orange eyes burning in the gloom. A majestic bird perched in the branches overhead, snow white with a tail that almost reached the floor. Another snow-white creature stood behind Tobe—a massive bull with golden horns. It stood beside two horses, one black and oily-looking, its eyes red and menacing, while the other was a freaking silver unicorn. There was an assortment of other creatures, from imps and gremlins to Santana's feathered snake.

The bull stamped its hooves, and the red-eyed horse started whinnying in a way that didn't sit well with me. From them, a bristle of unrest started to work its way around the creature horde. No sooner had they started than Tobe began to sing, his voice flowing through the trees, hypnotizing and sweet. He worked his way through several verses, each one somehow different in tone. The beasts immediately quieted down and dropped their heads in a sign of obedience to their Master.

"I have never heard your song, Beast Master, but I have heard *of* it," Kadar said. "It's quite something."

"It is the only way to maintain authority," Tobe replied. He looked remarkably calm considering the mess we were in. But that was Tobe in a nutshell, more stable and stoic than anyone you'd ever meet. "My friends, it is wondrous to see you all again. I hoped you would find your way to me with Alton's assistance, but the time passed and there was no sign of you. I confess, I began to worry." His voice carried a subtle hint of relief, letting me know he wasn't quite as calm as he appeared on the surface.

"We're here now, and that's all that matters." Alton forced a smile onto his sickly face.

"Are you unwell, Alton? You look pale." Tobe approached him, but Alton held up his hands.

"I'm fine, Tobe. Just a little worn out." *That was putting it lightly.* Alton looked like death warmed over.

"Well… if you are certain." Tobe frowned, his gaze settling on Kenzie. "Did you bring another Purge beast? Who does it belong to?"

Finch smiled. "This is one of our pals. Kenzie. She got stuck mid-morph, so she's kind of a cat until we all get our Chaos back."

"Ah." Tobe gave a courteous bow. "My apologies, Kenzie. I pray your recovery is swift." The cat mewed in response, rubbing her face against Finch's neck.

"Could you not?" he muttered. "We talked about this. Cats freak me out, especially when they do that rubbing thing." I could've sworn Kenzie laughed, as she continued to rub against him.

"Slinky!" Santana squealed, distracting us all from Finch's complaints.

She rushed forward and knelt in front of the feathered snake, who looked just as happy to see her. It had definitely grown since the last time I'd seen it. It came up to her shoulders as it swayed on its coils. Its gaudy feathers ruffled up with delight, and its scaly face rubbed against Santana's cheek in the same way Kenzie was doing with Finch. It was weirdly sweet to see her bonding with her Purge beast, though I was keeping one eye fixed on Murray. *Oh yeah, I remember you, you ugly jerk.* I doubted I'd ever get over the fact that he'd destroyed my beloved Daisy, even if Wade had repaired her. And that name would always drag up memories of my kindergarten bully—the one who'd put chewing gum in my hair, leaving me with a bowl cut for four months of my life.

"Would you like to introduce me?" Kadar smiled as he walked toward Santana. Slinky reeled back as if it were getting ready to strike, a hiss susurrating from its lips as its tongue lashed out.

"I don't think he likes you," Santana replied with a smirk. "He's got good taste."

Kadar shrugged. "His loss. I'm still not letting Raffe have the reins."

"What do we think of that, Slink?" Santana scratched the serpent's brightly colored throat. It darted over her shoulder and snapped its fangs at Kadar, making him stagger backward in surprise. Careful to keep his distance, Kadar sulked his way back to the group while Slinky continued to bask in the affection of his purger.

"What has happened in my absence?" Tobe asked. "I stayed in the coven as long as I could, but it became necessary to take action when Chaos was taken away from the magicals. I released the beasts from their boxes to create a diversion while we escaped the SDC. I am of far more use to you here than I would be at the Bestiary, forced to bend to Katherine's will... Although, I have been worried for the rest of my creatures."

"What sort of beast dad would you be if you weren't?" Santana replied as Slinky wrapped himself around her body, his head bobbing over her shoulder.

"So, you really can control these suckers even when you're not in the Bestiary?" O'Halloran looked over the beasties, his hands gripping tighter around the handles of his daggers.

Tobe nodded. "I can, O'Halloran. It is why I sing. Each of them has a song they respond especially well to, and that serves to keep them at heel. It is the gift of a Beast Master, and they will serve alongside us in whatever you may have planned. Most of these creatures are formed of pure Chaos. While they may not be able to perform magic, they are still able to wreak havoc and put up quite the fight, if required."

"I guess they know they're better off here with you than back at the Bestiary," Garrett said.

"Precisely." Tobe smiled. "They understand the horrors that will unfold under the reign of Katherine, and they know they will be used for energy until they have nothing left to give. A disgusting display of power. Anyway, I have promised them their freedom as long as they do not interfere with the human world. They know the consequences of disobeying me. Now, if you are here, then I suspect you have a plan of action in mind. Please share your ideas. I am eager to know what has happened, and where you all have been."

Stepping forward, I gave him the short version of the otherworld debacle, Katherine's desire to use my body for her own ends, my unexpected Purge, what happened after Chaos left us, and our whistle-stop visit to Marie Laveau and everything we found in the Grimoire. "So, we've got this three-part spell to use against Katherine, but no Chaos to actually use it. That's where the Hermetic Batteries come in. We need to draw some power from the cultists to get the Hermetic Batteries to work, so I can get going on Katherine's demise. And we were sort of hoping you might have some more. Alton said you might."

He nodded. "I have several on me. You are welcome to them, though they are also empty. I haven't had the opportunity to replenish them."

"That's okay. We've got a plan for that." I smiled.

"How are you able to use them?" Kadar frowned.

"I was given an energy signature by Selma, at the beginning of my life, that permitted me to use them," Tobe replied.

"Why would you *need* to use them?" Finch wondered. "You're powerful, right?"

"Sometimes more power is required in certain circumstances that concern the Bestiary. I draw Chaos from Alton and other powerful magicals, with their permission, of course, and utilize the Hermetic Batteries when I require a surge of energy to repair the atrium and such."

Tobe trailed off, and a moment passed as he shifted slightly on his feet. I watched him, trying to gauge his expression, but the Beast Master was hard to read, and even harder to read without my Empathy.

"Could I have a word with you in private, Harley?" he finally asked, his deep eyes fixing on me.

"Uh. Yeah, sure." *That can't be good, can it?*

I followed him toward the shore, leaving the crew in the near distance with the monsters. Slinky was still clinging to Santana, lashing his tongue out whenever Kadar came too close, while Tatyana approached the oily black horse with the red eyes. I watched in awe as she put her head against its neck and the horse started whinnying softly, like it felt some kind of affinity with her. Dylan, on the other hand, was keeping his distance. A second later, I stifled a giggle as the handful of gargoyles swarmed around Finch, trying to lick him with their slavering tongues. Murray seemed particularly excited to see him again, but they had a history—that was always going to happen. As he struggled to fight off their stinky, wet affection, I turned my attention back to Tobe.

"What's up?" I asked.

"There is something you must understand, something that I could not say in front of my creatures," he whispered back. "In order for your body to withstand the power of a Child of Chaos, you will need a considerable amount of Chaos within yourself, prior to the deal being struck."

I nodded. "That's what the Hermetic Batteries are for."

"I am afraid they will not be enough, Harley," he replied. "You need a large quantity of raw Chaos within your veins just to endure the might of taking Erebus in. Otherwise your body will break down, just as Katherine's is doing. You will not be able to hold it without *considerable* levels of Chaos."

I stared at him. "Then what am I supposed to do? I need to do this spell. Can't I just ask Erebus to give me my Chaos back as part of the deal? Would that help?"

"I doubt it, Harley. It is my suspicion that Katherine is deliberately holding onto your Chaos, instead of dispersing it amongst others, so that it would be impossible—let us use Erebus as the example—for Erebus to give it back to you instead as part of your deal. If it belongs to another Child of Chaos, Erebus cannot take it back on your behalf.

Katherine has been preparing for this for a long time, and we may be certain that she has taken all the necessary precautions to lessen her obstacles."

My heart sank again. *Cheers for the blow, Tobe.* "Then what are my options, if the Hermetic Batteries won't be enough and I can't ask Erebus for my Chaos back? Where can I get..." My voice trailed off. Tobe was looking at me strangely.

"I will have to sacrifice some of the creatures that I brought with me. I have not done it before, as it is on the darker side of magic, but I have a means of aiding you with an item in my possession. That is all I am willing to say, for the moment. But it is the only way you will succeed without causing yourself undue injury." He sighed sadly. "You mustn't tell a soul about this. If my creatures catch wind of the plan, even by accident, they will scamper off before such a fate can befall them, promises be damned."

"You can do that?" I felt so sorry for him. We were all having to sacrifice for this, even Tobe and his creatures.

"I—" His eyes turned skyward, his words dropping off completely.

Something was tearing out of the clouds, hurtling downward, heading right for the Rag Team. *Gargoyles.*

"They are from the Bestiary," Tobe announced. "Katherine must have let them loose to seek me out. I suspect she wants me back there!"

"Well, that's not going to happen." I balled my hands into fists. *Not on my watch, Shipton.* "Can't you sing to get them to stop?"

He shook his head. "They are under Katherine's control. They wouldn't listen to me now even if they wanted to."

"Right then, looks like we're doing this the hard way."

He nodded. "Indeed it does."

With Tobe by my side, I sprinted back up the shoreline toward the others, the blood pumping through my veins. If Katherine wanted to bring a fight to us, then it was a fight she was going to get.

FOURTEEN

Finch

These leathery critters didn't look like they were coming in for a cuddle. Thundering down from the clouds, they looked like a horde of flying monkeys. Was the Wicked Witch of the West with them? I freaking hoped not. I mean, I didn't see her anywhere, and I doubted she'd be risking too much with her body crumbling like moldy cheese, but she had a nasty habit of popping up at the worst possible moment.

"Get ready!" Wade shouted.

He'd lost his knife, which meant he was going bare-knuckle. *Typical.* I'd managed to hold onto my baseball bat. Santana had her shotgun aimed up while she delved into her pockets for her last few shells. Dylan was using his crossbow, and Tatyana had her knife raised—and it looked like she knew how to use it. Meanwhile, Garrett and O'Halloran had their shiny magical weapons ready to go.

I glanced at Harley as she took out her switchblade. Again, she really looked like she knew what to do with it. *The perks of a rough childhood.*

Alton had retreated, which was probably for the best. I didn't want to call him dead weight, but... he was dead weight. And he'd be plain dead if he entered this fight.

"Hadouken!" I howled. It felt right.

Wade frowned at me and shook his head. "What he said!"

The front line of gargoyles hit us head on, with Tobe and his monster mash leaping into action beside us. That awesome white bird zoomed through the air, its talons tearing into the shoulders of the nearest gargoyle. The creature screeched as the white bird dragged it around. At the same time, Kadar jumped higher than any human ever could, smoke billowing out of him like steam from a train. He grabbed one of the gargoyles by the throat and wrestled with it as he landed on solid ground. Before my very eyes, he ripped its head right off. I didn't know whether to clap or be sick.

Even Kenzie was getting involved, riding on Tobe's shoulders. She sprang at the gargoyles as they flew past her, clinging to the backs of their heads so they couldn't easily reach her. She bit and scratched until they had no choice but to land. There, she really gave them hell. I could hear the shrieks of frustration from here as she darted here and there, tying them in knots, and her sharp howls attracted the rest of Tobe's land-based critters. They swarmed around the gargoyle she'd downed, and the unicorn stabbed it right in the chest. *So, not all rainbows and glitter?* That horn was a killer weapon, and that beast was using it to deadly effect. Turns out, unicorns could be pretty terrifying when they wanted to be.

As the rest of the suckers dropped out of the sky, I ducked out of the way of their gnashing fangs. All I could see were shiny black eyes and ugly-ass faces. Twisting around, I brought the baseball bat down on the back of one of their heads. A yelp squeaked from the back of its throat as it hit the deck. Naturally, it didn't stay down. Jumping right up again with its wings flapping like mad, it swept toward me. I felt the bite of its claws as they raked across my chest. Hissing air through my teeth, I smacked it again and again. All around me, the others were giving everything. As it turned out, Dylan was a pretty nifty archer. He didn't have many bolts, but he was making each one count.

"Come on, you slimy little creeps!" Harley yelled as she swiped her blade in front of her. It slashed across the tongue of one of the beasts. The end of it dropped to the ground with a wet plop. *Ugh.*

"You tell them, Sis!" I yelled back. My gargoyle just wouldn't stay down. I kept hitting it, and it didn't make a difference. It kept getting up. *Seriously, learn when you're finished, pal.* I whacked it on the head again for good measure. This time, it struggled to get back up, so I hit it again to make sure it stayed put.

Tobe was the most impressive soldier on the field. I'd never seen anything like it. He kept swooping and soaring, plucking gargoyles off left, right, and center. His talons were ripping into them while his claws finished the job. Between the shotgun pellets, the crossbow belts, and the two fliers, things weren't looking so dire. Although, it was pretty baffling to see a leprechaun clinging to the neck of a gargoyle, trying to pummel it with his tiny hands. It almost looked like he was riding the gargoyle. It would've been funny if we weren't in the middle of a battle. And my freaking gargoyle had just dragged itself up again.

"Stay down!" I smacked it again. This time, it didn't move. Instead, it lay still and began to crumble. Flakes of ashy black started to peel away from the creature. The beastie was disintegrating. *Good.*

"Tobe, did you bring any Mason jars?" Wade shouted. I'd forgotten about those.

"No. There was no time," Tobe shouted back. He divebombed the swarm of gargoyles, scattering them like frightened pigeons. The white bird picked a few of them off, digging its glinting talons into their leathery bodies. Soon enough, there weren't any left in the air, but there were still plenty to contend with on the ground.

Santana and Slinky were working as a deadly duo, the feathered serpent wrapped around her like some weird harness. Every time Santana fired a shot, the serpent slithered away to finish the job. Like a terrier racing after pheasants that some posh-bloke had shot out of the sky. *I bet Davin likes a bit of blood sport.*

Slinky hadn't quite gotten over his hatred for Kadar, though. Whenever he got close, he made sure to nip at Kadar's ankles. Just to keep him on his toes.

Just then, I noticed Alton bend over double. He'd swung a massive branch at one of the gargoyles, downing it. Readjusting my grip on the baseball bat, I ran to help him. Evidently, he'd decided to join the fight. I'd almost reached him when I had to dive out of the way. That creepy black horse thundered right past with Tatyana on its back. *Whoa…* Leaning from side to side as though it was nothing, she slashed her blade at the gargoyles. And, man, did she make an impact. They didn't stand a chance, between her knife and the stomping hooves of that thing she was riding.

"You chose the wrong day for a fight, gargoyles!" she screamed. *Yup, she's got a point.*

One of the gargoyles leapt up into the air, making for Tatyana's head. "Get down!" Dylan yelled. A second later, a crossbow bolt shot right through its wing and brought it to the ground. Garrett appeared through the mass of gargoyle and Muppet Baby, and sliced the gargoyle in two with his fiery sword.

I hated to say it, but I was super jealous of that thing. Finch and the Avenging Angel—now there was a comic book I could get on board with. All my life, that'd been my sanctuary. Comic books. All of them. Every kind. Marvel, DC, Dark Horse, everything I could get my hands on. Ironic, really, that it'd taken me so long to realize I was on the villain's side when my entire childhood had been heroes and villains. Then again, there'd always been gray areas—Magneto, Thanos, Loki, Adam Warlock, the Punisher. They believed in their causes. Katherine had been the same. No wonder I'd been sucked in. But, finally, I was standing side by side with the honest heroes. The Captain Americas of our world. *Yo, you want to snap out of it?* My brain jolted me back into focus. We still had a battle to win.

O'Halloran was making a total mess of a trio of gargoyles that had targeted him. He had some mad skills with those daggers—they definitely belonged to him. The way he moved made me wonder what his military training had involved. It was like he wasn't even O'Halloran anymore. He was hyper-focused, ducking and diving and twisting like a dancer. I was so busy watching that I didn't notice the gargoyle coming at me until it sank its fangs into my shoulder.

"Son of a—!" I dropped the bat and grabbed it. Dragging it off me, I felt my skin tear. *That's going to hurt in the morning.* As I slammed it into the ground, I elbow-dropped it right in the chest. It wheezed, and a glob of oily slime landed square in my face. Harley appeared out of nowhere, bringing her switchblade down. The gargoyle screeched as it died, its body disintegrating.

"You okay?" Harley helped me up. "You looked like you were miles away."

"Katherine stuff," I muttered, wiping the gunk off my face. How could I be a hero if I needed my ass saved?

"You're going to need to clean that up." She nodded to my bleeding shoulder.

"Thanks."

She put her hand on my arm. "You sure you're okay?"

"I'm fine. Come on, let's get these leathery swine." I flashed her a grin as I snatched up my bat. Together, we reentered the fray. Scarlet Witch and Quicksilver—the baddest brother-and-sister team in existence. And they'd started on the gray side of the morality scale.

Working as a unit, the Muppet Babies made quick work of the remaining gargoyles. Katherine clearly thought we were weak and powerless, but we had other ideas. Sure, we were still targets, but we had something she didn't—nothing left to lose.

Tobe and his monster crew were doing a terrifying job of ripping the creatures apart. Apparently, there really was no sympathy between Purge beasts. The changelings were morphing into all kinds of petrifying beasts. Big, bulky bears, fiery phoenixes, and smaller versions of

Tobe himself—he was their general and they were obeying his every command. Even that scary wee leprechaun was a force to be reckoned with, having produced a wooden hammer-looking thing that he was wielding like a wild man. A shillelagh, if my memory of Irish culture served. I witnessed things I never wanted to see again. Mainly things involving that red-headed little punk and a gargoyle's eyeballs. *Ugh.*

Soon enough, there were no gargoyles left. Not from Katherine's side, anyway. We'd lost one of our own, and one of the changelings had fallen. But, aside from that, we were intact. The underdogs had won again. And, man, did it feel good!

"Is everyone well?" Tobe retracted his claws and looked at the rest of us.

"A few scrapes, but I think we're good," Wade replied.

"Anyone know how infectious gargoyles are?" I forced a smile.

Tobe approached me. "May I?"

"May you what?"

His fangs flashed in a grin. "Help sanitize your wound."

"Uh… sure?" I frowned at him. Major discomfort gripped my chest as he leaned in. Was I about to get a smooch from a big furry cat-bird? His tongue licked the bite wound. It felt rough and weird, like an actual cat's. And everyone was staring. "Yo, you want to buy me dinner first?"

Tobe laughed. "My saliva has powerful antiseptic properties. I wouldn't want you to get a nasty infection. Gargoyle bites are notorious for creating gangrenous wounds."

"Right… well, thanks, then." My cheeks were burning with embarrassment. "I never thought you and I would be getting up close and personal."

"Neither did I," Tobe replied. "You should be well now. Is anyone else wounded?"

As Tobe went around, literally licking our wounds, I noticed Alton sitting on the ground. He was breathing heavily, but his eyes were shining. There was some color back in his cheeks, at least.

"You okay, Alton?" I walked over to him.

He nodded. "I feel invigorated."

"Yep, that's adrenaline for you. You want to be careful it doesn't pack your ticker in, though."

"I have no idea what you just said." Alton laughed. "But I'll be careful not to push it too much. You may not believe me, after everything that's happened, but I do know my limits."

I arched an eyebrow. "You wouldn't be here if you did."

"I am not running on fumes just yet, Finch, though I thank you for your concern." He smiled up at me. "You know, once upon a time, this would have seemed outlandish. You standing here with the others. But now I couldn't picture the others without you. Is that strange?"

"No... I don't think so." I tried to hide my happiness. If even Alton thought I belonged, then that had to be a good thing.

"So, looks like we were right about needing Tobe and his Purge beasts." Harley wiped the sweat off her forehead as the crew gathered. "They give us the edge we need. Especially that white bird. What is that, by the way?"

"That is a Caladrius," Tobe replied. "She has rare healing powers, which may prove useful in the fight to come. Although, they tire her, which is why I have taken on the healing role for the time being."

"And what's that thing Taty's been riding on?" Dylan asked.

Tobe smiled. "A Kelpie. A horse of death."

"Right. Makes sense, I guess." Dylan glanced at her as she dismounted. Her whole kolduny world revolved around death. Of course she'd pick the death horse.

"I would like to assign a creature to each of you," Tobe continued. "They will defend you to the death, if need be. Santana, you should have Slinky, as you already have a bond. Tatyana, you should have the Kelpie, given your affinity with the beast. Dylan, I thought you might be best suited to the Cretan Bull, given your former Herculean abilities."

The white muscle-bound bull stepped forward and bowed in front of Dylan.

"Cool." Dylan tentatively stroked its head.

"O'Halloran, I thought the leprechaun might suit you. He may be small, but he is fierce." Tobe pointed to the terrifying little thing.

"Ye best watch who yer callin' small," the leprechaun sniped, startling all of us. I hadn't expected him to speak.

"My apologies, Diarmuid." Tobe chuckled as the tiny ginger strapped his shillelagh onto his belt and stalked up to O'Halloran, with way more swagger than anything his size should've had.

"The Irish have to stick together," O'Halloran replied.

"Aye, yer about as Irish as me arse," the leprechaun retorted. "Ye've likely never set foot in the homeland, so dint be callin' yerself Irish unless ye want te lose yer eyes."

O'Halloran frowned. "Are you and me going to have trouble?"

"Not if ye keep yer small jokes and yer Irish chat te yerself." The leprechaun clambered up onto his shoulder. "And dint try te hold me like a baby, else I'll bite ye. And dint be askin' fer no pot o' gold neither, 'cause I don't got mine no more."

"Noted." O'Halloran looked like he wanted to throw the tiny man into the river.

"Alton, I thought you could use the Caladrius. She may be able to keep your energy levels up if they fall below a certain threshold, at least until you can fill the Hermetic Batteries. Garrett, I will give you Striker the gremlin. He can spit fireballs, so I thought it might be a useful combination with your sword. Wade, I thought you could use one of the changelings, who goes by the name of Uzo." Tobe gestured to the changelings as one of them stepped forward.

"Like the booze?" I grinned.

Tobe ignored me. "As for you, Finch, I thought you might be best suited to one of the gargoyles. Argo has the best temperament. And, Harley, Murray seems keen to protect you, so I think he may be your best choice."

Harley paled. "Murray? No... anyone but him." The gargoyle mewled as it padded forward, clambering right up to Harley and nuzzling her legs. She looked about ready to launch the beast across the forest.

"He seems to have chosen you." Tobe laughed.

"Well, he's got a lot of making up to do." She looked at the creature. "I haven't forgotten about Daisy, do you hear?" Murray bumped his head into her arm.

"The Hermetic Batteries likely won't give our old abilities back," Alton said. "Just allow us to cast attack and defense hexes and curses once we've filled them, which will mean delving into the spells you've all been taught during your time at the SDC. So the extra monster heft will certainly come in useful. It will also aid us in getting the Chaos from the cultists."

"I may be able to alter the Hermetic Batteries to grant you your former abilities once more. It is a matter of syncing the batteries to your Chaos signatures," Tobe interjected. "But I won't know for certain until they are charged. There may not be time for such alterations."

Harley nodded. "Speaking of that, we should get the heck out of here so we can find some cultists to steal from." She took out her phone and started to dial.

"You calling up a few cultist pals?" I chuckled.

"No, I need to check in on Ryann and the Smiths. I texted them in New Orleans, but I haven't heard back. I just want to make sure they're still okay," she replied.

A moment later, her eyes went wide. A voice echoed out of the phone, which she'd clearly put on speaker. And it definitely wasn't Ryann or the Smiths.

"I have been awaiting your call, Ms. Merlin." Davin's voice drifted across the line, making my blood run cold.

FIFTEEN

Harley

———

"Davin?" My heart was about ready to explode out of my chest. "H-How?"

"That is for me to know," he replied smoothly. "The many tricks of a skilled Necromancer."

"Wh-What have you done with them?" I choked, still barely even believing who I was hearing. "Where are they? Put them on the phone, now!"

A harsh cackle echoed through the loudspeaker. "You are in no position to make demands, Miss Merlin. Allow *me* to dictate your options. If you wish to see your family alive again, I will need you to be at the Halidon Inn in Northern California by midnight. Either you surrender to me then, or the Smiths will be executed."

I couldn't speak. My hand trembled as it gripped the phone, and my knees were shaking. I'd been so focused on this part of my family—the Rag Team—that I realized I hadn't done enough to secure the safety of my other family. *My human family.*

"How did you find them?" I needed to keep him talking while I figured out what on earth I was going to do.

Another bitter laugh splintered through the phone. "How do you think?"

"I… I don't know."

"I imagine you thought you had nothing left belonging to them. Well, it is curious what secrets the thorough search of someone's room can reveal. The smallest object can become the key to a previously locked door. And a key, an actual key, can do the same thing."

My stomach dropped. I still had my key to the Smiths' house, stowed away at the back of one of my drawers at the SDC. I'd totally forgotten it was even there, because I hadn't needed to use it. It had just been gathering dust, a memento of my past life that I hadn't been able to part with.

And Davin had found it, so he could use a tracking spell to find the Smiths. That was the only way he could have traced them, considering they had no Chaos signature to follow. *You idiot!* I should've known they would go to every despicable length to get to me. And now, my heart was breaking all over again. I wouldn't lose them… I couldn't.

"Harley." Wade came to my side, and I quickly muted the call.

"What else can I do?" Angry tears sprang to my eyes. "I can't let them have the Smiths."

"If you go there tonight, you know what will happen." Wade's voice was tight with worry.

"It means Katherine will be one step away from taking me down," I whispered.

"She'll be waiting for you," Wade said.

I nodded. "I know. I know that, of course I do, but what am I supposed to do? Do I just let Davin kill the Smiths?" I gripped his hand. "I can't do that, Wade. The Smiths are innocent. I dragged them into this. If I let them suffer, then how am I any better than Katherine?" I'd made that dumb promise to the Chains of Truth, but, in action, it was a different story.

"Then we fight," Finch said. "We take the fight to her. We get in, we have a scrap, we get out with the Smiths, and we keep going. Katherine is weak without you, remember? She won't risk tipping herself over the edge, no matter how much she wants you. She needs to still have her body in order to take yours."

Wade squeezed my shoulders reassuringly. "We're all on your side, Harley. We'll fight."

"Okay… okay, then we fight." I unmuted the phone and put it to my ear, my hands still shaking. "I-I'll see you at midnight."

Davin snickered. "I look forward to it."

I hung up and leaned into Wade, his thumbs brushing away my tears. Anger and fear and grief rippled through me, making it hard to breathe. If it hadn't been for his arms around me, I definitely would have crumbled. That seemed so stupid. I'd been through so much and stayed standing, but this was one step too far. I hated the idea of putting everyone else in danger. Both of my families would be in the line of fire, and I had no idea how it would turn out.

Taking a breath, I forced myself to focus. *There's no other way.* I *couldn't* leave the Smiths to die.

"I know where we can get our Chaos from, for the Hermetic Batteries," I managed.

"You do?" Tatyana stepped forward.

I nodded. "Clearly, that slimy piece of crap is bursting with mojo. Either he was never actually dead—which I find *very* hard to believe, given the state of him—and found the strength to survive, or, *somehow*, he managed to resurrect himself. Either way, this means we can kill two birds with one stone."

"It is possible," Alton murmured.

"What's possible?" Garrett asked.

"That he managed to resurrect himself," Alton said slowly.

I stared at him. "Huh? I thought you said it *wasn't* possible."

"It is impossible in terms of one's *own* Necromancy, but… Necromancers have always sought immortality. Perhaps Davin found something to help himself. Perhaps he has figured out a way to make it possible… Perhaps Katherine's newfound power has had a hand in it.

That probably makes the most sense." Alton furrowed his brow. "Of course, this poses a problem: If Davin can't be killed, then how do we get rid of him for good?"

"Plus, the massive problem of Katherine being there to grab Harley," O'Halloran added.

"Nope, not going to happen," Finch said. "Like I said, Katherine won't be willing to risk the body she has left in case it all falls apart. She might've been listening in, but she'll be waiting for Harley to be delivered to her. She won't do any unnecessary work herself. She's got enough minions now that she doesn't have to worry about the dirty work."

"You're sure of that?" Wade asked.

He shrugged. "No, but it's a strong feeling."

"Either way, we'll need to scope the place out first," I interjected. I was inclined to believe Finch, but Katherine was an unpredictable creature. "We need to save the Smiths and get Chaos out of Davin. After that, we can decide what to do with that snaky son of a bitch and find a way to *keep* him dead."

It looked like my wobble was only temporary, because all of that anger and grief and terror had transformed into something else—pure, raw, visceral determination. Katherine had made the wrong choice by threatening my family, and she'd find that out soon enough.

"So… ?" Garrett prompted.

"So, next stop, Northern California." I glanced around at the new roster of the Rag Team. "We're going to need a watertight plan for this. Davin is most likely going to expect some kind of offensive."

Finch smirked. "Yeah, but he's not going to expect Tobe and a butt-load of monsters."

No… no, he's not.

SIXTEEN

Harley

Waiting was the worst part, though I guessed it was a gift as well as a curse. Davin had told us to meet him at the Halidon Inn at midnight, which gave us a few hours to cement our plan of action, even though concentrating was proving to be impossible. All I could think about were the Smiths and how I'd messed up.

When I'd left the Smiths', I hadn't taken a whole lot with me. Not that I'd had much in the first place: a few posters, some room ornaments, a few items of clothing that I'd borrowed from Ryann's wardrobe. And what was left had been more or less lost when that sweet, sweet first apartment of mine had been ransacked by gargoyles. *Yeah, I'm looking at you, Murray.* Frankly, I had no clue why Tobe had made the slobbering brute my personal bodyguard. Maybe he thought we needed to build some bridges, considering our checkered past with one another.

But there was the key. I couldn't believe I'd left that in the drawer. Though I could believe Davin had sniffed it out. Turned out he wasn't just Katherine's lapdog—he was her bloodhound, too.

"So where exactly is this Halidon Inn?" Kadar's voice broke through my thoughts.

We'd been moving through chalk door after chalk door for hours, trying to pass the time, as well as stay ahead of any cultists or gargoyles that might happen to be on our tail. Darkness had fallen a long time ago, and we were currently taking a breather in rural Wyoming, not too far from the border of Yellowstone but far enough to avoid unwanted attackers. We sat at a rickety picnic table, eating the last of the food we'd picked up at our previous location—a one-horse town somewhere in Wisconsin.

Looking around, everyone seemed like they were dead on their feet. A few of us had tried to sleep, but there was too much adrenaline running through the Rag Team in anticipation of tonight to really settle down.

"Sacramento," Garrett replied, his brow furrowing. "Imogene put me up there while I was helping out in LA, when I was out in the field instead of back at the coven."

"You mean Katherine," Santana corrected.

Garrett nodded. "Yeah… Katherine. Man, I keep forgetting." He gave a visible shudder. "It's a nice enough place, kind of out of the way in what's basically a strip mall. The only people I ever saw were businessmen coming off the I-80 and rich teenagers in Range Rovers pulling into the Starbucks for a unicorn frappe. It's got free channels and average room service."

"I bet you made the most of those free channels, eh? While the cat's away, etcetera." Finch flashed a wink.

"I mean the sports channels." Garrett rolled his eyes. "Anyway, I can help you picture it, Ra—uh, Kadar, so we hit the right spot."

"Much appreciated," Kadar replied.

I checked the clock on my phone and saw that it was a quarter to one in the morning. With Wyoming being an hour ahead of Los Angeles, I knew it was time for us to move.

"Kadar, would you care to do the honors?" I asked.

He grinned. "I was wondering when we would finally get down to business. Garrett, help me with the location." Garrett walked over to him, and the two of them started discussing while I turned to the others.

"Does everyone know what we have to do?"

"Get in, get the Smiths, get out, don't get killed?" Finch replied. "Oh, and make sure Davin stays dead this time?"

I smiled nervously. "Yeah, that's pretty much it. Does everyone know their teams?"

The group nodded.

"Kadar will be with me, O'Halloran, Diarmuid, the Kelpie, and a handful of other creatures," Tatyana said. That leprechaun was a law unto himself, and I felt sorry for whichever sucker was going to have to face him and his shillelagh. Well, not that sorry. I sort of hoped he might leap on Davin and scare the living daylights out of him.

Santana smiled. "And Dylan and Garrett will be with me, as well as Slinky, Striker, and Bullwinkle, plus extras." Dylan had named the Cretan Bull that had been instructed to guard him, though I wasn't sure the name hit the right note. "Bullwinkle" didn't exactly strike fear into my heart.

Dylan snorted. "I still think that's a killer name."

"You would," Finch said under his breath.

"And I will be joined by Alton and the Caladrius," Tobe added. "And a quarter of the remaining beasts, as well as Miss Kenzie."

"Which leaves the A-Team." Finch grinned. "My sis and my future bro-in-law, Wonderboy, with two badass gargoyles and Boozo the changeling." The gray-skinned, glowing-eyed beast scowled at him.

"Don't listen to him, Uzo," Wade urged, patting the changeling awkwardly on the shoulder. "And easy with the brother-in-law talk." He cast me a shy glance which made me smile. We were both still a bit young for that kind of thing, and we needed to survive Katherine before we could even *think* about the future.

"The door is ready when you are." Kadar gestured to the doorway he'd opened up against the wall of an unused restroom nearby.

As soon as he turned that handle, I felt certain all hell would break loose. And so, it was a bit of an anti-climax when we actually stepped through and found ourselves in the grim, empty lot at the back of the Halidon Inn, with no sign of anyone at all. *They're probably lying in wait for us.*

However, the worst thing we had to face was the rancid smell of the dumpsters that lined the alleyway and the scurry of rats, which quickly detected Kenzie and ran for their lives.

With Murray slapping his feet on the concrete beside me, I crept toward the end of the lot and peered around the wall. The road beyond was completely devoid of people—even the I-80 that stretched past the hotel like a big, fat, tarmacked snake—lending it a post-apocalyptic feel. There should have been people out here. I mean, we were practically *on* the freeway, for Pete's sake. I definitely smelled a rat, and it wasn't coming from the dumpsters. Then again, the King Rat himself was somewhere in that hotel, just waiting for us to appear.

"Does Astrid have eyes on Katherine?" I whispered, returning to the group. Murray didn't seem to want to leave my side, his leathery shape my constant shadow. *You've still got a lot of groveling to do, pal.*

"I'll call her, see what she can see." Wade took out his phone and dialed. "Astrid? Yeah, we need a location for Katherine. Is she anywhere near Sacramento? Right... okay... okay... yeah, I can wait. You have her? Okay, thanks." He gave a small smile. "We'll be careful, I promise."

Hanging up, he heaved out an anxious sigh. "Astrid has live camera footage of Katherine. She's in Purgatory. Apparently she's been there for a few hours, in the warden's office."

I frowned. "Doing what?"

"Nothing. She's just sitting there."

"What? That doesn't make sense," Santana said. "Is Astrid sure it's not on a loop or something?"

Wade nodded. "The footage is live and in real time; she said she double-checked. It looks like Katherine has got some kind of control over the warden, since his eyes were glowing. And he's doing the rounds as we speak, presumably making sure all the rebels are secured for Katherine. That's what Astrid thinks, anyway."

"Did she say anything else?" Garrett's voice carried a note of eagerness.

"Yeah, she said Katherine hasn't performed any magic for a while. Like I said, she's just been sitting there, letting everyone else run around doing her dirty work for her." Wade paused. "And she keeps adding some... stuff to her face every half hour or so. Astrid described it as 'skin goop,' so I'm guessing she meant some kind of makeup."

Understanding hit me like a bolt of lightning, and it looked like I wasn't the only one putting the pieces together.

"Her body must really be running on fumes," Alton said, before I had the chance to speak.

"I was just about to say the same thing." Tatyana shook her head. "It must be why Davin is doing all of this at her instruction—bringing Harley in for her."

O'Halloran grinned. "The lass *can't* do it herself. She can't do anything but sit on her ass and wait."

"Call yerself an Irishman. It's *arse*, mate," Diarmuid muttered. "But I happen te agree wit yez—sounds like dis Katherine wench is havin' trouble keepin' her bits together."

"I imagine that is why she sent those gargoyles after me, also." Tobe nodded. "Using even the smallest quantity of Chaos would cause further damage to her already fragile form. I doubt she is even able to open a portal on her own without crumbling to pieces. Or gaining another large crack in her façade."

Finch smirked. "She's finally getting the face she deserves. Looks like Mama wasn't listening closely enough—everyone knows Chaos comes at a price, and she's paying off a crap-ton of debt right now."

"Then this is it." I steeled myself. "If Katherine isn't coming, and my neck is on the line, then this really is our last shot. And we need to make sure we get it right. I'm not saying it'll be easy, but at least we don't have to worry about Eris the Uber-Bitch rocking up and making things ten times more difficult."

Wade's phone began to ring. He picked it up and swiped the answer button. "Hello? Astrid? Is everything okay?" He paled as he listened to her. A few moments later, he hung up again.

"What's up?" I peered at him. If this was another dollop of bad news just as I was getting into my groove for the fight to come, I was going to scream so loud it'd bring half of LA to a screeching halt.

"It's your Purge… thing," Wade said.

"Beast," Tobe corrected.

"Yeah, usually I'd agree with you, but Harley's Purge is harder to describe, Tobe. You'll understand if you get the chance to see it." Wade turned his attention back to me. "Something's happening with it. Astrid says it keeps lighting up, as if little explosions are erupting beneath the fog. And all the vegetation around the lake is growing at a crazy pace. Already, she said the woods around the cabin have grown twice as tall and twice as thick, and she said there are all kinds of beautiful and weird plants growing. One of them tried to bite her when she went out to take a closer look at the fog."

"What the heck did you squeeze out, Sis?" Finch gaped at me.

I shrugged in alarm. "I really don't know."

"That's not all," Wade continued. "Astrid said she spotted some strange animals in the woods, too—animals she's never seen before. She even checked a few against Smartie's systems, but they weren't recognized as known species."

"This is some John Wyndham crap, right here." Finch's eyes were bugging out of his head. "With a touch of Lovecraft."

"Funnily enough, Astrid did say it was starting to look like a sci-fi novel out there," Wade replied.

"Is it aggressive? The Purge thing, I mean? We'll forget about the bitey plants for now." My heart hammered in my chest. What had I created? What if we defeated Katherine only to have the world destroyed by this insane foggy stuff that I'd poured out my veins?

Wade shook his head. "Astrid just said it was peculiar, but she didn't sound scared. Well, aside from the man-eating shrub. It's just sitting there on the lake, doing its thing."

What's it's 'thing,' though?

That was the worrying part. But I couldn't think about that right now. There was no room for distraction—not until we'd put Davin on his ass and gotten the Smiths out of this shady hotel.

"Okay, then it's time." I swallowed my nerves. "The plan is to cause several diversions, right? We need to split up in our teams and come at them from all angles. Protect the Smiths when we find them and take down Davin and however many cultists he brought with him."

A murmur of agreement rang through the Rag Team.

Well then, the only thing we had left to do was get on with it. I imagined the Halidon Inn had seen some pretty grisly things in its time, but this was about to top them all.

SEVENTEEN

Harley

We quickly split into four teams. Tatyana's team and Tobe's team flanked the hotel, using the fire escape and the main entrance to get into the building, while my team and Kadar's headed for the staff entrance. Wade had his phone out to check for updates from Astrid on Katherine's activity, and Astrid was also supposed to be transmitting a real-time feed of the hotel for him to monitor anytime now. My nerves jangled as we broke through the doorway, with a bit of effort from Kadar.

The hotel was completely silent, not a mouse stirring. Evidently, the cultists had been instructed to be quiet, presumably so we wouldn't know how many were actually here. Together, we crept along the service corridor, past the kitchens, and moved up to the first floor of the hotel.

Wade put his hand up, signaling for us to stop. "She's sent me the feed, jammed their access to the cameras, and put their monitors on a loop," he whispered. "There are cultists on every floor."

"How many on this floor?" I whispered back.

He stared at his screen. "Eight."

"Okay, you wait here and launch your attack on this floor once I've made it to the right room," I said. "Be stealthy. I'm sure they already know I wouldn't come alone, but we might get lucky." I glanced at Finch, who stood on my right side. "I'm going to call you, Finch, and leave the line open. You should be able to hear everything that's going on."

He nodded. "The best kind of butt dial. Got it."

"Be safe, but remember… this is our last chance."

I had to take this first step alone, but it didn't feel so overwhelming knowing I had the Rag Team at my back. *To think I tried to keep you all away…* I offered them a reassuring look, my gaze lingering a moment longer on Wade and Finch's faces, then took a deep breath and strode down the corridor, trying to muster all the courage I possessed.

Rounding the corner, I came face-to-face with the first group of cultists. They raised their palms, ready to defend themselves. A moment later, they lowered them, evidently remembering that I didn't have any Chaos anymore. None of us did. But that didn't mean we'd go easy on these punks. And that was the greatest advantage we possessed. They thought we were broken, but we were anything but. *I* was anything but.

"I'm guessing you know where that British ass-wipe is?" I channeled a bit of Finch, trying to catch them off guard. The nearest two cultists frowned in confusion. "I mean Davin, you idiots. Where is he?"

The first cultist smirked. "Second floor, room 202."

"Thanks." Sarcasm dripped from my words. "Oh, and I don't need an entourage, so I wouldn't bother trailing after me like a bunch of lost puppies. This is between me and Davin, and that ridiculous woman you call a goddess. Funny, isn't it, that she hasn't bothered to show her face? Not much of a goddess, is she, if it's taken all this to try and get me."

With that I pushed through, relishing the bemused looks on their faces as they stepped aside. *That's right, Merlin, sow the seed.* If I could get even a handful of them to start doubting their mighty goddess, perhaps they'd start to realize that she wasn't so mighty after all.

Climbing the stairs to the second floor, I breezed past another bunch of cultists. They parted like the sea for me, both reluctant and agitated in equal measure. From the looks on their faces, I could tell they wanted to be anywhere else. To them, this was nothing but blind duty in the hopes of gaining some kind of reward. *As if you'll ever be anything but minions.*

I let all of that anger and bitterness flow through me as I pressed on, keeping my head high and my determination primed. Reaching the door of room 202, I paused for a moment. From the floor below, I heard a few muffled grunts and a couple of satisfying thuds. My team and Kadar's team were in place. Hopefully, that meant Tobe's team and Santana's team weren't far away. We were going to need all the heavyweights for this next step.

"I believe I'm expected." I shot a cold look at the two guards outside room 202.

"Davin is waiting for you," the first guard said tersely.

I snorted. "Isn't that what I just said? Stand aside. And I hope, when Katherine and her cult fall apart, that the door doesn't smack you in the ass on your way out."

"Eris is eternal," the second guard protested.

"Oh yeah? And I'm Ziggy Stardust." I smiled at them. "You can run if you want to. I won't tell. In fact, I'd encourage it. When Katherine's empire falls, you'll want to be as far away as possible."

They exchanged a worried look.

"No. Eris will prevail," the second guard insisted.

"Don't say I didn't warn you." I pushed past them and knocked on the door. I could've made a dramatic entrance, busting through the door like something out of a high-octane action thriller, but that wasn't my style. That was Katherine's style. No, I wanted him to stew awhile. I wanted him to invite me in, so that he had nobody else to blame when the monsters descended on them all.

"Come in." Davin's slick, slimy voice echoed through the door.

I smiled to myself, letting the anticipation spur me on, then turned the handle and walked in.

The room was dingy and didn't look like it had been redecorated since the seventies, with weird stains streaking the walls and a film of dust across the windows. If anyone brought a blacklight in here, they'd have run screaming. I could handle that.

What I couldn't stomach was the sight of Ryann and the Smiths, huddled and tied up in the corner. It was suddenly like the Ryder twins all over again. Their faces were pale and drawn, and Ryann and Mrs. Smith's eyes were rimmed with red. Mr. Smith was trying to be brave for his family, but even he looked like he was on the edge of breaking down. A bruise blossomed across Ryann's cheek, and they had a few more scrapes between them—though thankfully nothing too serious.

"Ms. Merlin, at last." Davin grinned. He was clearly enjoying the power of harming defenseless humans.

"Sorry to keep you waiting. You did say midnight, didn't you? Although, if you're waiting for me to turn into a pumpkin, you're going to be very disappointed." It took everything I had to keep my cool, with Ryann and the Smiths shivering in the corner.

"As amusing as ever, I see." He smiled dryly. "Oh, and my apologies for the unfortunate state of your human family. They put up quite the fight. Indeed, nobody was more surprised than I was. Sadly, that meant they needed a little roughing up. They simply wouldn't stop squirming and struggling, and you know I prefer the path of least resistance. Nevertheless, they are alive, as promised."

"I'm surprised you know how to keep a promise," I retorted.

"For the right person, my loyalty is unwavering."

I smirked. "Then you're a terrible judge of character. Although, we already know that."

"Excuse me?" He wrinkled his nose.

"Sidling up to Katherine like a desperate little leech." I shrugged. "Desperate Doncaster, that's what they should call you."

"Always so droll," he said sourly.

"What's a bit of humor when my life is on the line?" I grinned at him. He wouldn't have the satisfaction of seeing me weak, not with the small, savage army at my back. "Come on, dude, think of it as my last request. A few giggles before I have to give up my body for that evil witch you worship. Man, I bet all you can taste is her boots, with all the licking you've done."

"Do not push me, Harley."

"What else am I supposed to do? No magic, remember? My sharp wit is all I've got."

I could see him getting more and more annoyed, and I couldn't have been more pleased. Meanwhile, the Smiths looked on in fear. This wasn't a laughing matter for them or for me, but I had to keep up the ruse. *You're getting out of this alive. All of you.*

"And you accuse my beloved Eris of delighting in the sound of her own voice," Davin said.

"Just making sure I've got your full attention," I replied. "See, there's something that's still bugging me. I'm sure you'll keep insisting that you didn't, but I'm pretty freaking convinced you helped us when we escaped from the Garden of Hesperides. Katherine said 'jump' and you didn't. Not immediately. I want to know why."

He paused for a moment, his forehead furrowing in thought, before a strange smile spread across his face. "My allegiance is always to myself, above all others. I stand with the strongest. Believe it or not, I thought you might impress me if you got a second chance. Yet, here you are, stupid and emotional and painfully human, sacrificing yourself for your family when your focus should have been on looking for a means to destroy Eris. Think of it as a test. A test that you have failed miserably."

I frowned. "Really? Then why don't I feel like I'm on the losing side?"

"Because you are a foolish little girl and cannot understand when you have been beaten," he replied. "Now, before we proceed, there is something that *I* would like to know."

I shrugged. "Shoot." *Talk as much as you want.* The more he spoke, the more time the Rag Team and the monsters had to rally.

"This spell that Eris keeps mentioning—is there truly something within the Grimoire that will allow her to inhabit your body, and bridge the gap between worlds? I'd hate for her to go to all this trouble only to find that it can't be done."

"Absolutely, but I'm not going to tell you what it is," I replied sweetly. "Katherine knows, otherwise she wouldn't be so desperate to get her claws on me. And I doubt she wants you in on her little secret. You're nothing but a tool to her. Ironic, really."

"You think you can deter me with your words? It won't work." Davin smiled. "I have Eris's complete devotion."

I snorted. "And I'm sure you've got the hickeys to prove it."

"What spell is she so eager for you to read to her?" Davin pressed.

"Hansel and Gretel."

He rolled his eyes. "Be serious, Ms. Merlin, for all our sakes."

"She wants me to read a summoning spell for our old pal, Erebus."

He frowned, obviously concerned. "But what does it say? Be specific."

"No, you know what, I don't think I'm going to tell you." Black smoke slipped through the windows behind Davin, pooling down to the floor like dry ice. "I'm not here to give up all my secrets, and I'm definitely not here to give up my body. Sorry to disappoint."

"Pardon?" A look of confusion passed across his stupid face.

"Is that really why you think I'm here?" I laughed bitterly. "Did you really think you could just set a trap and I'd walk right in? You haven't been paying attention, Desperate Doncaster."

He grinned. "Ah, you think because Eris isn't here, you have a fighting chance. I did wonder why you were so calm. However, if you think that, then you are far more idiotic than I thought."

I looked toward the Smiths. "Actually, I'm not here to save my family, though it's a very welcome bonus. Sorry, guys." They flashed me a confused trio of frowns, but this would all make sense to them soon.

"I don't follow," Davin murmured.

"No, you really don't." I peeled back my sleeve to reveal the empty Hermetic Battery clamped on my forearm. It was on the opposite arm from my nasty apple tattoo. "I'm here to steal some of that tasty Chaos that Katherine let you keep."

Davin stared at me as Murray took his solid form right behind him. He had no idea a gargoyle was about to bear down on him, especially as a couple of well-timed thuds made his head snap toward the door.

Murray lunged, his oily fangs bared, and sank them right into Davin's shoulder. Davin howled, trying to grasp at Murray as the creature sprang up and powered back down, hitting Davin in the face with his leathery body.

A second later, Kadar kicked down the door and burst through, providing the dramatic entrance I hadn't given. He held a pair of Atomic Cuffs in his hands, given to him by Tobe, who always had a few spares tucked away in his wings.

All of a sudden, the tables had turned, and it didn't look good for Davin.

"Get this thing off me!" Davin roared.

But there were no cultists left to come to his aid. He put up his hands to try and use Chaos to get Murray off him, but Murray was too quick. He sank his fangs right into Davin's forearm, his claws swiping at his other hand. Davin tried to tug his arm away, dragging Murray around, but Murray just clung tight like the scrappy critter he was. This gave Kadar the chance he needed to dart across the room and wrestle Davin to the ground. The djinn clapped the Atomic Cuffs on the idiot before he could lift his palms again.

"Katherine's not going to be happy about this." I stared down at Davin, who lay helpless on the floor, scarlet with rage. His face had almost turned the same shade as Kadar.

"You are making an *enormous* mistake!" he growled, as Murray gave him another nip for good measure.

"No, Davin, *you* made the mistake when you underestimated us," I shot back.

I let Kadar wrangle him, while Murray stood guard, licking his lips with his long, black tongue.

I had a moment to breathe now, and I hurried to the Smiths. Kneeling beside them, I untied them as quickly as my shaking hands could manage. The rest of the Rag Team were spilling through the door, all of them bruised and battered but victorious, their monster bodyguards standing right beside them. There was nothing quite as impressive as watching Tatyana stomp through the door on the back of that death horse. I had no idea how she'd even gotten the beast up the stairs or how it had managed to squeeze itself through the doorway, but this was no ordinary horse. I guessed it had used some magical trickery to bust through. As for Tobe and the rest of the monsters, I guessed they were still outside stopping any cultists who'd tried to run. At least, that was what the muffled cries from the street below suggested.

"I'm so sorry," I said, once the Smiths were finally free. "Saving you was always part of the plan; I was just saying that to distract Davin."

"Oh, Harley." Mrs. Smith put her arms around me and pulled me close. She was shaking, clearly trying to appear calmer than she really was. I sank into her shoulder, gripping her tightly. A moment later, I felt Mr. Smith and Ryann close in, making it a group hug.

"Your world is a scary one, kiddo," Mr. Smith said, his voice catching. He looked pale, all the color drained from his face. He was trying to be brave, too.

I gave a dry laugh. "That's not even the worst of it."

"If we'd known you'd be in this much danger, we'd never have let you strike out on your own." I couldn't tell if Mrs. Smith was joking or not. "I'm sorry they tried to use us against you."

"Hey, *you've* got nothing to be sorry for." I pulled away, looking at them all. "I should have kept you safe. I should've done more."

Ryann smiled nervously. "But there's more to this than just us, right? This is a whole new, terrifying level of weird, but you didn't put us here, so don't you try and say you're sorry. You can't save everyone all the time, no matter how much of a badass you are. Which you are, by the way. That idiot wanted to use us against you, like Mom said. I'm guessing, since he stooped that low, he was running out of options. Am I close?"

"That's what we're hoping, yeah," I replied.

"Then what more could you have done?" Ryann said. "You *did* keep us safe, aside from a couple of bruises, but bruises heal. And, going by what you just said to the guy, we did you a favor by getting kidnapped. You need something from him, right?"

I sighed. "Yup. Chaos."

"Then everything worked out." She gave me a brave grin. "Where do you go from here? World domination?"

I chuckled. "Stopping it, actually."

"What?" Mr. Smith frowned.

"It's a very long story, and I don't have a lot of time." I smiled at them all. "But I'll explain everything to you when it's all over." *If I'm still here to tell the tale.*

"Are these your friends?" Mrs. Smith nodded to the Rag Team. Her voice trembled, like she was trying to find the normality in this totally abnormal situation. One of the most endearing parts of the human condition.

"No… they're my family. My other family. Well, I guess they're my *other*, other family, in the grand scheme of things." I smirked. "These are the guys who are helping me save the world."

"Where can I get me one of those?" Ryann asked suddenly.

I glanced over to see she was staring at Finch.

I almost choked. "Say what now? I thought you had the big, sexy Canadian?"

"What big, sexy Canadian?" Mrs. Smith looked horrified.

Ryann shot me a half-amused, half-mortified look. "I mean the *flappy thing* that keeps biting that man!" she hissed.

I realized that Finch was standing in front of Murray—and Davin—and my cheeks started burning with embarrassment.

"So much for sisterly secrets," Ryann chided, nudging me with her elbow.

I glanced over my shoulder at Davin, and quickly snapped back to the present. "Actually, speaking of the man that Murray keeps biting, I've got something to do."

"Murray?" Ryann asked.

"He's my flappy thing," I replied.

She shook her head. "What kind of world do you live in, huh? It's going to take me weeks to wrap my head around all this."

"You get used to it after a while." Getting to my feet, I returned my focus to the task at hand. These Hermetic Batteries needed filling, and we finally had Chaos on tap.

EIGHTEEN

Finch

Davin couldn't budge an inch thanks to Kadar and Harley's gargoyle watchdog, which was exactly what we needed to get these Hermetic whatsits filled. The five of us who had one unclipped them from our forearms and handed them to Kadar, who now had the ability to get these puppies filled up, thanks to whatever the heck Marie Laveau had done to him.

I watched Kadar closely as he dipped his head down and closed his eyes. A moment later, bronze light glowed through his palms and a massive spike emerged from a hidden contraption in the middle of the cuff. I stared at it. That thing looked *nasty.*

"Don't you dare!" Davin raged.

"What are you going to do about it?" Harley snapped at him.

She had a point. Kadar still had his mighty djinn knee shoved into Davin's chest to stop him from getting up. It didn't stop him from squirming, though. *Like the worm you are.*

Turning the cuff over, Kadar jabbed the spike into Davin's arm. I expected blood to flow. Instead, slivers of sparkling light began to spiral out of Davin's cut. They entered the battery through two silver nodules, one at either end. Through the glass windows in the cuff, I could see the battery filling up with all of that awesome energy.

This was just the ticket for what we needed. Harley could do all the Grimoire-reading she wanted after this. Davin was a Necromancer—the magical equivalent of the Hulk, internally speaking. Plus, Katherine had probably given him a dose of extra oomph to allow him to dart here and there, doing her bidding. He was her little pet, after all. Man, it was going to feel so friggin' good to have some Chaos back. Even temporarily, I wouldn't be Billy No-Magic anymore.

"Eris will make you pay for this." Davin looked like he wanted to smash us all to pieces.

I smirked. "Add it to our tab."

He continued to writhe and complain as Kadar filled the rest of the Hermetic Batteries and handed them back to us. Only Garrett and O'Halloran didn't have one, but they didn't seem to mind. After all, they were the ones with the magical weaponry, while the rest of us had the barrel scrapings from Santana's family cabin.

Harley picked up a Hermetic Battery and immediately carried it to Alton. He took it gratefully and clapped it on his forearm. Now that it was full of juice, it wasn't just a garish fashion statement. The network of veins beneath Alton's skin pulsed for a second before fading again. His skin quickly returned to its usual fleshy pink.

"How do you feel?" Harley asked.

"Exhausted." Alton gave a sharp laugh. "But I think it's doing something."

"Good. That's good. Stay with us, okay?" She looked worried.

He nodded. "I will."

I turned back as Kadar brandished one of the cuffs at me. I took it from him and put the item over my forearm. Immediately, a jolt of energy exploded through me. My own veins flashed like a backyard firework display, and my heart felt like it might burst right out of my chest.

The feeling disappeared as quickly as it had arrived. One intense pulse to let us know these things were working. *Nice.*

"That should tide you all over for a few days, if you're careful not to use them too freely," Kadar said. He filled up the last battery and handed it to Harley, who took it and put it on her forearm. That same flash lit her up for a second.

"Whoa," she whispered.

"It feels good, right?" I said.

She grinned. "Yeah... it does."

"We should get to Tobe and see if he can tweak them," Wade suggested.

"We've got to deal with *him* first." Harley glowered at Davin. We might not have had our abilities, but we had plenty of learned spells to use as a substitute. See, books could come in handy. And Davin wasn't going to get out of here without having a little courtesy sample.

His eyes widened. For once, I saw real fear on his smug face. "You don't need to hurt me."

"Didn't you just say Katherine would make us pay for this?" Harley shot back.

I joined the rest of the crew in a circle around him. We'd gone from being flimsy humans to his worst freaking nightmare. This was the greatest 360 in history. I didn't agree with my mother on a lot of things, but having power really did feel good.

"You caught me by surprise, that's all. I didn't know what you planned to do with me," Davin replied. The dude sounded desperate. "Set me free and I won't say a word about this. I will give you a third chance to prove your might against Eris. Remember how I paused in the Garden of Hesperides? I didn't want to admit it, but there was more to it than I explained. I admire you, Ms. Merlin. I wanted to see just how tough you are, and you have shown yourself to be a fearsome adversary. I underestimated you, but I will not do so again. Please, allow me my life, and I will—"

"You'll what?" Santana interrupted. "Turn on your beloved goddess? I don't think so, *pendejo*."

"I will. I will turn against Katherine if you allow me to join your service." He'd turned as white as a sheet. "Did I not say to you, Ms. Merlin, that I desired to be on the strongest side? And that my loyalty was to myself, first and foremost? Well, you have shown me that you are the stronger side. Let me live, and I will pledge myself to you."

"If you think we believe you, then you are far more stupid than we've given you credit for." Tatyana glared down at him. "We saw what you and the rest of Katherine's minions did to the covens and their inhabitants. My parents were among them."

"Then let me help you find them," Davin begged. "I have the means. You know I do."

Tatyana shook her head. "As much as I wish that were true, none of us are foolish enough to listen to a word you say. You've just proven you have no loyalty to anyone." Her eyes lit up suddenly. "You'd say anything to get loose."

"Easy there," I warned. "I know you're hurting, but we've got to be smart with these things."

The light faded from her eyes. "I apologize."

"O'Halloran, could you take the Smiths outside somewhere?" Harley's voice was razor sharp.

He nodded. "It'd be my pleasure."

"Well, I ain't missin' the show," Diarmuid muttered from his shoulder, slipping down his arm and landing on the floor. He was almost as scary as Katherine, but pint-sized. I didn't know if that made him scarier on a terrifying-by-square-inch level.

Leaving the leprechaun, O'Halloran ushered the Smiths out of the room. All three of them looked back at Harley. My heart wrenched. That was the look I'd always wanted to be given, all the way through my miserable childhood and beyond. Unconditional love. They were worried about her.

But I'd be more worried about Davin, if I were you. There was only one reason she'd be asking O'Halloran to take them outside—things were about to get biblical.

The moment the door closed, Harley snapped her head back around. She'd gone into full warrior mode. Right now, the top terrifying spot was entirely hers. Even Diarmuid had the sense to take a step back. As she lifted her palms, tendrils began to twist around her fingertips. They sparked and hissed like hot coals, fed by her anger. And Davin... he was well and truly crapping himself.

"I'd rather die myself than have a duplicitous worm like you on my side," she spat. "Whether you can come back to life again, I don't know. But if I kill you, at least that'll put you out of order for a while." She smiled, ice cold. "Oh, and you can say goodbye to your cultists while you're at it. The monsters got rid of them this time. The poor things were starving; it was only right to feed them. Actually, I'm pretty sure Diarmuid is digesting a couple eyeballs as we speak."

The leprechaun belched loudly. "Aye, ye can say that again. They repeat on me somethin' terrible, though."

Ugh. Just when I thought he couldn't get any more alarming.

"Please, Ms. Merlin, have mercy." Davin looked up at her with fake puppy-dog eyes.

The tendrils around Harley's fingers glowed brighter. "It's too late for that, Davin. You'll get the same mercy you showed all those innocents," she replied. *"Et ossa vestra conteram corpus ruina. Ne tenebrae vos sumo. Est digna est tibi. Egredere de terra hac."*

I didn't know the spell, but I knew it wasn't going to turn him into a magical princess. It wasn't even going to turn him into a toad. He had that covered all on his own.

Davin screamed as the spell hit him. Harley's eyes literally glowed, and her mouth contorted into a grimace as she pummeled the Chaos into him. His body arched and his limbs cracked, putting him in a position no mortal being should have been able to twist into. This was contortionism on another level, and no circus would've wanted to see this. I wasn't even sure I did.

Another howl tore from Davin's throat as the spell did its work. And then, there was silence, the howl cut off mid-shriek. Weighty, eerie silence.

All of us were speechless. This was *not* an after-school special. This wasn't even R-rated. It was something far worse.

It felt like Katherine's manipulation seeping into my sister. Katherine had pushed her to her limits, and this was the result. Harley's dark side in vivid surround sound and technicolor. A broken woman with no boundaries left. And that was the most dangerous place to be.

You deserve better than this, I mentally screamed at her. Harley was standing at the top of a very slippery slope, one I'd seen so many people tumble down in my years as a cultist. If she kept on down this road, she'd never forgive herself for what she'd done in order to defeat Katherine. She wasn't like me. She hadn't already shrunk her heart by doing evil things. She was good, and she was pure, and this would destroy her in the long run. I knew no matter how much you repented or tried to make things better, the memories would always cling on like barnacles. I worried what else she might have to do before this game ended.

"Harley?" Wade stepped forward and put his arm around her, energy still pounding into Davin. "You can stop. It's over."

Davin was dead as a doornail, and he wasn't getting up again anytime soon, resurrection or no resurrection. It looked like it'd take him ages just to put his limbs back where they were supposed to be. Either that or he'd be dragging himself around on permanent crutches with his arm twisted around his body like a corkscrew.

Harley blinked at Wade like she'd forgotten any of us were there. That was a bad sign. "Sorry..." she murmured. She pulled her hands away sharply and stopped the stream of energy, before glancing at the gauge on her Hermetic Battery. "I-I didn't use too much."

"Not sure Davin would agree with you." I was trying to make a joke, but she just looked at me blankly. Another bad sign that the mental gremlins were starting to creep in and make their home in her head.

"Things are looking up, right?" Dylan chimed in. For once, his chirpy positivity was welcome.

Wade nodded reassuringly, though he looked somewhat unsettled. "We've got enough Chaos to cast spells, and we've got some monsters handy, too. Plus, the Smiths are safe. So we should get down to Tobe and let him know it's all over. And see what he can do with these batteries."

Harley finally seemed to come back around at her boyfriend's words, a bit of life coming back into her face. *Good... that's good, Sis. Don't let the gremlins win.*

She met my gaze, and I offered her a smile. A look of overwhelming grief passed across her features, and I recognized it. It was starting to hit her, what she'd just done. But I kept smiling, and I hoped she understood what it meant. I was going to be here for her until the bitter end. And I wasn't going to let her fall. Ever.

That was unconditional love.

NINETEEN

Harley

I turned as Tobe and his pack of monsters entered the room. Evidently, they'd come to see if everything had worked out, since things had probably gone a bit quiet.

I couldn't look at Davin. At the terrifying *mess* I'd made of him. *Did I really do that?* I'd definitely performed the curse and it had definitely come out of me, but it was hard to stomach the violence I'd conjured to kill him. I'd fed my Darkness again without even realizing I was doing it. Understanding lingered like a black cloud over my head. I really had done that, and that was going to take some time to come to terms with. Time that we didn't have right now. *Compartmentalize.* It was the only way I'd be able to deal with unleashing that kind of cruelty on another living being.

Tobe stared at Davin's body, giving nothing away. One of the changelings, on the other hand, doubled over and vomited, a blob of oily black spitting onto the carpet. I didn't envy the maid who got assigned this room.

"Is it done?" Tobe asked, approaching me.

I nodded, trying to fix my eyes firmly on the Beast Master. "It's done. The Hermetic Batteries are filled, and Davin is… well, he's out of the picture for now, as you can see."

"I am pleased to hear that," Tobe replied, his fangs flashing in a brief smile. "Now, if I may take a look at those batteries, I will see if I can alter them to give you temporary control over your former abilities. If I can make the right changes, they should be able to pick up on the residual Chaos signature inside each of you and tune into the echo of it."

We all lined up dutifully as Tobe tinkered away at each battery, twiddling knobs and pressing buttons I hadn't even noticed embedded in the metal. All the while, I kept trying not to look at Davin's body, but it was like a magnet, drawing my eyes back to it again and again. At least I could use the sick feeling in my stomach when I looked at him to keep my Darkness in check. And, after all, it had been a necessary evil. It wasn't like I planned to go around doing that to every cultist who stood in my way. Doing that would only make me more like Katherine, and that was the opposite of what I wanted.

Plus, there was a chance Davin would shake it off like a bad hang-over and go back to being his usual, irritating self—run straight back to his beloved Katie to tell her what we'd been up to. An idea flitted into my head at that thought, and a small smile turned up the corners of my lips as it developed.

"There you go," Tobe said, turning the last dial on my Hermetic Battery. "That should enable you to tap into your former abilities, though I must reiterate the need for all of you to be cautious. Do not overexert them, or you will need to gather more Chaos from more cultists. And you, Harley, should be extra careful, as you will require the most Chaos for the spell to come."

"Thank you, Tobe." I nodded, then paused. "Actually, could I ask you for one more favor?"

"By all means."

"Could you get the Smiths and take them somewhere safe?" I took out my piece of charmed chalk and gave it to him. "They should be downstairs with O'Halloran. Please send him up once you've taken over. We need him with us for the next step."

"Of course, Harley." He made a majestic bow before giving a stern look to our bodyguard creatures. "Ensure that you protect these people with your lives, do you understand? They are to be kept safe. If you try to harm them, or if I hear of you attempting to escape, I will have no choice but to sing the Song of *Volumina Fumi* to you. And I don't want to do that."

The creatures looked rattled.

"Aye, we'll protect 'em. And I'll be keepin' these buggers in order fer ye, so dint ye worry. No singin' necessary, just grand old discipline." Diarmuid flashed the other monsters a creepy grin, which made the creatures shudder even more. Even Murray edged closer to me, as if I could protect him from the leprechaun.

"Gratitude, Diarmuid." With that, Tobe left the room.

I wished I could go with him to say a proper goodbye to the Smiths, but I supposed being reunited momentarily and seeing them safe would have to do for now. Time was ticking, and we had to get a move on.

"How do I look?" Finch smiled, using some of his Chaos to turn his hair back to a strawberry shade of blond.

"Tobe said we had to be careful with our Hermetic Batteries. I'm not sure changing your hair color counts as being careful," Wade replied with a roll of his eyes.

Finch shrugged. "I'll keep an eye on the gauge, don't worry. I refuse to be ginger, and that's all there is to it."

"Are we heading for Stonehenge?" Kadar asked. "That is where Marie Laveau said we needed to perform this spell."

"Yes, but not quite yet. There's something else I want to do first." I glanced at the Rag Team. "Can I have the room for a minute, guys? Wade, Finch, I need you to stay. It won't take long, there's just something we need to discuss."

"What?" Garrett eyed me suspiciously.

"I just… It's between the three of us, okay? Please give us a second. We'll be out before you know it."

The others looked at each other, as if weighing their options.

Dylan replied first. "Sure, why not? Just shout for us if that punk suddenly comes back to life."

He led the way, and the others followed him reluctantly, monsters and all—even the ones who had sworn to protect Finch, Wade, and me. At the door, Santana turned back for a second, a slightly wounded look on her face. That stung, but it was better if there were fewer people to hear what I had to say. And I'd only kept the people I knew would go along with it. Well, that was my hope, anyway.

"What's up?" Wade sounded worried. "Is it bad?"

"*What's* between the three of us?" Finch frowned.

I drew in a deep breath. *No point beating around the bush.*

"I'm going to open a chalk door straight into the warden's office in Purgatory and chuck Davin through. I've still got half of the stick I gave to Tobe." I took the piece out of my pocket. "Call me stupid, but I want to really piss Katherine off. She's put us through so much, and it's time for some payback."

Wade gaped. "Are you insane?"

"It'll just be a quick job," I replied. "And if it gets her riled up, it means she'll be open to an outburst that might buy us more time. The weaker her body gets, the better. So, we open the door, we throw Davin in, then we head straight to Stonehenge. If we linger too long, we're screwed."

Finch and Wade eyed each other as if they thought I'd lost my marbles. Who knew, maybe I had. But then, the most wonderful sound rippled out of Finch's mouth. A deep, genuine laugh. His eyes shone with mischief—that was the Finch I knew.

"I like it, Sis. I like it a lot. It's creative, I'll give you that." He grinned. "And it's a surefire way to get her seams to pop."

"I'm not going to dissuade you, am I?" Wade sighed, but I could see a flicker of amusement on his face, too.

I smiled. "Afraid not. If you don't want to help me, you don't have to, but I'm going to do this. Even if I have to drag Davin through the chalk door solo."

"Hey, I wouldn't leave you vulnerable like that," Finch said. "And the look on her face will make up for about five years of my childhood."

"I'll help, too," Wade said. "But we'd better be super quick."

"Then pick Davin up and get ready to toss him." I gestured to the body on the floor.

"Oh yeah, give us the grunt work." Finch chuckled as he headed toward Davin, grabbing his messed-up body by his mangled arms. Wade followed, grasping Davin's crooked legs. As they lifted him, Davin's body swung between them as if they were in the middle of a children's game of swing boat.

Moving toward the nearest wall, I drew a chalk door and focused on the warden's office. With it fixed in my mind and my heart pounding like a stampede, I whispered the *Aperi Si Ostium* spell. The edges of the chalk burned, forging the three-dimensional doorway that would give us our fleeting satisfaction. It felt incredible to have Chaos back at my disposal. I had no words to describe just how amazing it was. The closest thing I could compare it to was having a sip of water after going without for days on end.

"Ready?" I turned back to the guys, who stood behind me.

"Ready," they chorused back.

I yanked on the handle and tore the door open. A split second later, the guys tossed Davin's body through the door. He sailed a surprising distance, landing square on the warden's desk with a thud. Katherine screamed in fright, almost toppling out of her chair.

She'd been holding a pot of what could only be described as fleshy goop, which dropped to the floor as soon as Davin landed. The whole thing smashed to pieces, sending the goo flying. Her head whipped around, her eyes widening in horror. Her palms were about to rise up when I grasped the handle of the door and slammed it shut. *Not today, Katherine.*

Panting with adrenaline, I grinned at Wade and Finch. "Man, that felt good!"

"Hopefully her head explodes." Finch snorted.

Wade nodded, chuckling nervously. "That was possibly the riskiest, most stupid thing we've ever done... but holy crap, I'd do it again."

"Come on, we need to go before she rallies!" Clutching the broken half of the chalk, I sprinted for the door with the other two racing after me. As we barreled out into the hallway, the others, joined by O'Halloran, stared at us.

"What just happened?" Santana frowned.

I smiled back at her. "I'll explain later. Right now, we need to get our asses to Stonehenge."

I quickly drew another chalk door and whispered the *Aperi Si Ostium* spell. Tugging on the handle, I opened the doorway and ushered everyone through.

Beyond, a drizzly landscape stretched into the distance, gray clouds swarming overhead. But I could see those prominent stones towering in their ancient circle—a monument that had baffled human historians for centuries. If only they knew what it was really for, and why it had been built: as a marker to highlight the gateway to Elysium, right under their noses.

For my part, I'd never seen anything more hopeful and anxiety-inducing than those stones in all my life. This was it, the moment we'd been waiting for. We had Chaos again, and we had the Grimoire. Now, we just needed to summon Erebus and Lux and get the third part of the spell on the go.

But as the others spilled through in front of me, I hesitated on the threshold, casting a glance back over my shoulder. I wished I could've been looking at something more meaningful, instead of the peeling walls of a dingy inn. But it wasn't the location that was making me pause. It was the importance of this step that I was about to take, this step through to Stonehenge.

Part of me knew I might die in this pursuit, that I might never set foot on home soil again. Maybe my body wouldn't be able to hold the energy and I'd crumble the same way Katherine was. Maybe Erebus would claim my life in return for his help, as per his usual deals. Maybe my death was already part of the deal, and I just didn't know it yet. Who knew? Chaos hadn't opened this path to me with a promise that it would keep me alive. It didn't care. It just wanted Katherine destroyed, and so did I, no matter what it took. But did that mean I was ready to die for this cause? No... I wanted to live.

But as long as Katherine is destroyed, it doesn't matter.

That was the unpleasant truth. I was a tool in Chaos's plan. I wasn't some otherworldly messiah or a gift to the magical people. I was just a girl with a purpose she'd never asked for, with no choice but to see it through regardless of the consequences. I'd already lost so many people, and Katherine was only going to keep hurting people for her own ends. If this stopped Katherine from wreaking more havoc on this earth, from changing it irrevocably, then it would be worth it, even if nobody knew what I'd given up to make it happen. Even if nobody ever knew my name.

It wasn't just myself that I was thinking about, though. Things had already taken a turn for the worse as far as the rest of the world was concerned, and it would've broken Wade's heart if he knew about it. Dylan's, too. While I'd been standing in line to get my Hermetic Battery tweaked, I'd gotten a text from Astrid. She'd spotted the Crowleys and Remington on the cameras in Purgatory following Katherine around like zombies. I knew there was no way they were serving her of their own free will. They'd never have pledged them-selves to her. They had to have been made her slaves... and Wade and Dylan didn't know. Astrid had told me not to tell them, for the sake of preventing distractions, but it weighed on my mind. She had an excuse for seeming cold and calculated, even if that wasn't her true self, but that wasn't me, either. Still, I had enough worry for them to keep my mouth shut. It would hurt them deeply, and I didn't want to add that to their strain. Grief could do terrible things to people, and I didn't want it making Dylan and Wade do something that might get them killed.

Plus, the bigger picture would give them their vengeance, hopefully before harm came to too many more innocent lives. If I succeeded with this spell and summoned Erebus and Lux, then I'd be able to end Katherine and bring everything back to normal, without Wade or Dylan ever having to suffer, knowing what she'd done to their families.

If I succeed. Doubt lurked like an old enemy in the back of my mind. I was ready to give this my all, but I knew it would never go away. Regardless, I fixed my eyes back on Stonehenge. Too many lives rested on my shoulders now. It had all become so much bigger than just me.

And, maybe, death isn't so frightening, now that I know there's something waiting after this life. Every cloud...

Taking a deep breath, I walked through the doorway and closed it behind me, shutting the door on everything I'd been up until that moment. This was the end of a long chapter, and I didn't know if I was about to write the final page.

TWENTY

Katherine

You have got to be kidding me. The nerve of her!
    I'd only just managed to get my breath back after recovering from the fright of having Davin hurled into the room like a sack of potatoes—by Harley, Wade, and my darling, wretched boy. If they thought I hadn't seen them, they thought wrong. A second longer and I'd have had them. But now, my magical makeup was all over the floor, and I had a corpse covering my desk.

To be honest, I was flitting between pure rage and total confusion, neither of which was doing my body any favors. It was taking all the strength I had left not to snap and bring this whole damn world down with me, drawing every last scrap into my vortex like a black hole. It was no less than they deserved.

My body was caving in. Cracks splintered like a web across every square inch of my skin. It was on its last legs, and LaSalle wouldn't have been able to conjure a vat big enough to fix what was showing on me now. Black ooze trickled down my arms, staining my dress, and I could feel a globule making its way down my neck. I swept it away in disgust, flinging the viscous substance at the wall. But it would only be replaced with more. And from the wider cracks, particularly in my ripped-up hands, light had started to shine through.

This wasn't supposed to be how things went down. *I should've been snug inside my new body by now!*

I wanted to scream until the windows shattered. *Harley figured it out.* She knew I was crumbling. How had I ended up one step behind her, when I'd been way out in front for so damn long? It was like being five yards from the finish line only to have a giant sinkhole open up in my lane. I was so *damned* close! I could almost smell the ultimate victory. It belonged to me. Yet Harley had the gall to do this—throw Davin through a doorway just to show off! Maybe she'd picked up a couple of lessons from me, after all. Oh yes, she was definitely trying to get to me, using my playbook against me.

And, what was worse, I was letting her.

"No more," I muttered to myself. "Keep your mind focused, or you'll lose it all. That louse will be gone soon enough if you just keep going."

Gathering myself, I stood up and leaned over Davin, whose body perched rigidly on the edge of the desk. I reached out and stroked his handsome face to help distract myself. There were no 'imperfections' here. Well, aside from the fact that his limbs were sticking out at obscene angles. But his face was as beautiful as ever. I concentrated on that as I brushed my fingertips across his cold cheeks, trying not to look too hard into his wide, vacant eyes.

Davin was handsome and smart, powerful and bold. He was exactly the sort of man to stand beside a goddess. And, being alone in the warden's office, I allowed my feelings to rise up.

I wasn't as empty as people made me out to be. I was still capable of love, and Davin inspired something like that in me. Lust might've been more fitting, but lust could lead to something more. And I didn't like seeing him like this, even if he had yet to come through for me.

"You said you'd swear fealty to me if I got my new body," I whispered to him. "I haven't gotten it, though, have I? You wouldn't be here otherwise. You've tried, and you've failed. Can I really blame you for not trying hard enough, knowing what you've been up against?"

Would you listen to yourself? Get a grip, woman! I'd never given anyone a free pass in my entire life... but I couldn't bring myself to just toss this one away. *What have you done to me?* Had he put some sort of spell on me? Love Potion no. 9? It would've been easier for me to come to terms with it if it could have been explained away as a simple curse. If it wasn't, then why the hell was I so soft on him?

"Is it love?" I whispered. Even with all this power, and after all these years of despising men and everything they had to offer, it turned out there was something more powerful than all of that. The one emotion that had almost killed me two decades ago. It had made me weak then, and it was making me weak now.

Closing my eyes, I remembered that night, when Hiram had cut ties with me to run off into the sunset with my sister, with no idea he'd put his spawn in my belly. I'd gone to the Brooklyn Bridge and clambered over the railing. Had I been drinking? Of course I had. I'd stared down into the black water below and almost let go. But then, I'd heard my grandfather's voice in my head, telling me I could be whatever I wanted to be. And I realized that didn't involve being a cautionary tale —a Jane Doe plastered across the next day's papers, some poor girl who'd killed herself and her unborn child.

No, that wasn't the way I wanted my story to go. It was in that moment that I made the decision to become a Child of Chaos and live only on my own terms. No struggling. No distractions. No weakness. That included Finch.

Which is why this has to stop.

I snatched my hand away from Davin as though he were on fire. He'd be awake soon, and there was no way I was going to let him see me like this. Only one man had ever seen me brought to my lowest point, and I'd never let that happen again.

Walking to the largest splatter of magical makeup, I scooped up as much as I could and smoothed it over the most visible cracks in my face and neck. When Davin woke up, he would see me as my usual, confident, determined self. He wouldn't see the fear that was creeping through me, or the extent to which my body was failing.

Sitting back down at the desk, I closed my eyes and tried to think. Where had Harley been when she'd tossed Davin through? It had looked like the Halidon Inn, but if she had any sense at all, she wouldn't be there anymore. *So where is she headed next?* And how had she managed to draw a chalk door? They had a djinn with them who could have done it, but I hadn't seen him. That didn't mean he hadn't been helping them, though, and keeping out of my line of sight. I needed to nip this in the bud once and for all.

I had to get to Harley first, and when I did, I'd pull the plug on my son. I'd force him under my control and make him my most versatile weapon. No matter how much I hated the way he'd come into this world, I still didn't think I could actually *kill* him. I'd already proven that to myself, time and time again. It was the same reason I'd never actually gotten around to killing Naima, even though I'd threatened it so often it had almost become a running joke. They were both part of me, and murdering them would have been like killing parts of myself.

But that didn't mean I couldn't eliminate Finch as a weakness by making him useful to me, more useful than he'd ever been before. I'd have preferred him to come willingly, but beggars can't be choosers. That Dempsey Suppressor inside him could be made to snap. All I'd have to do, once I had my new body, was click my fingers, and that Suppressor would evaporate quicker than a pigeon in a hurricane.

"You will stand at my side, where you belong!" I hissed.

Until then, however, Harley was still walking, talking, breathing, and laughing in my face. With every continued beat of her heart, she was thwarting me. And I didn't like to be thwarted. When I finally had her body as my own, I'd get that long-suffering vindication for what Hiram had done to me, the last slice of justice I'd been eager to devour for twenty years. *Eat that, Hiram.* He was as responsible for all of this as I was.

"Your goddess requires you!" I barked toward the door.

Immediately, two cultists came running. Naomi and Tank—my beefiest bodyguards, both of them barely fitting through the doorway.

"We are here to serve you, Eris." Naomi bowed her head.

"Go to the Halidon Inn," I instructed. "Find the room where Davin was supposed to make his exchange. Use a tracking spell to find out where Harley and her band of merry idiots have gone. If that doesn't work, use whatever means necessary. They must be found, and they must be found now."

I got up and walked toward the two of them. Lifting my hands, I pressed a palm to each of their temples and let Chaos filter through me, imbuing them each with an extra level of magical clout. It was a heightened variation of the Sensate skill, which I'd taken to calling a "bloodhound ability."

Harley was a fox on the run now, and my bloodhounds would track her down before the day was over. Then, I would be the one to make the kill... well, not a kill, per se, but I'd get what I wanted from her. Her body. Even if half of *my* body was hanging off in flakes of skin and ooze, I wouldn't miss out on that for the world.

TWENTY-ONE

Harley

We'd been in place for a few hours, gathering all the necessary paraphernalia to perform the three-part spell. So far, everything was going according to plan. The monsters, Kenzie, and Kadar, led by Tobe, had done the collecting, using chalk doors to dart in and out across England. Meanwhile, the Rag Team and I had stayed here to prepare the rest of the spell. I needed to come to grips with the words because I had no idea if the whole "automatic reading out" thing would kick in, given that I was still technically Chaos-less at the very core of my being. The Hermetic Batteries couldn't change that.

Fog rolled across the open expanse of rural England, creeping around the obelisks that towered around us in wispy waves. Sunlight tried to peer through the dense cloud cover overhead, but more swelled in front of it like a barricade to keep that warmth from shining down on us, lending a strange darkness to the landscape. I didn't know if that was a bad omen. It was early morning, and a chilly breeze had whipped up, whistling through the stones. It nipped at our cheeks as we scoured our surroundings for any sign of unwanted cultists while a fine rain drifted downward, splashing icily against our faces.

Kenzie jumped down from her latest perch on Tobe's broad shoulders, landing with a soft thud on the grass. The Beast Master had arrived not long after we first came through, using his own chalk door. He told me he'd placed the Smiths somewhere safe, though he hadn't gone into detail. I figured the fewer people who knew where they were now, the better.

Kenzie moved away before anyone thought to stop her, leaping up one of the obelisks with effortless agility and settling on top of it, where she could get a better feline vantage point.

There was something about this place that felt mystical, and that hadn't changed as time passed. I didn't know if it was the eerie gloom casting shadows that seemed to move out of the corner of my eye, or if it was the icy drizzle, or the dense fog that clung to the grassy floor, but it seemed as if we'd walked into a strange otherworld already. The air around me thrummed with energy, powerful and unseen, as if the very particles of this place were vibrating in excitement. Stonehenge might've been impressive in its own right, but it was the feel of it that struck me the most. This place was drenched in Chaos. I could actually feel it, even without my natural Chaos at the helm. It resonated, somehow.

The monsters took action first, heeding Tobe's command to protect us. Together, they spread out, surrounding the monoliths in a bestial front line against anyone who might try to stop me from performing the three-part spell.

We couldn't put it off any longer.

Settling down in the very center of the ancient circle, I opened up the Grimoire and started instructing the others to position the ingredients in the required spots. There were two silver bowls, each of them filled with different items. On the left we had black onyx, belladonna, sumac, cordyceps, black oil-plant seed, quicksilver, hollyhock, and hellebore. On the right, the bowl held powdered opal, dendrobium orchid, agrimony, water violet, willow bark, vervain, milk thistle, and clove oil. Two of the Sherlock's Eyes sat in front of each bowl like a soothsayer's crystal balls.

"Is that everything?" Wade asked as he walked toward me.

I nodded. "Yeah. The only thing left to do is read this thing out." Frankly, I was terrified of what came next, but I knew it had to be done. No matter what the cost.

I glanced at Tobe, who gave me a brief bow.

"Everything will be ready for you," he said.

I didn't know what that meant, exactly, but I remembered his warning that the spell would have to come at the cost of some of his beasts. A pang of guilt twisted my stomach at the thought. This wouldn't be easy for him, and I was sorry that it had come to this. I cast him a bittersweet look of gratitude, knowing that, thanks to the unwitting sacrifice of his beasts, my body wouldn't start falling apart like Katherine's. The effects would be the same if he couldn't conjure up the energy to stop Erebus from tearing my body to pieces.

"Thank you, Tobe," I managed. Looking around at the rest of my friends, I gave a nervous smile. "You should probably get a safe distance away in case this goes badly."

"No chance," Santana replied. "We'll stay close. We've come this far together; we're not abandoning you now, *mi hermosa*."

Kadar's skin turned from red to olive. "We can protect you better if we're nearby." He'd relinquished Raffe for a moment, probably because he wasn't a fan of the mushy stuff, and this was about to get emotional.

I had no way of knowing if I'd see my friends on the other side of this. It only seemed right that we had a moment to say goodbye, even if we didn't say the actual word.

"You need to stand back," I insisted. This spell reeked of power, and I didn't want them getting caught in any accidental crosshairs.

"We're not budging, Sis," Finch said sternly. "We'll take a couple steps, but that's it. Non-negotiable."

Tatyana nodded. "We love you, Harley. We're not just going to leave you here to go through this alone."

"Besides, if anyone tries to stop you, we're going to need to form a defensive line around you," O'Halloran added with a reassuring smile.

"This is the best place to be, from a logical standpoint." Garrett wielded his sword, swiping it through the air. "You know, just in case Katherine's gotten wind of this."

"Erebus will be too focused on you to worry about us." Wade sank to the ground beside me, placing his hand against my cheek. "So don't you worry about us, either."

"We've got your back, Harley," Dylan affirmed. "To the end."

Tears sprang to my eyes. I knew it wouldn't do any good to keep asking—they'd made their decision, as I'd made mine. But, still, I couldn't get rid of the horrible feeling that they would get hurt if they stayed within this stone circle. The "prophecy" of the Chains of Truth hadn't come true in the Garden of Hesperides, but that didn't mean it wouldn't here.

Maybe I'd read it wrong. Maybe I'd assumed it was the Garden of Hesperides. But what if it was here instead? What if this was where I sacrificed everyone and everything to end Katherine, just the way I'd promised I would?

"Hey," Wade murmured. "Don't disappear on me now, Harley. I know you want to shield everyone, because you wouldn't be you if you didn't. It's one of the things I love most about you, just how much you try to protect the people you care about. But this is our fight as much as it is yours. Katherine has taken people from all of us. And we'll be here protecting you so you can crush her, because that's all we can do. So... let us do this. Let us be useful to you."

"I'm just so scared," I whispered.

"I know, my love." He put his arms around me and pulled me close. "But you don't have to be scared for *us*. This is where we're supposed to be. And I know you didn't ask for any of this, but there's a reason Chaos chose *you*, Harley. It chose you because you're the kind of person who's impossible not to love. It chose you because it knew your spirit was never destined to be alone—you were always meant to be surrounded by people who would give everything to see you succeed because you're everything to them: a friend, a sister, the other half of their soul. It's because of your heart that it chose you. And it's because of our hearts, and our love for you, that we chose you to stand by and protect. All of us have lost so much, and we're ready to win… because of you. Because we believe in you."

Sniffles susurrated around the group, everyone wiping tears away as Wade held me tighter. I clung onto him as I looked over his shoulder at my friends, beyond grateful that they were part of my life. I even managed a small smile when I noticed O'Halloran bawling like a little kid, wiping his nose on the back of his sleeve.

"Ach, that were rousin'. Me eyes are leakin' like taps." Diarmuid was bawling alongside O'Halloran, the two of them a complete mess. "All of ye get in there and give the lass a hug fer cryin' out loud."

The Rag Team moved in, all of them putting their arms around each other, laughing and sobbing and looking at one another as if this might be the last time. Raffe leaned over and kissed Santana, a subtle pulse of red letting me know both he and the djinn were saying goodbye, if only for now, while Dylan and Tatyana shared a tender smooch. Diarmuid threw his tiny arms around O'Halloran's neck, landing a weird kiss right on his lips.

Dylan pulled away slightly from Tatyana and looked at me. "Harley, you know I'm a fighter, and I don't want to die today. But, if this does all end today, then you should know… it's been a hell of a ride. Hasn't it, guys?"

"It sure has," Santana replied, gazing at me. "And we'd all be answering to Katherine right about now if you hadn't come into our lives with the determination and the power to stop her. We believe in you, *mi hermosa*."

"I don't plan on seeing any of you in the spirit world," Tatyana added. "So, take strength from us and succeed. We started this together and we're going to finish it together."

"You were always remarkable, Harley." Alton spoke up. He looked stronger than before, a bit of color in his cheeks. His voice was stronger, too. "The moment you set foot in the SDC, I knew you were destined for great things. I could never have anticipated *this*, but the fact remains—you have made your mark upon all our hearts, and now it's your time to make your mark upon this world. Break those chains, Harley."

Tobe mopped his face with his paw. "Your strength is beyond anything I have witnessed in all my long life. To have been trampled so many times only to get back to your feet again and again, never letting anything keep you down—Selma would have championed you if she were here. As she is not, I hope my pride in you will suffice."

"I love you, Sis." Finch's voice caught in his throat, making my own throat tighten. "I didn't know what it felt like to have a family. I still wouldn't if it hadn't been for you. You would've had every reason to leave me to rot in Purgatory, or put me back there after Eris Island, especially after all the things I've done, but you took a chance on me. You saw something in me that I didn't know was there, and it made me want to be a better man. You fought for me when nobody else would. Now it's my turn to fight for you."

Tears trickled down his cheeks and fell to the ground. I reached up for his hand and squeezed it tight.

"This is our last shot at freedom and salvation," Wade said, kissing my neck gently. "And we'll do everything we can to help you make this happen."

I pulled away from him slightly, positioning my hand so I could hold his face. Staring deep into his eyes, I leaned in and kissed him. He kissed me back, his lips pressing hard against mine, as though they were trying to tell me everything he felt inside, things he couldn't say in front of everyone else.

"I love you," I murmured.

"I love you, too." He kissed me again, to the point where I didn't want him to let me go. But he had to. I had to. Or we'd never get this done.

Releasing him, and noticing that everyone had turned their heads away to give us a private moment, I addressed them all.

"I love you all so much. Live through this, do you hear me?" I smiled through my tears. "I want to see every single one of you on the other side, and I don't mean the afterlife. Now, let's do this."

"You heard her." Finch offered me a tearful grin as he broke away from the group hug.

He took a few steps back and took up his position behind me. The others followed suit, forming a horseshoe around me in the center of the stone circle. Only Wade lingered a moment longer, kissing me one last time before I started something that would end with either the world's freedom or its demise. The coin was about to be tossed, and I wouldn't know where it would land until the last moment.

Staring at the monolith ahead to focus my mind, I took a deep breath and picked up the matte-black lens. With nothing left to do, I began to read. Although the words had transformed into English through the lens, the words that came out of my mouth were Latin:

"*Commotae Erebi exaudiet me cum clamavero ad te in tempore necessitatis. Hoc est officium ad respondendum. Et non neglecta sunt. Venite ad me et ego audiam quid dicam. Liberi flectatur. Tenebrae rursus oriri ex vobis finem et pactum, quod non requiritur.*"

The words echoed out in a voice that wasn't quite my own. Each syllable ricocheted between the stones as if a message were being relayed.

I paused when I came to the end of the first paragraph that would summon Erebus. The moment I stopped, the skies darkened as if I'd just called down the apocalypse. The clouds whipped across the sky at lightning speed, forging a thicker barricade across the sun, blocking it out completely until it was so dark that it could have been the middle of the night. Thunder grumbled in the near distance. The storm clouds unleashed their heavy load, and a driving torrent lashed down out of nowhere.

All the birds that had been flying wheeled around and soared away from this place in a mass exodus, while the trees on the horizon swayed wildly. It was getting hard to see; my eyes were blinded by the hammering rain. And where there had been rolling fog, the wispy mist had turned jet black, like black smoke drifting across the landscape, withering every blade of grass it touched.

As the winds picked up and howled through the stone circle, I glanced over my shoulder to see how the Rag Team was doing. Some of them were struggling to stand. Garrett was stabbing the ground with his sword and gripping tight to the pommel to keep upright. Kadar was crouched, his claws buried in the earth, and Santana had crouched behind him, using him as a windbreaker. Wade had linked with O'Halloran and Alton, the three of them bent almost diagonal, while Diarmuid was gripping O'Halloran's hair to brace himself. Tatyana was ducked down behind the head of her death horse, who was bearing the brunt. All of the monsters were buckling down to weather this supernatural storm.

The air thickened like the stilted pause before a true thunderstorm, the atmosphere within the stone circle thrumming violently. I could almost feel the particles of Chaos slamming into me as I tried to keep my focus on the spell.

Suddenly, just ahead of me, a whorl of that same black smoke rose up, twisting like a monstrous tornado that looked like it could've knocked every single one of these monoliths down like dominoes.

Erebus was on his way.

Crap. Turning my attention back to the Grimoire, I started to read the second paragraph. I needed to be quick, or Erebus would start taking lives before I'd even managed to get Lux here. Straining against the din that surrounded me, I screamed the words, letting them pour out of me:

"Mater exaudiet me cum clamavero ad te in tempore necessitatis! Hoc est officium ad respondendum! Et non neglecta sunt. Venite ad me et ego audiam quid dicam. Liberi flectatur. Ex lucem surgere et qui credita habebant bargain hoc requiritur. De mediato et statera haec commutation!"

The sky tore open as soon as I finished the second incantation, an enormous rip slicing through the storm clouds. With an explosion that blasted outward, searing light overwhelmed the darkness and forced it to retreat. The clouds sped backward as if they'd been put in reverse, leaving the sky blue and clear and the sunlight shining down. The winds and the rains stopped abruptly, and an eerie silence echoed across the landscape.

The newly emerged sun wasn't the only light in the sky. From the giant tear, which still gaped overhead, liquid light poured down like a waterfall, almost silver in color. It hit the earth without a sound, repairing the damage the black smoke had caused. In its wake, emerald-green grass and brand-new flowers sprang up, each blade and bloom glowing vibrantly until the whole world was a mass of pulsating bioluminescence, painted in colors far too bright to be natural.

From beneath the earth, another tear erupted, creating a fissure in the ground. That same liquid light burst out like a geyser, and the droplets splashed down onto the ground around Erebus's black tornado. I had to shield my eyes from the light as it flashed outward. Through splayed fingers, I watched as the two forces seemed to battle it out, the liquid light spiraling up around the black smoke until there was nothing left of it at all. As soon as the last fronds of smoke dissipated, the rest of the liquid light fell to the ground, making the grass glow.

Did it work?

I waited anxiously, slowly pulling my hands away from my face. Squinting, I held my breath as two figures emerged from the monolith ahead. They were humanoid, but not in the same way Gaia had been. One was made from dense black fog, while the other was made of liquid silver that ebbed and flowed across her body as she moved, following the flow of the muscles that should have been there. The figures held hands as they approached.

Behind me, I heard a collective gasp from the Rag Team. And I knew exactly how they felt. This was scary, unknown territory, and I had no choice but to feel terrified and awestruck in equal measure.

Lux and Erebus paused in front of me, summoned together just as

Marie Laveau had said they would be. My deal partner and our media-tor, standing side by side, their hands locked as if that was the only thing keeping Erebus from lashing out at me. I didn't dare speak.

Fortunately, Erebus didn't stay silent for long. He glared at me with red eyes that flashed through the dense, black haze.

"You're lucky you learned the rest of that trick, Ms. Merlin. Other-wise, I would've torn you all to shreds."

TWENTY-TWO

Katherine

I glowered at the dusty wasteland that used to be the Garden of Hesperides.

I'd come here because I was tired of sitting around in the warden's office. Some of my cultists had carried Davin through, and I was alone now with his body. At least here, the toll on my body didn't seem to be as great. I could breathe a bit. I'd instructed the cultists to come to me here once they had Harley, but two hours had passed and there was still no sign of them.

Davin suddenly wheezed, and I practically leapt out of my flaking skin. I staggered back, almost tripping over the head of some ancient statue.

His back arched unnaturally as life started to flow back through his veins, his blood glowing purple as the resurrection took hold. This wasn't exactly at the top of my list of sexy behaviors. *But if it brings him back to me...* I had a quick word with myself to cut off that thought. What had I said literally two hours ago? No weakness. No love. No affection. NO distractions.

Davin's limbs cracked as they snapped back into place, his broken arms flailing like jellyfish tentacles for a moment before they smoothed back out to looking the way they were supposed to. His legs slotted back into their sockets with a nauseating crunch, and his back flattened against the ground. A few seconds passed, but there was still no sign of life behind his eyelids.

With a frustrated sigh, I stooped to his level and slapped him hard across the face.

"Wake up!" I barked. "Stop messing around."

His eyes snapped open and he sat bolt upright, heaving in a raspy breath. "Eris?"

"Right here." I tapped my foot on the ground impatiently.

He turned to me, still breathing erratically. "How long was I gone?"

"A couple hours."

"That was a long one, then." He fumbled through his pockets and pulled out an amber amulet in the shape of an ankh. He grinned and kissed the object before tucking it away in another pocket.

"Should I give you two a private moment?" I asked dryly.

He gave a nervous laugh. "My apologies, Eris. Just showing gratitude that I am again in the land of the living."

"Well, welcome back." Sarcasm dripped from my words. Most of it was for show, but he didn't need to know that. I wanted him to be scared, but not too scared. A keeping-him-on-his-toes kind of thing. If I suddenly went all sappy on him, he'd be the one running for the hills, wondering if I'd had a lobotomy while he'd been out cold.

He looked around in sudden confusion. "Wait... how did I get here? Last I remember, I was at the Halidon Inn."

My gaze hardened. Time for a few home truths. "You failed me again."

He gaped like a beached fish. "My goddess, if you would allow me to—"

"Did I sound like I was finished?" I snapped, my cracks flashing. *So unflattering.*

"No, Eris. My apologies." He bowed his head like a good, obedient little boy.

"You failed me again, and that Merlin bitch had the audacity to chuck your body through a chalk door, just to rub it in my face." I took a breath to calm myself down. "I brought you to this place because my body doesn't seem to be as susceptible to crackage here. Although, being here isn't going to stop it indefinitely. The clock is still *clanging* in my ears."

Davin jumped to his feet with surprising ease, considering his legs had been sticking out at ninety degrees and his arms had been wrapped around his body like an over-amorous octopus about two seconds prior. "I have not failed you *yet*, Eris. I'll go directly after that redheaded fiend. I will not be humiliated like this! I refuse!"

"Hold your horses, Frankenstein's monster." I folded my arms across my chest. "What do you mean, 'humiliated'? How did she humiliate you?"

"She took me by surprise, my beloved Eris. She had Purge beasts on her side, as well as that Beast Master you've been searching for. I would have succeeded if it had simply been Ms. Merlin and her chums. I was ambushed and have the bite marks to prove it." He pulled the collar of his shirt along his shoulder to reveal two livid purple welts, and just a hint of tantalizing collarbone. "It was a gargoyle, and it wouldn't stop gnashing at me. And don't even get me started on that brute of a djinn!"

I sighed in irritation. "So that's where Tobe went? I'd hoped to capture him before he reached her, but nothing seems to be going my way at the moment, so I guess I shouldn't be surprised that this is yet another *screwup* to add to an ever-expanding list." The words rattled out of my mouth like gunfire. "But that's okay. Nothing to worry about. And, since my gargoyles have yet to return, it's probably safe to say they're all dead. But that's okay too. Nothing I can't handle. The Bestiary won't need Tobe anymore after I have my new body, and the cult can manage until then. Any other tidbits to add, while I'm processing?" I shot him a warning look. He better not have anything else to add.

He lowered his gaze. "The Smiths were freed."

"Well, I already know *that*. I sent cultists to the Halidon Inn to try and track Harley. They said there was nobody there, and they couldn't pick up the scent of the Smiths. So it's probably safe to say we've lost them, too."

"I am sorry, my beloved goddess." He'd stiffened, as if he thought I was going to lob his head off there and then. *If only.*

"This was a colossal screwup, Davin, even by your standards. And, while I may be fond of keeping you around, in my own way, I'm not the kind of woman who can be played. You know my rules surrounding failure. You're not an exception to any rule, no matter how highly you might think of yourself."

Davin's head snapped up, his eyes wide. "Give me a second chance, my darling Eris." Evidently, he understood the danger he was in. *Good.*

"That was your second chance," I replied. I wasn't really going to kill him, but I wanted to enjoy watching him squirm awhile. Call it personal curiosity, to see just how far he'd go to please me.

"Might I have a third?" His piercing eyes twinkled mischievously, a throaty chuckle escaping his throat. It was a bit on the nervous side, but I *was* threatening to kill him.

I smiled despite myself. "I suppose I would miss having that face to look at now and then…"

"I will not disappoint you again, my divine goddess."

I shrugged, keeping it blasé. "Fine, you can live, but you won't be disappointing me again. I'm going to make sure of it. This time, I'll be coming with you in your pursuit of Harley. I've come to the conclusion that I'd rather go out in a blaze of glory than keep pacing this depressing wasteland while putting my trust in your clearly useless hands. We find Harley, you open a portal to her, and we go together."

"But… your body, my love?"

"It doesn't matter now," I replied. "I'll take the risk. We'll portal directly to where Harley is, so I'll be close enough to that bitch to take her body for myself, once and for all."

I pulled out my phone and sent out a mass text, calling the cultists to the Garden of Hesperides, on the double.

Only a few seconds later, the first of them began to appear, portaling right through into the Garden of Hesperides. A formidable army. I smirked as Mallenberg emerged with a big group from Purgatory, with the Crowleys and Remington in tow.

"Harley and her misfits won't stand a chance against this crew, monsters or no monsters," I announced. This was going to end my way, exactly as I'd planned for all these years. A few hiccups and hurdles would only make it more satisfying when I finally took my place as the Goddess of Discord, reigning over the magical world, the human world, and the otherworlds, too, if I felt so inclined.

I was about to cast the spell to find Harley's whereabouts when I spotted the Children of Gaia watching me from the horizon. Their hatred for me was palpable, even from this distance, but they could shove their useless emotions up their Elemental asses. They weren't getting their mama back. And if I didn't manage to succeed, they'd be just as stuck with me as I was with them. A happy little family, trapped in this desolate place for the rest of time. *You should be cheering me on if you want to be rid of me that much!*

"Scowl at me all you like," I yelled at them. "This world is already mine, and soon the mortal world will be, too. Soon enough, you'll all bow down to me. I'll even wipe my boots for you, so you've got something clean to lick!"

I awaited their furious response, but it didn't come. Instead, their heads whipped around, all of them growing still, as if they were listening to something I couldn't hear. A moment later, their heads turned back around, smirks toying with the edges of their weird lips.

The next second, they were gone, vanished into thin air.

What the...?

That was suspicious behavior if ever I'd seen it. What had they heard? Who was talking to them? I didn't know, but it sent a strange shiver of anxiety through me. I hadn't even realized my body was shaking until Davin put his hand on my arm, his expression concerned.

"Are you all right, Goddess?"

Before I could reply, a portal opened right next to me and one of my cultists came barreling through, pale as a ghost and sweating profusely. I knew instantly that this wasn't one of the cultists I'd called for. They were already gathered and ready to go. No, this was more bad news. I could feel it.

"What now?" I snapped, draining what little color remained from his features.

He trembled in front of me. "Goddess, there's... there's movement in... in England. The Chaos gauges are showing... strange behavior, and England is... is the point of origin." He was shaking so violently I thought *he* might crumble. "A lot of powerful Chaos is moving... moving in one direction. It is all pooling in... in Stonehenge."

"Elysium," was the solitary whisper through my lips, like my last breath. The truth smacked me right in the solar plexus, knocking the wind clean out of my wilting sails.

This couldn't be good.

Elysium was the neutral realm of the Children of Chaos, and if Chaos had been picked up on the gauges as gathering in Stonehenge, that meant they were coming through the gateway between worlds *en masse*. And I doubted they were coming to join my side.

Oh, Chaos, you devious little wretch.

TWENTY-THREE

Harley

I stared at the humanoid figures, hardly able to believe they were actually here. This was the moment everything had been building toward. All the blood, sweat, and tears that my mom and dad had poured into this book had finally culminated in the two of them—Lux and Erebus—standing in front of me. Not quite in the flesh, but close enough. Dread and excitement hurtled through my veins, as I rode a wave of adrenaline.

There was only one part left to make this weird trifecta complete. I had to strike a deal with the Child of Darkness himself, to give him my body, so together we could destroy Katherine. That prospect was only marginally less inviting than handing my body over to Katherine herself, but between this rock and that hard place, I knew which was preferable.

Lux spoke. "He would have destroyed you all, and that is why I am here." Her voice was sweet where Erebus's was gravelly. It sounded like a Sunday morning chorus as it reverberated around the stone circle. And yet, it wasn't all sweetness and light—there was a cold edge to it that kept me on my toes. I mean, she was a super-powerful being in her own right, and I was just a measly mortal with a cuff on her arm pulsing temporary Chaos into the void Katherine had left behind.

"I should have known she'd never have the gall to call me on her own," Erebus boomed, his voice shaking the ground beneath me. Of the two of them, his intentions were clearer. He turned his glaring eyes toward me. "I have half a mind to call you a coward."

"Now, now, let us not begin with name-calling." Lux smiled through her silvery, shifting face. "As young Harley well knows by now, given the former war within her own mind and body, a balance between Light and Darkness is always a necessity. While both veins may be able to exist autonomously in the magical world, that is only a mirage, masking the real truth—it is still balanced, even in those who are one or the other. A receiver of Light will be paralleled in this world by a receiver of Darkness, ensuring it is always evened out. It is the same where Children of Chaos are concerned. You cannot summon one without the other, or else there will be nothing but destruction and misery."

"It is why we have been heralded into action, I suppose, now that the forces of Light and Dark have been taken away from their natural sources of delegation." Erebus's red eyes assessed me. "It is a true shame that it has come to this. Magicals without magic, pleading to the Children for help. Not all of us hope to be gods and goddesses who have to deal with the mortal realm. Some of us were happy enough as we were, striking deals when they came up and keeping to ourselves for the most part."

"Sorry to disturb you," I managed to reply, not entirely without sarcasm.

"Oh, believe me, I'm only too happy to play my part," Erebus retorted. "I just wish you had come to this conclusion sooner. If you had understood earlier that you would never have been able to stop Katherine from ascending, you would have focused your energies on reaching this particular moment much faster. And we would not have had to twiddle our thumbs, watching the mess unfold."

I stared at him. "And you're blaming me? Was I supposed to have some crystal ball to tell me this was going to happen?"

"Don't flatter yourself. My blame lies entirely with Chaos for allowing those ridiculous rituals in the first place. This is what happens when you grant mortals an opportunity to be more than they are. They ruin it for the rest of us." Erebus laughed, his eyes burning brighter. "I'm simply saying you should have been wiser in where you placed your focus."

"Well, I'm grateful that you're here." I forced the words out.

"I'm sure you are," Erebus replied with a hint of cruel amusement.

"Do not aggravate the child." Lux shot him a warning look.

This only made Erebus laugh harder. "You can mediate, Lux, but you can't censor me. I am stating the facts as I see them: mortals are idiotic. All of them. Without exception. That is why I am here, to make sure that Katherine remains in her lane. She may think she is beyond the realm of mortality now, but there is more to being a Child of Chaos than everlasting existence."

"That's why I summoned you." I concentrated on what I wanted to say. "I need you to help me end Katherine once and for all. I can't do that as I am, so you must give me what I need in order to make this happen. For all of our sakes, by the sound of it. You don't want her; we don't want her."

Erebus smirked with his dark, swirling mouth. "We understand why we were summoned, mortal. Our maker essentially wrote the spell you just chanted, using your parents to put it to paper. So, I suggest we start making moves, since you have already wasted such a colossal amount of time."

"Easy now, this is not a simple 'let's get on with it' sort of deal." Lux gripped Erebus's hand tighter, sending little shards of light through his smoky arm. "I wouldn't want Harley entering into something she is not clear about. She needs to understand what she is getting herself into, first, and how little she will know about your end of the deal before she has to make her choice. She needs time to think, without you rushing her."

"How little I'll know?" I frowned. "What do you mean?" Marie Laveau hadn't been able to tell me the minutiae of what was going to happen during this exchange, but I guessed I wasn't going to like it. This wasn't supposed to be easy.

"We will get to that in good time," Lux replied. *In good time?* We didn't have a lot of that right now. "Just to err on the side of caution, I am going to summon some more witnesses to this exchange. I will call the other Children of Chaos… aside from Katherine, of course. Nobody wants her here. She is not, and will never be, one of us."

I smiled. "I almost wish Katherine *were* here, just so she could hear you say that."

"Let us not tempt fate," Lux warned.

She closed her eyes and began to pulsate. As she did so, silver tendrils emerged from her face and hands and began running across the earth before disappearing into the distance. A hum began to vibrate through the air, growing to a deafening volume that made me cover my ears and close my eyes, as if that would help. There was something about Stonehenge that amplified every magical sound and sense and sight. But just when I thought my eardrums were about to explode, the sound disappeared completely.

Blinking my eyes back open, I almost gasped aloud. Gaia's Children had arrived—Earth, Air, Water, and Fire. They'd shrunk from their titan forms to fit the scale of Stonehenge, but that didn't make them any less impressive. I could almost feel the heat of Fire from where I stood.

Three other Children had appeared, too, standing in the gaps closest to Erebus and Lux, making it five in total. I didn't recognize these newcomers, but one of them had to be Nyx. The first new Child was made of an oily darkness speckled with flecks of golden light, while the second was a strange shade of blue and violet, composed of wispy gasses swirling over one another within its humanoid form. The third was formed of liquid metal with a slight rosy tinge and looked as if someone had boiled down a bunch of rose gold and poured it over someone's body.

"This is my twin, Nyx." Lux gestured to the oily, speckled figure. "And these two are Uranus and Eros. They will have no say in what occurs here, but it is respectful to have them present."

"They can't get involved?" My heart sank a bit. Having a small army made up of Children of Chaos could've been useful.

Lux shook her head. "No, they cannot. It is why Gaia's Children were reprimanded for their attack upon Katherine prior to her ascension. Such behavior, which goes against the instruction of Chaos, cannot go unpunished."

The Children of Gaia lowered their gazes, making it seem as if Lux had been the one to do the reprimanding. From my brief knowledge of her, she definitely appeared to be a by-the-book kind of Child of Chaos. Erebus, on the other hand...

He chuckled darkly, as if on cue. "You should be encouraging such emotional displays, Lux. We are all forbidden from killing Katherine, obviously, but surely they're entitled to an impassioned reaction after what she did to their mother? Our sibling, in case you were forgetting?" He smirked. At least, I thought he did. It was hard to tell with the Children's ever-moving features. "After all, what is the point of loopholes in Chaos if they can't be used? Harley would not be here if Chaos wanted to be entirely strict on that subject."

"If we become lenient with all rules, where will we be?" Lux retorted. "We are not all like you, Erebus, who would be only too happy to toss the rulebook out of the window."

Erebus nodded. "I've always said it is a shame there aren't more like me."

I couldn't quite believe that I was sitting here in front of the two of them, watching them squabble like... well, lovers or enemies. It was hard to tell. And what was with these two new Children of Chaos? All this time, we'd been working under the assumption that there were only four, but apparently there was a lot more for us to learn about the Children of Chaos and their wider world.

"You." Erebus suddenly boomed.

I glanced over my shoulder to see what had drawn the Child's attention. It was Finch standing there, looking stunned that he was being addressed.

"Me?" Finch pointed to himself.

"It must be hard to follow the supposed 'chosen one' while being imbued with the same blood, isn't it?" Erebus smiled.

Finch shifted nervously. "Not really. My sister is hard as nails. She's got the pure heart. Mine's full of holes."

"I commend you," Erebus replied.

"You do?" Finch frowned.

"It takes a certain type of strength to wriggle out from under Katherine's poisonous thumb."

Finch looked at me. "Not when you've got an alternative who's worth fighting for. Easiest thing I've ever done." He glanced back at Erebus. "She had the hard job, learning to trust me. Like I said, hole-y heart. Even the Chains of Truth had a hard time letting me through."

"Did they, though?" Erebus chuckled, letting his reply linger in the air.

I waited, but he didn't elaborate. A nagging curiosity filled the silence. *What was that supposed to mean?*

TWENTY-FOUR

Finch

———

"Uh… yeah, I'm pretty sure they were of two minds about letting me get through the door," I replied. "I mean, they shoved my ass back once, so I'd say I gave them a hard time."

Erebus shrugged. "Whatever you say."

"You think differently?" I figured I might as well get some kind of scoop out of Smokey while I had him here. How often did anyone get this kind of opportunity? He had a direct line to all things Chaos.

"That is none of my business," he replied. "That is between you and the Chains. I am merely speculating for my own amusement."

"Oh… okay." *Thanks for that, Shadowman.*

As Erebus returned his focus to my sister, a noise beside me made me turn. Kadar was growling like a rabid dog, his skin red and pulsating. Being this close to Erebus seemed to be having a weird effect on the kid. Raffe was way under there, buried deep, and clearly couldn't scrabble back to the surface. Djinn were Erebus's homeboys, and Kadar was reacting accordingly, getting all hyped up like he was about to spring into full rage mode.

But that wasn't the only thing worrying me. Behind us, trying to be discreet in the shadow of a monolith, Tobe was up to something mega shifty. It was noticeable because Tobe didn't have a shifty bone in his fluffy body. He was singing quietly, clearly trying not to attract attention, but I could hear a few notes under the crazy vibrations of this place. They were ancient and eerie, like the panpipe music played in shops hawking overblown herbal remedies and gemstones to help you sleep or whatever. Only, this music *actually* sounded powerful, like I was hearing centuries of sad history poured into a single song. The Purge beasts had all frozen to listen, as if hypnotized.

I noticed a small glass vial in Tobe's right hand. It shone brightly and was covered in carved charms. On the bottom of the vial, a diamond glimmered. As he continued singing his haunting tune, the Purge beasts started to sway. Tobe closed his eyes, and I could see the pain etched on his face. As he opened them, I saw two streaks of tears matting the fur under his eyes. I didn't understand why he was so broken up. Well, not until a moment later, when he moved toward the first Purge beast.

He touched the glowing vial to the nearest creature—Striker the gremlin. Immediately, the beast evaporated in a wisp of black smoke that got sucked right into the small vial. I wanted to ask Tobe what the heck he was doing, but that would only have brought attention to him. I sensed this had something to do with Harley. Tobe loved his beasts. He wouldn't be doing something that upset him or his creatures if it didn't serve a purpose.

As soon as he'd absorbed Striker into the vial, he moved on to the next beast. With his signature stealth, he continued to walk inconspicuously around Stonehenge, tapping the monsters like he was in the middle of a game of duck, duck, goose. The other monsters started to hiss and growl, clearly realizing what Tobe was doing, but they were still held by the sound of his song, so there was a limit to how much they could protest.

The Purge beasts' anger spurred Tobe on to sing louder. His voice seemed to calm them down until they were completely catatonic again. *What is he doing?* I watched as he worked his way around half of them, tears falling down his cheeks in big, ugly blobs. I wanted to keep watching, but Erebus's voice distracted me.

"Are you willing to do this?" His attention was entirely fixed on Harley.

Harley nodded. "I wouldn't be here if I wasn't."

"Are you *really* willing to do this?" Erebus pressed.

She lifted her chin like the warrior that she was. "I am."

"A deal will be made, and I will set the terms. You must choose to accept or refuse me now before we continue, as once the last passage of the spell is uttered, there will be no turning back. No changing your mind midway because you decide you don't like the terms. No flaking out."

No take backsies, we get it. I was trying to convince myself that this would be okay by making light of it, even though my insides felt like jelly. It seemed so totally unfair that Harley had to do all this alone. Erebus almost sounded like he *didn't* want Harley to accept this deal— it worried me that he was building up the stakes like a house of cards. What was he going to ask of her that had to have all this preamble? Erebus seemed to be circling his prey like a scavenger.

"I am not entirely pleased with the terms of this arrangement," Lux chimed in. "If you wish to back out, you can do so now, while I am here to mediate. Erebus is not fond of altruism, and he has already conveyed to me how irritated he is by the thought of being summoned without any benefit to himself. So, you may rest assured that he *will* want something. Hence, it is only fair that you have an objective warning prior to your decision."

As if I wasn't already panicking enough for my sister. What the heck did Erebus want? I wanted to make a big gesture of brotherly protection by striding up to Erebus and demanding answers, but that probably would've ended with a Finch-sized puddle on the floor. Or my entire body getting splattered on the monoliths of Stonehenge. Lux was here to mediate for Harley, not for the rest of us.

"So… I don't get to hear the terms first?" Harley's voice wavered a touch, and my heart damn near broke. "That hardly sounds like a fair deal."

"Didn't you read the spell's small print?" Erebus retorted. "Nowhere, in any of this, did anyone say it would be fair."

Lux yanked on Erebus's hand like an exasperated girlfriend. "There are repercussions to entering a deal with Erebus, and one of those is not knowing what the deal will be until it is struck. So, make your decision. This is your last chance to refuse."

Harley sat in silence and dipped her head back down to the Grimoire. If I hadn't been able to see her body shaking, I'd have thought she'd gone back to studying it. And maybe she had. But she was scared—*really* scared. And there wasn't a single thing we could do to help. If we told her to quit, what then? Katherine would get what she wanted. If we told her to do it, what then? Nobody knew except Erebus. *Sly weasel.* Man, I hated this Erebus dude. He was like the smug kid everyone at school disliked.

"She can't do this," Wade whispered from my left. There were tears in his eyes.

"Don't say a word," Santana breathed. "We're here to support her!"

"She has to do this," Tatyana added. "We may not like it, but she has to. Otherwise, what are our options? Katherine's new world order?"

I nodded. "Let her decide. We're spectators. It sucks, but that's why we're here. And think about it: it's not much of a choice, but who do you think Harley would rather have in her body? Erebus or the psycho aunt? It's like life or death, Wade." Even with the deal, it could still spell death. I didn't want to think about that now. I had to hope Erebus would choose to keep her around. He knew power. Surely, he wouldn't just dispose of her. *You better not...*

Wade shook his head and exhaled. "I know... I know. It has to be a Merlin. She has to be the hero. She's all we've got. I just... I just can't *lose* her."

"None of us can," Santana replied softly, her eyes filling with tears.

A Merlin... A hero...

A lightbulb went off in my head, eureka-style. An idea screamed in the back of my mind. What if there could be another option? I'd just presumed, since the Grimoire didn't want to let me in and I had a bad rap sheet, that I wasn't worthy of this ordeal. But if it was just about bloodlines, maybe there was something I *could* do? I'd been thinking about a million ways to get back at Katherine, and this… this somehow made sense. But before my mind could process it further, Harley lifted her head.

"I will go through with this, no matter what the consequences," she said, her voice strong. "The entire magical and human worlds hang in the balance, and I can't let all the lives Katherine has claimed go in vain. My own fears aren't significant anymore. The witch needs to be destroyed by whatever means necessary. That's all there is to it." She gave a small smile that let me know she was still fighting like hell. "Just don't screw with me, Erebus, okay?"

He chuckled. "I have always enjoyed your spirit, Harley."

He looked as though he was about to say more when a portal suddenly tore a hole in the fabric of space and time. *Oh, come* on! Katherine stepped through with one hand on Davin Ass-wipe Doncaster's shoulder.

How are you not dead, you absolute noblet? I wanted to unleash Kadar on him like a furious pit bull until there was nothing left of him to resurrect. If it hadn't been for the *army* of cultists pouring through more portals opening one by one nearby, I would've tried.

"No…" Wade gasped beside me.

"That bitch!" Dylan yelled. It took a lot to get the Duke of Laidback to panic, but something had riled him up, something above and beyond Katherine's sudden entrance, from the looks of it.

"What? What is it?" I scoured the newly arrived throng. There were some familiar faces. Instantly, I understood. The Crowleys were among the army, and so was Remington Knightshade. Their eyes were glowing purple. *So, they're not here of their own volition.* I knew what purple, glow-y eyes meant. It was enslavement, pure and simple.

Katherine was smiling with her usual smug self-satisfaction. That was, until she saw us standing there, forming a protective horseshoe around Harley. Surprise rippled across her cracked, mangey face. *You look like crap, Mom. Like a steaming, messed-up pile of cow dung that's been left out in the sun too long.* There was something so very rewarding in seeing that shock register on her face, if only for a split second. *What, did you think we'd let her do this alone?*

It was in that moment that I realized just how in over her head my mom was. She might have had followers who'd been bent to her will, but Harley had something more. She had people who genuinely cared about her, who would literally give their lives to save her. Did my mom have that? No way. These minions would run the moment they saw a hint that she might not make it through.

Katherine's eyes then darted to the Grimoire on the ground, slap bang in front of Harley. And the strain started to show a little more. *Come on, Mother—crack that face wide open. What are you thinking?* She looked like she was trying to say something, her eyes hypnotically drawn to the book. It held the spell she thought she could use to fix her case of crumbling-cookie syndrome. From what I knew of said spell, Chaos had made a bit of an error by not adding any fail safes or small print. The whole body-switching shebang was meant for a Child of Chaos. Any Child of Chaos. It was our kill or cure for ridding the world of Katherine's infection. But that meant it could be my mother's, too, to become the goddess she wanted to be. Now, we had two horses in the race. Erebus and Katherine. But the latter could go ahead and take a long walk off a short pier—she wasn't getting Harley.

"Aww, I have to say, I'm touched." Katherine forced a smile onto her makeup-caked face, snapping out of her trance. "I wasn't expecting a welcome party from my new Chaos family. Looks like you even invited the long-lost cousins everyone likes to forget exist. Although, it's customary to send an invite to the person you're congratulating. Did mine get lost in the cosmic mail or something?" She glowered at the gathered individuals, letting the daggers of her eyes cut into Uranus, Eros, and Gaia's kids. *As if they're scared of you.*

"This is not a celebration, Katherine," Air replied in a faraway voice, proving my point. "Nobody wants you here, and nobody wants to welcome you into Chaos, no matter how hard you try to force your way through. You are an embarrassment."

Erebus chuckled. "She doesn't know."

Katherine shot him a dirty look. "What don't I know? That's very presumptuous of you."

"I can feel your fear from here, Katherine," he replied casually. "You don't know why Harley is here—not with any specificity. You know there is a spell within the Merlins' Grimoire that has been carefully crafted with the sole purpose of defeating you. But you do not know the details of the spell."

"Again, your presumptions lack evidence. I've done my research, you can count on that!" she shot back. My mother was nothing if not diligent, but it wasn't as though you could just check out a book from the library on this kind of thing. How much *could* she actually know from inflicting torture on poor Odette?

"But you don't have all the pieces, Katherine." Erebus grinned through his smoky mouth. "You think you do, but you don't. Ransacking someone's brain by force is always going to create holes— holes that will not be apparent at first."

Ah... that's more like it. Erebus, despite being a scary brute in his own right, was making me feel a little more hopeful about this entire thing. At the very least, he was getting in some jabs, and that was always satisfying to watch. A squirming Katherine was the best kind of Katherine.

She snorted like an allergic horse. "I have the pieces I need, and that is all that matters. I know it will work. I have it on good authority. You have no idea how skilled I am at torture, Erebus. There were no holes, and your attempt at making me doubt myself won't work."

"Ah, so you would conduct this spell without the need for mediation?" Erebus eyed her with amusement. "A bold move. One I can admire. Although, I suppose you and I already have something of a deal, which I suppose makes you think you are immune to my power?"

"I know you can't hurt me without injuring yourself," she retorted.

What does that mean? Memories of the deal she'd struck with Erebus way back in Tartarus came flooding back. Had that somehow granted her protection from him? I dug a little deeper into my mental fortress, and what I knew of the laws of Chaos and Chaos deals, and realized with a sinking feeling that it might be true. *Ugh.* No matter what she did, she always landed on her feet. A deal with Erebus should've limited her. Instead, it was protecting her.

"But you plan to use Harley's body, which means we have a conflict of interest," Erebus replied. "You want to use the third part of the spell. It goes something like this:

What's yours is mine, what's mine is yours. Hold dominion over me, and take what is owed, to see this tyranny brought to a close.

What's mine is yours, what's yours is mine. You are invited, at my behest, to put this evil firmly to rest.

What's yours is mine, what's mine is yours. Take temporary control, and cross the divide, within my body may you reside.

What's mine is yours, what's yours is mine. We make this last stand as one, you and I, to ensure that our peace will never die.

What's yours is mine, what's mine is yours. I have the blood, you have the power. Help us overcome in our final hour."

Out of the corner of my eye, I saw Harley's eyes bugging out of her head. "Why are you telling her that?! She didn't know what the third part actually was; she just knew it existed! What the heck are you doing?!"

Erebus shrugged. "It's for my own amusement, obviously."

I rolled my eyes. *Seriously, Erebus?* Now wasn't the time for playing games.

This was my second time hearing the passage out loud, and it left a sour taste in my mouth. There was definitely no small print, and no distinction that it had to be Erebus. It still aligned with Katherine's vision: the person reading the spell just had to channel it toward the right Child of Chaos, and hey, presto, that individual's body would belong to them, to do with as they pleased. He'd just given it all away, like a broken candy machine. *Son of a...*

Katherine grinned, like the Kat who'd gotten the cream. "Was that supposed to dissuade me in some way?"

Erebus shrugged. "I don't dictate how you see things. It is a matter of personal perspective."

"All that talk of last stands and tyrants and a final hour is just fluff," she said with a smirk. "As you've said, it's a matter of perspective. Harley may think of me as the so-called 'evil.' But I think of the evil as the restraints on this magical world, and of the human dominion over us. I think of 'our peace' as my new world, in which we'll be the ones with absolute power. Ensuring that our peace never dies is all part and parcel to what I have planned. With me as goddess, peace will prevail. Now, I am certain this is the best course of action for everyone."

"Even now, you still believe that?" I said loudly. "Look in a mirror, Katherine. You *are* the evil. And all of that malevolence is coming to the surface, so everyone can see what you really are. Black goop where your face should be is everything you deserve."

"Cultists, take your positions!" Katherine commanded, as if she hadn't heard me. Though from the twitch in her jaw, I was sure she had.

Obediently, they spread out, surrounding Stonehenge and everyone inside it. Tobe's beasts snarled and hissed, but they clearly knew that if they struck first, they'd be faced with a losing battle. Well, either way they'd be faced with a losing battle, but this way they got to weigh up the enemy a smidge.

I glanced over my shoulder and noticed Tobe creeping back toward us, pushing through until he reached Harley. There, he leaned down toward her and spoke quietly into her ear.

"Whatever you must do next, you must do it quickly," he told her.

"Signal to me when you near the end." I could just about hear him, but I doubted Katherine could over the din.

"Oh, Beastie? I wouldn't mutter such things if I were you." Katherine smiled at him coldly. *Damn, she's got the ears of a bat. An ugly bat.* I expected another speech about doom and gloom, fire and brimstone, and our imminent demise. Instead, she returned her focus to Harley and the book.

Harley lifted her chin and stared back, and there didn't seem to be much fear on her face. Instead, there was an eerie calm, accompanied by a frown of... determination? *Yes, you give it to her, Sis!*

"You left your shot at becoming a goddess too late, Katherine," she said. "You let us get too far ahead."

Katherine snickered. "Hiram and Hester couldn't stop me, and neither will you. They wrote an entire book dedicated to me, and yet all of *that* came too late, not me. Chaos messed around, and now you're here, on your last legs, making a desperate attempt to fix its mistakes. Your bloodline ends here, with me, right now."

Erebus gave a sudden belly laugh that almost made me jump out of my skin. "But it wasn't solely Hiram and Hester's work, Katherine. Chaos itself co-authored this spell. You think it failed, and you keep saying it made a mistake, but it anticipated that someday, a Merlin might have to kill a Child of Chaos. Surely, you understand what that means." He grinned, his red eyes flaring. "Even Chaos did not want you. It did not fail; it was merely biding its time."

"Why do you think all the Children have come here?" I asked, unable to resist the urge to get in another left hook of my own. I glared at her, my hands balled into fists. "Because they, like us and Chaos, want to see you dead. You think you're some beloved goddess, but you're not. You're hated on an omni-dimensional level. Who else can say that? Literally every being in existence wants you gone. But you can't get that into your thick skull, can you? You're loathed, Mother. When you don't love anyone or anything other than yourself—how could you ever hope to be anything but hated?" She wasn't the only one who could make a decent speech. I watched my words hit her, her face contorting in a mask of pain. However, she quickly recovered, as per usual.

She turned to Davin, leaning close to his ear. "Do whatever you have to in order to secure our victory." She kissed his neck gently, making me want to hurl. "And the same goes for the cult members. A new world will rise from blood and ashes, and I don't care how much gets spilled to achieve it."

"As you wish, my divine goddess." Davin bowed his head and prepared to alert the troops.

The message spread rapidly through her army like a vast game of telephone. I could tell right away that Davin had altered the terms. They weren't nearly frightened enough to have been told verbatim what Katherine had said. These suckers would fight this battle until the bitter end. And so would we.

"What do you say we take this party to more neutral ground? We wouldn't want to freak UNESCO out by ruining Stonehenge now, would we?" Katherine smiled as she lifted her hand and snapped her fingers. The click echoed through the stone circle.

A moment later, the world began to shift around us, spinning like a vortex. The blue of the sky bled away, color splashing across it like a chromatography experiment. Sunset pinks and burnished oranges replaced the ordinary blue, while the grass beneath my feet transformed into a vivid, azure expanse. *Weird.* Stonehenge remained, though the monoliths morphed into obelisks of solid bronze. It was the gateway between Elysium and Earth, a natural portal of sorts, one which any Child of Chaos could activate. Including Katherine.

However, her little Thanos click came at a cost. A chunk of flesh sloughed away from her face. It fell to the ground, where it exploded in a flurry of golden sparks. I had to dig my nails into my palms to stop myself from shuddering. It was satisfying, sure, but seriously gross.

She turned to the obelisk on her left, which had transformed into solid metal. Her body froze in shock, and a stifled scream hissed out of her throat. *Aren't you a beauty?* Elysium had put up a mirror for her, so she could see the gaping void that used to be the left side of her face. It had crumbled away from beneath her eye to the bottom of her jaw, though her lips were still intact, making it even creepier. Oily black ooze spilled down onto her chest as flecks of bright light started to force their way through the remaining darkness, making that side of her face look almost galactic—and not in a good way.

How much longer can you hold on, Mother? Judging by the state of her, she didn't have a lot of time left. And she knew it.

TWENTY-FIVE

Harley

My head swam from the world spinning around us like a kaleidoscope and then spitting us out in this strange, beautiful otherworld. Even without the ability to truly feel Chaos anymore, I could sense this whole place dripping with it. My bones were vibrating, my teeth were chattering, and my every hair was standing up on end as I was bombarded by the pure essence of magic in its rawest form.

The grass was a vivid blue, the sky a perpetual sunset even though there was no sun to be seen, and the trees in the distance were covered in a rainbow of leaves. Smaller creatures howled from the boughs, while larger beasts approached the tree line to witness what was going on. They weren't like any animals I'd ever seen before, giving the weirdness of the Purge beasts a run for their money.

There were deer-like beings with two sets of white, fiery eyes and six sets of golden horns, adorned with the same leaves that covered the trees. Small bear-like creatures covered in silver spines left a cascade of golden sparks wherever they walked. Huge purple birds flew in the air, with tails and wings that were literally on fire, burning with a violet blaze. Giant mammoths with snow-white fur, speckled with crimson-

and-pink spots, and tusks that gleamed like they'd been crafted from mother-of-pearl, strode around the land. Some of the creatures were the usual quadrupeds, but others had more limbs, in varying sets and arrangements.

Katherine was on the other side of the stone circle, staring into one of the bronze monoliths. Half of her face had fallen away, leaving a horrifying void with an eye and half a pair of lips sticking out.

I looked quickly and anxiously to the Rag Team, who'd somehow gotten dispersed when Stonehenge spiraled us up into this place. The cultists hadn't wasted any time lunging into action. Weaselly Davin was barking out orders, his chest puffed out. *How are you still breathing, you evil prick?* He didn't seem to be experiencing any after-effects of the mess I'd made of him. His limbs were back where they were supposed to be, and that smug smile was fixed on his mouth again. As if we could ever have trusted a snake like that.

"Attack!" Davin cried out. The cultists moved in formation, closing in on my friends. My heart lurched as I saw the Crowleys and Remington trudging forward obediently, no longer in control of their own bodies. I so wished I could have protected Wade and Dylan from seeing them like this.

Using the Hermetic Batteries and whatever else they had at their disposal, the Rag Team launched into their own defensive strategy. I spotted Wade lifting his hands to hurl Fire at the oncoming mass, his eyes showing his pain as he tried to avoid his parents. He wouldn't be able to do that forever, not if they kept advancing. Beside him, Dylan seemed to be doing the same, hitting everyone around Remington but trying not to inflict any damage on his uncle.

"On your left!" Santana yelled to Kadar, who'd gone on a total rampage. I wasn't even sure if there was anything left of Raffe right now, thanks to the presence of Erebus. Kadar barreled through the army of cultists, sending them flying before they had a chance to retaliate. I could see the line he made through the throng as bodies arced upward and took down others as they landed.

"Garrett! Three o'clock!" O'Halloran boomed.

Being the only two without Hermetic Batteries, they were relying on their magical weapons, which seemed to have taken on a life of their own in this place. The Avenging Angel was burning brighter than ever, the flame licking with a blue edge that hadn't been there before. And O'Halloran's daggers were glowing green as he wielded them skillfully, slashing left and right as he tore into the cultist army. I saw Diarmuid leaping from enemy to enemy, following O'Halloran's path and enacting his miniature reign of terror.

"Tatyana! Remington!" Dylan called to Tatyana, who sat astride her death horse.

Nodding, she charged through the crowd and pummeled the enemy with her regained powers, thanks to the Hermetic Battery, drawing spirits to her. Shimmering entities moved alongside her, making the cultists freeze, as if they'd been touched by a ghost. She rode in a semi-circle around Remington, trying to break him away from the group.

Wade looked like he was trying to do the same thing with his parents. "Tatyana, cut my mom and dad away from the group!"

I couldn't even spot Finch.

I turned back to Lux in desperation. "Is Katherine allowed to do this? Can she intervene?"

Lux shone brightly, the turbulent movement of the light within her revealing hidden anger. "Yes, she can intervene in this manner. She can do as she pleases until you finish chanting the third part of the spell. You must proceed or lose the opportunity altogether."

I snatched up the Grimoire with trembling hands, just as Lux's words seemed to bring Katherine's focus away from her reflection. She turned to face me, giving me a full view of her nightmarish form.

"I've come too far, and worked too hard, to let you spoil everything at the eleventh hour," she rasped, her voice carrying strangely through the air now that her lips had been compromised. "I told you, time and time again, that fighting me was futile. I will always win, Harley. Always. Today is no exception."

Steeling myself, I began to read, letting the Latin variation of the full, combined spell flow out of me:

"Accipio te in universo multum, et dabo tibi quæ oportet enim haec postrema comprecer hora. Quid enim tuum est meus, ut quid debeatur: ego dabo tibi"—A strange whisper hissed in the back of my head, but with my focus on the spell, I could hardly make it out and kept going—*"Quid est hoc malum meum uti facillime superare potest. Ego reddere pretium. Venite ad me fili chaos meum et corpus et animam. Tolle eam—"*

Tendrils of Telekinesis wrapped around my body like pythons. The Grimoire tumbled from my hands and I went flying, Katherine launching me right out of the Stonehenge formation. I hit the ground with an almighty thud, the air knocked out of me.

I knew the last part of the incantation by heart—I hadn't wasted my time while Tobe and his monsters had been out searching for the ingredients. But none of that mattered if I couldn't get back to the book with the silver bowls in front of me. All the pieces were needed to make the spell work.

I scrambled to my feet while Katherine came to a halt a few feet from me. That burst of Telekinesis had taken its toll, and another chunk of skin fell off her face, sliding off like a broken piece of porcelain from an ancient doll in a thrift store. This time, it left a gaping hole in her forehead, the black ooze trickling down over the rest of her face like dark blood. Bright light was pouring from the thinner cracks in her chest and neck. It was coming through her dress, too, making it obvious just how far her self-destruction had gone. But she wasn't going to quit. She meant every word of what she'd said—she'd come too far to stop now. And I was the only thing standing between her and victory.

"This is one fight you won't win, Katherine," I snarled. "Look at the state of you! I could sneeze and you'd evaporate."

"I still have plenty left to give, Harley. And I will give it all to get the body I deserve. Only one of us will emerge from this, and I know who I have my money on." She grinned, the specks of light in her oily darkness glowing brighter. "It would be easier for both of us if you just gave up now, but you're too like me to do that, aren't you? You think you only have your mother's goodness in you? Think again. I've seen the evil you're capable of, and it makes me almost proud to be your aunt. Now, give me what I'm owed."

"You said it yourself… I'm not giving you anything without a fight."

"Then what are you waiting for?" Katherine grimaced.

Gathering Chaos into my palms using my Hermetic Battery, I sent out a barrage of Fire and Earth which hit her head-on and from underneath in a single blow. Spiked plants shot up from the ground and tried to strangle her with their vines, but she swept her hand and disintegrated them in an instant, while a shield wall stopped the Fire from getting through.

A violent orb of Fire came hurtling back in my direction. The heat of it singed the top of my head as I quickly ducked. Another one tore toward me and forced me to twist my body out of the way as I lifted my hands and shot a barricade of Air at her. She blocked with another waft of her hands, as if it were the easiest thing in the world. If it hadn't been for the flakes of skin that were dropping away from her like ashes, I'd have believed it was.

"*Et ossa vestra ut vincti concrescant frigore sanguis currunt. Tace, et non turbabitur amplius. Nihil sentis. Hoc lacerata est. Resurrecturi non sino.*"

I tried something different, using one of the spells I'd gotten from the memory dump. The Chaos from the Hermetic Battery sent the attack spell toward Katherine, but she was too quick. She broke it apart in a matter of seconds, the fragments of the spell drifting away on the tepid breeze.

"One of my favorites," she taunted. "You see, you *are* more like your dear aunt than you know. You're even choosing the spells that I would choose. You could have been at my side, if you'd only had more sense. But at least you'll get to see my reign from the back seat of your mind, once I've taken the rest of you. We'll both share an immortal life—

symbiotically intertwined for the rest of time. Come on, don't tell me that doesn't fill you with excitement?"

"I'd rather kill myself!" I yelled.

"A shame you won't have a choice, then." She launched a dense wall of Fire at me, forcing me to try out a defensive spell from that same catalogue in my head.

"*Protege me ex hoc. Protegas me. Ad formare bulla circa hoc mihi ut superesse.*" A shimmering forcefield manifested around me, and the wall of Fire bounced off.

"You've come a long way since our first meeting, Harley." She chuckled coldly. "Last time we fought like this, one-on-one, you created a giant sinkhole. Do you remember? Back then, you didn't even know what you were capable of. You thought you were a Mediocre. But now… I commend you. I'm going to enjoy taking all of that energy for myself. The perfect vessel, crafted from my own sister's womb, put there by the lover who spurned me. You were made for me, Harley. You are my justice—my revenge. It's only a matter of time before you realize that."

"Then you'd better hope that if you get your hands on my body, my consciousness doesn't stay awake," I shot back. "Because if it does, I'm going to chatter on and on and on about my mom and my dad and everyone you've ever hurt, until it drives you insane."

She smirked. "Oh, you won't be alive, Harley—not in any tangible way. Your body will be a shell, and it'll be all mine, no chattering voices to worry about. The chrysalis for my glorious butterfly."

With that, she lifted her hands, and a tendril of Telekinesis pierced straight through the forcefield I'd created. It wrapped around my chest and squeezed tight.

TWENTY-SIX

Katherine

I flung Harley upward, sending her body soaring in an arc before it crashed back down to the ground.

Rage and power burned through my veins like wildfire, pumping me up on wave after wave of tantalizing adrenaline. It felt beyond delicious.

Payback was the most satisfying thing on this planet. And this was the result of twenty years of endurance, building my empire to this point of complete triumph. This was the culmination of all of that anger and pain and bitterness, finally being pummeled right into the offspring of the people who'd caused it.

This was what I'd promised myself on the Brooklyn Bridge, even though I hadn't known of Harley's existence then. I'd promised to be great, and now it was within my grasp.

Back off, lover-boy. I shot a cold look at Wade as he tried to push through my army to reach her. Another sweet, sweet slice of satisfaction came my way as the Crowleys bore down on him like good little zombies. They grappled him to the floor, crying every step of the way.

"We're sorry, sweetheart. We're so, so sorry," Felicity wept. *Ugh, spare me the soppy ending.* She was sending blast after blast of Air into her darling boy while Cormac had a lasso of Telekinesis around his handsome son's neck. My zombie spell wasn't perfect at keeping them zombified. Intense emotion could reignite a sliver of consciousness, but it wouldn't stop them from hurting Wade. They'd just keep on attacking, as they'd been ordered, even after they'd killed their beloved son.

"Forgive us," Cormac rasped.

"Kill us! Stop us!" Felicity begged, imploring the cultists around her.

All the while, I kept up my own barrage of attacks on Harley, until she lay curled up on the ground, barely flinching as the Telekinesis smacked into her and tossed her around like a rag doll.

"Stop..." she wheezed.

But I was too far gone for that. I'd keep going until she was on the verge of expiring. Then, and only then, would I manipulate her mind into reading that spell for me. The one that would make all my dreams come true. *I'm my own damned fairy godmother.*

"Katherine... stop," Harley rasped.

I smiled. "No, I don't think I will. I'm enjoying myself far too much, and I deserve a little amusement after everything you've put me through. Shall I tell you what you're missing?" I looked out into the sea of battle and spotted the rest of her pals. I looked back at Harley with glee. Telling her the play-by-play would be fun.

"The Russian is in bad shape, Harley. Right now, she's panicking as hands reach out for her. Her spirits are failing. They can't protect her anymore. Ooh, would you look at that—they're flickering out of existence. And now, my cultists are grabbing her. She's struggling, as you'd expect, but it's pointless now. Yep, there it is. They've yanked her down from the back of that disgusting horse."

I paused for dramatic effect as the girl disappeared into the throng. The moments passed, and she didn't come back up for air. "I hate to say it, but I don't think she's going to make it." Just then, I heard the

Russian scream, and so did Harley. I could see it on her face as it twisted up and tears poured down her cheeks.

"Tatyana!" Dylan howled, but he was too busy fending off Remington to go to her aid. "Kadar—get Tatyana!"

"This should be interesting," I mused. "Kadar is charging toward Tatyana. He's tossing my cultists left, right, and center. Wait... what's that? Davin has him in a trance. Oh dear, looks like your star player is about to be taken off the field."

Sure enough, purple tendrils spread out of Davin and surrounded Kadar, binding him in sparking ropes of violet energy. He tried to fight them, his red skin pulsing, but the ropes held him fast. Smoke billowed, temporarily blinding the cultists and Harley's friends. Davin strode through the fog like the majestic, sexy beast that he was. He was chanting something under his breath, and Kadar's red flesh was turning black.

"He's dying, Harley. Davin is killing him. Soon enough, he'll be nothing but dust, and the djinn will take your friend down with him."

"Stop this!" Harley yelled, her voice strangled as I tightened my grip on the Telekinesis around her.

"Pardon? You'll have to speak up. I can't hear you over the sound of your friends dying." I chuckled. "Now, who else can I spot? Ah yes, looks like O'Halloran and Garrett are having some trouble. O'Halloran should've stayed with me."

The two of them were backed against a monolith, looking weary as they swiped their blades. They were covered in blood, and both of them were breathing heavily. They weren't wearing the same cuffs as the others, which meant they didn't have any Chaos at their disposal.

"They're easy pickings for my army, Harley. Yep... O'Halloran just got hit, and he's not getting up. It won't be long before he's O'Dead."

Garrett was faring better with that big fiery sword of his, but I wasn't going to tell Harley that. Actually, I wouldn't have minded having that sword for myself when I rose as the Goddess of Discord. Then, I could be the Avenging Angel that this world deserved.

Harley tried to turn to look at the fray, but I twisted her back around, making her cry out in pain.

"It's rude to interrupt. Didn't your mother teach you anything?" I smiled. "Oh, that's right, you never had one, did you? I'd say I was sorry about that, but I'm not. She got what was coming to her. It's heart-breaking really, but at least your mother isn't about to murder you, so I spared you that. Wade's is, though. His dad, too. Can you hear your beloved gargling as his father squeezes the life out of him? Come on, concentrate. It's tricky, but you can just about hear him straining for breath if you try *really* hard."

"I won't read for you," Harley hissed through her teeth. "I made a promise. I'm keeping it, no matter what you do to me or to them." She should have been wavering by now, but that annoying determination was still etched on her face.

It didn't matter. A few more minutes and she'd be weak enough to bend to my will. I could make it happen without exerting every last scrap of energy I had left. I'd manipulate her mind, force her to recite the deal part of the spell, and call out my name instead of Erebus's.

Speaking of which… those useless ingrates were just standing around, watching the mayhem. Even the Elementals had the sense to know when they were defeated, apparently.

"Now, who do we have left?" I glanced across the horde and found Finch.

My stomach lurched involuntarily. He was fighting to the death against Davin and my cultists—the former having left Kadar on the ground in an unmoving black heap.

Even now, I didn't want Finch to die. Not at the hands of Davin, and not at the hands of my cultists.

But Davin knew that—he knew what he had to do, as per my request. He knew I wanted Finch alive so I could make him suffer, and so that he could learn from his mistakes.

"Alton is almost on his knees, you'll be pleased to know," I contin-ued, turning my attention away from Finch. I'd never have expected my son to make such a promising warrior. It looked like all of those endurance tests in my fighting arenas on Eris Island had finally paid off. *See, Finch, your mother always cared.*

"Tobe is being singed to within an inch of his life, and I don't see any more of his precious beasts. That bird high-tailed it out of here the moment things started to go south. Gargoyles are loyal. The rest, not so much."

"You haven't mentioned Finch." Harley grinned up at me, spitting blood onto the blue grass. "And I'm guessing they're putting up a better fight than you're letting on. Otherwise, you'd let me see." She tried to turn again, but I twisted her back around. She'd just have to take my word for it.

"Actually, no. Finch is trying to protect Alton, and he's getting his ass handed to him. He's just staggered back after taking a fireball to the chest." It pained me to see it, but I knew Davin wouldn't let him die. He wouldn't fail me again. If Finch died, so did Davin.

Another fireball slammed into Finch, sending him sprawling back against one of the monoliths. "Ooh, I felt that one. Didn't you? Your friends aren't in good shape at all, Niece."

"Says you? Have you seen the state of your face lately?" She chuckled darkly, wiping blood from her nose.

I sneered at her. "You've lost another one."

"What?" She gasped, wavering at last.

"That Catemaco bitch is down. Poor thing tried to run to her djinn lover to help him, and now she's getting smashed into the ground by a Herculean."

I watched it unfold, Orishas dancing in the air around the Mexican witch as they tried to help. But there were just too many cultists, and they were all swarming Santana like flies, joining in with the Herculean's bloodlust until she looked like a mangled shell of a person. Apparently, I'd be taking out the Catemaco heiress today, too. A nice, neat package deal.

"She isn't getting up, niece of mine. Mincemeat would be a good way to describe her right now. And now Kadar has blinked his little red eyes awake. Oh, and he's looking at her so mournfully. Is... is the djinn crying? I think he is. Well, that's a new one for me. So, the beast can feel, can he? Ordinarily, it's supposed to be beauty that killed the beast, but in this case, it looks like the beast killed the beauty. It's so poetic, isn't it? Honestly, I really wish you could see this. It'd crush you, it really would, but I'm kind enough to spare you that. What sort of aunt would I be if I let you watch as your friends died, all because of your actions? You did this, you know. You killed them, just as much as my cultists."

Harley gripped the grass, her knuckles whitening as she screamed into the earth. It sent a shiver up my spine. That was the cry of the truly devastated—the rare individual who had nothing left but grief.

I'd screamed in that same way once before, and I'd almost forgotten what it could sound like.

As her scream cut off, I took a step toward her, realizing this was my moment. Her mind was on the edge of collapse, which would make it all that much easier to slither in and get her to do what I wanted.

I was about to lift my hands to start the process when a rush of air swept across the landscape. A portal tore open, right in the center of the stone circle. I hadn't noticed that Nyx was missing, but that wispy devil was the first one to walk through, followed by Levi and a bunch of fresh meat, ready for carnage.

So, you can't intervene, but you can bend the rules a little?

No doubt they'd say this was just an innocent invite. *Innocent my left ass cheek.* Nyx had known just where to go and who to find. The whole Catemaco clan had come along to the execution, too, and Tatyana's parents were standing at their side. Plus a dozen other magicals whose names I didn't care about. Somehow, they had all gotten their hands on Hermetic Batteries.

I was tired of toying with my prey. It was time to finish this.

Closing the gap between myself and Harley before Levi the Useless and his eager group could head in my direction, I brought my boot down on my niece's throat. Now, *this* was poetic. She was looking up at me with that same lost, broken expression that her mother had worn when I watched, from the shadows, as Hiram ended her. A sweet little echo of the past to spur me on. It was the divine understanding of one's mortality coming to a close. Hester had known it, and Harley knew it now.

Leaning down, I took out my ceremonial blade and carved the symbol of Hecate's Wheel into Harley's forehead—the black spot marking her demise. She cried out as the blood began to pool, but I paid her no mind. The carving reminded me of a labyrinth with a star in the center. A perfect symbol to reflect the complex journey I'd taken to reach this point. And Harley was my star, in the middle of it all, waiting to be plucked from the heavens.

Next, I grabbed her hand and began to carve more symbols, remembering what I'd seen in Odette's mind—the clues that had led me to this. I didn't need Harley's combined spell; I just needed the third one. The one I'd stolen from the Librarian. But that shortcut required a bit of extra prep on my part; hence the carvings. I didn't mind a little more work to get what I wanted.

From left to right, on her right hand, I etched the key symbol, a circle with a horizontal line through it. The lantern symbol came next, which was a simple, empty circle. The sun symbol followed, which looked like a rudimentary star, and then came a circle with a vertical line and a tail of sorts to represent the stars. On Harley's thumb, I etched a circle with a vertical line through it, no tail necessary, to emulate the moon. And in her palm I drew a fish, with four crosses beneath and a triangle with a plus sign underneath it.

This was the Hand of Mysteries—the alchemical symbol of apotheosis, used to transform man into god. Or, in this case, woman into goddess. This was my gateway.

I tucked a strand of Harley's sweat-dampened hair behind her ear, marveling at its color. It was the same shade of red as my own. She'd been through enough. Time to put her out of her misery.

"It's almost done now," I whispered. I could almost taste victory on my tongue, and it beat any bottle of champagne you could've thrown my way.

TWENTY-SEVEN

Finch

There's a turning point in every fight, no matter how big or small, where you realize you're more or less screwed. We'd flown past that point about ten minutes ago. Outnumbered, outmagicked, outmaneuvered.

Santana and Kadar were down. Tatyana was being trampled under fifty pairs of feet. O'Halloran was on his knees. Wade was struggling with his zombie parents, who were weeping as they tried to squeeze the life out of him. Not to mention Harley, who was curled up on the ground outside the stone circle, being pounded by Katherine's Chaos. To get to her, we had to get through an army, and things were starting to feel dire. Our window was closing, and it was closing fast.

"I have been looking forward to this." Davin kept approaching, though Garrett, Tobe, and I were doing our best to keep him back. Alton was helping us too—the Caladrius had come back to defend him and had given him a surge of vitality. He looked almost normal again, his cheeks flushed with an angry red. Either that, or he was crazy feverish.

A blast from Alton's palms sent Davin flying, slamming him into the nearest monolith. Our window had opened a crack. It was now or never.

"I have to finish what Harley started." I glanced at Tobe on my left side.

"What?" he shouted back, as though he hadn't quite heard me. With the commotion going on, I wasn't surprised. Either that, or he couldn't quite believe what I'd just said.

I could see the Grimoire from here, a short distance in front of Stonehenge's twelve o'clock, with the army circling around it. There was so much power in that thing that even the enemy didn't want to go near it. Then again, it wasn't as if they could—the Grimoire could only be touched by those it gave permission to, and those it wanted to be touched by. And it wasn't about to give permission to a bunch of cultists.

What kind of irritated me was the Children of Chaos standing around like spare parts. Surely if there was a time to break ranks with Chaos's ridiculous rules, it was now? Katherine was going to win if they didn't. But it looked like they'd made their choice. *Leave it all up to us, why don't you?*

As if responding to my criticism, a huge blast of air whipped across the stone circle. I stared in shock at Alton, wondering if he'd unleashed some crazy magic, but he looked just as surprised as I did. As I followed his gaze, a portal tore wide open, just outside the left-hand curve of the stone circle. Nyx stepped through first, with reinforcements in tow.

You beauty! I was glad to see *someone* was doing something. Levi was leading the new crew, and I'd never been happier to see the pathetic slug in my life. Astrid was there, too, with a fresh swarm of drones, echoing her mode of attack in the Garden of Hesperides. She'd tucked herself behind a monolith, but still—what the heck was she thinking? This was no place for a mortal. I realized the irony in that, but she didn't have a Hermetic Battery she could use. Garrett had paled. He was clearly thinking the same thing, though you had to admire her courage.

Krieger and Jacob weren't here, so I guessed they'd stayed back to watch over Harley's Purge oddity. But Levi knew about the Hermetic Batteries and what we'd learned from Marie Laveau, thanks to the wonder of burner phones. How they'd gotten hold of some Batteries, *and* managed to fill them, was beyond me, but they had enough to make a dent. Perhaps they'd found a way to give Zalaam the same marker Marie had put in Kadar. Whatever the case, they were already on the attack.

"I have to go now while everyone is distracted," I shouted louder.

Tobe's eyes widened in surprise. "You?"

I nodded. "My bloodline is the same as Harley's, and that's all Erebus needs, right? Sure, I don't have her insane powers, but I don't think that's the important part anymore. The key is in my blood and in my heritage." I looked to Katherine, who had taken out a knife and started carving things into Harley's face. My eyes flew wide in horror. "And she won't see it coming!"

"Yes… yes, I believe that may work." Tobe took out that weird vial he'd been pouring his creatures into. "Drink this before you allow Erebus to take over your body. I had been planning to wait until Harley finished the third incantation, to allow it to work at its maximum efficiency, but we never got to that moment. You will have to drink it now."

"*Drink* it?" I shuddered. The inside was filled with an unsettling black goo. No doubt some concentrated jelly of Purge beast remains. *Ugh.* Couldn't it be cough syrup, or cordial cherry juice?

"It is the only way your body will withstand the influx of Chaos," Tobe warned. "Especially as you lack Harley's powers, it will take even more of a toll upon you. This should protect you if I have made the correct calculations."

"If? Tobe, this isn't a time for ifs."

He smiled nervously. "I *have* made the right calculations. It will protect you from being torn apart by Erebus's might."

"That's more like it, Beast-Man." I took the vial and slipped it into my pocket. "Garrett, how do you feel about putting that sword to good use? I'm going to need some backup if I'm running this gauntlet." I nodded to the Grimoire, which lay a good ten yards away.

Garrett lifted his blade. "Lead the way. I've got your back."

We jumped in, tearing through the throng that separated us from the Grimoire. I shot bolts of Telekinesis at anyone who came too close, sending them sprawling backward. They knocked down clusters of anyone they fell into. Even so, there was an endless swarm to force our way through. Behind me, I heard the swish of Garrett's sword as he cut down anyone in our path who might try to attack from the sides.

Meanwhile, my eyes were fixed dead ahead. I could still see Harley, and she was in a bad state. Purple light was pouring out of the bloodied circle in the center of her forehead. Her eyes were glowing a weird shade of orange. Katherine was chanting something which made Harley's disfigured right hand pulsate with a creepy red glow. I had no idea what underworld, evil hexes Mother Dearest was performing, but I knew why she was doing it. This was her way of getting Harley to read out the body deal spell.

My sister's face was twisted up, like she was trying to fight it, but although Katherine's body was falling apart, her mind and energies were more powerful than they'd ever been. This was a calculated risk for her, and she was putting everything she had left into Harley. I had to muster every ounce of willpower to stop myself from sprinting directly for my sister to try and save her from Katherine. If I did that, we'd never stand a chance of getting the last part of the spell completed.

A cold surge of anger swelled in my veins, but I ploughed on through the fight. At least Tatyana had reappeared from the horde and sat astride her death horse again. That would never not be terrifying. It looked, weirdly enough, as if a tag team of Diarmuid and Murray had been the ones to free her. I could tell from the gouged eyes of those stumbling blindly around her, all of them covered in oily bite marks. Diarmuid now stood on the Kelpie's head, popping an eyeball into his mouth, while Murray hovered above, divebombing at random. *Good thing I didn't eat today.*

O'Halloran had managed to reach Santana and had her slung over his shoulder. He sliced at anyone who dared approach, looking like a total badass. I watched him make his way toward Dylan and Kadar, who was unconscious on the ground. I couldn't see Remington, but since Dylan had managed to get away, that didn't bode well for our tattooed friend. *Shame.* Remington had been a good guy. He wouldn't have done this willingly.

Dylan quickly used his Chaos to undo whatever hex Davin had put on Kadar, following instructions O'Halloran bellowed at him. Bronze light twirled out of Dylan's palms and sank into the djinn. It freed Kadar from his immobilized, unconscious state, and he immediately jumped up and roared. The sound echoed through Stonehenge, making everyone pause for a split second. Kadar, on the other hand, didn't pause. He plunged into the army, picking up right where he'd left off.

Levi, the Catemacos, and the Vasilis family were making mincemeat out of the cultists, who'd clearly messed with the wrong people. I saw Tatyana notice her family, and a wave of relief washed over her face. But she was too busy fighting the cultists around her for an emotional reunion. As the Catemacos and the Vasilis family edged forward, making more of a dent in the throng, they managed to drag the Crowleys off of Wade. He wriggled free, gasping in breaths as he stared in surprise at his saviors.

I surged on, pummeling the cultists who flooded around me. Garrett's blade was doing some major damage, too. I heard the cries as the cultists went down behind me. *Come on, a few more yards!* I could see the Grimoire clearly. It was so close. One more push and I'd have it in my grasp. I just prayed it would grant me permission. I'd heard its whispers before, which gave me some confidence that it didn't entirely hate me. And, besides, this was for Harley. And to end Katherine. *My intentions are good, Grimmy. Please, realize that and let me in.*

I'd just sent out a barrage of Telekinesis when I heard a scream that made me stop dead in my tracks. It wasn't a normal scream. It was like the scream that had come out of my own throat when I'd found out Adley had been murdered. I whirled around to find Garrett flat on the ground behind me, face down. A sparking purple dagger was lodged between his shoulder blades, the whole thing morphing into violet tendrils that slithered into Garrett's body.

I looked up to see Davin smirking, his hand still raised in the position of throwing the dagger. I stooped to turn my friend over. His eyes were staring up blankly, devoid of life.

"You son of a bitch!" I howled, my heart clenching. Davin had killed him. I'd seen death enough times to know when someone wasn't coming back. Even with Davin, there was always that half-smirk on his dead-ass face to let me know he was going to wriggle free of death somehow. A giant "screw you" every time he came close to it.

Utter devastation coursed through my veins, but I couldn't stop now. There wasn't time to grieve. That could come later, when all of these lowlifes were gone. When Katherine was dead and they all started scuttling away like rats.

As Tobe lunged at Davin, descending on him with his claws bared, I turned around and ran. With a blockade of Telekinesis in front of me, I didn't stop until I'd reached the Grimoire.

Skidding to my knees, I snatched up the book and raised the lens to my right eye. I had to use this window of distraction or lose it forever. The enemy was too busy contending with the freshly arrived allies to bother with me. And the Children were just watching, with a mixture of concern and apathy. *This would all be over if you just DID SOMETHING!*

I channeled all my rage into furious concentration as I stared at the book. And, somehow, the words made sense to me. I could hear the book whispering as I held it, like it wanted to let me see.

"Can I finish the spell for Harley?" I fixed my gaze on Lux and Erebus, who were standing just in front of the twelve o'clock monolith. "I have her bloodline. My heritage is the same as hers—from the Primus Anglicus. And I have the words of the spell right here. It's letting me see them. That's got to be a good thing, right?"

Erebus flashed something close to a grin. "Oh, I love a twist, don't you? Keeps things exciting. Yes, you are a Primus Anglicus descendant, as Harley is. So why not? Knock yourself out."

"Are you sure you want to do this?" Lux cut in. "The same terms apply, and you will not know the ties that bind you until you have already accepted, by reading out the last part of the spell."

I rolled my eyes. "Enough with the 'are you sure' crap! You can see what's happening behind me, right?!"

"Yes, we can, but—"

I didn't let Lux finish. Ripping the cork out of Tobe's glass vial, I chugged the black goo in one gulp and tried not to gag as it slithered down my throat like a wet slug. It tasted like moldy dirt with a hint of acid that burned my throat.

No sooner had I sucked it down than I could feel power rushing through me like a billion tentacles. They spiderwebbed out of my chest, splintering down every limb and appendage, invading every cell and vein until I was full to the brim of what felt like raw Chaos, in its purest form. But, somehow, it didn't feel like it was helping.

It felt like it was breaking me apart from the inside out. The intensity turned to agony, my skin fiery hot, like I was going through the worst sunburn of my life. My lungs were ignited next, every breath feeling like my last. It hurt to drag oxygen inside, as though I was swallowing acid instead. My whole body started to throb, each pulse sending a jolt of piercing pain through every limb and organ, down to the last damn capillary.

But Tobe had sworn it would work. I trusted him.

Still, for a split second, I had a creeping doubt. What if Katherine had gotten to Tobe first? What if this was her backup for her backup for her backup—a way of stopping Harley before she could pull any tricks? Only, I'd downed the goo instead.

I glanced back to try and find Tobe in the crowd. He was flying overhead, an earnest look on his face. "You must proceed!" he shouted. "It hurts, but it will protect you!"

Okay then… I picked up the book and found the last paragraph. Taking a shaky breath as my whole body burned and vibrated with the strain of controlling all this juice, I started to read:

"Accipio te in universo multum, et dabo tibi quæ oportet enim haec postrema comprecer hora. Quid enim tuum est meus, ut quid debeatur: ego dabo tibi. Quid est hoc malum meum uti facillime superare potest. Ego reddere pretium. Venite ad me fili chaos meum et corpus et animam. Tolle eam et uti eo ut telum. Transeunt mortalitatis distinxerint Divinum et destruunt quod minatur. Quod est meum tuum est. Tolle quod debetur. Accipio te paciscor." I paused as a whisper crept into my head. One word. *Erebus.* Immediately, the spell's ending changed in my head. I knew what I had to say to make this work. *"Quod est meum tuum est. Tolle eam Erebo deferre nefas."*

There was no information actually written in the spell that said I had to call for Erebus, but he was the one I wanted to make the deal with. And that whisper had refused to be ignored, urging me to say those words. So I did.

I turned to face the dark Child. "So, what do you say? Don't keep a guy waiting. I've read the spell, I've accepted your deal, so give me the terms so we can get on with this!"

He smirked. "Of course." He snapped his fingers. A pulse blasted out of him in a dark wave that sent up a protective shield around the three of us—me, Lux, and Erebus.

Try getting through this, Mother.

I saw it catch her attention, and she turned away from Harley to stare in horror. They were all on the outside, looking in, with no way of stopping what was to come. I couldn't stop it either, in fairness, but I'd made my promise a long time ago. Would I sacrifice myself for my sister if the moment came? *Of course I would. I'd do it a thousand times over, if it meant saving her.* I couldn't ask to be the hero and change my mind if I didn't like the consequences. That wasn't how being a hero worked. And this was one hell of a redemption arc.

The fight had come to a screeching halt. Davin was frozen in astonishment. And Katherine couldn't move, she was so shocked and horrified. She hadn't seen this coming, just as I'd hoped. She knew, firsthand, that nobody could touch the Grimoire unless expressly permitted. She hadn't been able to. Her cultists hadn't been able to, when they'd tried to steal it for her. So she'd left it out in the open, confident that she was beating seven bells out of the only person who could use it. And she'd gotten it way wrong.

"Don't you *dare* do this, you ungrateful, spiteful little boy!" She pummeled the shield with wave after wave of Telekinesis, but it didn't do a damn thing. It just gave a pretty dramatic percussion accompaniment to what was about to happen. Her demise, straight up.

I smirked back at her and flipped her the bird. I thought about saying something eloquent, but why bother when this sent the perfect message?

She was the one who was out of time now.

"Come on, Erebus," I said, swallowing my nerves. "Let's finish this before Katherine does something neither of us can fix."

TWENTY-EIGHT

Harley

I was teetering on the brink of unconsciousness. Blood filled my mouth, and I could feel more of it congealing across my face, where it had trickled down from the sigil she'd carved right into my forehead. My hand stung and my whole body ached. Every muscle hurt from the torment Katherine was intent on putting me through. I'd felt helpless and broken... until I saw Finch and heard his voice drifting across Stonehenge. I'd heard him finish the spell.

My heart had jolted in fear for him, but there was a huge swell of relief knowing that someone had done it. Even if that someone wasn't me. I could hardly believe that he'd taken that step, and that Erebus and Lux had permitted him.

Katherine hadn't twisted me back after her last round of violence, so I lay there looking at the mayhem within the stone circle. Time slowed down, and my eyes took in every detail I'd missed during Katherine's brutal punishments.

Garrett was dead on the ground, the cultists having parted to reveal him. I heard Astrid's screams from somewhere in the near distance, that shivering, bloodcurdling sound bringing pain and a faint flicker of hope. If Astrid was screaming, then it meant she was feeling something. I just wished it hadn't taken this to let her experience emotion again.

Santana was injured, O'Halloran moving her down off his shoulder and cradling her like a baby. Tatyana was streaked with blood, her hand covering a wound to her chest, but she was still sitting astride her horse, staring at the cultists who'd frozen suddenly. Meanwhile, Kadar spurred back into action, ploughing through the mess, his focus on total destruction. It seemed to break the trance, forcing the cultists to defend themselves, and mayhem erupted again.

Tobe was hovering low over the veiled dome where Finch was making his deal, though his fur had been singed in places and there were cuts and tufts of matted fur all over his body. Alton seemed to be in better shape, with the Caladrius flying close to him. And Dylan was standing with the Catemacos, about to face off against Remington and the Crowleys, who were relentless in their pursuit. Somehow, Remington had resurfaced, and he didn't seem to be showing any signs of backing down. Dylan and the Catemacos intervened and pinned the Crowleys and Remington to the ground, along with a few others who'd been zombified by Katherine.

It's all coming to an end. Finch just had to finish this, and we'd be home free. I spotted Wade in the crowd, his face bruised and battered, a painful-looking circle of red around his neck. As soon as our eyes met, he started running toward me. The cultists were too distracted by the reignited battle to understand why; he was just another sprinting soldier.

"Wade!" I gasped. I wanted to tell him to get back, but the words wouldn't come out. My voice was nothing more than a faint rasp.

As he broke through the edge of the stone circle, Katherine hurled a pulse of Telekinesis right at him. She probably knew the end was nigh, but that only gave her more reason to fight back. Wade sailed through the air and hit one of the monoliths with a sickening crack that shivered right through me. He slumped against it, his head drooping.

"NO!" I tried to cry, but only a croak came out. A second later, Katherine turned her focus back to me.

"I will get what I came for!" she spat, grabbing me by the neck and squeezing tight.

"No... no, you won't," I wheezed. "You'll fall apart before you can... make me read anything. And I'm going to watch everything you've worked for... tear you to pieces!" It hurt to speak, but she wasn't getting the satisfaction of seeing this through.

She loosened her grip slightly and responded in a low hiss. "I have more strength left than you think, parasite. Plenty, in fact, to get what I want."

"I'll die first." I clawed in a breath as air flowed back through my throat. "I was already ready to give everything to stop you... that hasn't changed. If all I've got to do is hold out longer than you can, then so be it. You'll be making my job way easier!" I had to push this out. I had to land the final blow to her doomed empire. I had to believe I *could* hold out longer than she could. She was already a mess, and making me read out the last part of that spell would mean using some powerful magic. Magic she might not have the strength left to conjure. "And anyway, that spell you want to use... it isn't for you."

"You must be desperate, to start rehashing *this* subject, Harley." Katherine sneered. "The third spell does not specify *which* Child of Chaos. That was Chaos's mistake, as we have discussed."

"But the Grimoire spoke Erebus's name. Not yours. Not the name of any other Child of Chaos. Just Erebus. It was hidden in the spell the whole time. The full spell. The third part becomes modified when it's part of the full one." There'd been nothing written about Erebus at all, but I guessed it was another preventative measure Chaos had slipped in. A secret whisper, so that only those with the proper intentions could use it. Another way of shoving Katherine out.

"I don't *need* the full one. That's what I'm trying to get into your thick skull." Katherine raised her palms to start her curse again. "The spell I took from Odette is a separate entity. It doesn't need to be combined. Hence the carvings on your face—I've already done what I need to do to get the added power to make my body spell work. All I need now is for you to speak the incantation. The separate one. Maybe *your* spell requires Erebus, but mine doesn't."

"Well, it doesn't matter either way. You've been beaten to the punch. Finch has beaten you to the punch." I braced for the impact of her hex, but it was taking some time. Evidently, she needed a lot of concentration to stop it from breaking the rest of her apart. "All he has to do is enlist Erebus before you can get anything out of me, and judging by your face, you're struggling."

Air hissed through Katherine's gritted teeth. "Shut your mouth, Merlin."

"Why, because you don't like the truth? Chaos made sure Finch was born. Another Primus Anglicus with Merlin blood who could perform the spell. *You* gave birth to your own destruction. The Grimoire decides who gets to read it, and it's allowed Finch to see the spell at last. It always whispered to him. I didn't understand why until now. It was keeping an option open in case I couldn't make it. And, since the final spell was specifically designed for a Merlin spellcaster, he fits the bill."

"You're wrong. Finch is too weak a magical to make it work, even with those Batteries and whatever tricks Tobe has up his sleeve!"

I smiled. "But it's not really about power, Katherine. It's about blood. All this time, Chaos conspired to bring us together—Finch and I —knowing you would get to this point. Finch was always meant to be waiting in the wings, it seems." I laughed lightly as realization seemed to dawn on Katherine's face. "It was never just me you had to worry about. My brother has everything I have, and, what's more, he has every reason to take you down. You gave him those reasons. Now, I'd call *that* poetic, wouldn't you?"

A cruel grimace twisted up her stunned face.

"Well, if that's the case, what use do I have left for you?" Purple tendrils shot out of her hands, wound down my neck, and grasped my whole body in a vise. "If I go down, Harley Merlin, you're going down with me. This started with you, and it ends with you," she hissed.

The tendrils gripped harder, and I could feel my bones crushing together. It felt like sucking air through a straw filled with cotton wool, and I could feel those tendrils sinking inside me, stealing the life from my veins and leaving a cold dread behind. Somehow, time seemed to slow down.

Seconds became minutes as I fought to survive, feeling every fiber of my being crushed tighter and tighter. It wouldn't be long before I started to crumble. All she needed was the right pressure point and I'd break. I could feel myself decaying the same way Wade had in Marie Laveau's garden on our first visit.

"Not so smug now, are we?" Katherine leaned in as I felt my skin suck inward like a vacuum. "At least I'll have this to comfort me in the long days to come. And I *will* find a way to release myself, you can count on that. Davin has already been instructed to scour the earth for any other powerful descendants of the Primus Anglicus if this fails, and he will summon me once he finds a suitable candidate—as I've said, Finch won't be strong enough for this. But his descendants could be. Even if it takes decades, Davin won't let me down. Even if I have to wait for my son's children, I will."

Taking some pointers from Echidna, there...

At least that would require Finch to make it out of this alive. Unless there *were* children from other Primus Anglicus bloodlines around. I hoped Chaos had enough sense to never allow anything like that to happen again once this was over—yet she was still so sure of herself, even now. It was worrying, but also slightly laughable that she still believed so much in Davin's loyalty. If she fell today, I couldn't see her ever hearing from the slime ball again. I would've staked my life on *that*, if she wasn't about to squeeze the last drop out of me.

This was it... this was the moment I died. I kept expecting Finch and Erebus to turn up to save the day, but they weren't here. And I couldn't turn to find out why they had stalled, with Katherine gripping me like this. Nobody would remember me once my friends were gone, but at least I'd played my part, right? I'd provided the decoy to give Finch a shot at getting this done, and that was all that mattered, wasn't it? So why did I want to live so badly? Why was I clinging on when the inevitable was seconds away? Surely, it would be easier to give up and go peacefully on to the next world?

Are you kidding, Harley? Was I really going to let this woman end me, after all of the struggles I'd gone through to get here?

No, she'd had me against the ropes for way too long.

There was an old saying that a tiger nearing death was at its most dangerous. After all, with time almost up, there was nothing left to give but everything. She could threaten to take me down with her, but two could play that game.

I gripped tighter to every shred of energy and consciousness I had left and used the agony that rose with it to fuel me. The pain turned to anger, and that anger fed the fire I needed.

I poured every emotion into gathering my strength, letting it rekindle my determination. My muscles felt like lead, but that was just too bad. I forced my hands up and pressed them against my chest, letting Chaos surround me, overwhelm me, saturate me to my last freaking breath. It was like jump-starting a car, and the zinging explosions of pain that fired through every vein in my body echoed the sentiment. It was like electricity, crackling through every inch of me, using the bare bones of the Hermetic Batteries to create something altogether more formidable. I was the tiger, and I was going to use it all to fight this bitch.

Breathless, I delved deep inside myself, straining to find the edges of my warring affinities—Light and Darkness. I hadn't sensed the divide between them as strongly as usual, since the Hermetic Battery paled in comparison to my natural Chaos. But all I had to do was coax the Darkness back out. It was still there, inside me, somewhere. *Feed the Darkness...* I closed my eyes and sought out its faint edges, feeling like I was trying to pick up a moth's wing without crumbling it in my fingers. A ripple of excitement coursed through me, as if Darkness was responding to my call. *There you are. Don't let me down.*

Tempting it out of its secret hideaway, I let the Dark energy flow through my veins and gave it permission to take hold. It burned like no pain I'd ever experienced, as if my entire body were melting away from its skeleton. But I had to keep going. I had to gather the Darkness in the pit of my chest until I couldn't hold it in any longer.

Once my ribs felt like they were two seconds away from blowing, taking my lungs with them, a giant blast of Telekinesis ripped out of me. I screamed, using the sound to vent some of the overwhelming pain and to keep from losing my hold on consciousness. The vise-like grip around me loosened completely as Katherine was thrown to the side.

"Obey me!" My voice came out in a strange, haunting echo. And I realized I wasn't controlling it anymore. Darkness had it. Or Chaos itself was calling. Perhaps the Darkness was feeding some residual link to the Grimoire.

The words ricocheted across Elysium. *Who are you talking to?* It became clear a second later, as Air in humanoid form appeared beside Katherine and crashed into her with full force. Water, Earth, and Fire joined her a second later, all apparently called to arms by my, or Chaos's, words. The Elementals were beautiful and ethereal in their physical manifestations, and I couldn't take my stinging eyes off them as they began their assault on Katherine.

I wasn't going to let them have all the fun. It felt like every heartbeat was tearing another chunk of strength out of me, but I forced myself to focus on the thrum of Chaos within me. I closed my eyes and grasped for those pulsing threads and clung on with every ounce of willpower I possessed. Pain throbbed behind my eyes, making it hard to see, but I knew exactly where Katherine stood. With a wrench that almost sent me tumbling to the ground, I forced out a barricade of Fire.

It careened into Katherine, and she shrieked and struggled to throw up a forcefield to stop it. She stared at me through the wall of flames, just about managing to fend them off. She was afraid, completely thrown for a loop. *Now let's see how you like it against the ropes.*

"Get her!" I commanded, in that same eerie tone. I forced one agonizing foot in front of the other.

"They can't kill me!" Katherine shouted back.

Fire stomped through her forcefield with a fiery leg, making her topple backward.

"Maybe not, but they can make what remains of your mortal life a misery!" I hissed, blood spitting from my mouth.

Fire pulled what I thought was a smirk and smacked into Katherine's face with a blazing punch. A strangled growl clawed out of her throat as her head snapped backward. Magic spiraled frantically out of her hands and surged toward Gaia's Children, but she was barely holding onto her body now. There was more black and speckled light than skin, and golden beams had begun to pierce through her dress. Big flakes of flesh sloughed away and crumbled on the ground, turning to ash. *Ashes to ashes...*

Heaving energy into my palms, I slammed an explosion of all four elements into her at once. Her mouth gaped as she tried to breathe through a tornado of water while simultaneously fending off my other three elements—and Gaia's Children who joined the attack. My lungs were on fire, my brain felt like it was going to burst out of my skull, and my legs had gone into shaking, stumbling autopilot. But the sight of her finally floundering spurred me on. That, and the knowledge that if I stopped now, so would my heart.

Because I wasn't in a much better state than Katherine. We were both hanging on by a thread, despite the Chaos driving me. And a creeping, terrifying cold was edging deeper and deeper into my core. Katherine no longer had her hold over me, but Death—the entity that came for all of us in the end—had been summoned, and he wouldn't leave without the life that was owed.

But at least I could make sure Katherine came with me.

TWENTY-NINE

Finch

"Now would work well for me. Y'know, anytime *in the next ten seconds, really!*"

We'd completed the spell, so all that was left was for him to reveal the terms. *Why the freakin' heck is he stalling?!*

I tried to keep the anxiety out of my voice. I wasn't scared about Erebus's deal—well, not really. I barely even wanted to hear the terms at this point. I was too petrified for Harley. She was struggling like hell against Katherine, looking like the living dead, giving everything she had. Every time she drooped, she dragged her head right back up again. But she didn't look like she had much strength left. And I wasn't going to stand here and watch her die. Stepping into her place was supposed to stop that! How she was doing this with just the Hermetic Battery, I didn't know. It was like something else had possessed her. Something raw and furious, forged out of survival itself.

Erebus chuckled. Everything seemed to amuse him. He clearly didn't get out much. "Why the rush? Surely it will be more satisfying if I make you wait a while longer?"

"Kind of on a deadline, Erebus. Emphasis on the 'dead!'" It was hard to read the expressions of these two Children, as their faces phased in and out of the smoke and liquid light they'd poured into their human molds.

"You should be careful what you wish for," Lux warned.

"What, are you genies now? Should I be rubbing your lamps?" I glared at the Children. "I need to get on with this, ASAP! So if you *need* to tell me the terms, spit them out so we can crush my mother into the dirt. Capiche?"

"You have such a fiery spirit," Erebus mused. "Even more tantalizing than your sister. But very well. Here are my terms: I want you to be in my service, indefinitely. You will serve me until such a time as I decide I am finished with you, if you want me to defeat Katherine. If you refuse these terms, I have the divine right to kill you, right here, right now."

I felt like the air had been sucked out of me. "But that could mean I have to serve you for the rest of my life."

"Your point being?" Erebus's red eyes flashed. "It would be a shame to have to kill you, so I hope you will accept without delay. You were the one rushing me, remember?"

I glared at him, trying to cover my fear. "Touché."

"There are *so* many things a Child like me can do when cutting a deal with magicals," Erebus continued. His smoke billowed as if he were enjoying this a little too much. "I draw power from them. And it also livens up immortality. Everlasting existence can get so very dull. I may not wish to traverse the land of the living and the land of the eternal beings the way Katherine does, but I like to dip my toe in every now and again. Striking these sorts of deals allows me that ability, when a need or a desire arises. So, what do you say?"

"Are you sure Katherine won't still be able to do that?"

Erebus shook his smoky head. "Not if you accept. Katherine will be killed in her mortal *and* immortal states. Sounds like an oxymoron, I know, but a Child is capable of killing that which is immortal if they take control of a mortal body. Complicated stuff, but it will make sense once you agree. Essentially, Katherine will be killed, and she will not be able to return in any form."

"If you want to save your sister, you must decide before it is too late," Lux urged.

So, I was going to let Erebus become my master. No biggie, right? *Yeah, right.* Of course it was a biggie, but I couldn't show him I was scared, and I couldn't worry about the minutiae now. I glanced back at Harley. Her face was so pale and drawn she almost looked like a corpse. I needed to swallow my personal anxieties and get on with it, before she caved in completely. Servitude was a grim notion, but at least we would both get to live if I did this. I might have been separated from my sister for nineteen-odd years, but we'd been put on this earth to fight together. The Grimoire knew that, and now I did, too. This was my purpose. Harley had been the hero for so long, and now it was time for someone else to take the weight. *I love you, Sis. Hold on... I'm coming.*

I sucked in a sharp breath, my mind racing. "If it means Katherine dies and my sister lives, then so be it." I nodded. An idea sprang into my head—one that might help Harley. "Yeah... let's do it. Let's do the deal. Although, can I add a proviso?"

"What?" Erebus eyes flashed again.

"Harley has to live, or all of this is null and void." If this was a deal, it was only fair I added my own terms. I needed Harley to survive.

"Fair is fair," he replied. "I agree to your proviso."

I smiled. "Then, I accept."

"Good. I was starting to think you were having second thoughts." He cackled in delight.

A moment later, booming thunder clapped above us.

"I approve the deal, with its proviso," Lux announced.

"So, what happens n—"

I didn't get to finish, as Erebus suddenly spiraled up in a tornado. He came hurtling down toward me and pummeled straight into my mouth until I couldn't breathe. As my eyes filled with black mist, the rest of me disappeared into deep, dark oblivion.

Goodnight, sweet prince.

I didn't know what I'd find when I woke up. It wasn't in my hands anymore. My hands, and everything else, now belonged to Erebus.

THIRTY

Harley

Katherine sent a shockwave of Telekinesis back through my own lasso. My hands jolted as if burned. The pain stole the breath out of my lungs, not that I had much to begin with. All of the veins beneath my skin pushed to the surface, threatening to explode, until there was a web of crimson throbbing just under my fragile flesh.

I was literally falling apart, just like Katherine.

A few of the veins cracked, the blood trickling out and dripping onto the blue grass. As I fought for air, the strands of my Telekinesis loosened, and Katherine dropped to the ground, conjuring a huge, swirling wall of protective magic. But I wasn't frightened by a little forcefield. I wasn't frightened of anything, anymore.

"Break it down!" I howled, my eyes bulging.

I felt a wetness on my cheeks and reached to wipe it away. When I brought my shaky hand back down, my fingertips were slicked with blood. *It doesn't matter... It doesn't matter...* I repeated the mantra as I pushed out strands of Chaos from my palms. The bronzed tendrils felt like broken glass within my veins as I drew them out, like they were being raked along my insides.

The Elementals obeyed my every word as if they were Purge beasts.

They hammered down on the forcefield, using every Elemental power in their playbook. Katherine glowered at them, singed and muddied and drenched, light pulsing out of her in a glaring fury. Well, she wasn't the only one who was pissed. Renewed anger pounded through me more intensely than any impact the Elementals could land, making my Chaos jitter violently as I joined them in attacking the forcefield. I screamed louder with every burst of energy I spent, feeling like I was hurling my body into a concrete wall each time, the ricochets rocketing through me until I felt my own skin start to rip. But I didn't stop. Adrenaline, Chaos, and rage kept me going, thundering blasts into the forcefield until shimmering holes started to appear in the fabric of it.

"Learn when you're defeated!" I shouted, my whole body trembling.

A giant tear split up the side of the forcefield, giving Air and Fire the opportunity to slip inside and dart toward Katherine.

"I'm still standing, aren't I?" she wheezed back, casting out a bombardment of Telekinesis that sent Air and Fire scattering.

"Barely." I blinked the blood from my eyes. "Earth, Water—get her!"

Obeying my Darkness' command, they stalked toward their prey, giving Katherine no choice but to retaliate. As she lifted her hands to defend herself, light burst out of her in a surging blaze of white heat and glaring sparks that made me cover my eyes to stop it burning out my retinas. But I knew what that meant. This wasn't an intentional outburst. She couldn't hold herself together any longer. She'd been clinging to her mortal flesh with both hands, but those were slipping away, too. Literally. As the glare faded, I couldn't help but look as she descended into a panic. It rippled across the remains of her face like a kaleidoscope of horror.

Glancing over my shoulder, feeling my neck crack as I turned, I saw Erebus disappear inside of Finch.

"You can stop smirking," Katherine hissed. "I'm not done with you."

"Aren't you? I think... you're about finished, if you ask me," I croaked.

She shook her head violently. "No! I won't let you take this from me. All these years of work and blood and sweat and tears—you're not ruining it now!"

Before I could lift my hands to stop her, she released another pulse of powerful energy. This time, I knew it was intentional. She really was going to fight to the bitter end, even though she had to have known this outburst would drain her resources down to the last few drops. The blast was so intense as it barreled into the Elementals that it forced them right back and sent them flying. Turning her attention on me, she sprinted at me, her mouth opening in a scream. She was barely a few yards away when she suddenly skidded to a halt. Another figure had entered the game.

Finch stalked toward her, having appeared from nowhere. The protective barrier had fallen, and now there was nothing between her and Erebus.

"I still have time... I still have time," Katherine muttered, but everyone knew her time was up.

"You have been a busy girl, haven't you?" Erebus's voice echoed through Finch's mouth, eerie and unsettling. "Can you imagine my surprise when I found a Suppressor in here? What have you been hiding, you devious little minx?"

I frowned at Erebus's words. "What are you talking about?" I looked back at Katherine, waiting for some kind of answer.

"As if I'd breathe a word to any of you!" Katherine snapped. "He's weak. He's always been weak. I just made sure he matched his mentality."

"Erebus?" I turned to *him* for answers.

"Finch was born powerful. More powerful than Katherine, before she ascended, and just as powerful as you, Harley," Erebus replied. "Evidently, she wanted to find a way to keep her beloved little boy under control in case he ever betrayed her. A Suppressor fits the bill. That's my guess, anyway."

"You shut your mouth! 'Beloved little boy'—don't make me laugh," Katherine screeched. "What would you know about it? What would you know about anything I've done? You had your deification handed to you. I had to work for it. I did what was necessary!"

"What?" I gasped, trying to stop my body from shaking. With no fighting to distract me, I was feeling the brunt of everything. I wished I could shut my brain off, so all the pain would go away, but instead I had to stand there and try to endure it.

"I should've killed Finch when I had the chance," she said, seething. "I should've known Chaos would try to screw me, yet again. I should've known Hiram would come back to bite me in the ass. His blood is rotten, and so is Finch's! I should've smothered him as a baby, to stop him from ever becoming a part of Chaos's little plan!" She glowered at Erebus. "My own son is going to kill me now, is that it? Is this Chaos's last dig at me, after screwing me royally from the get-go?"

"You've got that right," Erebus replied.

"Do you expect me to beg for mercy?" Bitterness glittered in Katherine's eyes, a smirk twisting up the corners of her broken mouth.

Erebus cackled. "No, you relinquished your right to mercy a long time ago. Now I'm going to give Finch what he has always been owed —the gift you took from him."

I could almost hear the Suppressor snap as Erebus took full control of Finch's limitations, ridding him of them completely to get hold of all that untapped power. Breaking a Suppressor was a violent and dangerous undertaking—my own struggles were proof of that—but this was a different ballgame altogether. Erebus had been the one to snap it, and I didn't know if that would make it better or worse. I hoped Erebus would be the one bearing the brunt of the release, because if anyone could withstand it, it was a Child of Chaos. But what if it was only a temporary measure, leaving Finch with the same struggles as I had when mine broke, once Erebus left him again? However this played out, I just prayed Finch would pull through it in one piece.

"All this… it was always supposed to lead to this…" A strange laugh strangled in Katherine's throat as she looked at Erebus. "Chaos made me believe I could become a goddess if I just jumped through the flaming hoops. Did I not do everything it asked of me? Did I not give everything to become this world's savior? Does it not see what I'm trying to do? Does it not see the bigger picture, in which magicals will reign supreme? Does it want us to be subservient to mere humans for the rest of our days? It has built me up, letting me believe dominion was possible... but it never intended to let it happen." She smiled sourly. "But perhaps I should've known. Myths and legends are mythical and legendary for a reason. There is no room for dreamers in this world. There is no place for those who want to shatter the status quo. Chaos is weak and cowardly! Chaos couldn't stand to see me rise to my true glory, so it decided to shaft me at every turn! It's jealous and feeble, and you're all fools if you believe you'll be better off without me!" Her voice rose to a fever pitch, and I stared at her in disbelief.

Even now, with her body on the brink of decimation, she couldn't accept she was wrong. But this was the closest to surrender we'd ever get. Her expression showed a defiant woman who would keep her chin up until there was nothing left of her. Nevertheless, there was nothing else she could do to stop this from happening. She knew it, and we knew it. This was it... the end of Katherine Shipton.

THIRTY-ONE

Finch

Sitting in the passenger seat of my own body wasn't exactly what I'd call a smooth ride. I was still there... sort of. It was like watching from the front row of a movie theater, everything too big and in your face, and kind of squiggly.

Actually, to be honest, it was more like I was Alex DeLarge in *A Clockwork Orange*—the movie, not the book—with my eyes pried open by some nefarious metal contraption, forced to do nothing but watch as Erebus did his thing. I could hear everything. I wondered if Mother Dearest knew that, given what she'd just admitted.

I'm... powerful? I got a bit of a hint when the Suppressor snapped, thanks to Erebus and his devil-may-care attitude. He'd busted that thing wide open without a care in the world. And, while I might have been in the passenger seat, I could friggin' feel everything. And that included a nuclear-sized explosion going off inside me. If it hadn't been for Erebus using his Child of Chaos clout as a buffer, I'd have been annihilated—black goo or no black goo.

With the explosion still pulsing through me like a relentless tidal wave, my cells jangling like windchimes in a hurricane, I tried to find a way to speak to Erebus.

"You realize I can feel that, right?" I sent out the mental message and hoped we were symbiotically linked enough for him to hear me.

"I had to break it," came his reply, in the form of a wispy echo. "I didn't want to limit all that glorious Chaos. You will thank me when I use it to end Katherine, as you desired."

Semi-satisfied, I sank back into my piggybacking position. If I was lucky enough to get my powers back after this, if Chaos was somehow restored to everyone it had been taken from, I was going to have a bunch of new things to learn. *Who knows what powers be lurkin' in this here body?* My initial thoughts were of excitement. But then the worry kicked in, like an over-attentive soccer mom. I'd seen Harley battle her way through the aftermath of a Suppressor snap, and it hadn't been pretty.

Then again, in my Reading, it'd said I only had Darkness in me. I'd taken that literally, as a sixteen-year-old kid with a psycho mother. But now, I finally understood that Darkness was more nuanced. It didn't mean you had to be bad. I only had Darkness to contend with, and since Erebus had borne the brunt of the energy snap, then maybe I'd be okay? Maybe it would be easier for me?

There was only one way to find out, and we had to get through this first.

"Are you prepared for this?" Erebus's voice echoed in my head again.

I smiled. Well, I imagined myself smiling, since Erebus had control of my face. "Oh yeah, you bet I am. This is two decades in the making."

Oh, the evil betrayal of it all. The control she'd wielded over me, all these years. Even now. I'd never have known about the Suppressor if Erebus hadn't snapped it for me. Yeah, she'd given birth to me, but that didn't make her a mother. She'd ruined my life in every way she could. She'd taken love from me. She'd taken family from me. She'd made me believe I was born wrong. Then, to add the evil sprinkles to the top of her cupcake of torment, she'd taken my true power from me. It didn't matter that I might get it back now. It was too late for redemption. She was all villain, right to the last page.

I had no mercy left, and no sympathy. Ironically, she'd torn that out of me, too. All I had left, as far as she was concerned, was hatred. A smattering of disgust. And a bucketload of anger. She'd manipulated me from day one. She'd been so afraid of a tiny baby that she'd made it her life's mission to make sure that baby grew up feeling lost and alone and devoid of affection, desperate and willing to do just about anything for a glimmer of love. *And worthless, let's not forget worthless.* Yeah, thanks, brain.

Katherine stared at me, her face huge on my internal screen. "Don't do this, Finch. I know you're in there somewhere, and I know you've got the power to overcome Erebus." Her voice trembled, which threw me for a loop. "You're my son. I've been a terrible mother to you, I know that, but that doesn't mean I don't love you. I've always loved you! I kept you alive because I love you, and I want you to be at my side again. It doesn't make sense without you, Finch. I realize this seems like some pretense to get you to call Erebus off, but it isn't. It's the truth. I stood on a bridge with you growing in my belly, and I didn't jump because I loved you too much. My life didn't matter to me then, but I couldn't bear the thought of ending yours before it had begun. Please, Finch… have mercy on your mother!"

One last shot at survival, Mom? She really was pathetic. It might have worked on me if I hadn't met Harley. Heck, it might have worked if she hadn't murdered Adley, then had Weeping Willow try to murder me. But there was too much water under the bridge, and she could drown in it for all I cared.

"Finch?" Erebus's voice echoed in my head again.

"She can go to hell," I replied.

"As you wish." *Is this guy sure he's not a genie?*

Erebus chuckled as if he heard what I was thinking. A moment later, my body moved forward. A surge of power detonated through me, explosions going off in every available vein. My body bolted forward at supersonic speed, with a crazy Child of Chaos at the wheel. I caught a glimpse of Katherine's shocked expression as Erebus, via me, barreled into her and tackled her to the ground. She was pretty much helpless, as she deserved to be.

Whole pieces of her body were falling away now as Erebus landed a sucker punch to her stomach. It was the first of many in a brutal barrage. She tried to fight back with the specks of energy she had left, but her attacks didn't even seem to touch Erebus. He just kept going. Every harrowing smack he delivered was loaded with burning white Chaos energy, vicious and sparking. Every blow broke off another slice of her until there was nothing left of her body but pure light, light seeping out of a thick, black ooze. Through my half-blinded vision, blurred by the bright light, I saw that her face wasn't much better.

"Stop this, Finch!" she begged.

"You did this to yourself!" I roared, my voice coming out of my mouth in Erebus's weird, booming tone.

"I'll be better. I'll stop. I'll stop all of this if you just let me live!"

"Did you stop when everyone you killed pleaded for their lives?" I spat back. She didn't mean a word of it. Did she think I was stupid? The moment I released her, she'd be off trying to get Harley's body again. Or mine. No, she'd made her damn bed. Now she could lie in it.

"I was wrong, Finch. I thought I could do this, but Chaos never wanted me to. I'll accept my fate. I'll be trapped in the otherworld for the rest of eternity, and I won't make a peep. Just let me live. Even in that form. Please, let me live!"

As Erebus landed another blow, the rest of her face fell away, leaving two eyes and a mouth in a void of oily black. She looked horrifying, but at least now her appearance matched the blackness of her soul. If she could hold a mirror up to herself now, she'd see what she really was. A dark, evil monster. And there was only one place for monsters to go. She was fresh out of second chances.

"Erebus, finish her," I said within myself.

"With pleasure," Erebus replied. He reeled back, his fists glowing bright white.

"This is for my father!" I shouted out of my possessed mouth as Erebus landed his punch. "And this is for my sister!" Another blow landed. "And this is for everyone you've ever hurt! And everyone who begged for their lives and were killed anyway!"

Erebus's glowing fist smacked into Katherine's chest. Only, the solid wall of flesh that should've been there wasn't anymore. It pummeled right through her chest and came out the other side, billowing with black smoke.

She gaped up at me, her eyes wide. The hole in her chest blackened further, blotting out the glowing beams completely. The darkness spread like a rapid disease, hardening the ooze and sputtering out the specks of light. Her mouth opened in a startled "O" as if she wanted to say something, but the disease hit her before she could, leaving her in that open-mouthed, silent scream as her entire body turned into what could only be described as charcoal. It started to crumble away immediately, leaving chunks and piles of black dust on the blue grass beneath her. Her chest then caved in, until there was nothing left but an emerald dress filled with ash.

That was it. That was the end of Katherine. It had all happened so quickly that it didn't seem real. I expected her to rise up again and give that telltale cackle.

But she didn't.

Her body stayed as dust on the ground, and a gentle breeze started to blow it away across Elysium. There was a weird irony to her final resting place. Elysium, in history, was supposed to be the heaven for great heroes and warriors, a reward for their good deeds on earth. It wasn't for evil, twisted wannabe goddesses who'd caused so much pain to so many people. Yet, here she was. Maybe she'd earned her place with infamy instead of heroism. This place was a mythological cemetery for legends, after all. And she would go down in legend, for sure, just not in the way she'd hoped.

Nothing was ever enough for you, was it?

I stared down at her cremated ashes. She could've lived, if she'd just accepted what it meant to be a Child of Chaos. She could have played her tricks, the way Erebus did. She could have dipped her toe into the mortal world, as Erebus had put it. But that would never have been enough for her. Even if she'd achieved goddess status, she'd have targeted the otherworlds next until she held dominion over everyone and everything. With that mindset, she'd been doomed from the start.

The funny thing was, as I kept looking at her scattered form, I found I couldn't blame her entirely. I blamed Drake Shipton for putting these thoughts in her head in the first place. I blamed people like Davin for encouraging her. I blamed my father, to some extent, for not being kinder. I blamed her family for the same reason. Compassion went a long way toward steering people off a certain path. I knew that firsthand. If it hadn't been for Harley's compassion, I'd still have been a furious, dangerous, embittered little man.

I wasn't saying that anything could've necessarily changed her course in life, but everyone had their turning points. And I wasn't saying that the majority of the responsibility wasn't on her shoulders. It was. But seeing her there, dead, made me think about what might've been if things had been different for her.

Would she have shown you the same sympathy? There was my trusty brain, kicking in again. The facts were these: she'd had every opportunity to stop, or to reach for a more attainable goal, and she hadn't. She'd harmed children to get here. She'd killed so many people. Her hands were drenched in their blood. And this was her reward. By trying to take everything, she'd received nothing.

It's better this way. You'd never have stopped.

One person had died so everyone else could live. Surely, that was a fair exchange?

And yet, suddenly, I felt tears streaming down my cheeks. Erebus was still in me, but he'd given the reins back. And in that moment I felt it all, in a gut-wrenching bombardment of emotion. My heart hurt like it had been stomped on. Killing anyone was awful, but killing the woman who'd given birth to me... that was never going to go down smooth. She'd turned my love to hate, but they were two sides of the same coin. I could feel grief over losing my mother, even if I'd been the one to end her. Even if it had been a necessity. It hurt. And I knew it always would.

But... I was free. We were all free. And for that, I could endure just about any pain this world, or any world, could throw at me.

THIRTY-TWO

Harley

I blinked in total shock as I stared down at the ashy remains of Katherine Shipton. We'd focused our lives on her for so long that I wasn't even sure what I'd do now that I didn't have to worry about her anymore. It was like Columbus-syndrome—everything had been conquered, so now what? It didn't feel real.

I kept staring at what was left of her, waiting for the other shoe to drop, but it wouldn't. Could she really be dead? Had a Child of Chaos really been annihilated? Or was this some warped dream that I'd wake up from in a moment, to find she was alive and we still needed to kill her? Maybe I was back in the French church and this was a complex version of Euphoria.

I kept blinking, but the vision in front of me didn't go away. Finally, the pieces started to come together, making some sort of sense. Finch had finished the job that I couldn't. He'd done it. But he'd made a deal with Erebus in order to do it. And I didn't know what the terms of that deal were.

I glanced up at him, my whole body trembling with agony. I was a mess, and that creeping cold sensation refused to go away. Death felt like it was still coming for me, even with the harbinger dead on the ground. Finch was standing over me, watching me with a mixture of concern and affection on his face. I wanted to believe it was Finch, but his eyes were a smoky black, making it impossible to differentiate between him and Erebus.

"For what it's worth, you're still one of my favorite products of Chaos." Erebus's voice boomed out of Finch's mouth. "I would have liked to take over your body for a while, but these things always have a way of surprising you. You have such potential, even more than you realize. And so does your brother."

"What are you going to do with him now?" I asked, my voice barely a whisper. "What deal did you make? If you kill him over this, I swear to Gaia, I'll come after you."

Erebus chuckled. "Why would I want to waste a perfectly good magical? I'm insulted."

"He will leave Finch's body." Lux stepped forward, grasping Finch's hand tightly. "The task is complete, meaning he cannot remain within Finch longer. As for the deal, Finch's servitude will commence whenever Erebus demands it."

"Wait. What... What do you mean by servitude? Will it... Will it include taking him over like this?" I was struggling to stand, let alone speak, but I needed to know. This was my brother's life and welfare they were talking about. He wasn't just some pawn to be used, and I wasn't going to let up until I knew what he'd gotten himself into.

Because of me. Maybe it was guilt. Maybe it was sisterly concern. Maybe it was both.

"An impressive question," Lux replied coolly. "No, Erebus cannot and will not take over Finch's body like this again. Whenever their collaboration begins, it will unfold in a very different manner."

"Different, how?" I pressed.

"That is all I can say on the matter." Lux's eyes flashed coldly, and I sensed I had no choice but to let the subject go. It wouldn't stop me from worrying, though.

Erebus turned toward the Children of Gaia. "You—you might as well make yourselves useful, now that you've already broken several rules. Wipe out the cultists who remain in Elysium, aside from those with violet in their eyes. These ingrates are just as responsible as Katherine and must be duly punished."

"Wait... no." I dragged in a painful breath. "I know they've done wrong, but *killing* them is what Katherine would've done. Can't you do something else? There's been enough death. I'm completely *sick* of it."

Erebus paused. "You wish to show mercy, after all they've done? Some of these are ruthless killers, in case you need reminding."

"I know. But I don't want to see any more death. Mercy is what separates us from people like Katherine." I stooped, feeling faint.

He shrugged. "Fine. Then take all the cultists to the Garden of Hesperides. Again, aside from the ones with purple in their eyes. As that otherworld will be vacant for some time, they can endure their lifelong sentence there. They can rebuild what they destroyed and sow the seeds that will see it brought back to vitality."

"Thank you," I wheezed. I had no love for these cultists, but I meant what I'd said—I didn't want any more blood spilled in Elysium. A life sentence in an otherworld was a far better punishment.

Gaia's Children leapt into action, sweeping through the masses and gathering up cultists like sheep. Fire opened up a hyper-powerful portal, way larger than any I'd seen before. Through the gaping hole, I could see the barren wasteland of Gaia's otherworld stretching into the distance, letting me know this was a different sort of portal. It was more like an interdimensional gateway that led instantly to the other-world, like a great big chalk-door.

Air and Water moved around the back of the horde like two massive sheepdogs, and the four Elementals started to usher the cultists through the portal into what would become their prison. I'd expected them to put up a fight, but they seemed to know they were defeated. Their leader was dead, and the world she'd promised had died with her.

There was one face I couldn't spot, however... Davin's. He was nowhere to be found. I supposed he'd cut and run, likely portaling himself out of there the moment it looked like Katherine was going to lose. I had no clue how he'd managed to portal out of Elysium, given that you needed a Child of Chaos to get in. Surely, it was the same to get out? Then again, he had his ways of worming out of almost everything, so him disappearing didn't come as too much of a surprise. Besides, his lover was gone, and he had no reason to keep fighting on her behalf. He'd never even pledged himself. He'd always stated that his loyalty was to himself, and to the winning side. Now that Katherine had fallen, he'd run off to be loyal to himself once more.

Maybe one day, we'll cross paths again. He'd stay low for a while if he had any sense, and at least he wouldn't be able to fulfill Katherine's wish of summoning her, since there was nothing left to summon. But I'd break that "no death" rule, just for him. He'd wanted to stand at Katherine's side, so I'd make sure he could do that in death.

Unless death claimed me first. As Gaia's Children swept the last of the cultists into the Garden of Hesperides and closed up the portal behind them, leaving only the enslaved and our allies, I finally gave in to the pain and exhaustion. My shoulders sagged and my chin dropped to my chest, my head lolling. My knees buckled, and I hit the ground with a sickening crunch. I'd pushed myself beyond mortal means, and this was the price I had to pay. I felt completely broken. My bones were shattered, every inch of my skin was covered in bruises and trickling lacerations, and there was blood everywhere. I couldn't move without gasping now that I'd slowed down, and every breath was getting harder and harder to take. My body couldn't hold me anymore.

"Harley?" Wade appeared on my left and sank down to his knees. His fingertips gently lifted my chin, sending a shooting pain right up my spine. I cried out, and I saw his face contort with grief. He didn't know what to do to help me, and neither did I.

"I think... I think I'm dying," I whispered. The moment I said it, I knew it to be true, without doubt. Everything was getting very heavy and cold, to the point where my body was begging me *not* to take another breath.

"Don't say that," Wade choked. He touched me so gently, his finger-tips nestling underneath mine. "You've come this far, Harley. Please, don't give up now. I love you. I love you, and I don't want to be without you. You have to fight, my love. Please, please, keep fighting."

Tears trickled down my cheeks. I couldn't even lift my head to look at him. "I want to live, Wade... but it hurts so much. I... I don't know if I can fight it anymore..."

I felt him put his arms tenderly around me. He didn't squeeze, even though all I wanted was one last embrace. A proper one, so I could sink into his arms and go to sleep. That didn't sound so bad...

"Harley, stay with me." Wade breathed against my cheek. "Please. Stay with me."

"I'm trying," I whispered. "I'm really... trying... Wade... Hold me... tighter..." If I could just cling to Wade and focus on him, maybe that would keep me here... maybe I could... hold on... a little... longer...

"Tobe, get the Caladrius!" Wade cried out.

"I'm sorry, Wade. The Caladrius will not be able to heal her. She is too far gone." Tobe's baritone voice caught in his throat.

"We have to try! We're losing her!"

Tobe's beautiful singing drifted into my ears, and a moment later, I heard the sound of flapping. Cool air blew against my face as the Caladrius landed next to me. But it barely stayed a minute. The next thing I knew, it had lifted back into the air.

I knew what that meant, and so did Wade. So did everyone around me. The Caladrius couldn't fix me.

"Let me think!" Erebus's voice startled me, sending another jolt of fiery lightning through my every cell and nerve until I would've done anything to make it stop. This was beyond pain now. This was unbearable.

"I know there's an afterlife, but you don't belong there. Not yet," Wade whispered frantically, kissing my face. "Just because the

Caladrius can't fix you doesn't mean you're going to die. You have to stay here, with me and everyone who loves you. You made it, my love. You made it, and you're alive, and you're still breathing. So keep doing it." He paused, choking on a sob. "Don't leave me. I don't want to do this without you."

"I... don't think I have... a choice." My voice was slurring, and my eyelids felt impossible to keep open. "I love you."

"Harley, no... No!" Wade tried to lift my chin again, but my head lolled back. I got to see his beautiful face one last time, though his eyes were glittering with tears. He was desperate, but there was nothing anyone could do now. Love couldn't save us. It didn't have the power. I was going to join Katherine after all, though not in the same place, I hoped. She'd wanted it to start and end with me, and after everything I'd been through, it seemed as though she was going to get her final wish.

"Fine, I'll do it!" Erebus barked as I sensed Erebus-Finch sink down behind me. "Stand back," he ordered Wade.

"What? No," Wade choked. "I'm not leaving her."

"Then she will die," Erebus replied casually.

"You must do as he asks, as difficult as that may be." Tobe landed with a soft thud beside me.

"How do you know he's not going to finish the job?" Wade shouted back.

Tobe smiled and put his hand on Wade's arm. "Because he wants her to live, Wade. He is fond of her. Come away and let him work, or you may lose Harley forever. And that is something none of us want."

Reluctantly, Wade pulled away and stepped back, Tobe clamping his paws down on Wade's arms in case he changed his mind.

I didn't understand what was happening. Everything was a hazy blur, my vision close to gone. I didn't want Wade to move away; I wanted him to hold me while I went to sleep. Instead, I felt Erebus-Finch gather me against his chest and put his palm across my forehead. A moment later, I felt warmth pouring through me like molten honey.

It slipped easily through my veins, and I could feel it... repairing... replenishing... fixing all the damage that had been done.

My bones were set back into place without pain, the bruises dappling my skin started to recede, and the wounds and fissures that had opened up began to close of their own accord. Even the hideous markings that Katherine had carved into my forehead and my hand were healing. I could feel the skin fusing back together as if it had never been separated.

As the glorious warmth continued on through my body, fixing every little detail, I heard a voice whispering in my head. The whispers weren't my thoughts, and they didn't sound like Finch's thoughts, either. No, it was Erebus, taking a moment to speak to me in private.

"Your parents did the best they could, and you have made them proud today. I commend you, Harley. They would, too, if they were here."

"But... I didn't do anything," I mumbled back. "Finch killed Katherine."

Erebus chuckled inside my skull. "You fought Katherine until your last breath, and you brought *him* here, Harley. Not only that, but you brought him here as a changed man, capable and willing to do the things that he has done. I'm not one for sappiness, but I must admit, it was your compassion that altered him, putting love into his heart so that he would have the ability to read the Grimoire. It would never have allowed him otherwise. His act of selflessness opened the book to him when it mattered. That would never have happened without you and your love for him. It was always about you, from the moment my father took hold of your father's hand and had him write this spell for us all."

His words filled my head, making my heart swell with a shy pride. I'd never felt enlightenment before, but this had to be something like it.

Erebus moved back, the warmth still throbbing in my veins in an oddly pleasant way. I felt giddy, all buzzed on whatever he'd done to me. This was better than any painkiller I'd ever taken. I could breathe again, and my body felt loose and free, with no more aches and pains to stab at my insides.

As soon as Erebus stood up, Tobe released Wade. Wade skidded to his knees beside me and pulled me into his arms. Now that there was no more pain, I could hug him back the way I wanted to. My arms looped around his neck, and my fingertips ran through his dark locks as he buried his face in my shoulder, squeezing me so tight. I could feel his tears soaking through the torn-up mess of my jacket, and I smiled against his neck, knowing nothing could separate us again.

Over his shoulder, I watched the black smoke of Erebus abandon Finch's body. It twisted out of his mouth and returned to the earth in a spinning cyclone, the edges tightening to create his humanoid figure again. As soon as the smoke was gone, Finch lurched forward, coughing and gasping for air as if he'd suddenly been saved from drowning. Tobe went straight to him, wrapping his strong, furry arm around Finch's shoulders to keep him upright.

"Are you well?" Tobe asked.

Finch stared at him. "As well as can be expected, considering I've just had the Lord of Darkness using me as a meat suit. I'm going to need flushing out completely. Every internal irrigation available, I'm getting it."

Tobe chuckled. "It sounds like there will not be any permanent damage."

"Jury's still out. I feel violated," he muttered, but I could see a small smile playing on his lips.

"I enjoy a jest as much as the next Child of Chaos, but I'd advise you to be careful." Erebus's eyes flashed a warning that rendered Finch silent. "That said, what you set out to do is done. I will come to collect the rest in due course."

"Can you give me a timeframe, so I can make sure I haven't booked a vacation or anything?" Finch asked.

Erebus laughed. "No, I cannot. It will likely come when you least expect it, as all things do."

Erebus's words sent a shiver of concern through me. But, in that moment, his earlier statement managed to overwhelm it all... *It's done.*

Those were the words I'd been longing to hear ever since we'd started on this insane mission to end Katherine. I glanced over my shoulder to where the Grimoire lay, still open to the page with the three-part spell. However, the book had started to shift things back to where they belonged, the ink fading through the paper and taking the torn-off pages with it. A moment later, the book slammed shut on its own, everything back where it was supposed to be. Just like Marie Laveau had said.

"I love you," Wade whispered.

I nuzzled into his neck again. He smelled of blood and sweat, but I didn't care. "I love you, too. So much."

He pulled away slightly and gazed down into my eyes. "I don't ever want to lose you. Ever."

I smiled softly. "Neither do I."

He leaned in and kissed me gently, his lips grazing mine. I pulled him closer, that tenderness giving way to sudden desperation. I didn't care if people were watching. I'd almost lost him today, and he'd almost lost me. That was cause for a passionate kiss if ever there was one.

I sank deeper into the moment, kissing him feverishly as I felt his hands smoothing across my neck. I clung to him for dear life, my lips moving against his in a hungry rhythm that I couldn't suppress. I didn't want to admit it, but I supposed I wanted to feel something, after having my Chaos taken had left me so empty. I wanted to feel alive, if only to remind myself that I was. And he was. And all of our friends were... well, almost all of them.

I wanted this to be our happy ending: the villain vanquished and the righteous surviving by the skin of their teeth. We'd done it. The scrappy underdogs had defeated Katherine. So why didn't it feel like a happy ending? I kept trying to force the feeling, but the more I did, the more reality set in. It was painful and heartbreaking. So many lives had been lost, and they didn't get to have Erebus swipe his magic hand over them to bring them back.

I didn't just mean the people I knew. I wasn't just thinking about Garrett, and Isadora, and Tess, and Louella, and Shinsuke, and Jacintha Parks, and Adley. I was talking about all those people on the video footage whom we'd seen cut down by the cultists, and all those people who'd been "in the way" during Katherine's endless missions across the globe. How could I feel anything close to happiness when I knew the cost of this freedom?

Never again.

Those two words popped into my head, and a small, tremulous wave of hope washed over me. It might not have been the ending I wanted, with not enough of us here to witness it, but it was still an end to Katherine's reign of terror. A reign that would never be allowed to happen again. We'd make sure of it.

And, maybe, in the years to come, when the dust settled and every speck of Katherine was removed from this earth… maybe this would all feel like it was worth the price that had been paid for it.

THIRTY-THREE

Finch

I leaned into Tobe as I slowly caught my breath—a bit of furry therapy to get me back on track.

He had pushed the boundaries of his moral compass to make our victory happen, and I'd forever be grateful to him for that vial of goop. Just as he'd said it would, it had held me together. My body was thrumming with all this new juju, but at least I wasn't cracking apart like a chick trying to escape an egg. I'd have been the egg in that scenario.

"Can you stand?" Tobe asked, looking concerned.

I nodded. "Yeah… I think so."

He held out his hands as if I were a baby taking its first steps. On shaky knees, I managed to stay upright. My entire being felt like a battleground—pain, grief, exhilaration, newfound energy, and a hint of relief, all warring for the top spot in my brain. I kept expecting to go into a Purge, but it didn't come. Nobody else was Purging either, despite the powerful spells they'd been hurling around. I wasn't sure if it had something to do with our Chaos being borrowed through these Hermetic Batteries. But at least we didn't have to deal with a fresh crowd of Purge beasts coming our way.

The lovebirds had finally broken apart, ceasing their slobbering display of gratitude. I'd thought about making one of my usual repulsed quips, but they'd earned the right to munch each other's faces off a bit. So, I just waited until I was sure they weren't about to delve back in for second helpings. They stood up, Wade helping Harley to her feet, and I seized my opportunity.

Closing the gap between us, I put my arms around them both and pulled them in for a group hug. I felt their arms encircle me in return.

"Are you okay?" Harley asked, her voice muffled in my shoulder.

"I will be," I replied. "I'm sorry I took your revenge from you. I just had to. There was no other choice. When I saw Katherine kicking seven shades of… uh, sugar, out of you, I realized I had to do something, or we'd lose our shot for good."

I felt her smile against me. "I understand, and I'm not upset. I'm just worried about you."

"About me? Pfft, nothing to worry about here." It wasn't the whole truth, but times like this called for some white lies. If it'd been anyone else, they wouldn't have called my bluff. But this was my sister we were talking about. She knew a fib when she saw one, especially from me.

"I'm worried about the deal you made. That's a huge price to pay, Finch."

"It's better than dying, right?" I pulled away slightly and looked into her eyes. There were tears there. Smiling sadly, I brushed them off her cheeks. "Erebus could've asked for a lot more. In the grand scheme of things, I'd say I got off lightly."

"I guess he likes us." She chuckled faintly, though the sadness lingered.

"Which is why he could've asked for a *lot* more." I flashed her a grin. "Honestly, it's all going to be okay. You'll see. Katherine is gone, and the world will put itself back together again. Humpty-Dumpty style."

She frowned. "You realize nobody could put Humpty-Dumpty back together again, right?"

"Ah… bad analogy. But you get what I'm trying to say. We killed her, and she's not coming back. The world can heal now, and I doubt we'll ever have to deal with anything like her again." I paused. "Not in our lifetime, anyway. There'll always be psychos, but they'll probably be someone else's problem. We've done our part."

"Erebus told me the Grimoire let you read it," she said. "I thought you might've just memorized the spell."

"I had, but my memory is like a sieve. It's a good thing the Grimoire let me in, otherwise I might've conjured a twelve-foot bunny instead or turned everyone into toads."

True understanding hit me then, that the Grimoire really had given me permission to read it. I'd heard it whispering so many times before, but I'd never been able to look at the pages. Not until that last moment, when I'd needed to most. Did that mean my heart was as good as my sister's? Or did it just mean she didn't have to blacken hers by murdering Katherine? Either way, I'd done it to save her. Maybe that gave me some brownie points on the cosmic scale of things.

"How do you feel?" She looked up at me with sisterly concern.

I shrugged. "Still figuring it out."

"We're all here for you, if things get a bit… dark," Wade interjected.

"Thanks, Wonderboy." I chuckled, but Erebus seemed to have removed my funny bone for the time being. I couldn't feel much humor about the situation, though I was going to keep forcing it until it came back.

"What about the new energy?" Harley glanced over me as if she were looking for some obvious changes.

I sighed. "Who knows? Our Chaos isn't back, so maybe I'll never find out. And this thing is drained dry, so it's not like I can have a test run." I lifted my empty Hermetic Battery cuff.

"A world without Chaos…" Wade let the words hover over us like a big, fat, ominous cloud.

"Way to kill the victorious mood, Crowley." I tried to make it sound like a joke. But it was pretty much a fact. We had no way of getting our Chaos back. If Erebus or Lux, or any of those other Children, could've done it, they'd surely have given it all back when Katherine took it.

That wouldn't have broken any Chaos rules. Since that hadn't happened, it looked like we were stuck this way. The supernaturals would still have it, and the cultists in the Garden of Hesperides would still have it. But we magicals… it looked like that part of us was gone forever. We were human now, for all intents and purposes.

What else could we do? Use the remaining cultists as cattle and milk them of their Chaos to fill these batteries? Nah, that was a Katherine thing to do. Plus, we didn't have anyone to write legislature anymore. The president was in the Garden of Hesperides. And, until new leadership could be ordained, we'd just have to get on with things as they were. Devoid of Chaos.

A sound distracted me from my ruminations. A soft whimper, whispering across Elysium. I turned to find Astrid on the ground in the near distance, cradling Garrett in her arms. Leaving Harley and Wade, I bolted over to my fallen friend.

Garrett was dead. Really, truly dead. His eyes were blank. Astrid held his body in her arms and was rocking him gently. She didn't have any tears in her eyes, but her pain was palpable. The anguish in her hushed, guttural cries broke my heart. It was even harder to watch knowing she was trying to fight to feel more than she was capable of feeling. A glimmer of emotion had come back, but that emptiness inside her was still present. I could only imagine how difficult that was for her. Then again, as awful as it sounded, maybe it was a blessing in disguise. I was fighting to keep a lid on my emotions and failing miserably. Grief hit me like a freight train, pulling at my insides far worse than Tobe's goop. Garrett was never going to come back. Astrid might've had things she wanted to say to him that she'd never get to say, but so did I. We'd never properly patched things up. I bit the inside of my cheek to stop the tears from falling, but I could feel them stinging at my eyeballs.

I was a mess; Astrid was a mess; everyone was a mess. And Stonehenge was a mess, too, for a different reason. I focused on that to try and stop the grief from overwhelming me. The blue grass was covered in blood and bits of dismembered cultists. Murray's doing, no doubt. He was standing guard over Remington and the Crowleys, nipping at them when they tried to struggle. Diarmuid stood on Cormac Crowley's head, whacking him with a miniature shillelagh every time he tried to break free. Those curses Katherine had put on them had clung on past her expiration. Someone would have to remove them.

"Zalaam? Kadar?" I looked to them. Kadar had calmed down now that Erebus was outside the stone circle, just watching us with his shiny sidekick. I didn't know why they were still hanging around. Maybe they liked watching human misery. Or maybe they were waiting for the right moment to kick us out, like polite hosts at a party they were totally done with. Anyway, a bit of humanity had come back into Kadar's red eyes, and his skin was no longer pulsing, which was a good sign.

"Yes?" Levi replied.

"Can you fix them?" I nodded to Remington and the Crowleys. *A good name for a… ah, forget it.* This was too sad an occasion for my brain to make stupid jokes.

Levi frowned. "That will mean unleashing Zalaam."

"And?" I hardened my gaze.

"I was just saying…" he muttered sheepishly.

With a sigh, he handed the reins over to Zalaam. His skin turned red, and I saw smoke billowing faintly from his shoulders. Levi had this knack for doing something completely selfish right after proving himself to be a reasonably decent person. Wasn't it worth it to let the djinn out to fix some people in need? *Priorities, Levi… priorities.*

With Zalaam now in control, he moved toward those who'd been enslaved. There were a handful more aside from Remington and the Crowleys. Taking his time, he touched his red palm to each of their foreheads. A moment later, they started hacking up black tar from their throats. Each doubled over and retched violently. Zalaam held onto the strands of tar and tugged on each one until they were all the way out of everyone's throats, a look of disgust on his face.

"These are the curses," he said, lobbing the globules on the ground. Or "globbing" them, as I'd now refer to it.

The purple tint slowly disappeared from the enslaved ones' eyes as they regained their faculties. While we waited for them to come back around, I glanced at the rest of the Muppet Babies. They were okay, for the most part. Tobe had come back over and was starting to lick wounds in that unsettling, overly intimate way. The Caladrius was also flying over the remaining crew, drawing the injuries out of them and taking their pain and blood into itself in a flurry of gray ashes. The wounds healed up almost instantly, much to my relief. However, there was one face that still looked off color. Alton had sunk down into a heap on the floor. The Caladrius fluttered down toward him, only to fly away again, the same way it had done with Harley. Had it used too much of its magic to heal the others, leaving it with not enough to keep restoring Alton?

They'll survive this. Alton will survive this. He just needs more Chaos. His Battery had to be running low by now, which was why he was flagging. If only I could've said the same for Garrett. No amount of licking or Caladrius power or Hermetic Batteries could fix him. I kept trying to fight back tears, but I couldn't stop them now—they streamed down regardless.

Something finally seemed to click with the Crowleys. They jumped to their feet and hurtled toward Wade and Harley, throwing their arms around the pair. Remington followed a moment later, heading straight to Dylan.

"I'm so sorry, Dylan. I'm so, so sorry." He sobbed into Dylan's shoulder, gripping his nephew tight. If Dylan had any hard feelings, he wasn't showing them. Instead, he melted into a puddle of tears and hugged his uncle back. Once they'd finished their bittersweet reunion, Remington moved around to the rest of the group and hugged everyone else too, grateful to be alive—and not to have killed anyone he cared about.

The Catemacos were with Santana, who'd come back to the land of the living, thanks to the Caladrius. They hugged and cried and hugged some more. Nobody came to me, but that was okay. I'd said my piece to my family. Harley. The only actual, flesh-and-blood family I had left. These were my friends, sure, but genuine family ties would always take precedence.

And so, I watched as even Raffe and Levi hugged. This was good. This was how it was supposed to be. It was better than nothing, considering none of us had expected to get out of this alive. We'd all pledged to give our last breath to the cause, but we were still breathing, and our mission was over. Surely, that had to be worth it?

It would've felt more worth it if I wasn't painfully aware of Garrett and Astrid. It seemed perverse to feel like such a failure over one single death. But the truth was, one death felt all the more agonizing when everyone else was still standing. It was like one person in a team not getting to finish the race. I couldn't do anything to hold my tears back anymore. I didn't want to.

Allowing them to pour down my cheeks, I sank down next to Astrid and took Garrett's hand. It was already cold. Did that mean his spirit had left? It didn't matter. Neither Erebus nor the Caladrius could bring him back. And Alton didn't look too good, either. I didn't know why, but the Caladrius seemed to have abandoned him. As if he were a lost cause.

I buried my face in my friend's palm and let the pain out. He'd been my closest friend, once upon a time. He was the only one who'd never judged me. He'd taken me back after the stunt I pulled at the SDC what felt like a lifetime ago. But what right did I have to feel sorry for myself, when Astrid had lost her love? They hadn't rebuilt their bridges. Even without a soul, that would've been killing her inside. So much unsaid, never to be said.

"I'm sorry, Astrid," I murmured.

She looked at me as if she wanted to say something, but her face just twisted up into a mask of total devastation. She buried her face in Garrett's hair and gripped him tighter, rocking him slowly. "Garrett…

come back. There's so much we didn't get to do, and… I want the chance. I should've let you in… Don't be gone… please, don't be gone."

I felt a fresh stab of pain as I remembered when I'd been in her position. Katherine had robbed me of the chance to hold Adley in my arms like Astrid now held Garrett, but that hadn't lessened the pain I'd felt. If anything, it had made it worse. Back then, I would've moved heaven and earth for the chance to hold Adley again.

Though, even if I'd held her, it still wouldn't have felt real. Death always seemed impossible to those who still lived. Even staring at Garrett now, I expected him to sit up. He couldn't be gone. He just couldn't be.

A movement behind me made me turn. Alton had stood up and was staggering toward us. His face was gaunt, but tears were spilling from his eyes. Seeing his daughter in this state… it must have been burning him up. Especially as he was the one who'd made her like this. When he'd brought her back after the Asphodel Meadows, he'd brought her back wrong. A huge part of her soul was still out there, somewhere. And the lack of it was making it even harder on her.

"Astrid?" Alton said softly.

She shook her head and kept her face buried in Garrett's hair.

"Astrid, there is something I can do," he continued.

She looked up in surprise. Meanwhile, the rest of the Muppet Babies and their extended Muppet families edged forward. Curiosity had them hooked, and I was dangling from the same line, eager to hear what Alton had to say.

"What?" Astrid murmured, a hint of nervous hope in her voice.

"As a Necromancer, I was taught many resurrection spells. My ability may be gone, but my knowledge of forbidden spells isn't. And I've learned a great deal more in recent days—spells that previously weren't known to me."

He took a small box out of his pocket. I recognized it immediately. The ghoul bones. "And I still have magic in this Hermetic Battery to perform two last spells. They are the closest I've ever gotten to pure

Necromancy. But they must be performed now, otherwise they won't work."

Astrid frowned. "I don't understand. You can save him?"

I understand... And I had a majorly bad feeling about it. I knew what those ghoul bones did, and I'd seen the condition Alton was in after the last time he'd used them. Davin wasn't here to share the load this time, and Alton was already a few steps from death's door. The Hermetic Battery and the Caladrius had been the only things keeping him going.

"Alton, I don't know if this is such a good idea," I said.

"I didn't want to say anything before, but I am dying. I can feel the cold setting in. It started the moment I resurrected Isadora. This path was already set when I chose to do that. I have been on borrowed time ever since." He paused with a sad smile. "As soon as the last of this Chaos is used up, I won't make it to tomorrow. And I would rather use what I have left in order to help my daughter. There are two parts to the spell. One will bring the rest of Astrid's soul back, and one will bring Garrett back."

Astrid's eyes widened. "Dad... no, you can't. The Caladrius... the bird can help you."

Alton shook his head. "The Caladrius could only ever be a temporary fix, sweetheart. I spoke with the Bai Gu Jing when I brought Isadora back from the afterlife, and she made me a deal—she said I could live to complete our task. Now that it's over, there's only so long I can stay. Even if I got all my Chaos back, my days would be numbered. I would have a year at the most." He paused, brushing a tear from his cheek. "However, I can ask one more favor before the Bai Gu Jing takes me. But I have to ask it now, while there's still a chance I can reach Garrett. She is a generous spirit, despite what was done to her, and she looks kindly on women and their suffering. I'll ask her for this, and then I'll go."

"Alton..." Harley had walked over to us, and she looked about ready to crumble.

Astrid shook her head vehemently. "There has to be another way! How can I lose you? How can I gain him and lose you?"

"Please, sweetheart." Alton knelt beside her. "Let me do this one last thing for you. I can see how badly you're hurting for him. And I can feel how much pain you're in, having to live every day with part of your soul missing. What kind of father would I be if I didn't do everything within my power and beyond to fix that?"

"But Dad... No. Dad... " Astrid reached out and grasped at Alton's shirt, pulling him toward her.

Alton kissed the top of her head. "I have to do this now, darling, before the Bai Gu Jing comes for me and takes me without giving me the chance to ask a favor, and before Garrett's spirit crosses over, which will make it all the harder to get him back. Not impossible, but I might not have the strength to do both if I wait too long."

"No, Dad... please... don't leave me," Astrid whimpered. This went beyond the emotions that a soul could muster. This came from the blood that bound them. This was a bond nobody could take away.

"Tobe?" Alton glanced at the Beast Master, who nodded. Obediently, he took Alton's place at Astrid's side and wrapped her in his strong, furry arms. He held her there, rocking her like a baby as she continued to whimper for her father. This gave Alton the opportunity he needed to move Garrett away. I helped, though it still didn't feel right. This was Alton Waterhouse. What was the world, and the SDC, supposed to do without him?

Alton and I had buried our hatchets. I respected him, and he respected me. And it stung like a bitch knowing we were all about to lose him. But there was some method to his madness. If you knew your days were numbered, why not go out giving one last gift to your loved ones? I'd been prepared to do the same thing when I'd read out the deal spell. Erebus could've asked for my life, and I would've given it. That would've been my last gift to Harley. So who was I to tell Alton what he should do with his last breaths?

We lay Garrett down in the center of Stonehenge. There, Alton sat with Garrett's head in his lap and rested the box of ghoul bones on Garrett's chest. To my surprise, in another show of humanity, Levi sat down behind him to support his body, so he didn't have to worry about keeping himself upright.

"I will be here for you, Alton," he offered.

"Thank you, Levi." Taking a deep breath, Alton closed his eyes and began to perform his last magic on this earth.

As he settled into the spell, Tobe carried Astrid over and stood as close as he dared. Keeping Astrid firmly in his grip, he made sure she didn't have to watch. Shielding her face with his hefty paw, he watched with tears trickling through the fur beneath his eyes. Tobe and Alton had been friends long before I'd come to the SDC. This had to be hard for the Beast Master, too. I mean, how many loved ones had he had to say goodbye to in his long, long life? People came and people went, and he remained, set to outlive them all. How he was still sane was a mystery to me.

"*Baigu ling, tingcong wo de haozhao. Wo wen ni de cunzai. Yi ni de zhenshi xingshi lai dao wo men zheli, yibian yindao naxie yijing likai wo men de ren de linghun. Baigu jingshen chu xianzai wo men miangian, bing jiang ni de shouti gongji wo men xiang yao de ren.*"

Alton had begun, and there was no stopping him now. This was the saddest damned thing I'd ever seen. I had to fight to keep control of my own emotions. Of all the people standing here, my tears were the least important.

"*Wo you liang ge ginggju. Gei wo zhexie zuihou de haochu. Jiang wo nu'er de linghun dai hui ta shenbian, ba zhege duoluo nanhai de linghun dai hui ta de shenti. Rang tamen tuanju, wo hui xingangingyuan de he ni yi qilai.*"

As soon as Alton stopped chanting, the bones began to rattle and started rising up out of the box. They floated up and twisted in a spiral, hovering over the top of Garrett's body. Next, they floated toward Astrid, hovering there for a moment before drifting back to Alton. After a brief pause, the bones began to click together, forming a tiny skeleton. Then that disappeared as limbs and a body began to form overtop, finally revealing a beautiful woman with long black hair.

She wore a white dress that billowed, even though there wasn't a breeze to be felt. I'd never seen anyone like her. She was ethereal and stunning. Her body was translucent and showed the monoliths behind her through her skin.

Alton bowed to her, and she bowed back.

"Why have you summoned me again?" Her voice came out as an eerie rasp that didn't fit with her beauty. "Did you not understand the terms of our agreement? I thought to give you some more time to wind up your mortal coil, and yet you call me of your own volition. Why?"

"I have a favor to ask of you," Alton replied.

"A favor?"

Alton nodded. "Bring the missing part of my daughter's soul back to her, from wherever it is. And bring this young man back to life. Then, I will go with you willingly."

"They are in love?" the Bai Gu Jing choked.

"They are, and she can't feel anything properly without all of her soul. I made a mistake when I tried to save her a while ago. I didn't bring all of her back." Tears spilled down Alton's cheeks. "I want her to feel again, and I don't want her to have to lose her father and the man she loves in one day. That's too much loss for anyone to bear."

Amen to that. This was almost too unbearable for all of us.

The spirit paused for a moment. "And you will come with me afterward?"

"I will," Alton replied.

"Very well. I will grant you this final favor."

With that, she twisted up into nothingness and disappeared. Purple tendrils of Necromancy began to spiral around Alton, turning his skin as black as coal. He was holding on... just barely. The rest of us waited. I could hear everyone holding their breath.

The Bai Gu Jing returned what felt like a lifetime later. Beside her, she dragged two shimmering spirits. It was hard to get a good look at them, as their faces kept phasing in and out. But there was something unmistakable about their faces when they did phase in—a translucent imitation of their solid selves—that let us all know that the right spirits, or whatever they were, had been collected. She took the first spirit to Astrid and forced the shimmering entity into Astrid's body, then lay the other one down on top of Garrett. The spirit sank in, melding with his lifeless form.

"I have done my part," the Bai Gu Jing said. "The rest is up to you."

Alton nodded, and she moved back.

Closing his eyes again, Alton began to chant. This time, the spell was in Latin.

"*Facere quod perierat vincire cuius corpus. Ceteros loco, anima et spiritus redeat ad virum commovebitur. Tumultus duo, nisi sint unum. Et resurgent qui enim mortuus est. Et restituere illud quod capta esset. Reduc illas. Reduc illas. Et extremum spiritum meum erit eis. Haec ultima est agere. Is enim libenter dedi.*"

The purple strands spilled out of Alton and poured into Garrett, while a few stray tendrils worked their way toward Astrid. I watched their veins pulsate beneath their skin, glowing with purple light. As Alton repeated the spell twice more, his body suddenly erupted in an explosion of violet, the light surging out of his chest. It swept right through the stone circle, a glittering veil clinging to Astrid and Garrett.

A small smile lifted Alton's lips. As he took his last breath, he sagged backward into Levi. In synchronicity, that same breath exhaled right out of Garrett's mouth in a purple spark that slipped between his lips.

Before anyone could fully react, Garrett took a sharp breath and sat bolt upright. He was alive, and Alton was dead behind him.

"Come now." The Bai Gu Jing held out her hand to another shimmering spirit that had appeared. Alton, in spirit form, turned to look at Astrid. She twisted in Tobe's arms to meet his gaze. Tears streamed down her face, and every emotion washed over her in wave after wave.

"Dad, don't go!" she bawled. "I don't want you to go!"

"I love you." Alton's voice reverberated in a faraway whisper.

"I love you! I love you! Don't go!" Astrid tried to wrestle free of Tobe, but he held her.

"Let him go, Astrid," Tobe murmured. "He has done his fighting. Let him rest now. He was a true warrior, and he has earned his peace."

Astrid stilled in Tobe's arms and stared as the Bai Gu Jing came up to stand alongside Alton. The two of them vanished a moment later. All that was left was a small pile of bones on the blue grass. Alton had given the ultimate gift, at the ultimate price. He'd given his last breath for his daughter and the man she loved. If that wasn't the true meaning of unconditional love, then I didn't know what was.

THIRTY-FOUR

Harley

A strange mood settled over the group in the wake of Alton's parting gift. We were all rocked to our cores by the actions he'd taken to help Astrid. Everything felt bizarre without him here, and we were all dealing with the grief in our own ways.

Nobody had said anything, though Levi was checking Garrett over to make sure he'd come back whole. It was odd to see Levi taking the lead, but I guessed it was giving him something to do, to distract himself from Alton's death. They might not have liked each other much, but they'd been reluctant colleagues for years. Tobe was similarly distracted with Astrid, letting her bury all her pain in him as he held her. He was good at that, and it comforted me to know she was in safe paws.

With blurry vision from gathering tears, I glanced around Stonehenge. Erebus and Lux were still there, standing at the edge of the circle, looking in. I supposed we were in their territory, which was why they hadn't left yet. We were the trespassers. The rest of the Children they'd brought along to witness were still watching, too—Nyx, Uranus, Eros, and the Elementals. I was still waiting for Finch to make some quip about the second one in the list, but he was uncharacteristically quiet. I guessed he had a lot to think about. He'd almost lost his friend and his sister, he'd killed his mother, and he'd just found out he was as powerful as I was. Plus, he had no way of discovering his new abilities, since most of our Hermetic Batteries had run out of gas and we had no moral way of refilling them.

As I looked at the Children of Chaos, irritation bristled through me, setting my hairs on end.

"Why are you just standing there, staring at us?" I raised my voice at the cosmic spectators, done with their constant observation. "Why are you still here? Are you going to help us? Surely there's something you can do instead of just gaping at us all!"

"Help with what?" Erebus replied stonily.

I shrugged. "I don't know. How about you start by helping us get our Chaos back?"

Lux shook her silvery head. "There is nothing we can do in that regard. We do not have the authority."

"Then who the hell does?" I snapped. Chaos rules could shove it. I'd had enough of all these restrictions. I mean, who was running the show if these Children didn't "have the authority"? Chaos wasn't a physical being, as far as I could tell. How could they blindly follow something that didn't even have a form?

"Chaos," Lux replied. I knew what she was going to say before she even said it. It was their answer for freaking everything.

"Well, can you at least give us a way of bringing Chaos back, then? A spell, a hex, an object—*something*?"

"We cannot," Lux said. "We do not—"

"Have the authority. Yeah, I'm starting to see a pattern." I shook my head in irritation. "So, if you're not here to help, and you don't have the authority to actually *do* anything, then what the heck are you good for? Why are you still watching us?"

"We are very good at kicking ungrateful humans out of Elysium, for starters," Erebus interjected.

I sucked in a breath, trying to temper my emotions. Yes, Erebus had helped us big time, but that hadn't exactly been out of the goodness of his heart. He'd made some sketchy deal with my brother, which he refused to give me details about. Still, it wasn't a good idea to get on their bad side.

"We're not ungrateful," I said, steadying my voice. "But surely you can understand how frustrating it is to have all these powerful beings around us who can't do anything to bring back our Chaos?"

Lux sighed. "I understand your frustrations, but that does not change anything. We cannot aid you in the way you desire."

A murmur from Garrett drew my attention back to the center of the circle. Levi had completed his checks and had apparently finished filling Garrett in on everything that had happened since he'd taken a magical Necromancy dagger to the back. Garrett blinked slowly, as if he couldn't quite believe it.

"Alton did that... for me?" he said, dumbfounded.

Levi nodded. "He brought you back with his last breath, and restored Astrid's full soul to her in the process."

Garrett immediately searched for Astrid, his eyes finding her nestled in Tobe's arms. "I can't believe it... I can't believe he would do that for me. Is it true, Astrid? Did he bring your soul back?" He looked like he wanted to get up, but Astrid's words made him sit right back down.

She stared at him with tears in her eyes over the top of Tobe's bicep. "I wanted you to come back. I... I wanted it so badly. There are so many things we never got to say or do. But..." Her breath hitched, and her face scrunched up in pain. "But I can't... I can't look at you... and not wish my father was here!"

Her shoulders shook as she sobbed, and her heartbreaking grief could be heard all around the stone circle. This was what it meant to have all of her soul back. She was feeling everything now, at a time when she probably wished she couldn't feel anything at all. There was a bittersweet irony to it that clenched my heart in a vise. Alton had done this to allow her to experience emotions again with the hopes that Garrett could help her to heal, but he'd opened a gaping wound that would take a lot of time and effort to close up again.

"Astrid…" Garrett looked lost and confused.

"Give her time, Garrett," Levi whispered. "She just needs time."

We should have been happier than this, but it was hard to feel victorious, given the circumstances. Too many people had died in the fight against Katherine, and there was a whole world out there, filled with magicals who had lost all their power. Not to mention dealing with the remaining cultists. There would certainly be some who didn't realize the fight was over. There would be so many who'd keep fighting in her name, even though there was no longer any point. They still had their abilities—they didn't have to worry about a life without Chaos.

"How do we get de covens back?" Tatyana's mother spoke up in her thick Russian accent, shattering the uncomfortable silence. It seemed a bit premature, but it was nice to have something to focus on.

"Tobe can still get inside the Bestiary, so that's one way in," Remington replied. He looked like a broken shell of a man, after his zombification.

"And we still have some Hermetic Batteries," Levi added.

"Aye, and ye've got us Purge beasts." Diarmuid nodded, wielding his shillelagh.

I realized that was why we didn't feel victorious yet, aside from the obvious losses. It hit me like another of Katherine's punches. We didn't feel victorious because we hadn't won yet. There was still so much to do to fix what had been broken.

But, one way or another, I knew we'd make it, now. We'd pushed through the hard part and defeated Katherine. All we had left to do was regain the balance in the magical world, which she'd shifted toward her end.

Easy… right?

THIRTY-FIVE

Harley

"Can you at least see the human world from here?" I turned back to Lux and Erebus.

Lux nodded. "I can."

"How much of a problem are we facing?" Wade chimed in. He stood beside me with his arm around my waist. Right where I hoped he always would be.

"The humans still do not know there is anything amiss—for the most part," Lux replied, still cool as ever. "Your warfare has not spilled out much into their world. Aside from the covens being populated with cultists, everything is fairly contained."

I sighed heavily. "So, we'll have to organize our troops, so to speak, and potentially wipe a few minds where possible. Katherine disrupted the balance, and it's our job to fix it. Chaos just doesn't feel right like this, since she dispersed abilities that belonged to other people. We need to find a way to… I don't know, what's the word?"

"Reset everything?" Finch said.

"Right, reset everything." I paused. "But at least Katherine is done and over with now. You cut off the head and the body is bound to flounder. There might be some stubborn limbs along the way, but we can deal with those as they arise."

"Does this mean we can have Elysium back?" Erebus grinned through his smoky mouth. "There has been far too much human influence here for my liking."

"Don't worry, we'll be on our way," I muttered, glancing at Lux. "Actually, can you please send us back to the lake beside the Catemacos' cabin?"

The others looked at me curiously.

"Why there?" Santana asked, having somewhat recovered from her battering.

"There's something I need to see." I was worried about Jacob and Krieger, for sure, but there was more to it than that.

"We'll begin proceedings in de human world, if dat suits you?" Tatyana's father replied.

I nodded. "We'll catch up to you once we're done in Mexico. Can you send us to two different places, Lux?"

She scoffed. "I know you think us useless, as we have little authority over your Chaos, but that is frankly insulting. Of course I can send you to two different places. Portal magic is simple."

True to her word, she promptly opened up two portals. They were the same kind I'd witnessed Nyx use to bring the cavalry in. Through the sparking edges, I could already see the place we wanted to go. I stepped toward it while the rest of the Rag Team gathered around me. They didn't need instructing. We'd started this together, and now we had to finish what remained together.

However, there was an empty space where Astrid should've been. She was still safely ensconced in Tobe's arms, and didn't seem to want to leave.

"You should go with them, Astrid," Tobe said.

She shook her head. "I can't... I want to make sure my dad is... put to rest."

"You will regret it if you do not follow them, dear girl. Take it from an old beast who knows what it is like to watch their loved ones pass," he said softly. "I know you are in pain, and I know that wound will not fade for some time, but you must keep yourself distracted. Do all you can in their name. It is the only way to keep their memory alive. And I am certain it is what your father would have wanted."

"I... I don't know if I can," Astrid whispered.

"You can, little one." Tobe smiled at her and mopped up her tears with his paw. "You can and you must. You are fearsome, and you will endure. Time does heal, though it takes a while. Be with your friends. Be with those who love you the most and begin that lengthy process. Allow me to deal with the arrangements for your father."

Astrid blinked slowly, the rest of her body unmoving. For a long moment, I thought she was going to refuse again. But then she wriggled out of Tobe's arms and dusted herself off. The tears still hadn't dried on her cheeks, but there was a sad determination in her eyes. Taking a moment to breathe, she stepped forward to join us.

Garrett reached out his hand to Astrid, but she dipped her head and swerved away. "I'm sorry, Garrett," she breathed. "I need... more time."

"I understand," he replied softly.

I felt sorry for him. There was no way he wasn't feeling guilty about what had just taken place, even if he wasn't to blame, and that had to be a heavy burden to bear.

"You will join us back in San Diego, won't you?" Mrs. Catemaco called, sounding worried.

Santana glanced back with a smile. "We will. We've still got a war to end."

With that, we crossed the threshold of the portal and stepped out onto the lakeshore in southern Mexico. The mist-covered lake lay ahead of us, undulating in that same weird way it had been doing when we left this place. I turned as Lux followed us right up to the edge of the portal. She lingered there, as if she wanted to step through, and gave us an elegant bow.

"Are you coming with us?" I asked, surprised.

"No, I will remain here to ensure your families and those who were enslaved are safely returned. If you wish to see me again, all you have to do is summon me." She chuckled faintly. "Which is why you should not forget this."

She tossed the Grimoire through the portal, and I caught it deftly in both hands, clasping it to my chest like it was a long-lost friend. This was testament to how tired my brain was. Even after Erebus's healing, I'd almost left it behind.

I bowed back awkwardly. "Thank you, Lux."

"It has been my pleasure." I thought she was about to close the portal, but something made her pause. It was hard to tell with a face like hers, but it looked like she was staring at the lake, and the mist that had settled across it. With a bright laugh that sounded like bells tinkling, she beckoned to Erebus, who joined her at the gateway.

"No..." Erebus gasped. "Can it be?"

Huh? Can what be?

"There is only one way to find out," Lux replied. "Hello there!"

The black mist rolled away from the lake and surged toward us. I held my breath, half expecting it to charge right into us, but instead it stalled a few feet away and gathered itself together in a strange, hazy shape. For the first time, I noticed the true change in this place. I'd initially been too distracted to see what the weird mist was up to, to take in the rest of the scenery.

Everything had altered, just as Astrid had informed us back at Kenzie's apartment. The grass leading to the lake was tinged with every color of the rainbow, and all the flowers had swelled to five times their usual size. Blooms were springing up in all sorts of weird and wonderful species. The trees had spread out and grown rapidly until the woods behind the cabin looked more like a rainforest, with flower-encrusted creepers and fluorescent cracks in the trunks that pulsated with rows of tiny lights.

No matter which way I looked, I was bombarded by color. Petals the size of my forearm lolled in the breeze, each one more vivid than the next—reds, yellows, oranges, purples, pinks. Some of the flowers had a petal of each color.

And the creatures lurking in that rainforest were beyond anything I'd seen before. They didn't look like they were of this earth. In fact, I'd seen some similar creatures in the forests of Elysium, though they weren't quite the same as these. Fantastical birds with huge wings of red and white fluttered from bough to bough, crying out what sounded like a warning. Snakes with scales of blue and striking yellow slithered through the undergrowth with fanned-out heads. I saw one of those deer-like creatures, too, that I'd seen in Elysium, sipping casually from the lake. It was silver, with horns of gold that were draped in vines of vivid, almost neon, green. Speckled along its body were crimson and violet spots, which had the same bioluminescent pulse of the trees— not to mention the six legs that were holding it up.

What on earth had happened here? Or, more appropriately, what otherworldly thing had happened here?

"It is done, my darling," Lux said to the bobbing mist in front of her. "It is time for you to assume your former role and come back to us. There is an otherworld filled with wrongdoers for you to deal with."

I staggered back as the mist began to grow limbs, stretching out until it formed a slender feminine figure. It was a feminine figure that I recognized, though I hadn't seen her in about four years.

The mist was me... well, a younger, teenage version of me, with much longer hair, and she was completely naked, though her flowing red hair went some way toward keeping her dignity. Somehow, it covered all the right places, no matter which way she turned. As she flashed me a glowing smile, I just gaped at her in disbelief.

"What the—?" Finch said what the rest of us were thinking as he shielded his eyes.

Lux laughed. "Harley's first Purge was Gaia herself, reborn. We should have sensed her, but somehow we did not. I suppose we had other matters to contend with. But she is as you see her, alive and well. Through you, Harley, Chaos was able to react to Katherine's destructive actions and see Gaia salvaged."

"But… she's a teenager?" I croaked, struggling to find my voice.

Lux nodded. "She is in her juvenile state, yes. Soon enough, she will regain her full strength and continue in her duties as a Child of Chaos."

Gaia smiled. "I was dazed and confused upon Purging, which is why I manifested as a mist," she explained. "It took me a while to remember who I was and what I was. And here I am." She stepped forward and embraced me, which would've been pretty weird even if she hadn't been nude. "Thank you, Harley. Without you, I would have been no more. I owe my life to you."

I patted her awkwardly on the back. "It was the least I could do… I guess?"

"And Finch." Gaia moved away from me and opened out her arms to my brother.

"Uh, I'll pass on the hug, if that's okay with you," he said awkwardly, still shielding his eyes.

Gaia chuckled. "You mortals and your fear of nudity. Is this not how you all came into this world?"

"Not quite," Finch replied. "I was way smaller, and my hair didn't cover all the… stuff. And I definitely didn't have the… uh… stuff that you have."

"Nevertheless, I am grateful to you, Finch, for your part in destroying Katherine. It pains me to see the destruction of any creature, but there may always be exceptions." She drew in a breath. "And now I am able to restore all of the imbalance that Katherine has brought to Chaos. Now, I can restore everything she sought to unravel."

I stared at her. "You mean give us our Chaos back? I… I thought Children of Chaos didn't have the authority." I shot a pointed look at Lux, who just giggled.

"*I* do, in this instance," Gaia replied. "When Katherine defeated me, she took over my position among the Children, including my power. I am the one who controls the flow of Chaos, generally speaking. I can take and grant Chaos, but I choose to let nature make those decisions. I do not like to toy with the natural order."

"Can you bring mine back, too? I know Katherine was hoarding it." I didn't know what I'd do if she said no.

"I can. Katherine did not absorb your Chaos into herself by way of a ritual, and so it will be restored in the same manner as everyone else's. However, there is a more pressing matter I must attend to," she replied.

"More pressing then getting our Chaos back?" Finch murmured.

She nodded. "Yes. One of you is injured. I must heal you."

I glanced around the Rag Team in confusion. All of our injuries had been lapped up or sucked up by Tobe and the Caladrius. And mine had been taken away by Erebus. *Who is still injured?*

Gaia moved through the group until she reached Astrid, and all of us quickly stepped aside. Gently, she placed her hand on Astrid's head, and I saw a silvery light flow directly into her. As Gaia drew her hand away, Astrid crumpled to the ground. Garrett hurried to her side and put his arms around her, and this time, she didn't reject his comfort. She just buried her face in his chest and sobbed.

"What did you do?" Wade asked.

Gaia smiled. "I gave her an open channel to her father's spirit, and just enough Chaos to keep it open for a while. I hope it will help make the transition into a life without him a little easier. It is my gift to her, for her work, for her sacrifices, and for her father's sacrifice. Such selfless actions, borne of unrelenting love, must be rewarded. She will never be a magical, but it is the least I can do for her human toil. Although, I suppose I can do a little bit more."

Standing still, Gaia put out her arms and released a deep sigh.

An eerie whisper rustled across the lakeshore and beyond, unblocking the dam that had hoarded everyone's Chaos. I jolted as a surge of magic flowed back into me, making my cells tingle and awakening all those dormant powers that had been stolen from me. Looking around, I realized everyone was experiencing the same thing.

Chaos had come back. All of it. Every last drop.

THIRTY-SIX

Finch

Holy crap! Those were the only words in my vocabulary that came close to what I was feeling. Insane power coursed through me like lightning strikes. And this lightning was definitely hitting the same spot twice.

The Suppressor was outta here! It took Chaos to a whole other dimension. Thoughts were rattling through my head like an express train to nowhere, and I was left with some crazy jitters. With that Suppressor gone, I had a whole bunch to figure out. Not only inside of me, but outside of me.

All this excess chutzpah had come way too late in the game. To be honest, I didn't have a clue what to do with it, but there was a fight going on in my innards. Not Light and Dark, like my sister had experienced. This was something else. This was just my body going "Huh?" at all this fresh influx. My fleshy confines had gotten so used to just a smidgen of power that this was throwing it for a loop.

Where was I going to direct it all? I had no mission—not really. Gaia had pretty much done our last bit of work for us. The magicals had their power back, and they'd take the cultists to church for trying to infiltrate. I had no mother, which wasn't necessarily a bad thing, but

I felt a gap, a palpable one. I'd spent so long under her shadow that it felt weird to be out in the sun.

So, I was all dressed up with no place to go. I didn't have much else, aside from Harley. But there was a conversation coming. I could feel it hanging between us like an ugly black cloud. I'd struck a deal, even if it felt like a different me had made it. I'd promised to consider going back to Purgatory, to clean my slate the "proper way." Whatever that was.

All I knew was that if I went back into a glass cell, I probably wouldn't come out again. I'd be so strangled by red tape that I'd never see the light of day, and Harley was naïve if she thought any different. I still had "Shipton" blaring at the end of my name like a burglar alarm. I couldn't just call myself a Merlin and hope the stigma of my past would fade away.

Maybe I should skip out now, retire to a tropical island.

Man, I was worried. Really worried. I didn't want to go back to Purgatory. I liked my life now. How could the magical community throw me in prison again after what I'd just done? Surely, saving the whole magical and human world was worth my freedom? Not to brag or anything. It didn't feel brag-worthy. But I really didn't want to get locked up again. Not now.

"I know what you're going to say," I said. Harley had turned to me with that "I've got good news and bad news, except, there's only bad news" look on her face.

"I didn't say anything," she protested. But her eyes gave her away. There was a reluctance there.

"You want me to hand myself in, right? Like I promised?"

She shook her head. "I wasn't going to put it that way, and I wasn't going to suggest you go back to Purgatory at all. That ship has sailed, Finch. There's no way you're going back there. I was going to say that we should make a case for you, to stop them from *dragging* you back there, but we have to go through the proper avenues, or they could find an excuse to put you back behind bars."

I winced as another explosion went off inside me. My newfound power was really upping the ante. As quickly as possible, I shrugged it off. I didn't want her getting all mother hen around me. I had this. If she could get through it, so could I. Especially since I didn't even have that major Light and Dark battle going on. I knew Darkness was the team I batted for, and that swallowed up any Light that might've been trying to make its mark. Somehow, that made it easier. Just a bit.

"You know I only made that promise to get out, right?" I gave her a nervous grin as the sudden jolt subsided.

"I do, but it's no longer relevant. And it doesn't change what I'm saying. Stay and make a *case* for yourself. You destroyed Katherine Shipton. If that doesn't get you a free pass, I don't know what will. Just make it right, okay? Don't go running off, because I swear you'll spend the rest of your life running, and I don't want that for you. You bulldozed into my life, and now you're staying in it."

"But a tropical island does sound *so* very tempting." I chuckled, but my heart wasn't in it. "And I can always bulldoze back in again when the dust settles."

She put her hand on my arm. "Finch, you know you have to do the right thing. Don't make yourself into an enemy of the state, because that's not what you are. You're a hero. You saved all of us. You jumped in and did something insane, and I'll forever be grateful to you for that. So, don't make me watch them hunt you down like a wild dog. You're better than that."

"And what if it fails? What if they don't care? What if they just want to make an example of me because I've got that stupid name engraved on me for the rest of time?" I lifted my sleeve. "I've even got this ridiculous apple. It doesn't look too good when you think of it like that, does it?"

She sighed. "Okay, so, worst-case scenario, you skip out and go into hiding. But don't do that yet. This is a new world we're facing, Finch. Order still needs to be restored, and some rules need to be rewritten. If there are good people in power, you'll be fine. If not, I'll help you get away. But, right now, there are covens without leadership, Mage Councils without Mages, a presidency without a president... It's a royal mess out there, and we need all the help we can get to fix it." She gave my arm a squeeze. "And maybe, with those extra brownie points, you'll get to go home a free man."

"Home?" The word lodged in my throat like a gobstopper.

"Yes, home." She smiled. "With me. With us. Where you belong."

"I must go now." Gaia suddenly drew our attention away from each other. I still couldn't look. *Geez, put a loincloth on or something.* Of all the slinky ladies I wouldn't have minded seeing in the buff, my sister was *not* one of them. As she turned around to enter the portal, I wanted to pry out my eyes. I supposed I could just add it to the list of things I needed therapy for.

Gaia stepped through without another word, leaving Lux and Erebus to leer through the void. Erebus fixed his gaze on me, and shivers ran down my spine. There was only one reason he was looking at me like that.

"I will call upon you later, when the time is right," he said. "I always collect what is owed."

With that, he turned and disappeared back into Elysium. The shivers didn't stop. I had a vague sense of what I'd gotten myself into, but still... it wasn't a nice feeling, having the Prince of Darkness and our desperate deal hanging over my head. Why couldn't he have asked for something else instead? Like chocolate, or poetry, or a pretty, ancient artifact? I could've gotten my hands on something like that, no problem. But an undetermined sentence of servitude? The only comfort I had was that it had been worth it.

It is over... It was starting to feel more real as time passed. Without Katherine lording it over everyone, we had the space to rebuild. We could fix what she'd damaged. Plus, she'd opened up a gap that hadn't been there before. Ironic, really. From her vision of a new world, we'd gotten a new world, just not the one she'd intended. With the entire hierarchy in pieces, there was room for fresh blood to be injected into a worn system, and a chance at reviving it and making it into something better. We could all start over and find our own spots in the magical world.

I glanced subtly at Harley. I wanted that for her the most. She'd been rogue for so long, lost in foster care, deprived of her family, and not knowing where she belonged. And yet, she still gave a damn. Her experiences hadn't broken her. Nothing had. Life hadn't turned her cruel or cold, and neither had our mission.

Maybe I *had* spared her that. I'd seen the horror on her face after she'd killed Davin at the hotel, so maybe killing one of the people on her list had done her a favor. At least she wouldn't have to think about it for the rest of her life. Not like I was going to have to. And maybe this new world was the home we'd both been looking for our entire lives.

I dropped my gaze as Harley launched herself at Wade for another round of "whose tongue is whose?" but I couldn't help the smile that was forming across my face.

Whatever happens, Harley will be happy, and she will be free. No more loneliness, no more isolation, no more feeling lost. She had Wade, she had me, and she had her friends. And maybe that was enough to keep the darkness away.

As for me... I'd figure myself out, one way or another.

THIRTY-SEVEN

Harley

A month had passed by like a minute. And, already, there had been enough changes to give me hope for the future.

There was new, better leadership across the board, unifying the country and the rest of the world and making the entire magical community stronger. We magicals were still a secret from the humans, but that had been decided on by the people, for the people, with them voting that it was for the humans' benefit. After all, if a bombshell like that got dropped, it would only lead to further unrest. Something nobody wanted, right after the mess with Katherine. Plus, more security measures had been put in place to make sure nothing like this ever happened again.

Meanwhile, the gateways to Eris Island had then been closed up, with all the cultists living there now disbanded and in custody. The humans who'd joined Katherine's cult were jailed in Purgatory for life right along with the magical cultists. Even those who'd been taken through to the Garden of Hesperides had wound up being sent back to face the music. Some were still on the run, but they'd all be caught soon enough, and every single one would answer for their crimes.

The empire Katherine had built, and the island she'd called home, were nothing more than empty dreams now, never to see the light of day again. I suspected the secret services would have plans for it, delving into all of Katherine's lingering secrets and her wealth of books, artifacts, and research, but that was on a need-to-know basis, and I wasn't in that secret circle. They'd probably have to do something with Drake Shipton's pruney, half-dead body, too. I was sort of glad I wasn't part of that disposal.

O'Halloran had taken up the position of director at the SDC and finally moved his wife into the area, though she still had no idea what he actually did for a living. She thought he worked in the military, in covert operations, though he told her he'd managed to get a desk job. Apparently, that was enough for her—no more questions needed. Meanwhile, Tobe had restored his Bestiary to its fully functioning prior state. All the magicals had started to settle back into life as they knew it, now that they'd had their abilities returned to them. Thanks to Gaia, things felt balanced again.

Juno Laurier, who'd been a member of the California Mage Council, and then one of Katherine's zombified victims, was the new director of the LA Coven and now sat at the head of the California Mage Council. Levi had been reinstated as a Council member, too. Meanwhile, Remington was in the running to become the next president of the UCA. Dylan wasn't amused by the prospect—Finch kept teasing him about it and bowing at every opportunity, just to make him uncomfortable.

"You'll be the FNOTUC. First Nephew of the United Covens. It has a nice ring to it, don't you think?" Finch smirked from across the table in the Banquet Hall. The news had just come in that Remington was the frontrunner in the polls.

"Shut up," Dylan muttered. It was the hundredth joke in a long line directed at him, and I could tell the humor was starting to wear thin. But there *was* a hint of pride in Dylan's eye whenever someone mentioned his uncle's rise to power, and we all knew there was nobody worthier of the position than Remington. A good, solid, wise, unbreakable person was exactly who we needed in a leadership position right now.

In the interim, as we waited to hear whether Remington would get the job, posthumous medals of magical valor were granted to those who'd been involved and had sacrificed throughout this entire Katherine mess. None of our victories could have happened without so many people, and we wanted the whole magical world to know. This time, the heroes wouldn't be forgotten. I wouldn't let that happen.

Nomura had been granted posthumous clemency for his previous actions, his name cleared in death. That one had had hit me hard. I was crushed when I found out what had happened to Nomura, and what Katherine had done to his wife. Remington had been the one to insist he be given a reprieve, and I was glad he'd done so. All Nomura ever wanted was to see his son safe, and now the Nomura line was gone. Another proud name knocked out by Katherine Shipton.

The real Imogene had also been granted a posthumous medal of valor, and her death had been mourned throughout the magical world. It had come as a shock when everyone discovered she'd been imprisoned for so many years, with Katherine masquerading as her. Everyone's guilt was tangible, as they were forced to realize they hadn't been able to tell the difference, but at least the real Imogene had been honored for her suffering and her courage. And she would not be forgotten.

Alton, Louella, and Isadora had been awarded posthumous medals, too. Astrid and Alton's wife had been the ones to accept Alton's medal, but his wife had moved away shortly afterward. It was too painful for her to be at the SDC without him, and she hadn't been given the same fleeting gift of an open channel with his spirit that Astrid had been granted. It was clear she needed the separation in order to rebuild her life without her husband. I didn't envy her that mountain to climb.

Jacob and I had accepted the medals on behalf of Louella and Isadora, and it'd been a tough ceremony all around. Not a dry eye in the house. Like Winston Churchill once said the last time a great evil had threatened to tip the world's balance, though I'm paraphrasing—never in the field of magical conflict was so much owed by so many to so few.

That was the curious thing about the aftermath of Katherine's destruction. Everyone seemed to realize that they'd dropped a pretty huge ball. Nobody was without some responsibility, not even me and the rest of the Rag Team. And that weight of regret somehow brought everyone together, uniting a global network that had been in pieces up until now, with everyone looking out for themselves instead of tending to the wider picture.

Weirdest of all was that Katherine had made it happen. This unity was her doing, in a way. Trying to destroy this world had only brought us closer together. She had made everyone realize what they stood to lose if they didn't work together. Not that I'd ever give her any props for her part in it.

So here we were, sitting in the Banquet Hall together—me and the Rag Team, all of us back together in a way I'd never have thought possible a month ago. We still felt Louella's absence, especially Jacob, but life as we knew it was starting to take on some normality again. We were sipping coffee and lounging wearily after a massive dinner, but our bellies weren't the only things that were satisfied. As Freddie Mercury would have put it, we were the champions.

Yep, Finch has definitely rubbed off on me. But you know what? It felt good. We hadn't allowed ourselves much pride or victory celebration over what we'd done, but as the pieces started to come back together and the loose ends were tied up, that sense of triumph managed to pop up every now and then.

"How's your dad doing with the whole getting ousted thing?" Santana asked, casting a loving smile at Raffe.

It was nice to see him back to his usual self. The djinn still made an appearance when he felt like it, but it seemed like he and Raffe had come to some sort of agreement. Raffe was firmly back in control. Although, saying that, we'd have been in dire straits if it hadn't been for Kadar. I guessed all of us, even Raffe, were warming to the djinn.

Raffe shrugged. "He hates it. Keeps moaning about it. Says O'Halloran isn't equipped for the position." He smiled back. "I think that's why O'Halloran is keeping Diarmuid around, like a guard leprechaun. Just this morning, he smacked my father over the head with that shillelagh thing when he tried to tell O'Halloran how to organize the registry. You should've seen my father's face."

"I think he's still bitter about losing his pot of gold, and that's his way of letting off steam." Dylan chuckled.

Raffe nodded. "Small-man syndrome at its finest." He took a deep sip of his coffee. "But, saying that, I think my father is secretly glad he doesn't have to run a coven anymore. Being back on the Mage Council is more than enough for him."

"What about Kadar and Zalaam? They doing okay?" I asked.

"They pick a fight now and again, but they're on their best behavior," Raffe replied.

"Pfft, that's what you think." Kadar rose to the surface for a split second, making all of us laugh.

Even Santana seemed fond of Kadar these days. I'd asked her a couple days ago how things were going between her and Raffe, and she'd just given me this mischievous grin and said, "What can I say, he's a bit of an animal." So it looked like djinn and magical relations were going pretty smoothly.

Santana and Raffe were stronger than ever, and so were Tatyana and Dylan. Just now, they had their arms around each other, and Tatyana was leaning into his shoulder. It looked like the most natural thing on earth.

As for Astrid and Garrett... things were still a bit rough for them. They hadn't gotten back together yet, and it'd probably be some time before they would. I guessed it couldn't have helped that Chaos had returned right after Alton had sacrificed himself, meaning she could have potentially had her father for another year. Her father's spirit had only been a temporary comfort. His voice had faded as the weeks passed, and now she couldn't hear him at all anymore.

Most nights, she came to my room, or Santana's, or Tatyana's, and the four of us would sit there and talk through everything until we were too tired to talk anymore. Astrid spent a lot of time at Waterfront Park, too, talking to her mom in Cabot's to try and process everything. They both felt his loss keenly, but her mom was trying to help out, championing Garrett as much as she could while struggling with her own pain. I liked to think it had helped, but bridging that gap between Astrid and Garrett was going to take time. If it could be bridged at all.

They still had feelings for each other. It was obvious in the small things. Before dinner today, Garrett had carried Astrid's tray and made sure she got the last of the Black Forest cake, because he knew it was her favorite. And a few days ago, Astrid had tracked Garrett down to give him the Avenging Angel. There'd been some discussion about what should happen to the magical weapons, but she asked O'Halloran to let Garrett keep it. She'd even cleaned it and mounted it, so he could have it on his wall.

Little moments that showed they cared. Maybe when all the grief had subsided and wasn't so overwhelming for Astrid anymore, they'd have a breakthrough. After all, that had been Alton's hope in resurrecting Garrett. He'd wanted Garrett to take care of his daughter. But it had to be hard for Astrid to look into Garrett's eyes and remember that he was here in her father's place.

"Anyone heard from Kenzie?" Wade asked, placing his hand on my knee. He was a conservative kind of guy, but he'd gotten more used to PDAs after Santana had called him out on it. I believe she'd said, "Geez, Wade, my grandma gives me more love than you're giving *mi hermosa*. What is she, your accountant or your girlfriend?"

Finch chuckled. "She's back to her old tricks. You can take the girl out of the ghetto, right? Well, I suppose she's still in the ghetto, but you ghetto what I mean."

Kenzie had managed to get back into her body when Gaia had restored Chaos, but, as with everything else, it hadn't been a cure-all for everyone's problems.

"How's her mom?" Astrid stared into her coffee, as if it held the secrets of the universe.

"I spoke to Kenzie yesterday, and she said she was going to take her mom to Marie Laveau soon," Finch replied. "Fight Voodoo fire with Voodoo fire."

I smiled at my brother. He was in a good place, even with all of the extra Chaos thumping around inside him. He'd had a few minor outbursts when he'd lost control of his new powers, like accidentally setting fire to one of Wade's best suits, dousing Santana and Slinky in a torrent of water, almost getting his eyes gouged out after unintentionally flinging Diarmuid across O'Halloran's office, and growing a giant oak tree in the atrium of the living quarters... But, otherwise, he seemed to be dealing with it like a pro. Plus, he was still here, which meant everything to me. We'd all made a strong case for him within days of returning from Elysium, and he'd been pardoned by the Supreme Court of the United Covens of America. It'd helped a teensy bit that Mrs. Crowley had been one of the judges presiding over the case. Wade had definitely had a few words with her before the trial. Whenever I tried to pry it out of him, he just gave me a cheeky wink and said:

"Hey, your family is my family now. And what's the point of family if you can't pull a few strings?"

Either way, Finch was free and spending most of his time delving into his new powers, to prevent any more little accidents from happening. As it turned out, he was a full Elemental like me, with an extra level to his Shapeshifting prowess that gave him the ability of Mimicry—the power to emulate someone down to the smallest nuance, taking on their voice, their mannerisms, everything, without any prior research. I guessed it was similar to the way I was given the ability of reverse Empathy after my Suppressor broke. And it meant he didn't have to be a redhead anymore. He'd gone right back to that strawberry-blond shade, and I had to say, it suited him much better than the red or the platinum blond. It was definitely better than the frosted tips, even though I was sad to say goodbye to nineties boy-band Finch.

He'd also ended up with a medal for his part in Katherine's demise, and he wore the ribbon of it sewn onto his jacket like a military officer. That ceremony had been far happier than the rest of them. Finch had tried not to cry as he accepted his medal, but I'd seen his lips trembling and noticed the slight flick of his head as he tried to fling the tears out of his eyes. Finally, there was some good to be associated with the Shipton name. At least, there would've been if Finch hadn't insisted on changing his name to Merlin.

I preferred him as a Merlin and was proud of him sharing our dad's name. But, in the eyes of the magical population, he would always be a Shipton, and maybe that wasn't such a bad thing now.

Finch was happy. At least, he seemed happy when he was around us. I didn't know what went on behind closed doors. But he was powerful now. More powerful than before, with a mass of potential that I could tell he was eager to keep exploring. And he had people who cared about him, and a place he could call home at the SDC, with fancy new digs in the living quarters. He was about as reformed as we were ever going to get him, and that was enough for me.

In the last week or so, he hadn't been around as much, though. That sucked a bit, I wasn't going to lie, as I was worried it might become a recurring theme. He'd said he had to travel, without specifying the destination or what he was getting up to. He wouldn't talk about it when he was around and had shut down every conversation I'd tried to broach on the subject. "I was just away, sorting stuff out," was the most I could get out of him.

An even touchier subject was Erebus, someone I suspected was related to his recent travel. However, after trying a few times with that angle, I concluded it was useless to try and force Finch to talk. He'd explain everything when he was ready, and I'd be here, waiting to listen. Was it frustrating? Sure. Could I deal with it? I had to.

As for the rest of us, there was a lot of happiness to go around despite the people we'd lost. Wade and I were going strong, too... better than ever, in fact. I'd finally faced that terrifying dinner with his parents after putting it off for about two weeks, and it hadn't been terrifying at all. Maybe it would've been different before the big Elysium fight, but, with all that already between us, they'd welcomed me with open arms, and I finally got to see just how cool his parents were.

Neither of them had come into this world with much, and they'd pursued a better life for themselves and their son. It had taken them a long way, and I could see where Wade got a lot of his determination from, even if he did have a privileged moment or two from time to time. Like telling me off for not buying the good brand of almond milk, or trying to slide the waiter a fifty to get a good table. Not that he ever got away with it. I was good at grounding him, just as he was good at grounding me.

Krieger had officially adopted Jacob, and the two of them were thick as thieves, always in the infirmary tinkering away, doing something or other. Jacob had taken an interest in medicine and alchemy, deciding he wanted to pursue that instead of engineering, which seemed to please Krieger immensely. The books that Jacob always seemed to be carrying were getting bigger and bigger with each trip he made to the infirmary. Dylan had offered to carry one particular monstrosity for him, as it had been weighing poor Jacob down on his way back to the living quarters, and he hadn't known the right spell to help him bear the weight.

But having a goal was good for Jacob, and it made me happy to know he had someone he could rely on again—someone who wasn't going anywhere anytime soon. Krieger was definitely a good role model for him. Sixteen was a tricky age for any teenager, and it helped to have wise, kind people around to keep him on the straight and narrow and to encourage his interests. He'd always miss Isadora and Louella—all of us would—but we were here to keep their memories alive. Suri's, too, if only for Jacob's sake. He really had liked that girl.

Speaking of teenagers, and children, for that matter, the rare magicals Katherine had used for her final ritual had been safely returned. Those who still had parents and foster parents had gone back to their former homes. And those who didn't—they'd been welcomed into the covens closest to where they'd come from, many of them finding their place in the SDC.

Sadly, their Chaos couldn't be returned after Katherine was destroyed—she'd basically eaten it up. But, O'Halloran had made some exceptions to the no-human rule in the hopes that maybe, one day, some Chaos would somehow find its way back to them. Astrid had been put in charge of them as the new preceptor of Human-Magical Relations. This kept her busy, and I suspected that was the sole purpose of giving her the job, to take her mind off Alton. Levi could say what he liked about O'Halloran, but the guy was doing an awesome job of fixing everything at the SDC.

In fact, Ryann had applied for an internship to join Astrid at the SDC as an advisor, as part of its new policy to open up dialogue with humans who might be aware of or interested in magical behavior, but only upon careful selection. There were still mind-wipes and cleanup crews going about their duties to keep magicals as much of a secret as possible, but there was definitely progress. And, I got the feeling that Ryann's law studies would come in pretty handy to push the envelope even further. Mind-wiping was a moral gray area, and if anyone could think of a better way, it was my adoptive sister.

After the battle in Elysium, all three of the Smiths had been returned to their house from the interdimensional pocket where Tobe had kept them safe. They'd settled back into normality surprisingly quickly, with their admirable tenacity. Mr. and Mrs. Smith hadn't had their minds wiped, either, and they were constantly texting me and checking up on me to see how I was doing. At first, they'd been apprehensive about Ryann applying for an internship here at the SDC, but they'd come around, safe in the knowledge that the threat of Katherine was gone. I appreciated their aftercare, and I tried to do my best for them, too, making sure they were okay after what they'd experienced. So far, there didn't seem to be any troubling side effects, and I hoped it would stay that way.

"Should we head out?" Wade's voice derailed my train of thought.

I smiled nervously. "Yeah, let's go. I don't want to be late."

After saying a quick goodbye to the others, we walked through the halls of the SDC together until we reached the Assembly Hall. O'Halloran was already waiting for us, with one of the mirrors showing the newly repaired foyer of the New York Coven.

"I thought I was going to have to come and get you myself." O'Halloran grinned.

"Sorry, we lost track of time," I replied.

"Yeah, Chef's food will do that to you." He gestured for us to step through, and we did.

I took a breath as I looked up at the gothic architecture of the New York Coven. I hadn't seen the state Katherine had left it in when she'd decided to destroy the place, but everything seemed to be back to normal. A little newer, perhaps, but I wouldn't have known anything had happened here just by looking.

Walking quickly, we made our way to the Grand Hall, where four officials were waiting for us. Now that I had my Empathy back, I could feel Wade's nerves radiating off of him, making my own nerves jangle.

This was the icing on the cake for me, but that didn't mean I wasn't scared of the outcome. Walking up alongside the officials, I turned to Wade and leaned in, kissing him for luck.

"You'll do great," he said, brushing his thumb across my cheek and placing a gentle kiss beside it. "And I'll be right out here waiting for you when it's over."

I nodded, gathering myself and taking a shaky breath. This wasn't the time for nerves. "See you soon, then."

With the officials leading the way, I headed into the Grand Hall. This meeting with the New York Supreme Court of Magicals and the Special Pardoning Committee of the UCA was just for me.

I had to do one more thing, and I had to do it alone.

THIRTY-EIGHT

Harley

I remembered the last time I was here, when I'd come to get permission to enter Special Collections the second time around. It had been intimidating then, but I sensed this was going to be twice as bad.

The hall echoed with my solitary footsteps as I made my way up to the table at the farthest end. A panel of judges and lawmakers from the magical world sat there, staring at me. Apparently, they hadn't gotten the memo that they were supposed to make folks like me feel comfortable. I didn't recognize any of their faces, which suggested they'd had a bit of a roster change-up in the aftermath of Katherine, too. Maybe that was because some of them had skipped off to the cult and were now in prison, or they hadn't survived the cull when this coven had been taken over. Either way, they were still intimidating.

A smaller table sat a short distance in front of the long one, and I saw my name on a metal placard. A few reporters had been allowed in, and they were standing along the edges of the hall, their notepads flipped open and pens poised for action. A magical stenographer sat at a bulky typewriter thing, her fingertips caressing the keys in an unsettling way. My stomach was doing somersaults as I approached my table, sat down, and tried not to fidget.

"Welcome, Miss Merlin," the elderly man sitting in the middle of the long table said. "My name is Quentin Millstone and I am the head of this council."

I nodded. "Hello, Mr. Millstone."

"Now, you are here to make a case for your father's record, is that correct?"

"Yes… that's right."

"Well then, you may begin," Quentin encouraged.

I took a deep breath and let everything I'd rehearsed flow back into my anxious brain. *Compartmentalize, compartmentalize... this is nothing compared to Katherine.*

"Well, I'm here to clear my father's name," I started. "I'm sure you've all heard the stories about him, and I'm here to tell you that you were misled. He had no control over his actions when he aided in the murders of the Shipton and Merlin families, including the death of his wife, Hester Merlin. My mother. He was under the manipulation of the *Sal Vinna* curse, which you should be able to see in Exhibit A."

I waited for them to rustle a few papers around and bring my dad's autopsy photo to the front.

"The markings on his neck corroborate what I believe to be true," I went on. "They are the type of markings found in curses such as this. Marie Laveau also corroborated that my father wouldn't have been able to fight a curse like this. Chaos helped him to write one last spell in the Merlin Grimoire, and then Chaos pulled itself out of his mind when the curse took hold. His last ounce of free will was used to put that spell into the book—the spell that saved us all from Katherine Shipton."

I paused to let that last sentence sink in.

"In fact," I continued, "it's because of him and my mother that we were able to destroy her. They created the Grimoire, with Chaos's help, and the whole book was full of ways to kill Katherine. By the time we used it, there was only one spell that was still viable. That was the last one I mentioned. Well, the last part of it, to be exact—the other two parts had been written beforehand by my mother. For his sacrifices and his work toward ending Katherine, I believe my father is owed clemency and deserves to have his name cleared."

"You say this," a stout woman to Quentin's right spoke up, after a moment, "but how are we supposed to know if that's true or not when we can't read this Grimoire for ourselves?"

I smiled. "Because Katherine is dead, and she was killed using the spell I mentioned. I can have a whole group of magicals come in here and testify to that. They all saw what happened, and they heard the words Finch Merlin spoke. They were the same words my father wrote to make the spell work."

"And you expect us to go to Marie Laveau and ask her to testify, too?" a man with a lanky frame and wispy black hair asked.

"No, but I do expect you to believe me. A month ago, and even beyond that, I jumped through hoops you wouldn't believe to bring Katherine's reign of terror to a close. My father's last spell gave us that chance. If it wasn't for him, we'd all be under Katherine's control right now."

"I know there are many of you in leadership positions who were under her influence without even knowing. Katherine spread those pills and her mental manipulation far and wide," I continued. "Does that make you as guilty as my father was? Does that mean you're responsible for the deaths of everyone who was killed before Katherine died? I doubt any of you would say it was your fault that people in this coven died. My father was under a far greater level of control. He didn't want to hurt the people he loved. He proved that, because he managed to keep me alive for so long afterward, even though the curse must have been eating him alive inside."

A third judge—an elegant woman with long blonde hair who

looked alarmingly similar to Imogene—spoke up. "Yes, and how is it that your father managed to withstand the curse throughout the time you were in his care? If Katherine had such control over him, how would that be possible? And why did he not try to kill his sister during that same time?"

My hands clenched around the table's edge. I had been expecting these questions. "First of all, I suspect my father was able to withstand the curse to take care of me because Katherine didn't know I existed. I wasn't on her list of people that needed killing, which somehow made me exempt. As for my aunt, from what I've gathered from people who know about hexes and curses—Preceptor Evangeline Chequers, to be exact, who's taken Preceptor Bellmore's place—when my father escaped Katherine, he stretched the scope of the curse. It gave him more control over his willpower again. However, as I've said, it continued to eat away at him. That's why he ended up leaving us. He knew he was going to die, and he didn't want the curse to overpower him again and make him kill Isadora the same way he killed my mother."

The judges sank into quiet thought, whispering to each other every so often.

"Preceptor Chequers also validated these markings on my father's neck—she said they weren't natural and had to be the result of a hex of some kind. I put her write-up into the evidence folder, so it should be there for you to read." I took a deep breath. "Also, there's one more thing."

"Go on, Miss Merlin," Quentin replied.

"If I can forgive him for what he did to my mother, surely you should be able to see past your judgment of him. He didn't take anything away from you, but he took everything away from me. And I forgive him, because I knew Katherine—I knew what she was capable of, and I knew he'd never have done those things willingly. Even with his last self-aware moments, knowing he had to go and do something he'd never be able to take back, he provided us with the means to end

Katherine. He's one of the heroes in this, and we don't spurn heroes; we celebrate them for their sacrifices. You forgave Finch, and you awarded him a medal of valor. My father deserves the same leniency. He did far less, but gave far more for this cause."

I was shaking by the time I finished, and a cold sweat was creeping down my neck.

For what felt like a lifetime, the judges said nothing. They just sat there and stared, their faces impassive. And then, a single sound echoed through the room. At first, I didn't know what it was. Then, turning, I saw that the stenographer had risen out of her chair and was clapping wildly. The reporters joined in, some of them struggling with tears.

My heart swelled in my chest as I sat in my seat, confused and elated and anxious. The judges didn't clap, but I knew I'd given my best.

All I could do now was wait and hope for the right outcome. I had a feeling it was going to be the longest wait of my life.

Wade was hanging around in the hallway outside, and he started running straight for me the second I emerged. He put his arms around me and held me tight before pulling away, a worried expression on his handsome face.

"So?" he asked earnestly.

I shrugged, my face deadpan. "It went the way I expected."

"Oh… I'm so sorry, Harley." He pulled me in again, smoothing down my hair with his palm. "You can always appeal, right?"

"I don't know if there's any point," I murmured into his neck.

"Hey, you can't give up on this. Your dad deserves to be exonerated, and we're not going to rest until he is. I'll speak to my mom again, see if there's something she can do to help."

I smiled. "No, Wade, there really isn't any point."

"What do you mean?" He held me at arm's length, raising an eyebrow.

"There isn't any point... because I did it! Hiram Merlin has been cleared of any and all crimes and has been reinstated posthumously in the New York Coven Hall of Fame, or whatever it is they have. It started out badly, and I didn't know if I'd be able to change their minds, but I gave them a few home truths and they agreed to exonerate my dad." Happy tears sprang to my eyes as I sank back into Wade's arms, letting him hug me close.

"Don't do that to me!" He laughed against my cheek as he placed a kiss there.

"Sorry. I couldn't help it."

Wade moved back slightly and tilted my chin up, leaning in to kiss me. His mouth grazed mine, and every remaining ounce of tension melted away, replaced with total contentment. My dad had been exonerated, and now I was exactly where I wanted to be: engulfed in Wade's arms and feeling as if I could take on anyone and anything and survive. I kissed Wade more deeply, his mouth catching mine again, the both of us totally oblivious to everything else around us. It was an interdimensional bubble all of our own, built from a love that only continued to grow with time.

Finally, we could both look forward to a future without fear—whatever that might be, and wherever that might lead. We could do anything, go anywhere, and find our places in this new world... together.

And, sure, we might have a kid one day, and Leviathan might call to collect on the bargain to name him or her. But, hey, what was the worst that could happen? Katherine had set the benchmark for terrible things, and I doubted there could be anything worse than what we'd already faced.

Our hell was over. No more pitchforks, no more fire and brimstone, no more chasing after the villain and worrying about what it would cost us.

I was back at the SDC. The Rag Team was going strong. And Finch was probably going to be just fine. The world was changing and we were changing with it.

What more could a Merlin ask for?

What's next?

Dear Reader,

Thank you for reading *Harley Merlin and the Mortal Pact*.

The wicked witch is dead!

But the SDC lives on, and Finch's adventures are just beginning…

Keep turning the pages for five exclusive *sneak-peek* chapters from Book 10: **Finch Merlin and the Fount of Youth!** (Releasing July 22nd, 2019).

Finch BONUS Chapters

FINCH MERLIN AND THE FOUNT OF YOUTH (HM 10)

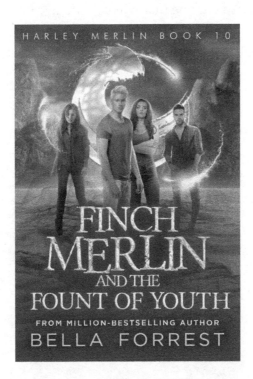

Releasing July 22nd, 2019

What's a guy gotta do to appease an evil god?

It's been a year since Katherine tried to take over the world, and Finch Merlin is itching to do something other than odd jobs for Erebus, God of Darkness. Erebus promises he'll free Finch of his servitude after he completes one final task—finding the Fountain of Youth.

Finch has no idea why Erebus wants eternal youth, since the guy is already an immortal being. All the secrecy makes Finch uneasy, but he has no choice but to obey.

He knows he'll get by with a little help from his friends, namely his old pal Garrett, who's still dealing with the whole "being resurrected" thing. There's also Ryann, Harley's foster sister, now a regular at the San Diego Coven. Whenever she's around, Finch feels butterflies in his stomach. Or maybe it's just a bad case of indigestion.

Together, they'll infiltrate the flashy world of the magical elite in search of a rare artifact, one that will help them capture a poltergeist— the angry ghost of famed adventurer Ponce de León.

Finch's adventures have only just begun, with plenty of old and new friends…and foes.

Chapter 1

FINCH

Well, wearing black was a bad choice. I'd been going for ninja vibes and now I was paying the price—baking in the Cuban sun, my T-shirt sticking to me like a slug on a window.

Smearing my sweat even further across my face with the back of my forearm, I paused beside the edge of a nearby wall and peered around it. This was my version of incognito sneaking, though I did have some cloaking magic at my disposal to make it easier.

Morro Castle was beautiful, all sandstone and cannons and fortifications that looked like they'd come right out of a George R.R. Martin novel. No dragons, though, unfortunately. Even though I'd seen an impressive array of creatures in Tobe the Beast Master's massive Bestiary, I still hadn't seen a dragon. Disappointing didn't even cover it.

Catching my breath, I looked over the nearest wall. The ocean crashed against the rock promontory below, on which this whole fortress had been built. Taking a dip in the chilly water would've been a mercy right about now—I didn't understand how there could be any sweat left in my body.

"Morro" sounded so very mystical and exotic to dumb foreigners like me, but the funny thing was, it just meant "rock." Rock Castle. Not very inventive, really. Still, it was crazy beautiful, standing alone on this outcrop where it had defended Havana against the British. Not that it had done a very good job. Those sneaky Brits had slipped in anyway.

I know of another slippery Brit I could mention. Davin Doncaster, the Necromancer and slime-ball extraordinaire who'd been a major pain in our asses during the Katherine campaign. He was still off the radar.

But that wasn't why I was here. And this place was just a tourist destination now, diminished to nothing more than an opportunity for vacation photos in front of a cannon.

Why did I never get to just enjoy these exotic places? Why didn't I ever get to pause and take selfies? Nope, this was no vacation, and sneaking through the narrow, boiling-hot paths of this fortress wasn't exactly my idea of a lazy Sunday.

I'd spent the past year doing insane errands for Erebus, the Prince of Darkness—my constant, irritating shadow. It was the price I'd paid for killing Katherine, but the debt was starting to wear thin.

I mean, how many more errands could Erebus possibly have left? Sometimes, I got the feeling he was just messing with me. Asking me to fetch the Easter Bunny had definitely been a joke at my expense. As it turned out, when I'd reached Easter Island, what he'd actually meant was a sacred jade rabbit that had been hidden there by Chinese magicals way back when. *What's next—the Tooth Fairy? Santa Claus? Meryl Streep?*

I had to keep telling myself that it was actually a pretty small price to pay. He could've asked for my life, or my sister's life, or one of my friends' lives. He liked death deals more than anything, and he had a weird obsession with making exchanges. So I supposed I should've been thanking my lucky stars, but there was only so much thanking a guy could do when he was hightailing it around the globe in search of a million bizarre wish-list items.

At least the magical world had recovered pretty well after my mother's demise, so I couldn't complain there. We had good leaders and a decent new setup, which seemed to be lasting. Our world was definitely in a better state than it had been pre-Katherine. That was how we defined time now—post-Katherine and pre-Katherine.

Magicals were still a secret to humans, which meant the biggest danger had been averted. If the humans had found out, it would've just caused more unrest, and nobody wanted that. In their eyes, we would have become a powerful threat that would need to be stopped, and they would've come up with some military tool to detect us all, like in the *X-Men* comics. Nukes, advanced weaponry, special cells, the whole shebang. I've said it before and I'll say it again—folks could learn a lot from comic books.

Seeing that the coast was clear, I hurried along the narrow path leading toward the lighthouse—the tip of the fortress, so to speak. Since I was armed with my cloaking magic and a bunch of knockout powders, this was finally going to go my way.

After a year's worth of in-depth research, and a whole bunch of antihistamines to stop my allergies from going crazy while digging through all those dusty tomes, I'd found out that this fortress was the resting place of Ponce de León's spirit. Now, most people thought he had been buried in San Juan Bautista Cathedral in San Juan, Puerto Rico, but those people hadn't endured sneezing fits and watering eyes after devouring book after book on the subject. They also hadn't endured going to San Juan and finding out they were wrong, the hard way. It was just one of many lies surrounding the conquistador's life and death.

"Conquistador" is a great word. Finch the Conquistador. Maybe one day, when I'd conquistador-ed my way out of my deal with Erebus.

This wasn't the first time I'd broken into a famous monument. San Juan Bautista Cathedral hadn't even been my first, and this wasn't the first time I'd broken into Morro Castle, either. I'd tried it five times. That's right, *five.* But I'd only gotten myself arrested once, so I was going to chalk that up as a win.

Those previous attempts hadn't been failures, though—they'd given me the opportunity to fully understand the layout of this labyrinth. How the British had done it on their first try, I wished I'd known. I supposed I had to give them props for that.

After my last attempt, now broke thanks to paying my bail, I'd realized there was one place I hadn't checked out—the very lighthouse I was edging toward, slow and steady, like the proverbial tortoise. It was the only place left to search through, which meant it had to be hiding what I was looking for.

Mr. Conquistador himself.

I rounded another corner, where the path opened out. Sand covered the ground, leading to a wall on my left and a Spanish-style chunk of the castle to my right. The lighthouse rose up ahead, like a proud...well, lighthouse. Now, why wasn't I doing this in the dark? A good question. I'd tried that, and it hadn't worked. This way, if anyone caught me creeping around, I could just pretend I was an idiotic tourist who'd somehow gone somewhere they weren't supposed to. But I hoped the cloaking magic would spare me that embarrassment.

I needed to get past the security guards to reach the lighthouse. The cloaking magic covered me visually, but if I touched anyone, they would feel it.

Heading back the way I'd come, I almost barreled into a pair of guards doing their rounds. I pressed against the wall again and waited for them to pass. They were almost clear when one brushed a hand right across my abdomen. I froze. He paused, too, looking around.

"Did you hear something?" he asked.

Crap.

I darted along the wall behind them until I reached an open expanse of path with no tourists or guards in sight. Turning, I sketched a doorway on the wall and whispered, *"Aperi Si Ostium."* The edges of the door fizzed and cracked, causing way too much of a scene. However, I'd started the process now, and no guards had caught up with me yet. As soon as the lines sank into the wall, forming a three-dimensional indent, I pushed it open and rushed through, slamming the door shut behind me.

Unfortunately, I'd misjudged the location of the far side of the lighthouse. I stepped through the doorway into air. The ocean crashed below, waves frothing up like jaws ready to devour me.

Dammit! I went into freefall, plummeting to a watery landing. Could I have been cool about it? Sure. Was I? No. I flailed frantically as the water rushed up to meet me.

Fortunately, I hadn't just spent the past year traipsing around completing Erebus's whims and fancies. Oh no. I'd also spent it sprucing up my newfound Elemental abilities, which had been in full force since Erebus had snapped my Dempsey Suppressor to smithereens. So I guess he had some uses.

Sending out a wave of Air with my hands, I created a cushion beneath me. It caught me like a pillowy cloud when I was just shy of hitting the water. *Ah, this is what it must feel like to be an angel.* I recovered quickly, forging another pillow of Air that I could jump to in order to get myself back to the edge of the promontory.

There, I ducked behind the fortification. I was crouched on the roof of what had once been part of the fort—a little house-like building that had now been reduced to a toilet for seagulls. And almost for me, after that little shocker. As my pulse returned to normal, I peered over the lip of the wall. The guards were standing right in front of the lighthouse door, chattering to each other in Spanish. I rolled my eyes. Couldn't they have picked a better place?

I sat down on the roof and tried to unstick my shirt from my skin as I waited for the guards to move. After all, I couldn't mess this up again. There was a pesky proviso in the deal I had with Erebus: no failures. I could die attempting a mission, sure—Erebus didn't give a hoot about that. But failure? Nope, not acceptable.

Still, I'd been using my time wisely. Since my end of the bargain showed no signs of arriving, I'd realized about six months in that I needed to start looking into ways of freeing myself. Loopholes, spells, hexes, even the viability of faking my own death. I hadn't found anything useful yet, though I'd read a *lot* of good stuff about the scammers of this world. Devious wives, spiteful husbands, psychotic parents —all the juicy, true-crime before-bedtime sort of stuff. I'd thought I'd known everything there was to know about psychotic mothers, but the Internet had proven me wrong.

Anyway, nothing useful had turned up. I wasn't trying to get away with murder or an insurance payout. I just wanted to be free of these shackles. I'd thought about asking Lux if she could help me, but I was still working up the courage. She and Erebus came as a pair. A bad pair, like two sour grapes on a vine. They made Antony and Cleopatra look like pussycats, and the War of the Roses look like a petty squabble. Love and hate times a million.

The frustrating thing was, you never knew which one was going to come out when they were together. I'd lost count of the times I'd had to duck as one chucked half a mountain at the other. I'd also lost count of the times I'd had to cough in an oh-so-over-the-top way to stop them from tonguing each other's faces off while I was standing right there! This was all the more impressive considering they didn't have real tongues. At first, it'd been a hell of a shock to see that side of things, since I'd presumed they were siblings. But, apparently, it wasn't literal. They were Chaos's kiddos, yes, but not actually related.

Pushing away the horrible memory, I looked back over the wall. *Yes!* The guards had moved on, giving me a direct line to the door of the lighthouse. I vaulted myself over the wall, checked to make sure nobody was watching, and sidled up to the wooden door. I smirked at a man standing in front of a nearby cannon while his girlfriend snapped a photo. *Attaboy.*

Pressing my hand to the lock, I fed a blast of Air through it. My new quartet of Elemental abilities definitely had some benefits. Well, my powers weren't so new anymore, but I was still getting used to them. It was hard to break the habits I'd learned over a lifetime.

The door lock mechanism clicked as Air pushed the teeth upward. Slipping into the lighthouse, I ran up the winding staircase.

Halfway up, I paused to drag in a breath. I might've been running around the world for a year, but I really needed to hit the treadmill. Using the spare moment, I took out the amulet I'd brought with me. The cops had given me a thorough pat-down during my last attempt at this, and even they hadn't found it. *Though nobody needs to know why.* Fortunately, I was back to using a conventional pocket to stow this thing away.

The amulet was a legitimate Eye of Horus, stolen about a month ago from Luxor by a tomb raider. That tomb raider had been me, minus the leg straps, pistols, tiny shorts, and curve-hugging tank top of the video game version. I only went after this amulet because Erebus had told me I'd have to actually speak to the Ponce. Naturally, that was all he'd given me. I'd asked for a little help in learning to use it, and he'd shrugged and told me to figure it out. Sweet of him to be so caring.

An amber bead lay where the Eye's pupil should've been. It was supposed to glow yellow in the presence of a spirit. I'd tested the theory in a couple of cemeteries with the help of Tatyana—the San Diego Coven's resident spirit whisperer—but whether Ponce de León would bite or not was yet to be seen.

I needed the amulet to speak with his spirit about the location of the Fountain of Youth. No idea what Erebus wanted that for, since the dude was already immortal.

Also, apparently this meant the Fountain of Youth was a real thing. Who knew, right? I was still wrapping my head around it. Next, he'd be sending me on a wild goose chase to the Isle of Avalon to have a chat with King Arthur, then sending me swimming in some lake to bring back Excalibur. Just to really bring that Merlin dynasty home.

I froze as I heard voices drifting down from a platform above my head. They didn't sound like spirits. No, it sounded like two jackasses egging each other on.

"Go on, I dare you," one guard said. My Spanish was muddy at best, but Santana had given me a crash course prior to this little jaunt.

"You go, if you're that worried," the second replied.

"No way, man! Everyone knows there's a spirit up there."

"So? It's daylight. Spirits don't come out in daylight."

"Who says? My mother saw one once, at, like, two o'clock in the afternoon."

"You sure she wasn't drunk?"

"Hey, you watch your mouth!"

"You brought it up. And I'm not going up there, so stuff it."

I glanced back down at the amulet. It was flashing yellow.

Chapter 2

FINCH

The amulet's glow intensified as I moved up the stairs. I paused on the platform where the guards were still egging each other on. It was too narrow for me to just slip past them. I watched for a moment, and then an idea popped into my head.

Edging forward, I held my breath and reached up. My fingertips tickled the back of the first guard's neck. He whirled around, and I ducked out of the way.

"Stop messing around," he muttered to his colleague.

"What are you talking about?" the other answered, looking annoyed.

"You're trying to freak me out, just because I said you weren't brave enough to go up there." He pointed to the top of the lighthouse.

My end goal.

"I didn't do anything," the other guard protested. I crept forward again and poked the nearest guy in the spine. He spun around again.

"Quit it!" he yelped.

"Quit what?" the second dude replied.

"Okay, that's it. I'm getting out of here. I don't care if you think I'm a coward. I'm not staying in this place."

He didn't wait for his colleague to answer. Brushing right by me, he jogged down the stairs, leaving the other guard with no choice but to follow. I pressed myself against the curved wall as he went by. I waited a few moments longer until I heard the lighthouse door open and close.

Nothing a little haunting can't fix. I chuckled, giving myself a moment to enjoy my triumph. Getting rid of the guards had been surprisingly easy, but the rest of my task wasn't going to be. Craning my neck to look at the top of the lighthouse, I shuddered. The amulet was glowing like a beacon and getting hot in my hand. That couldn't be good.

Why couldn't it have been an artifact-finding mission? Artifacts were easy. Some digging here and there, maybe a bit of thievery, and the job was done. Spirits were crafty, and I didn't like them one bit.

Steeling myself, I made my way up the rickety stairs. With every step, the amulet glowed brighter. I wished I could've been back at the SDC, learning more about the ins and outs of my newfound abilities. Things were pretty much peaceful there. No dramas, no ghosts, no missions… just plain old coven life. Even when jobs came up, they were nothing compared to Erebus's endless list of tasks. Man, I envied Harley and the Muppet Babies.

This was the price. You know that. Right on time, my brain swept in with a sharp reminder. I'd taken my pills that morning, but sometimes my brain liked to chatter away of its own accord.

I reached the last landing, where a wooden ladder disappeared into a dark hole above. *What could possibly go wrong?* Crumbly ladder, pitch-black trapdoor, a twenty-foot drop to the ground below, and Ponce de León shivering everyone's timbers at the top. Bad, good, scary, angry— it was anyone's guess what kind of spirit I'd be facing.

Taking a deep breath, I gripped the middle rung of the ladder and started to climb.

Eventually, I emerged from the trapdoor, grateful not to have plummeted to my death. The lantern room curved around me, with uninterrupted windows on all sides and a huge bulb in the center. As it was daylight, the lantern wasn't lit to warn ships, but the room gave one hell of an ocean view.

The waves churned and seagulls wheeled, and I could see ships in the distance, big ones, small ones, all kinds. I was about to step forward to get a better look when a shadow made me freeze. Someone stood on the other side of the lantern, looking out at the sea.

The figure wore a cloaked hood of some kind. They seemed to suck all the light out of the room. It should have been glaringly bright, with the sun shining down. But it wasn't.

I looked down at the amulet. It was so bright now that I couldn't look at it without risking my retinas. *Yep, I'm definitely dealing with a spirit.* I lifted the amulet toward the hooded figure, and the amber stone vibrated in my hand.

I cleared my throat. "Am I in the presence of Juan Ponce de León?" At least I didn't have to worry about trying to speak in broken Spanish to this guy. From my research, spirits were beyond the limits of languages—they could understand and converse in any tongue.

I figured it was best to get straight to the point. This had to be a super-powerful kind of spirit if I, a meager non-Kolduny, could see it with my bare eyes.

"Hello? Mr. Ponce de León?" I spoke again, since the shadow didn't seem very chatty. "Or do you prefer Juan? Mr. Juan? How about 'Conquistador?' Just so I know." I took a step closer and saw a waxy sheen of gray skin underneath the hood. The fabric covered half of his face, but I could make out a pale mouth. *Suitably ghoulish.*

I waited, but he didn't say a word. "See, the thing is, I was hoping you could help me out with something. I'm looking for the Fountain of Youth. I bet you're tired of hearing that, huh?"

I gave a nervous laugh. "I mean, that's quite a legacy, right? The man who found the Fountain of Youth. It's better than 'Pie-Eating Champion 2010,' anyway. Sorry, I babble when I'm excited. You're a legend, sir. You pretty much invented Florida, you explored the Caribbean, you governed Puerto Rico, and you're one of the most famous explorers of all time. You're a heck of a guy, Mr. Ponce de León, even without the Fountain of Youth stuff. But, unfortunately, I *am* here for the Fountain of Youth stuff. Erebus sent me to speak to you. He wants to gain some intel from you, via me."

I stopped again. The spirit had to be ready to answer me now that I'd just jabbered my way through an introduction like Mr. Bean on steroids... right? Plus, I'd dropped the big name, and that usually got folks talking. But the shadowy figure just stood there, staring out at the sea.

A spark of anxiety shot through me. I was getting a *very* bad feeling about this. Had I missed something important? Was I supposed to collect something else before I came here? A gift, or an offering, or something? Erebus hadn't said anything about it, but then, he wouldn't have. I tried to think back just in case, but the only thing on my to-get list had been this amulet.

"Can you hear me, Mr. Ponce de León?"

I held my breath as he turned. A ghastly face appeared under the hood—skeletal and drawn, with sunken cheeks and hollowed eyes. He opened his mouth, as if he was finally going to say something, only his mouth kept getting wider and wider, unnaturally wide, as if he were made of putty. The long sleeves of the cloak billowed out.

His entire being expanded like a swelling cloud. I stared as his gray skin morphed into a tempest of black tendrils with a vaguely skull-like head hovering in the middle.

"*GET OUT!*" it roared.

I staggered backward, dropping the amulet into my pocket—and forgetting about the trapdoor in the floor. My legs fell right through it, and my hands snapped out to stop the rest of me from following suit. I gripped the side of the trapdoor with every ounce of strength I had and hauled myself back up into the lantern room. I needed to slow down on the Wile E. Coyote mistakes, otherwise this would be the last mission I ever went on for Erebus.

Don't speak too soon. Judging by the seething mass of shadows dead ahead, it still could be.

"I'm here on behalf of Erebus!" I shouted, my voice snatched away by the wind that howled around the room.

"Leave this place!" the spirit boomed.

"I can't leave yet! You need to tell me where the Fountain is!" I ducked as a chair whizzed over my head and smashed against the back wall.

Ah. Poltergeist. It made sense now. I'd been able to see the spirit, which shouldn't have been possible. That meant it was another type of spirit—a pissed-off poltergeist.

A table came at me, full force. I dove out of the way, slamming into the lantern. Chunks of wood and steel and stone hurtled at me next, the poltergeist seizing whatever was handy and chucking it my way. I rolled and ducked and dove, but the attack just kept coming. Putting up my hands, I shot a blast of Telekinesis at the spirit, but it passed straight through him.

Okay, that's not good. How was I supposed to fight a spirit?

I hid behind the lantern, trying to catch my breath. A chunk of the ceiling fell away above me, giving me a split second to lunge forward before it crashed into the ground. It landed right where I'd been crouched. It would've brained me if it had hit its mark.

I stole a glance around the lantern to see the poltergeist shudder strangely. Its skull face disappeared. Long, black claws extended from its wrists. Before I could dart away, it charged at me. Those long claws raked right across my chest as my body was halfway turned.

Pain like no other erupted inside me. White-hot and searing, it spread out across my chest and up my throat.

I need to get out... I need to leave before it kills me. A sixth attempt might have to be my lucky charm. I scrambled toward the trapdoor. I needed more information about poltergeists before I went up against this creep. He was out of control, howling and raging, claws primed and ready to slash again.

My face twisted in agony as I ran, trying to reach the trapdoor before the poltergeist launched a second attack. But no matter where I went, the shadow appeared in front of me, like the worst kind of Whack-A-Mole. It was blocking my exit out of here.

I sent out a wave of Fire followed by a gust of Air to knock the thing back. It barely flinched, and I was starting to feel lightheaded. I hurled another barrage of Fire. Finally, the poltergeist reeled back for a moment, giving me a direct line to the trapdoor. My knees almost gave way as I ran for my life.

Man, I should not feel this weak... this... tired.

Something weird was definitely going on here. I was weakening way too fast for it to be natural.

Tumbling over the edge of the trapdoor, I caught one of the rungs with my foot and scampered down as quick as I could. Another chair followed me through. It careened right past me and plummeted the twenty feet to the ground. I heard it shatter on impact, though I didn't dare look. Vertigo wouldn't have been too helpful, when I already felt dizzy as hell.

"Get out! *Get out!*" The poltergeist's voice thundered through the lighthouse, shaking the walls. I sprinted down the spiral staircase, feeling the whole thing shudder underneath me.

So much for conversation. The poltergeist really didn't want to talk, and a deal was definitely off the table. I just had to hope I didn't die before I made it out of here.

Ponce de León's rage followed me all the way down, deafening me. Glancing over my shoulder, I saw darkness descending. *He* was following me down, his claws eager for another bite.

But he couldn't follow me out of the lighthouse, surely. Spirits like Ponce were supposed to be tied to a location.

I barreled out of the building, my thighs burning and my muscles aching. The searing pain across my chest made it hard to breathe. It was working its way higher up my throat. My ankle hurt, too, from landing awkwardly on the ladder rung. Fortunately, there were no tourists around to see me burst through the door. In fact, the fortress had become eerily empty and silent since I'd entered the lighthouse, the sky overhead now dark and ominous.

But that was the least of my concerns.

A powerful gust of wind exploded out of the door and smacked me in the back. I toppled forward, landing in the dirt, right on the ragged cut. And, inside my head, I heard the most terrifying scream:

"Never return here!"

Dragging myself to my feet, I staggered away from the lighthouse, my body barely able to hold me up as I lunged for the nearest wall. I needed to get away. All that screaming was too much, making it feel like my head was about to blow, as well as my chest.

I was almost at the castle wall when a shadow appeared in front of me, blocking my path. *What the—? How is this even possible?*

Gasping for breath and fighting to stay on my feet, I gave it one last burst of energy. I ran for the wall, getting a second scrape across the chest as I tore past the poltergeist. The pain as he raked the already-raw flesh was indescribable. A howl escaped my throat, every vein in my body ablaze with agony.

Struggling to stay upright, I fumbled for my trusty charmed chalk, then scraped the shaky lines of a doorway into the wall and choked out the *Aperi Si Ostium* spell. I looked over my shoulder to see the spirit surging toward me. I lifted my palms one last time and sent out a blast of Fire and Telekinesis.

Yanking at the handle, I pushed it open and lunged through. I got a final glimpse of the seething shadow mass as it zoomed toward me, missing me by a millisecond. I took a moment to assess my surroundings, to make sure not even a wisp of that thing had managed to get through.

I'd escaped it… just barely.

"Finch?"

Krieger was staring at me from his workbench. He held a screwdriver poised mid-air, frozen like a substandard mime. Jacob sat beside him, similarly stunned. What could I say? I knew how to make an entrance. A natural gift from my dearly departed mother.

I looked around and saw that they were working on a bronze device. Presumably, the one they'd been tinkering away at before I left for Cuba. It was supposed to be another magical detector to replace the one Katherine had stolen, just souped up a bit. An enhanced version based on Krieger's memories of the last one, complete with a finger-print scanner so only vetted magicals could use it.

O'Halloran had been the one to suggest it. As the new and improved SDC director, it made sense that he'd want new and improved things. He thought we could use the device to find rogue magicals and keep them safe, especially after the Katherine debacle. Or "the Blip of Eris," as I liked to call it. No more cults, thank you very much.

"Yep… sorry about the rough entry," I said. The strip lighting of Krieger's office stung my eyes as I braced my hands against my thighs. I tried to pull in a decent breath. Had the air here turned to slime while I'd been gone? It felt like it.

"Are you okay?" Krieger scraped back his stool. The sound splin-tered through my skull, as if I'd spent last night downing shots of tequila. I kept trying to breathe, but the pain in my chest was over-whelming.

Exhausted, I couldn't stay upright any longer. My knees buckled, and I crumpled to the floor, panting like a dog.

Jacob leapt up and ran with Krieger to my side.

I winced as they hauled me up by my pits and carried me through to the infirmary. They settled me down on a gurney, buzzing around me like flies. Krieger was tearing things out of a drawer, pulling out reams and reams of bandages as if he were a magician at a kid's party.

"We need to stop the bleeding," he said, glancing worriedly at me.

Okay, so maybe I lost more blood than I thought. That was another problem with black clothes—it was hard to tell if you were gushing your lifeblood all over the place.

"Come on, how bad can it be?" I croaked.

"Very bad," Krieger replied. "What on earth did you go up against, to get injuries like this?"

I smiled. "Tobe Hooper, 1982."

"What?" Krieger frowned. "What has this got to do with Tobe?"

"Not Tobe. Tobe *Hooper*."

Jacob gasped. "*Poltergeist?*"

"See, and you said making you watch all those old movies was pointless," I wheezed.

"Are you saying a poltergeist did this?" Krieger paled.

"In my usual roundabout way... yeah." I sucked air through my teeth as Krieger pressed a wad of gauze against my wound. "You want to go easy there, Krieger? I'd like to keep my ribs intact, if that's okay with you?"

"Jacob, get Marianne Gracelyn here immediately." Krieger ignored me, giving Jacob a pointed look.

"What's she going to do?" I muttered, trying to stop my head from spinning.

"As the preceptor of Wicca and Herbalism, she'll know far more about poltergeist injuries than I do," Krieger replied. "They're not regular injuries and require special concoctions and herbal treatments to temper the wounds. If not treated correctly, you may..." He trailed off, visibly uncomfortable.

"You can say it, Doc." I smiled weakly. "I might die, right?"

He sighed gravely. "Yes, you might. A poltergeist's attacks are infused with dead-men's poison, otherwise referred to as 'concentrated death.' It's lethal if left untreated."

"And here I was, thinking you were going to say it was something serious." I stared up at the ceiling, trying to hide my gathering fear. I could put on a good show in front of most people, but this wasn't something I could laugh off. This was scary... genuinely scary. And I couldn't help thinking:

What the hell had I gotten myself into?

Chapter 3

FINCH

It took Marianne an hour to finish patching me up. She threw all kinds of poultices and potions at me in the hopes of drawing out the dead-men's poison. The stench from the goo she pounded up in a mortar and pestle was almost worse than the idea of dying from this wound—something like the bottom of a dumpster. But, apparently, it was good for me. Vile medicine for a vile injury.

She bandaged up the rest of me, too, where I'd gotten a few scrapes and cuts that I hadn't even noticed. The poltergeist had hurt me more than I'd thought, landing a few surprise blows. An Egyptian mummy had nothing on me right now. My ankle, thigh, hip, chest, and shoulders were neatly bound and stinking to high heaven.

"You'll have to wear these for the next twenty-four hours," Marianne instructed in her odd, musical voice. It was hard to feel negative when she was around. She buzzed with positivity. *Stick some of that in a drip for me, would you?*

"No showers, no water, and no exerting yourself. Take it easy over the next couple of days," she continued.

As preceptors went, Marianne was an emblem of the new order, young and beautiful and insanely smart, even though she'd been at the SDC pre-Katherine. She had long, red hair that was fastened in a braid to her waist, with feathers flowing down as if they were part of her locks. Not like my sister's red, and not like my real shade of ginger, which I kept permanently under a strawberry blond façade. It was more of a true red, like it had come out of a box instead of nature. She looked like she had old Woodstock photos on her walls and listened to Bob Dylan on repeat. Right now, she wore bright yellow bell-bottom cords, a tie-dyed T-shirt, and more beads than New Orleans at Mardi Gras.

"How easy?" I replied.

Taking it easy wasn't exactly an option for me. I had work to do, and Erebus didn't accept delays. And this definitely wasn't the first time I'd had to get on with a task while recovering from a plethora of injuries. As it turned out, being Erebus's messenger boy was a bigger risk to my health than being Katherine's sidekick.

"Basically, you need to stay on your back and rest." Marianne smiled as she stowed her many herbs and potions back into a big leather bag. A veritable hippie Mary Poppins.

I rolled my eyes. "I was worried you'd say that."

"She means it, Finch," Krieger interjected. "You must rest, or you won't get better."

"Okay, okay, I heard you the first time." I tried not to sulk.

"I wouldn't have taken you for a troublesome patient." Krieger chuckled, clearly relieved that he'd been able to help me out. For a doctor, there were some definite holes in his expertise. Then again, I supposed poltergeist attacks were fairly niche in his line of work.

"Where were you when this happened?" Jacob distracted me from my sulking. He sat to my left, in one of those ancient vinyl chairs that all hospitals seemed to have. "Which poltergeist was it? Do you know?"

I smiled. "How about you mind your beeswax and get back to tinkering with the shiny new magical detector?"

"Actually, he makes a valid point." Krieger folded his arms across his chest. "Where were you, and what on earth were you doing?"

"Will it make a difference to my healing?" I replied.

"Well, no, but—"

"Then it's none of your beeswax, either." I grinned. "No offense."

Krieger frowned. "I really think you should tell us."

"And I really think Marianne told me not to exert myself. Talking is making me so very weak." I closed my eyes as if I was going to sleep, only for them to fly open as the door to the infirmary burst inward and Harley came crashing through. Wade ran alongside her.

"Oh yeah, I might have called them," Jacob whispered.

"Snitch," I hissed back.

He gave me an oh-so-innocent shrug. "I thought she should know. She's your sister."

"Yeah, I don't need reminding." I sighed.

Harley hurried straight for me and threw her arms around me. I rolled my eyes.

"Ouch! Wounded invalid over here." It did hurt, but I was secretly glad to hug her again after my brush with death.

She drew back. "Are you okay? What happened?"

"It's nothing, I'm fine. You didn't have to come all the way down here to worry over me," I replied. "It was just a work accident. Stuff happens, but it's all good now."

"Stuff happens?" Wade asked. Harley arched a disapproving eyebrow at me. They were tag-teaming this in annoying couple fashion.

Krieger glanced between the three of us. "On that note, there's something I need to talk to you about. Marianne, Jacob, if you could join me in my office?" He led the way, with the other two following. Jacob was a little more reluctant, but Krieger was his adoptive dad now, so he had to do as he was told.

At least the good doctor still knew how to take a hint. It was considerate of him to leave me alone with my sister and Wonderboy Wade so she could whip my ass in relative privacy.

"How's everything in paradise?" I dove in first, before the questions could start again.

Harley shook her head. "Stop deflecting, Finch."

"Who's deflecting?" I smiled sweetly.

Paradise entailed Wade and Harley being at the top of their game and still nauseatingly in love. They'd moved into a shared, bigger office in the coven to run their taskforce. They'd also moved into a shared, bigger room in the living quarters, but the less said about that, the better. I was still her brother. I'd already had a few choice, brotherly words with Wade about their living arrangements, but he'd just laughed.

As part of their ongoing duties within the SDC, Harley and Wade had been appointed as Special Coven Agents. They had sparkly new uniforms and everything. Which meant, while I was out hunting down all of Erebus's whims and fancies, they were out hunting down rogue Cult of Eris members still at large, among other things. Frankly, I would've given anything to have their job.

As for the rest of the Muppet Babies, they had the easy, stress-free task of bringing new, undiscovered magicals into the coven.

"Finch!" Harley said sternly.

"Harley!" I mimicked. I knew it irked her when I did that.

"What happened to you?" Her tone softened. "When Jacob called, I was so worried."

Wade nodded. "We both were."

"Which is why he shouldn't have called you. Like I said, there's nothing to worry about. Hazard of the job, that's all." I grinned up at Wade. "Although, I'm touched. Wonderboy was worried about me— there's something you don't hear every day."

"Be serious, Finch," Wade replied. "Come on, just let us know what happened. You got injured by a *poltergeist*. That's not some simple occupational hazard. You could've died today."

I shrugged. "But I didn't, and I can't tell you. So it'll be easier for all of us if you both just let it go."

I wanted to tell them more, I really did, but I didn't want their pity. Or their self-pity, for that matter, particularly Harley's. She'd beaten herself up enough about Katherine's demise and the way things had gone down. I wasn't going to drag them into my troubles. I'd chosen this. I could do it on my own, the way I was supposed to. And, if there came a time when I couldn't anymore, then I'd reach out for help.

"We already know it's because of Erebus, Finch." Harley perched on the edge of the bed and held my hand.

I didn't pull away. Just because I wouldn't ask for their help didn't mean I didn't appreciate some sisterly comfort. I liked having her nearby. Maybe it was because of some residual abandonment issues, or maybe it was just because I finally had family, but it made me calmer when she was here.

Wade nodded. "You're always so secretive about the jobs you do for him, but sometimes it's best to ask for help before things get too dangerous."

"Are we forgetting how Harley tried to end Katherine on her own?" I regretted the words as soon as they slipped out, but I wanted them off my case. Not for me, but for their own sakes.

"And what did you do about that, huh?" Wade replied. "You followed her around like a puppy until she gave in. I'm glad you did, don't get me wrong, but you might need a better example."

I narrowed my eyes at him. "Touché, Crowley... touché."

"You've been going at this by yourself for a year, Finch. Surely, it's time you let us take some of the weight?" Harley paused. "Or, if not me or Wade, then someone else you trust? You almost got snuffed out by a poltergeist today. We almost lost you. Please, just ask for freaking help."

"It's not that simple—" I started to protest, but she cut me off.

"My guess is, you needed something from that spirit—something Erebus wants—and you clearly can't get it on your own. I'm not saying you aren't capable, because I know you're capable of just about anything, but this may be biting off more than one person can chew." She gave my hand a squeeze.

Wade smirked. "I wouldn't say he's capable of just about anything. He still has trouble keeping his hair the same color."

"Pfft, says you. You've got enough product in your hair to baste a duck," I shot back.

"Don't say 'baste.'" Wade shuddered.

"Why not? Baste, baste, baste."

Harley rolled her eyes, though a smile tugged the corners of her lips. "Can you not do this now?"

"I wasn't doing anything," I replied, though I felt better. Making fun of Wade always made me feel better. "I know you're concerned, but I really do have this covered. I'm fine, honestly."

"Why don't I believe you?" She gave me a long look and sighed. I squeezed her hand back in response.

"You know I'm always here if you need support, and I know you've got some demons to work through, on top of this creepy servitude." Harley's eyes and voice were solemn and kind. "But I just want you to let me help you, if you ever need it. I know what you sacrificed to finish Katherine, and I hope that, one day, you might let us share that responsibility."

"As soon as my ass needs saving, you'll be the first to know."

I looked down at Harley's hand holding mine, my eyes drifting up to the leather cuff on her forearm, which covered her golden apple tattoo. She never went without her cuff. I wore a similar cuff whenever I didn't feel like shifting over my two apples—the first one that I'd willingly gotten, and the second one which I'd had poured onto me while gussied up as Pieter Mazinov. The cuffs served as a constant reminder for both of us of what we'd been through. We'd never have made it to the bitter end if we hadn't worked together.

So maybe she was right. Maybe I did need some help for this task, if

I ever wanted to finish it. This wasn't Katherine-Shipton-level evil, but it left me with the same sick sense of dread.

A job shared... right? The sooner I got this over with, the better. And I had just the person in mind, someone who didn't share my sister's savior complex.

Chapter 4

FINCH

The next morning, my eyes opened to daylight nagging me to wake up. I groaned and shoved my head back in the pillow. *My sweet, squishy love...* I'd deliberately refused to set an alarm, but the sun had transformed into a stressed-out mom ready to kick my ass if I didn't get up and ready, pronto. I dragged my second pillow over my head like a sandwich to block out the glare.

My body felt like it had been hit by an eighteen-wheeler, or like I'd downed a bottle of Diarmuid's secret brew, which could kill a grown man but, apparently, not a leprechaun. Everything hurt. No exaggeration. My skull throbbed, my limbs felt heavy, my wounds stung, and, man, did I stink. Those poultices should have come with a biohazard warning. I'd dragged myself to bed, not wanting to spend the night in the infirmary. Now, I wished I had. My sheets would never be the same.

Coffee... My delicious, caffeinated mistress will fix this. That and a hefty dose of painkillers, which Marianne had packed me off with. A stack of them sat on my desk. Grumbling a number of choice expletives under my breath, I removed the upper layer of my pillow sandwich and hauled myself out of bed. Every step took effort.

Padding over to the mirror, I took a long, hard look at myself. My skin was pale, and my hair was sticking up at all angles. My body hadn't fared much better. Bruises were blooming all over the visible parts of my chest and stomach, and the bandages that were keeping my dignity had turned a rank brown color thanks to the poultices.

It was weird how quickly I'd settled into life at the coven. This bedroom brought me that homey kind of comfort that people loved to harp on about—home is where the heart is and whatnot. I guessed my heart was in the SDC now. Plus, I'd done a killer job of decorating, if I did say so myself.

I had a red feature wall with framed comic books hanging on it. Rare copies, of course—first appearances, key issues, all the good stuff. There was a packed bookshelf on one side with all my favorite reads, from the classics to contemporary and everything in between. Harley liked to mock me for my copy of *Wuthering Heights* and my Austen collection, but I called her a philistine and that shut her up. A guy could enjoy whatever he wanted, and I liked to think of myself as a bit of a Heathcliff.

I had the rest of the usual suspects—a desk, a chair, a few knick-knacks. There was a collection of still-boxed figurines on the shelves and a wardrobe with my meager selection of clothes. Yeah, this was home. Well, when I actually got to spend some time here. I'd lost count of the countries I'd been to in the last year, thanks to Erebus.

Walking to said wardrobe, I took out jeans, a T-shirt, and some fresh boxers. My daily uniform. As I got dressed, wincing every time I bent the wrong way or brushed one of my many new injuries, I looked at the pictures on the desk. There was one of me and the Muppet Babies, all together, outside the Fleet Science Center. It had been Jacob's idea, during his brief foray into photography. We were all smiling in the photo. Yes, even me.

Santana wasn't looking at the camera and appeared to be laughing at something Raffe had said. Dylan had scooped Tatyana into his arms and hoisted her in a fireman's lift. The shock in her eyes was captured for eternity.

Wade and Harley were standing as if they were trying to take a nice photo for prom, Wade's arms around her waist. Astrid and Garrett bookended them with strained smiles, as far apart as it was possible to be. As for me, I was crouched in the middle, giving it the rap-star vs. no whiff of a lover in sight. Well, not really.

I sat cross-legged in front of the mirror and dragged a comb through my hair. Staring at my reflection, I sighed. It was nice to see people happy, sure, but I would've liked to have someone, too. You know, someone I could vent to at night, or relax with when I was tired of missions and magic and all that malarkey.

Yeah, but you had yours. My brain came in with a sharp reminder. And maybe one was all a person got. I'd loved Adley more than I'd known, and it had taken my stupid head too long to realize it. I ruined it with her, so maybe I didn't get to have a second chance with someone else.

Just someone *else, eh?* I reached up to the top drawer of my desk and took out a packet of my special pills. My brain was being a little too chatty right now, and it was time to put those pesky gremlins to sleep for a bit. It had a point, though. Every morning, I woke up thinking about a certain woman, and every night, I went to sleep thinking of her.

Why did it have to be her? Harley would feed me to Murray if she found out I was crushing on her adoptive sister. And the psychological implications were borderline Ancient Grecian.

Not that it mattered. Between my mind gremlins and my servitude to Erebus, I wasn't exactly a catch. And I wasn't about to drag someone else into my world. Especially not Ryann Smith. Plus, whenever we met, I morphed into Finch the Jackass or Finch the Deathly Silent. Whichever my mind preferred that day. Oh, and I could never resist the urge to make fun of her towering Canuck moose of a boyfriend, Adam, which didn't exactly make her warm up to me.

But I couldn't help it. That guy riled me up, giving me all sorts of inferiority complexes. He looked like he spent all day at the gym, he'd gone to Harvard, he was interning as a pediatrician. *I mean, come on!* And it definitely didn't help that he was so damn nice. Like *too* nice. Like serial killer nice. And I'd never be like that.

I threw down the comb and lay back on the carpet, staring up at the ceiling. I blamed the Smiths for this—Mr. and Mrs. Smith, to be precise. They'd smothered me with love after the Blip of Eris was over. Mrs. Smith, the mother hen, had truly scooped me under her wing. I had an open invitation to their house, and Harley had hauled me along at every possible opportunity.

With all the cakes and homecooked food and watching Mr. and Mrs. Smith canoodling constantly, how could I not have fallen for Ryann? They'd set the mood, being all loved-up all the time! I didn't go over there as much anymore, but I was invited to the occasional Sunday barbecue. Which Captain Serial Killer was always at, too.

Okay, enough wallowing. I rolled over and stiffly got to my feet. Dispensing with all thoughts of Ryann, I hobbled into the bathroom to wash that girl right out of my... face. I couldn't shower. Marianne's orders.

Running the faucet, I splashed the cool water on my skin, along with some soap, and started to brush my teeth. After sticking my head under the faucet to rinse my mouth out, I straightened to take another look at myself.

A scream nearly squeaked out of my throat as I stared at the words that had appeared on the mirror. Bloody writing spelled out the ominous message:

"I summon thee."

"Oh yeah? Well, I summon you to stick your summons up your butt," I muttered, breathing sharply and bracing myself against the sink to stop myself from having an all-out heart attack. Why couldn't he just text me, or call, or send a letter? Even a friggin' carrier pigeon would've been better for my nerves than this.

It pissed me off... and scared me, a little bit. I was in no condition to face Erebus right now, especially after my colossal failure with Ponce de León.

You'll have to wait, sunshine. I needed a breather. And, anyway, what was the worst that could happen?

Chapter 5

FINCH

An hour later, fresh as a daisy, I sat in the Banquet Hall for breakfast. I had coffee. I had pastries. Life was good. I always appreciated the spread they put on here. No matter what time of day it was, you could always swipe something tasty from the kitchens.

The Muppet Babies were assembled, looking annoyingly chirpy. Then again, they hadn't gone twelve rounds with a poltergeist.

"How are you feeling?" Tatyana asked, sipping delicately at some herbal nonsense.

"Ah, I see the news spread quickly," I replied. "I'm fine. I'm going to have some super-manly scars, but I'll live."

"Poltergeists are very dangerous, Finch." She eyed me sternly.

I smiled back. "So everyone keeps telling me."

"Did they get all the poison out?"

I nodded. "Apparently. Turns out, Preceptor Gracelyn is pretty nifty with her Wiccan mumbo-jumbo."

"It's not mumbo-jumbo. Wiccan magic is very powerful, and very legitimate," Santana said pointedly. She and I were still not quite in the realm of friendship. We'd been making progress, but then I'd doused her and her feather boa. Accidental, of course, but she had a big wet chip on her shoulder about it.

"Nothing wrong with a few scars, buddy," Dylan chimed in, as positive as ever. Honestly, I'd gotten used to his eternal optimism.

"At least you're not possessed or anything," Raffe added through a mouthful. *Charming.*

"And what's that supposed to mean?" Kadar rose to the surface for a moment.

Raffe rolled his eyes as he shifted back. "I didn't mean anything by it. Like Tatyana said, poltergeists are dangerous business. I was concerned for his welfare, that's all. You don't have to take everything so personally."

"Can poltergeists possess someone?" Jacob looked up from his bowl of technicolor puffs of cereal. He might've liked to pretend otherwise, but he was still a kid.

"They can if they're pushed to it, or they have a reason for it," Tatyana replied.

"I can think of a few reasons it'd want to possess Finch." A new voice in our group spoke, casting me a terrifyingly girlish smirk. Saskia Vasilis, Tatyana's sixteen-year-old sister, who'd have given Regina George a run for her money. I blamed Ryann and Harley for me even knowing who that was. They'd made me sit through *Mean Girls* on one of our evenings at the Smiths'.

Tatyana shot her a look. "Saskia!"

"What? I'm just saying." She pretended to pout, while fluttering her eyelashes at me.

Not in a million years, jailbait. I really hated teenagers, with the exception of Jacob, for the most part. Tatyana wasn't too happy about this teenager, either. Saskia had been sent here on the student exchange program, and Tatyana was trying to be sisterly about it. But Saskia was proving to be a heck of a nuisance. She'd already spent part of the morning poking Garrett, who had buried his head in a newspaper to avoid her.

I jumped as something brushed against my leg, and I slammed my knee into the underside of the table. I hissed through my teeth and ducked down to see what it had been. I half expected to see Saskia's leg trying to play footsie with me. Instead, I came eyeball-to-eyeball with that friggin' Purge beast of Santana's, Slinky.

"Do you have to bring your feather boa to breakfast, Santana? It's trying to cop a feel." I tucked my legs right under the bench so it couldn't have another lick of me with its hissy little tongue.

"I imagine he smelled you and wanted to figure out what had died," she shot back.

I smirked. "Well, can you call it back? I'm trying to eat, and having a reptile wrap itself around my legs isn't good for my digestion."

I'd seen that slithery pet way too much for my liking of late. Wherever Santana went, it went. Apparently, she was trying to train it to be a Familiar of sorts, although I got the feeling she liked bringing it everywhere just to freak me out. That thing had gotten *big* since Elysium. It was about the size of a mature boa, with a bright ruff of feathers around its neck. Not the same color as Quetzi, and not quite as massive, but he'd get there one day.

"You afraid he might bite?" Santana grinned.

"Actually, yes." As if to prove my point, Slinky lunged upward, nearly making me fall back off my seat.

"Aww, he just wants to say hello."

Santana knew that *wasn't* what he was doing, but the creepy creature decided to stroke its head against my cheek anyway. A snaky joke. I shuddered. I wasn't a big fan of snakes in general, but Slinky and I had a mutual dislike of each other.

"Yeah, well, if it could slink away from my face, that'd be great." I shoved the Purge beast in the side of the head to get it to move and received a loud hiss for my pains.

"Hey, don't touch him!" Santana snapped.

"Then stop letting it sneak around under the tables, or I'll have to report it for inappropriate behavior," I replied.

Saskia batted her eyelashes. "I think Slinky has the right idea."

Save me, someone. Right now, I was fodder between Saskia, who delighted in making innocent folks like me as uncomfortable as possible, and Santana's beastie.

"Saskia! I'm not going to tell you again," Tatyana chided.

"Tell me what?" she replied sweetly.

"I mean it."

"Mean what?"

A muscle twitched in Tatyana's jaw. "Just… behave yourself."

"Killjoy," Saskia murmured under her breath.

"So, how did you end up toe-to-toe with a poltergeist?" Dylan asked, evidently eager to draw the attention away from his nightmarish potential sister-in-law.

I shrugged. "How does anyone end up dealing with a poltergeist?"

"No, seriously, what were you doing when it happened?" Raffe pressed.

"Oh, this and that," I replied. The King of Nonchalance.

"What does that mean?" Garrett finally spoke. "What have you been up to?"

"You know, just keeping busy." They weren't going to get anything out of me.

Garrett pulled a disgruntled face. "Clearly you were up to something. People don't just bump into poltergeists by accident."

"Maybe I'm the first." I smiled stiffly.

"If you're having some kind of trouble, I'd be happy to answer a few questions," Tatyana said. "I know a lot about poltergeists, after all. We studied them in depth while training to become a Kolduny."

That got my attention. "You did?"

"Yeah, a whole month on them," Saskia interjected. "I nearly broke my jaw in half, yawning through the lectures. It wasn't like they were teaching me anything new. I'd read all about poltergeists by the time I was five."

Tatyana gripped her mug until her knuckles whitened.

"Careful, you might smash it," I teased.

Her expression relaxed slightly. "What my sister is trying to say is, we're well-versed in poltergeist lore. We know a thing or two that other people don't. So, if you do—"

"If you need some help, I'd love to volunteer." Saskia cut her off again.

Tatyana stared at her sister, and even I was a bit frightened. These Kolduny women were scary, but for very different reasons. "You're not getting involved in anything that is tied to Erebus! Nothing. I mean it. If I hear so much as a whisper that you've disobeyed, I'll have words with O'Halloran."

Saskia glared back. "Ooh, you'll go running to the teacher?"

"I. Mean. It." Tatyana held her sister's gaze until Saskia sank back in her seat, admitting defeat with a petulant scowl on her face.

Just then, Ryann rushed over with a croissant and a coffee. How had I missed her coming in? That wasn't like me. My Ryann radar was usually primed and precise. All this poltergeist business must have been knocking me off my very poor game.

"Morning, all," she chirped, sliding onto the bench beside Harley. "I don't have much time, but thought I'd say hi before I dart off again."

"Ryann? What are you doing here?"

The words came out colder than I'd intended. She'd surprised me, that was all. Last time I was here, she wasn't. Her internship with Astrid in the shiny new department of human relations had finished, and she hadn't said anything about applying for another position. So I'd presumed that was the last of that.

She didn't seem to notice my brusqueness. "I've just started a summer internship with Miss Miranda Bontemps."

I nodded. "I bet you'll have a Bontemps with that."

She gave a pity laugh that made my insides curl up. "Hah. Good one."

"Yeah, good one, Finch." Wade smirked at me.

Does he know? No, he couldn't. I'd been so suave and discreet in my nonexistent displays of admiration.

"I'm focusing on human rights in the magical world," she continued.

Her face positively radiated with pride and enthusiasm. *Come on, Finch, say something cool and encouraging.* "So, how will you explain this to Ted Bundy?"

The Muppet Babies stared at me like I'd grown a second head.

"He means my boyfriend, Adam." Ryann chuckled, and the entire group relaxed. "Such a joker, isn't he?"

"He sure is." Garrett snorted.

"And Adam is wonderful," Harley added pointedly. "Definitely not a serial killer."

"That we know of," I said in an undertone. "Anyway, what are you going to tell him? I'm guessing he doesn't know about your toe-dip into the magical world. Or the magical world at all, for that matter."

Ryann smiled. "I'm still getting used to that word—magical. Although, some folks seem more magical than others."

The Muppet Babies snickered. *Does she mean me?* Pfft, I was plenty magical. More magical than everyone at this table, Harley excluded. I wanted to peacock a little, but Adam wouldn't have done that. He was modest, on top of everything else. Ugh, I hated him. Still, it stopped me from boasting about my magical prowess.

"Have they made you sign an NDA?" I asked, recovering.

"They have, but it's okay. I'm just grateful to have this opportunity, and O'Halloran gave me some pointers about how to keep things quiet without jeopardizing a relationship."

She had an answer for everything. That was one of things I liked most about her. She kept me on my toes. Sometimes so much so I felt like she had me en pointe.

"Hey, what happened to you? Did I miss something?"

I looked up as Ryann's expression softened and she gazed at me with concern.

I shrugged, cool as a cucumber. "It's nothing. Took a tumble, that's all."

"You don't look good. Should you be up and about?"

"It looks worse than it is," I replied.

"I could ask Adam to look at you on Sunday." She paused. "Although, I suppose Dr. Krieger has you covered. I keep forgetting you guys have everything you need right here."

I frowned. "Sunday?"

"Yeah—don't tell me you forgot! Mom invited you to Sunday dinner, remember?"

"Oh... yeah. I'll see how I feel." If Jack the Ripper touched me, I'd roast *him* on the barbecue.

Ryann nodded, looking a little disappointed. "Of course. If you're not feeling up to it, that's fine, but I know Mom and Dad are looking forward to it. They've been missing their adopted third child." She gave me a small smile that made my throat close, and I tried to think about Jacob to distract myself. Harley had tried to encourage him to reconnect with the Smiths, even if they couldn't remember those days. But he'd refused, coming up with countless excuses. The real truth, however, was much simpler. It hurt too much.

Harley put her hand on Ryann's forearm. "I'll make sure he comes along."

"Okay. Well, I need to be going. I'll see you all later." Ryann slid from the bench and got up, coffee and croissant still in hand. I tried to think of something to say that would make her stay longer. I wanted to ask her what she'd been up to, and just shoot the oh-so-casual breeze. I guessed it would have to wait until Sunday.

She turned, and my heart leapt. *She's going to stay, after all.* "Oh, and Finch?"

"Yes?" My pulse was raging.

"You know I think the world of you, but can you please leave Adam out of our conversations? I know you think it's funny to call him all those things, but there's really nothing funny about serial killers. It's beneath you."

I withered like a shrub in an arid desert. "Sure. No serial killer jokes. Got it."

"Wish me luck!" She smiled again.

A ripple of "good lucks" passed around the table as she turned and left, leaving me to stew.

"It's not like you to pass up the chance for a witty comeback," Santana said.

"She got you good!" Dylan laughed.

I tried not to meet anyone's gaze. "I didn't want to be rude."

"Did that poltergeist lobotomize you, as well?" Wade grinned.

"Are you sure you didn't meet a changeling instead?" Garrett added. "Where's the real Finch? Come on, where are you hiding him?"

"How's that for sympathy, huh?" I replied. "*You* try being Class A hilarious after having your chest gouged by a psycho spirit."

"Poltergeist," Tatyana corrected. "There's a big distinction between spirits and poltergeists. You see, a spirit is a—"

Saskia rolled her eyes. "Geez, Taty, don't bore him. He just escaped one near-death experience."

As the sisters scowled at each other, I glanced at Harley. I was waiting for a dig, but it didn't come. Instead, she offered a sympathetic smile. A comforting barnacle in a sea of ridicule. *Does* she *know?* Had she and Wade been gossiping in secret? See, this was why I needed someone. Everyone else had a person they could spill their secrets to, but I had to keep mine locked up for the gremlins to feed on.

I stared down into my coffee, only to jolt back. There was no coffee in this cup anymore. It had filled up with blood. Scarlet trickles sloshed over the sides. I looked around frantically, but nobody else seemed to have noticed.

Erebus. Another one of his hallucinatory tricks to put me on edge. A sign because I was keeping him waiting. Man, that guy sure was persistent. I guessed I couldn't put him off anymore, not unless I wanted a nasty surprise in my bed. Or something worse.

"I should get going, too." I clambered over the bench.

"Can't handle the heat, huh?" Santana grinned. "You can give it but can't take it?"

"It's got nothing to do with... never mind. I'm just tired." I balled my hands into fists. "Garrett, do you want to meet up later?"

He nodded. "We can swing by the burn unit, if you like."

I scrunched my face into a sarcastic smile. "I'll text you the details."

"Call me if you need anything," Harley said, saving me again. "And get some rest. Sister's orders."

I gave her a small nod before exiting the Banquet Hall, leaving the laughter and stinging puns behind. They hadn't meant anything by it, but their jabs made me feel like I was being pushed to the edges of the group again. Sometimes I wished I could be more a part of their group. But all of this Erebus stuff made me feel like an outsider, anyway. Until I was free again, I couldn't be part of their world... *Geez, am I going to start singing Under the Sea, next?* All I needed was a shell bra.

I trudged back to my room and went straight over to my desk, taking out an antique ring that Erebus had given me. It was a chunky gold monstrosity with a fat ruby in the center and strange etchings in the metal band—sigils and charms specific to the Lord of Darkness himself. But it wasn't just a gaudy accessory. Oh no. This was a modified portal opener with a direct line to Tartarus, crafted by an ancient servant of Erebus.

Wishing I didn't have to, I slid the ring on the middle finger of my right hand. The moment it was on, the world swirled around me in a dizzying vortex. The walls, the ground, everything all fell away.

The next moment, I landed in the darkest depths of Tartarus. As soon as I set foot in the shadowy otherworld, unable to see my own hand in front of my face, the noises started. Soft at first, they grew into a crescendo of growls and snarls and snapping jaws.

I formed a ball of Fire in my palms to light my way through the pitch black. I only had minutes to get to Erebus before the night-crawlers came a-hunting.

Ready for more?

Harley Merlin 10: Finch Merlin and the Fount of Youth releases **July 22nd, 2019.**

Visit: **www.bellaforrest.net** for details.

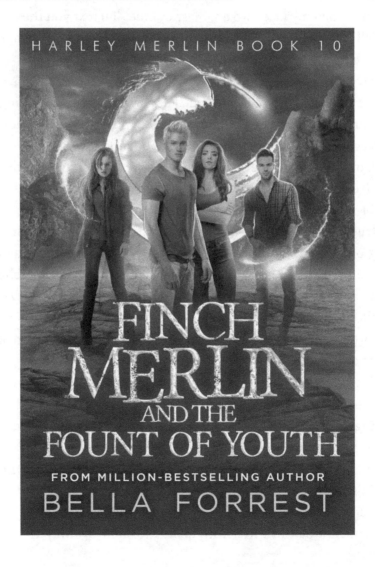

Thank you for reading, and I cannot *wait* to see you there!

Love,

Bella x

P.S. Sign up to my VIP email list and you'll be the first to know when my next book releases: **www.morebellaforrest.com**

(Your email will be kept 100% private and you can unsubscribe at any time.)

P.P.S. Feel free to come say hi on **Twitter** @ashadeofvampire;

Facebook www.facebook.com/BellaForrestAuthor;

or **Instagram** @ashadeofvampire

Read more by Bella Forrest

HARLEY MERLIN

Harley Merlin and the Secret Coven (Book 1)

Harley Merlin and the Mystery Twins (Book 2)

Harley Merlin and the Stolen Magicals (Book 3)

Harley Merlin and the First Ritual (Book 4)

Harley Merlin and the Broken Spell (Book 5)

Harley Merlin and the Cult of Eris (Book 6)

Harley Merlin and the Detector Fix (Book 7)

Harley Merlin and the Challenge of Chaos (Book 8)

Harley Merlin and the Mortal Pact (Book 9)

Finch Merlin and the Fount of Youth (Book 10)

THE GENDER GAME

(Action-adventure/romance. Completed series.)

The Gender Game (Book 1)

The Gender Secret (Book 2)

The Gender Lie (Book 3)

The Gender War (Book 4)

The Gender Fall (Book 5)

The Gender Plan (Book 6)

The Gender End (Book 7)

THE GIRL WHO DARED TO THINK

(Action-adventure/romance. Completed series.)

The Girl Who Dared to Think (Book 1)

The Girl Who Dared to Stand (Book 2)

The Girl Who Dared to Descend (Book 3)

The Girl Who Dared to Rise (Book 4)

The Girl Who Dared to Lead (Book 5)

The Girl Who Dared to Endure (Book 6)

The Girl Who Dared to Fight (Book 7)

THE CHILD THIEF

(Action-adventure/romance. Completed series.)

The Child Thief (Book 1)

Deep Shadows (Book 2)

Thin Lines (Book 3)

Little Lies (Book 4)

Ghost Towns (Book 5)

Zero Hour (Book 6)

HOTBLOODS

(Supernatural adventure/romance. Completed series.)

Hotbloods (Book 1)

Coldbloods (Book 2)

Renegades (Book 3)

Venturers (Book 4)

Traitors (Book 5)

Allies (Book 6)

Invaders (Book 7)

Stargazers (Book 8)

A SHADE OF VAMPIRE SERIES

(Supernatural romance/adventure)

Series 1: Derek & Sofia's story

A Shade of Vampire (Book 1)

A Shade of Blood (Book 2)

A Castle of Sand (Book 3)

A Shadow of Light (Book 4)

A Blaze of Sun (Book 5)

A Gate of Night (Book 6)

A Break of Day (Book 7)

Series 2: Rose & Caleb's story

A Shade of Novak (Book 8)

A Bond of Blood (Book 9)

A Spell of Time (Book 10)

A Chase of Prey (Book 11)

A Shade of Doubt (Book 12)

A Turn of Tides (Book 13)

A Dawn of Strength (Book 14)

A Fall of Secrets (Book 15)

An End of Night (Book 16)

Series 3: The Shade continues with a new hero...

A Wind of Change (Book 17)

A Trail of Echoes (Book 18)

A Soldier of Shadows (Book 19)

A Hero of Realms (Book 20)

A Vial of Life (Book 21)

A Fork of Paths (Book 22)

A Flight of Souls (Book 23)

The Chain (Book 3)

The Keep (Book 4)

The Test (Book 5)

The Spell (Book 6)

BEAUTIFUL MONSTER DUOLOGY

(Supernatural romance)

Beautiful Monster 1

Beautiful Monster 2

DETECTIVE ERIN BOND

(Adult thriller/mystery)

Lights, Camera, GONE

Write, Edit, KILL

For an updated list of Bella's books, please visit her website: www. bellaforrest.net

Join Bella's VIP email list and she'll send you an email reminder as soon as her next book is out. Visit: www.morebellaforrest.com

CPSIA information can be obtained
at www.ICGtesting.com
Printed in the USA
LVHW091026070220
646192LV00002B/3